Paula Boer has been passionate about horses all her life and believes that humans are no more important than any other animal. She lives on 500 acres of forest in the Snowy Mountains of Australia. Inspiration for her stories comes from the natural world and she loves travel to wild places, many of which she has experienced on horseback, such as riding in Mongolia.

Paula has been a regular contributor to horse magazines and has had many animal short stories published. Her best-selling *Brumbies* novels for middle grade readers, following the adventures of two teenagers catching and breaking in the wild horses of Australia, are based on her own experiences.

For more information about Paula and her books, visit www.paulaboer. com.

T0288788

The Equinora Chronicles by Paula Boer

The Bloodwolf War
The Stealthcat War
The Harbinger of Death

The Harbinger of Death

The Equinora Chronicles: Book 3

By

Paula Boer

This is a work of fiction. The events and characters portrayed herein are imaginary and are not intended to refer to specific places, events or living persons. The opinions expressed in this manuscript are solely the opinions of the author and do not necessarily represent the opinions of the publisher.

The Harbinger of Death

All Rights Reserved

ISBN-13: 978-1-922556-86-8

Copyright ©2022 Paula Boer

V1.0

This book may not be reproduced, transmitted, or stored in whole or in part by any means, including graphic, electronic, or mechanical without the express written consent of the publisher except in the case of brief quotations embodied in critical articles and reviews.

Printed in Palatino Linotype and Badloc ICG.

IFWG Publishing International
Gold Coast

www.ifwgpublishing.com

For my beloved Pete, without whose support I would
never have become a writer.

Acknowledgements

I thank everyone who has helped me on my journey, not only writing
The Equinora Chronicles, but also through the grief of losing my
beloved Pete. You all know who you are. Thank you again with all my
heart.

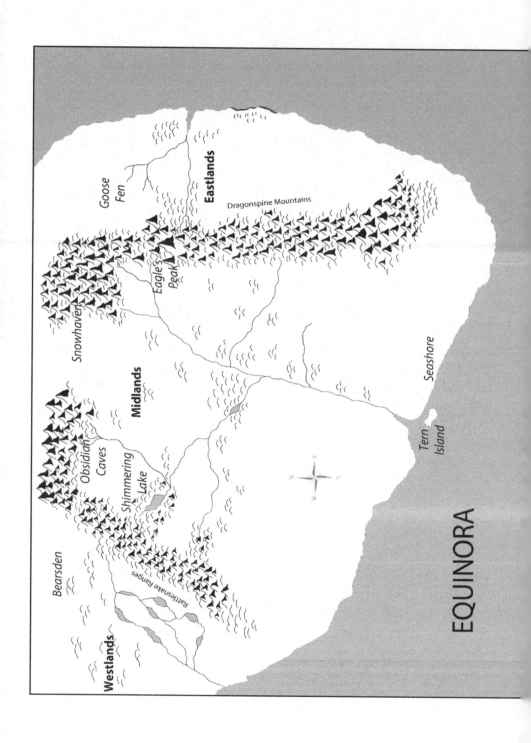

EQUINORA

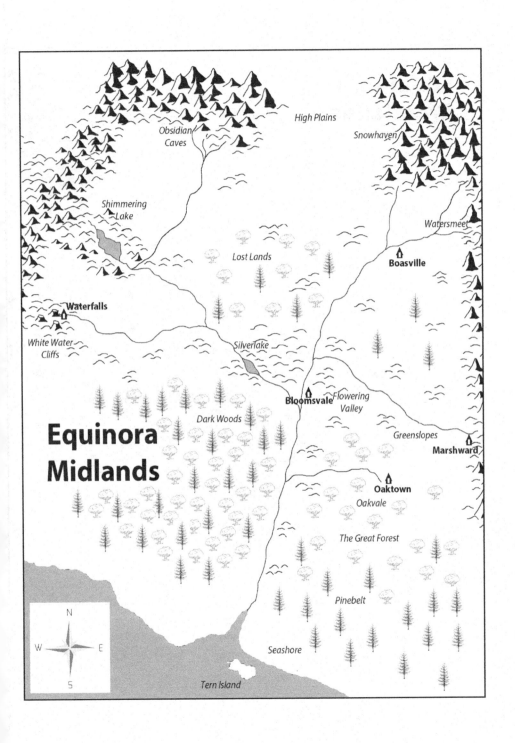

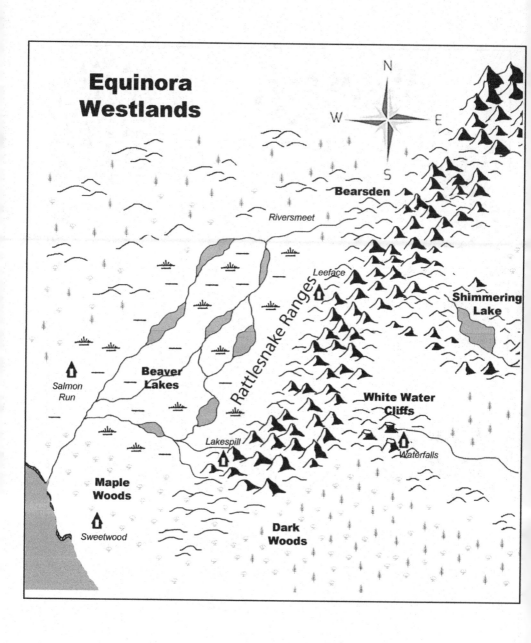

Prologue

Mares with young foals dotted the pastures among the daisies and buttercups, the horses' coats sleek and their rumps round. Shadow surveyed his herd with contentment, proud of all those he had brought to Eagle's Peak and the strong offspring carrying his blood, and delighted with the regeneration of his territory after its destruction in the stealthcat war. With his power enhancing the land and protecting the hidden valley from the ravages of snow and wind, and him being the strongest stallion in all of Equinora, many mares had chosen to stay with him rather than return to the freezing winters and scorching summers of the eastern plains.

The scent of oestrus wafted on the breeze. Shadow pricked his ears and widened his nostrils, keen to detect which mare had come into season. None of those grazing alongside the creek showed any interest in him. A couple of older colts played in mock battle on the far edge of the herd, squealing and rearing, nipping each other's necks, and prancing in circles. A buckskin filly cavorted around them, flicking her toes out as she pranced with her tail held aloft, sure signs of her readiness.

At last. Chase had grown into a magnificent two-year-old, broad of chest with strong bones and a grace that belied her size. And those eyes. Her black eyes. They had mesmerised him from the first time he'd seen her, the eyes of one he'd loved before—Dewdrop, the Air Unicorn—dead because Aureana had been too weak when creating her; dead because Jasper interfered in Shadow's aid; dead from being unable to cope with Shadow's power coursing through her frail body.

But now Chase was his and ready to mate. No other stallion would have her. She would produce magnificent foals for him, regardless of where her warmblood came from. Her black eyes proved she had strong unicorn ancestry, probably from both her dam and her sire. Mixed with his power, greater than the strength of all six unicorns combined, their offspring would populate all of Equinora. He trotted down the grassy slope and whinnied to her.

Chase peeled away from the colts and cantered towards him, head high and tail flicked over her back. Even as a maiden, she knew this game well, having watched him pair with other mares over the last two springs. Her turn had come.

He drew close, her musk heightening his anticipation, his blood running hot. He arched his neck to display his muscled crest, poising mid-air between strides in a display of supreme vigour.

She veered around him and raced up the hill. Her black hooves flicked up clods of fresh earth, the sweet scent of damp soil and crushed grass mingling with her intoxicating aroma. He sprinted after her, letting the wind whip back his crimson mane and forelock, his matching tail streaming behind him. The sun warmed his black coat as much as the excitement, raising a gloss of sweat and filling him with power.

The meadow changed to forest and the ground steepened. Trees closed in overhead, their wafting branches creating dapples of light on Chase's rump. Soft grass gave way to a deep bed of pine needles matted with oak and maple leaves, springy beneath Shadow's hooves. He raced after Chase. Through the narrow trails they galloped, their breathing drowning out any birdsong, squirrels and voles scurrying away beneath their feet.

Shadow could easily catch her. His speed surpassed any normal horse, any unicorn even. The last of Aureana's creations, he was the goddess's equal, made in her form, the most powerful creation in Equinora since she had departed forever. To him, his twin horns marked him as superior to the unicorns, but he no longer wished to rule the entire land. After generations of imprisonment at Obsidian Caves, he was content to luxuriate at Eagle's Peak with his herd, revelling in the warmth and abundance of feed. Not that he needed to eat, able to draw energy from the sun, the wind, and the earth, but why forego such simple pleasures?

He let Chase draw ahead, not wanting to tire her by pursuing her too closely. He had plenty of time to enjoy her, not only this season but in the years ahead. No other stallion would dare challenge him.

Chase dropped to a trot, small stones rolling away beneath her hooves. As she climbed higher, trees dwindled to shrubs, disappearing altogether on rocky ground. The wind chilled and blew stronger, whistling between craggy outcrops, tugging her mane and tail into tangles. Shadow followed at a steady pace, up and up. Chase slowed to a walk, scrambling over boulders with the sure-footedness of a goat. Never had Shadow followed a mare for so long, so far from the herd, so distant from his valley. Did he scare the filly? He halted.

She stopped and bent to face him, her upper lip twitching. "What's the matter? Are you scared of heights?"

He snorted and continued his pursuit. "Take care. These ledges can be treacherous."

Chase half-reared. "But the view is fabulous! The herd look like ants. The valley is an emerald amid the snowy hills. Don't you like admiring your domain?" She sprang onto a rock shelf, flicking her heels and tossing her tail.

They continued to climb the tower of obsidian for which Shadow had named his territory of Eagle's Peak. An enormous eruption had flattened the top of the spire. Thick layers of ash packed hard on the mountainside among rivers of solidified lava, barren of any life. Their hooves clattered on the hard surface, the sweat on their hair freezing into sparkling crystals.

With a final lunge, Chase reached the summit, staggering with the force of the wind. "This is amazing! It's—"

Her words whipped away to join the eagles looping upwards on unseen thermals, their wings held out with only the tips angled to direct their glide.

Shadow stood by her side, his original mission secondary for the moment as he gazed over the country below. Ranges of mountains paled to the horizon, valleys bisected by foaming rivers of snowmelt, and fresh shoots cloaking waves of trees in myriad yellows and greens.

Chase strutted around the perimeter of the platform, exuding warmth, her arousal obvious. Reminded why they had climbed out of the valley, Shadow sprang after her. She tossed her tail over her back and swung her rump toward him. Egged on, he rushed at her.

She side-stepped.

Fuelled by renewed desire, Shadow leapt and mounted her, scraping her spine with his forefeet.

Chase hollowed her back and ducked away from beneath him, spinning her hindquarters away.

Too pent up for patience, Shadow snatched her neck with his teeth and held her as he climbed over her hip. Again she slid away from him, the tang of blood sharp in his nostrils as his teeth tore free.

Keeping her head towards him, Chase backed up, almost sinking to her hocks as she skidded on the smooth rock in her haste.

He pursued.

Chase threw up her head. Her rump sank down. She whinnied as her hooves scrambled.

Only then did Shadow retreat, concerned that he had pushed her too fast. The echo of stones bouncing down the mountain rattled in his ears. The mingled scents of sweat and lust changed to those of fear and pain. Chase slipped backwards.

Shadow lunged forward to grab her neck, this time to save her.

Too late. The cliff crumbled beneath her weight. She slipped over the edge. Shadow peered over the rim, front legs splayed. Chase's body bounced against protruding rocks. Her screams echoed and then receded with her fall. A shower of obsidian shards smothered her flailing legs as she tumbled.

Shadow sped across the platform to the track they had climbed and galloped at breakneck speed down the mountain, cutting across the scree and ash as close as he dare to follow Chase's descent. An eagle screeched above, the only sound other than the blood pounding in his head.

Shadow discovered Chase's immobile body smashed on an over-hang, two-thirds of the way down the rock-face, high above the tree-line. He scrabbled up beside her and dragged energy from the life-force of the rock, the heat of the sun, and the strength of the wind. He ran his lips over her body from her muzzle to the tip of her tail. He breathed life over her with all the love he could summon. He even called to Aureana in the spirit world, ignoring his pledge to never contact her again after she had banished him to a life of dark and cold.

Nothing worked. Chase remained dead.

Shadow raged through the forest, blasting pines to splinters as slender as their needles as he passed. His hooves gouged great chunks of earth as he galloped, his anger scorching the branches that scraped his hide. A racoon darted along a branch at head height; he blasted it to shreds, leaving fur and entrails dangling among a trail of devastation. He reached the valley floor, snorting through inflamed nostrils, sweat creamed on his neck, chest, and flanks.

Mares lifted their heads and skittered out of his path, neighing to their foals to follow.

Shadow ignored them and tore along the creek, anger and self-hatred whipping him faster, harder, further. He climbed out of the valley at the other end of Eagle's Peak and surged up a steep-sided gorge, bounding over boulders that blocked his path and splashing through white water as the river tumbled around him. The roar of a waterfall drowned out the thumping of his heart.

When he crested the ridge, he slid to a halt. Ducks and geese rose from a tarn in a flurry of white feathers, their honking alarms maddening Shadow. He blew at the surface of the water, the shallows warmed by the spring sun, offering a tempting drink.

A frog hopped onto his muzzle.

Shadow reared in fury. Channelling all his frustration and heartbreak into his power, he drew the water from the lake, sending it spiralling to the sky in a climbing vortex, sucking up the fish, the frogs, and their spawn. Clouds massed overhead, dark thunderheads roiling with life as the tarn emptied. When not a drop remained in the pool, Shadow flung the entire overhead mass westwards on a wind strong enough to carry the storm across Dragonspine Mountains, across the rolling hills of Midlands, and across Rattlesnake Ranges, on to the land of lakes.

Drained of energy, sapped of strength, and emotionally void, Shadow hung his head. Nothing would alleviate his sorrow. No good would come of destroying his territory. He looked back to Eagle's Peak and the mares huddled at the far end, no longer grazing. No foals gambolled among the marigolds. Even the birds had deserted the skies. Destroying Eagle's Peak wouldn't bring Chase back. Only one thing remained for Shadow to do. He would follow Chase, and Dewdrop, to the spirit world.

He retraced his hoof-steps back through Eagle's Peak, still ignoring the mares and their queries about what had happened, where Chase had run to, and why he fretted. He no longer cared for their welfare. They were of no use to him where he intended to go. One of his warriors would rise to fill his place. The offspring he'd already sired would grow big and strong, their ancestry enabling them to win territories and rule in his stead. He had no worries for them.

Slower this time, Shadow ascended the obsidian spire, weighed down by grief. He perched at the edge of the platform where the wind whistled around him, failing to stir his body or his resolve. He peered down at the ledge where Chase's body had lain, now out of sight, whether taken by scavengers, the goddess, or gravity, he didn't know. It didn't matter. He would be with her soon.

Empowered by the strength of the tower of rock beneath him, Shadow shoved off from the platform into the air, leaping far enough out to ensure he landed far below without snagging on the high ledge that had smashed Chase. He spun head over tail, his legs flailing, his forelock lashing his eyes, and his tail tangling around his hocks.

And fell. And tumbled. And fell.

Trees rushed by in a blur. Hawks swooped, unable to match his speed of descent. For the first time since Aureana had trapped him at Obsidian Caves, Shadow welcomed the release of all cares. No more would he crave for revenge against the unicorns. No longer did the need to reproduce drive him to seek mares. Never again would he pull power from the elements to improve Aureana's creations.

He continued to fall.

The ground rushed towards him with finality.

Shadow roused, every muscle screaming in agony, every bone smashed into fragments. Enough blood pooled around him to refill the tarn he had emptied. Clouds hazed his eyes. Was he in the spirit world? Where was Aureana? Would she come to welcome or chastise him?

The pain lessened. He groaned and stretched his neck. As he raised his head, his sight cleared. Pines and spruce, interspersed with ash and oak, lined a hill above him. A creek spilled over a granite ledge in a shower of sparkling droplets that caught the last of the setting sun to form myriad tiny rainbows. A parade of ants bypassed him as they tracked along a well-worn trail to their temperate burrow before nightfall. The surroundings were at once familiar and strange, enveloped by a descending mist.

Shadow struggled to his feet and shook from head to tail in a cloud of dust. Already his bones had healed. His muscles ached as he walked forward, but their stiffness loosened with every step. The fuzz in his head dissipated.

A whinny carried on the air, at first inquisitive, becoming more anxious when no reply rang out. Breeze, Chase's dam, called for her filly.

So he wasn't in the spirit world. He remained in Equinora, in Eagle's Peak. He couldn't even die successfully. Damn Aureana! Having created him in her likeness, she had made him immortal.

For the third time, Shadow climbed Eagle's Peak. If he couldn't kill himself, he would do what he could to send a message to Aureana. Power through his hooves shook the stone beneath him. A tremor rippled through the valleys, trees toppling and rocks cascading as an earthquake snaked north. Great fissures gaped between the mountains, rending them apart. Further to the north, avalanches boomed and clouds of ice billowed up from Snowhaven only to be obscured in black ash as the spires of Obsidian Caves erupted, destroying Shadow's former prison.

Fed by the enormous energy pumping through his legs, Shadow intensified his onslaught. Dusk drowned under his wrath, yet far to the west stars blinked to life, mocking him. Using every power he could, he pulled them out of alignment. He knocked moons out of orbit and upset the magnetic fields of planets. He sucked comets and meteors from their trajectories and smashed them to pieces. He combined space-dust into missiles and sucked them down to Equinora.

Let Aureana's precious world know and suffer the depth of his fury.

Chapter 1

A bear as tall as a rearing horse staggered on his hind legs along the crystalline beach, slashing the air with massive claws and snarling at the flies that buzzed around his face. Pendulous growths hung from his bedraggled coat like ripe fruit, dried pus crusted on bald patches of his sagging hide, and festering sores oozed from his contorted face. With a gargled bellow, the bear sank to all fours before rolling on his side in the deep sand, his ugliness contrasting to the rainbow colours of the tiny dragons that skimmed the surface of the water.

Prism trotted over to the fallen beast, snorting at the foul smell, her nostrils distended to reveal glistening red linings. "Who are you?" How had a sick animal come to Shimmering Lake without being detected at the boundary? Normally the border dragons alerted Mystery or Gem, her sire and dam, to the arrival of any animals in need. She quivered. Had the recent earthquakes somehow damaged the protective veil?

A taint of rotting vegetation and decomposing meat wafted from the bear. Prism lowered her head to protect herself with her crystal horn in case the beast attacked. She had never seen a bear so enormous. "Why are you here? Do you intend to harm those under the protection of the unicorns?"

With a groan, the giant bear struggled to sit up, his giant paws slipping in the sand, his strength all but gone. "I'm no threat. I need help."

Prism stepped closer and sniffed at the bear's sores. He was certainly very sick. He must have come because he'd heard that her dam healed any animals who sought refuge at Shimmering Lake.

Prism called Gem by mind message. *Can you come to the lake? A bear needs your aid.*

I'm up in the hills mending a deer's broken leg. How urgent is it? Can Laila and Meda help?

Prism dithered. As rare as it was for more than one creature to need aid at any one time, with three healers in the valley, no-one need suffer. But the bear was enormous, and Laila only a human without powers from the goddess. Would she be safe?

The bear groaned again, his rasping breaths shallow. Surely he didn't pose a threat in this condition, and Prism couldn't let him suffer. "Stay where you are. I'll fetch a healer."

Prism raced along the shore in search of Laila, sending out a message to Meda, the healer dragon, as she galloped. *Meda! I need you and Laila. Where are you?*

A tiny voice in her mind described a meadow a short distance away. Directed by the dragon's response, Prism galloped to where Laila gathered herbs. Meda rose from the woman's shoulder in a flutter of jewelled wings as Prism skidded to a halt.

Mystery, Prism's sire, grazed nearby and raised his head at her sudden appearance. "Whatever is the matter?"

"A giant bear. He's very sick. At the lakeshore."

Mystery trotted over and nudged Laila. "Jump on. Bring your medicines."

Without questioning, Laila gathered up the soft deerskin pouch she used to store her treatments and sprung onto Mystery's back, accustomed to riding him every day.

Hastening back to the shore, Prism galloped ahead of Mystery, with Meda flitting above her ears. The prone bear remained where she'd left him. She slowed to a trot to avoid kicking sand over him.

Mystery whinnied as he neared. "Kodi!"

The guardian bear? Prism's mind spun with the implications of his arrival. Like the unicorns, the bear was one of the goddess's chosen creatures and should have been able to share the life-force of the land to prevent becoming ill or cure any injuries. What was he doing here, so far from home?

Laila slid off Mystery and ran to greet Kodi, flinging her arms as far around his bulk as she could stretch, heedless of his weeping sores and rank fur. "I never thought I'd see you again. What's happened?"

Gem cantered up, her emerald coat glistening in the morning light, her opal horn and hooves flashing as she skidded in the sand. "I came as fast as I could. Who's this? How did he get here?"

Before Prism or Mystery could explain, Meda landed on the bear's head, her scales transforming to emerald as she gained strength to perform a healing. She held out her delicate wings to shield the sun from his crusted eyes. "Lay still!"

Prism had never seen an animal so wasted and sick. Only Kodi's power must have kept him alive to travel such a long way. Meda would need all the love that she, her parents, and Laila could send in order to help the stricken bear. Anxious to hear what had caused the bear's plight, Prism fidgeted at his side as Gem called other healing dragons to his aid.

One by one, the bat-sized creatures arrived, settling along Kodi's body. Like Meda, they transformed from their usual rainbow colours to emerald, and huffed over his body to heal his sickness. While the three unicorns powered their love into the dragons, Laila applied salves to the bear's wounds and dribbled pain-killing tinctures on his swollen tongue.

By the time the sun hung overhead, they were all exhausted. Most of Kodi's sores had closed, but he still struggled for breath and his lean frame trembled with pain.

Prism snuffled close to his face. "I can't believe you're not fully recovered."

The bear groaned, his eyes tight shut and head drooped on his chest. "I only struggled this far to warn Mystery. I've failed as guardian. Let me die."

Mystery pawed at the jewelled sand. "Don't talk like that. Follow me and swim in the lake."

Empowered by Gem, the waters of Shimmering Lake provided sustenance for all the creatures who lived in the territory. Mystery encouraged Kodi to stand, prodding him gently with his nose. When that failed to rouse him, he poked the bear's rump with his horn. "Get up. Hang on to my tail." As Kodi obeyed, Mystery dragged the stricken animal behind him and plunged into the healing waters.

Prism and Gem joined them while Laila and the healer dragons rested on the beach. Aquadragons dived and blew bubbles around

Prism, singing their trilling tunes of welcome through fluted snouts. Tongues of wild celery lapped her legs and pondweed reflected sunlight in green and yellow mats. As she swam to deeper water, trout as long as her forelegs wove through the currents, their scales glimmering as they pulsed past. Smallmouth bass circled, their red eyes gleaming like fire-dragon scales.

The warmth seeped into Prism's flesh and the water buoyed her as if she were flying rather than swimming. Flying. The only winged unicorn, the third-generation and therefore supposedly more powerful than her parents, she should be able to fly. But her wings had yet to hold her aloft; she had never experienced the three-dimensional freedom of the air like the fish enjoyed in water. Mystery and Gem no longer asked whether she had been successful when she came back from her attempts from the hilltops, avoiding her gaze and swapping looks of anguish, no doubt thinking she didn't notice.

What if she never learnt to use her wings? Were they merely for show, her freakish golden feathers mimicking those of the goddess, but without any power? What would Kodi, the guardian of the goddess's feathers, think? Why was the bear here? Perhaps she was meant to give him her feathers, or use them to heal him. Was that what they were for, not flying? Deep inside, she knew the answer, but refused to acknowledge it.

Shoving aside her sense of foreboding and self-doubt, she rose and splashed, dived and played chase with the olive and gold walleyes, delighting in the energy that enveloped her. She could never stay glum for long in the depths of the lake.

Reinvigorated, she followed Mystery and Gem when they returned to the bank and led Kodi to their favourite rolling spot, sharing the hollow in the coarse sand.

Kodi stretched and showered a cascade of sand from his renewed coat, new flesh padding out the loose folds, and tawny bristles like mink fur adorning his healing scars. "That feels better."

Mystery nuzzled the bear's shoulder. "Are you able to tell us your story now?"

Kodi squatted on his haunches and scratched his rump with a forepaw. "You won't like what I have to say, but yes."

Gem snorted. "This is no place for long tales. Let's seek shade."

For Kodi's sake, they kept to a steady pace as they headed to their favourite resting-tree. The mighty oak arched resplendent with the green leaves of summer as well as the oranges and reds of autumns. At Shimmering Lake all seasons combined, excluding winter. Blossom emitted the delicate whiff of spring concurrent with ripening acorns.

Kodi's breathing laboured. He collapsed against the trunk of the tree and launched into his news. "The last of my treasures has been stolen."

Mystery tossed up his head. "The goddess's golden feather? From your cave in Snowhaven? That's terrible news. Who can have taken it?"

Prism shuffled her feet and blew through flared nostrils. "It must have been a brave and clever creature to get past you. I wouldn't venture into your cave uninvited."

Kodi huffed, hung his head, and settled onto his haunches to tell his tale. "It was during a massive avalanche. The whole hillside collapsed."

Not having ever seen snow, Prism couldn't picture what that meant. "Couldn't you dig the feather out? Maybe it's still buried there."

Groaning, Kodi wiped a paw across his face. "I would have felt its power. It's gone. I knew it as soon as I escaped the fall. I've travelled far in my search, even all the way to Bearsden in Westlands. The bears there tell me a giant eagle with golden wings brags of having the treasure. But I can find no trace of him or the feather."

Mystery stamped a hoof and switched his tail in agitation. "Claw! He used the three feathers buried at Obsidian Caves to enhance his powers of flight. He's one of Shadow's creations."

Kodi harrumphed. "So I gather. Anyway, I journeyed further, following the rumours. I've been unable to locate him."

He paused. His lungs wheezed. His eyes glazed. "I encountered devastation like you wouldn't believe. Rivers drained and valleys flooded. Mountains turned to rubble and others newly born, still steaming. Vast lakes of rotting weed, rivers of dying fish, and forests littered with animal corpses." He paused. "The pestilence west of Rattlesnake Ranges is enough to curdle anyone's blood."

Prism tossed her golden mane, stunned at how far Kodi had travelled. No wonder he had been so unwell, though he still appeared sick in body, and there was no doubt his mental health was little better. "Could the earth's upheaval cause a plague? Perhaps foul air from the depths has poisoned the world. Or could the eagle use the goddess's feather to do damage like you speak of?"

Mystery walked around them, circling the tree. "I can't see how Claw could sicken the land. Something else is going on. Not even the first-generation unicorns have ever told of eruptions and quakes like those in recent times. But I can't imagine that the goddess would be doing this to Equinora, her own creation."

Kodi scratched at the last of his drying scabs with massive paws, his claws longer than Prism's hooves. "What about the duocorn? He's caused havoc in the past."

"Shadow? I doubt it, even if he did have that much power. He's content at Hidden Valley. I swapped messages with him when Prism was born. He was happy to boast about the strength of his offspring from the warmblood mares. He'd have no reason to hurt Equinora, especially Westlands where the devastation seems worst."

Gem nuzzled his shoulder. "Could Shadow have sired another hotblood?"

The idea confused Prism. "I though there could only ever be six of us."

Mystery halted and twitched his muzzle as he pondered. "Six unicorns, yes. But what if he has sired another duocorn? Or enhanced one of his colts? They would have a high percentage of hot blood and could present a formidable danger. There's nothing to keep them at Eagle's Peak. By now, some would be old enough to leave and establish territories. They may have gone west."

Gem struck the ground with a hoof, sending tremors that rattled the leaves on the nearby trees. "I knew the recent earthquakes couldn't be natural. A great force is at work, no matter where it comes from. Even the weather is affected. There have never been such cold winds here as we've experienced this last moon. And there have never been so many falling stars. Every night they rain down. Why has the goddess abandoned us? She didn't grant us powers to deal with these types of problems. We must call her before the whole of Equinora succumbs to whatever Kodi has seen plaguing the west."

Despite the implications of pending doom, Prism's heart raced with excitement. She gazed at the disappearing horizon where the sky reflected the rich sapphire of the lake. "The moon will be full tonight."

She had never participated in a ceremony to contact the goddess. All six of the unicorns must be present, and Diamond, Gem's dam, had the power of translocation. When the need arose, she could carry others with her. "Will there be time for Diamond to get everyone here?"

Gem snorted in disgust, ears flicking and eyes rolling. "Tempest won't come. He refuses to have anything to do with us since Moonglow went to the spirit world to be with the goddess. Anyway, Diamond has gone overseas to search for Echo. He hasn't responded to any messages for a long time. He must be out of range. We'll have to make do."

Mystery threw up his head. "Only three of us? Will we have sufficient power?"

"You and I are second-generation. Prism is third-generation." Gem sidled up to him and nuzzled his shoulder. "We have more strength than all the first-generation unicorns ever had between them."

Mystery returned her loving caress. "I suppose we have no choice."

"We must find the mushrooms." Gem searched around her. "Laila, can you help?"

The young woman acknowledged that she knew where the hallucinogenic fungus grew.

Mystery nudged her hip, the signal for her to mount. "I'll take you while Kodi finishes recovering. Then we need to hear more of his story before tonight."

Prism coughed. "What can I do?"

Mystery pointed out all the animals who had gathered to hear Kodi's story. "Build a bonfire, at least as high as your ears. Everyone here can help."

Prism directed the animals to collect firewood. The smallest brought dried moss and kindling in their mouths, the larger dragged sticks and logs with their teeth and paws. By the time Mystery and Laila returned to the lake, a huge pile towered in preparation for the ceremony. Blaze, a one-of-a-kind dragon larger than a unicorn, dropped the last log from his claws on top of the heap before flapping down to settle next to Prism, wings folding with a clap. His jewelled scales glinted with all the colours of the rainbow, those on his torso larger than Prism's eyes, graduating down in size along his muscular neck, down his spine, and continuing to his tail that wrapped around his scarlet legs, their colour indicating his power over fire.

Prism thanked him. She and the dragon had become close friends, her dapples matching the dragon's armour. Her crystal horn sparkled like the spray from a waterfall, and her mane and tail ruffled like her golden wings with the merest breeze. But unlike Blaze, she couldn't fly, even though that must be her power. With Prism being the Spirit Unicorn, created after Moonglow died, her parents had assumed she would receive Moonglow's power of prophecy, but no visions had ever come to her. What was her power to be? Gem was the Air Unicorn; why wasn't she the one with wings?

The full moon rose causing the stars to lose their shine, disappearing one-by-one until even the shadows on the hillsides shrank under the glare. Exhausted from recounting his tale, and still not fully recovered, Kodi settled beside Laila under the mighty oak. Prism consumed her share of the bitter mushrooms before Mystery asked Blaze to light the fire.

The mighty dragon's scales glowed as he absorbed love from the unicorns. When his whole body shone crimson, he expanded his chest beneath outstretched wings and snaked his head forward. A gush of flame spurted from his gaping mouth as he emptied his lungs of power.

The dry timber flared as it crackled to life. Heat radiated in a burst. Even the moon dimmed in submission to the blaze. With the whole pile of wood alight, the three unicorns stood at equidistance around the pyre and touched the tips of their horns over the centre, stretching their necks through the licking flames, oblivious of their scorching forelocks and manes. Sparks danced like fireflies, singeing Prism's dappled coat with pricks of heat like scorpion stings. She braced her legs as her mind spun.

Scenes played in her eyes of the foulness in the west—the putrid water and bloated corpses, the malignant growths on plants and animals, and the suffocating fetid air. Her tongue thickened and nausea swamped her guts. More images flashed through her brain—enormous beasts with monstrous horns, amphibians spewing noxious bile, and swarms of insects devouring swathes of land. Pain shot through her legs and her heart ached as she watched trees topple into rivers, rivers reroute from their normal course, and mountains crumble into dust.

As the horrors receded, a mighty golden unicorn on outspread wings swept over the dying land. The goddess's tears showered down, searing Prism's skin as she galloped below. She cried out in her mind for the goddess to stop, to teach her how to fly, to show her how to save Equinora. The goddess pulled ahead and disappeared into the setting sun, her mental instructions hanging behind her like mist rising from the lake at dawn on a hot summer's day. Then she was gone.

Prism shook her head in a froth of golden mane to clear the vision from her drugged mind. As the fire dwindled to embers, she shivered, more from despair than cold. Breaking contact with Gem and Mystery, she reeled towards the lake to wash away the taint and heal her burns.

Gem staggered beside her. "It's no good. I didn't see anything. The goddess didn't come."

Mystery sipped between swollen lips beside Gem. "Did we do something wrong? Maybe we did need all six of us."

Dropping to roll, Prism tried to shift the sickness that spread from her head, over her ribs, through her guts, even befouling the muscles in her legs. Her hooves trembled as if another great earthquake assailed the land. "We didn't need the others. I saw the devastation. I tasted the rot. I smelled the plague. You were right; the falling stars were an omen."

Mystery and Gem stared at her, waiting for more.

"I met the goddess. She said—" She gulped, dreading what she had to share, with no way to soften the goddess's orders. "She said that I must go west and find the source of the problem. I must be the one to save Westlands."

Gem reared and lashed out with her forelegs. "No! You must have it wrong. You're too young. Mystery and I will go."

Prism stepped around the fire. "No, you mustn't. The goddess demands that it be me. This is for me to do." She crept close to Mystery. "I'm happy to go. You were no older than me when you went east to save the warmblood mares."

Mystery reluctantly agreed. "I wish I could spare you from whatever evil lies over Rattlesnake Ranges, but following a quest does seem to be the way our family gains our power. Fleet saved

Midlands, and I helped Eastlands. If this is what the goddess—"

Gem barged between them. "No. Mystery, you and Fleet are stallions. Prism is a young mare. We can't let her go."

Shaking out her golden wings, Prism glanced between her parents. "Consider the good news. I've come into my power of sight. I was the one the goddess spoke to."

Stamping the ground, Gem snorted. "Any of us could have received the vision. That's what the ceremony is for. Moonglow didn't need to eat mushrooms or light a fire to prophesise. Anyway, I no longer believe your power is the ability to see visions. It's that of flight, else why did the goddess give you wings? The fact that you can't fly yet proves you're too young for this mission."

Mystery nuzzled Gem's neck. "The goddess has spoken. Our daughter must eradicate the evil. You know Prism wouldn't lie about what she saw and heard. This is the goddess's wish."

Prism waited.

Gem acquiesced with a sigh. "Only if Kodi goes with her. He knows the territory."

The guardian mumbled his assent. "I've as much chance of finding the lost feather there as anywhere."

The lost feather was the least of Prism's concerns. She inhaled deeply before sharing the last of the vision. "There's more. The goddess said a unicorn...a unicorn...must be the harbinger of death!"

Chapter 2

Dense pines obscured any view of the rugged peaks the steep hill-sides suggested, their trunks leaning upwards towards the ground as if seeking to hug the land to prevent toppling. Few creeks bisected the slopes on this side of the mountains, the seasonal storms dumping their burden on the westward side of the range. Instead, craggy outcrops of grey granite jutted amid the forest providing the only break in the canopy, revealing rare glimpses of scudding clouds. No breezes stirred the air. No birds tapped holes or shrilled warnings. Layers of shed needles, twigs, and cones muffled the paths created by generations of hooves and paws, adding to the stillness of the dim interior.

Prism wound along the trails that zig-zagged up and down the slopes, her ears pricked and eyes scanning for movement. Years of scurrying animals had cleared the easiest pathways around massive boulders and through rugged passes, yet she rarely saw one of the creatures. Unlike at Shimmering Lake, here the tiny mammals and reptiles kept hidden, wary of strangers.

Or perhaps they were all gone.

Prism trod with care, ducking under low branches and weaving around fallen timber. Frustrated at the slow pace, she wanted to go faster to explore this new territory, inhale the scents of conifers and lichen, and meet the residents. So far, few clearings had offered the chance to canter and stretch her legs, and she had to keep her pace down so she didn't leave Kodi behind. Unlike the unicorns, the bear couldn't rely only on energy from the land. Why had Gem insisted he come along? This was her mission, but Kodi was positive that the missing feather and the plague were linked. Who could be the harbinger of death? Did the feather give them extra powers?

The guardian padded on all fours behind her, snatching at green shoots to eat, chewing and slobbering as he sauntered, seemingly in no hurry despite his previous urgency for help. His full strength had returned after a few days at Shimmering Lake, during which time Prism had sought as much information as she could about where they were to go. Instead of returning to Bearsden in the north, they had decided the best course of action would be to commence searching further south for the source of the horrors.

Excited at the prospect of adventure, Prism had been impatient to get moving and prove herself as capable as her ancestors. Although Kodi had cheered up since healing, he obviously didn't relish returning to the west, probably feeling guilty for allowing the goddess's feather to be stolen.

And he was so slow.

Why couldn't Blaze have accompanied her instead of the guardian? But the dragon wouldn't be able to navigate the tight pathways, even if she had been able to convince him to leave Shimmering Lake, his joy at being with other dragons too much to ask him to leave.

Lost in her thoughts, Prism only noticed the tiny paw marks of a small mammal when she encountered the black and white creature, its fur fluffed up and tail erect. She stopped in surprise. "Well met, little fellow. I'm glad to meet you."

"You speak skunk!"

"I can speak with everyone." Prism twisted her head to make her crystal horn sparkle and tossed her golden tail over her back. "I'm Prism, the Spirit Unicorn."

"Get away! I'll spray you!"

"That's no way to greet me. I'm on a quest to save Westlands. Have you seen any other unicorns?" The notion of a fellow unicorn being the source of all the suffering that Kodi had experienced and she had seen in her vision was still hard to believe. But the goddess had explicitly stated that a unicorn must be the harbinger of death. Is that why the skunk was scared of her?

The animal faced its backside to her, its brush twitching. "I've seen nothing. Go away."

Saddened at the skunk's rudeness as much as the lack of news, Prism stepped around him and carried on. Further down the trail she encountered a porcupine, its quills bristling. This animal at least lowered its spines after she introduced herself. "Have you seen or heard of any illness among the other residents of the forest? Are the plants you eat still healthy?"

The porcupine scampered up a tree to Prism's head height, clinging to a branch with long claws, its fathomless eyes revealing nothing. "All's well here. Should we be worried?"

"I hope not. There's news of terrible things happening at Bearsden. I'm on my way to sort it out."

"Good. I...look out! There's a bear!" The porcupine raced further up the tree, disappearing among the branches in a cascade of needles.

"Don't be frightened. He's with me." No amount of cajoling would bring the creature down. Prism sighed and sprang into a trot. She'd learnt nothing.

Further up the trail, a log as high as Prism's withers blocked the track. She halted with a snort, neck arched, and nostrils distended to test the air for any threat. Tangled branches stretched both sides of the fallen tree. She shoved the trunk with her chest, to no avail. She rammed it with her rump and lashed out with her hind legs. Her hooves thudded against the wood, but failed to move the obstacle.

Kodi caught up with her. As she considered her options, he plucked leaves from the surrounding bushes to munch. She studied him, gauging his bulk. "I might be able to jump over, but that won't help you get by. We'll waste time if we have to backtrack."

Kodi squeezed next to her and studied the barrier. "I'll see if I can lift it." The muscles along his forearms bulged as he tugged and heaved. Twigs and bark showered his head making him sneeze. He let go. The tree sprung back horizontal.

"Make room for me." Wedging her rump underneath the jam, Prism worked alongside Kodi. As she wriggled her hindquarters further under, he used his shoulders. They gasped and moaned. The trunk creaked and groaned. The root end rolled off another log with a crash, flinging the topmost branches in the air. Leaves and branches tremored as the tree shook.

Prism poked Kodi with her horn. "Quick. Go under."

Following the bear, she ducked and scrambled beneath the log before the tree could settle back and block the path again. Brushing against the rough bark, she only just made it through before another loud crack preceded the trunk crashing to earth. She let out her breath in a rush, trembling with relief.

Getting past obstacles would be much easier if she could fly. Gem and Mystery had hoped she would gain her power of flight when her horn emerged. That had happened two years ago, when she was six moons old, yet she still couldn't leave the ground. Her wings remained useless, but it had nothing to do with a lack of power. She pushed the thought away and concentrated on why she was here. "I can smell water ahead. I'll see you there."

The track widened enough for Prism to float into an extended trot, her crystal hooves flicking tree litter in her wake, her mane and tail rippling and shimmering with gold at every stride. Encountering a mossy clearing, she gave a huge buck and galloped across the springy ground. A movement caught her eye. She skidded to a stop and peered into the thick growth at the edge of the clearing. "Who's there?"

Only crashing vegetation answered. Prism glimpsed a pair of wide horns as the bulky shape merged with the gloom. She stepped to where she had seen the beast and stretched all her senses. A strong odour lingered and deep depressions in the mud showed where the animal had leapt away. Although she hadn't seen its full shape, she'd never encountered anything like it. Except in her vision—an enormous beast with monstrous horns!

Her heart raced. Leaping across a tangle of branches, she hurried to follow. Which way? She had no idea. No telltale hoof-prints marked the spoor. No snapped twigs revealed a direction. No sight or sound of what she'd seen remained. Had she imagined it? But the rank smell still hung in the air. Maybe it could translocate like Diamond. If so, continuing the chase was pointless, and she couldn't leave Kodi.

She trotted back, her pulse racing faster than the effort required. "I saw a beast. Huge and horned. We haven't even crossed the ranges yet."

The mighty bear sniffed the air. "What did it look like?"

"Almost as tall as me. Flat horns out to the sides. Dark brown, shaggy."

"Did it have a big rounded nose?"

"Yes! Is that what you saw near Bearsden?" Prism shivered with excitement. "If it hasn't disappeared, we need to find its trail. You can track better than me. Hurry."

Kodi scratched his thick hide and rumbled deep in his throat.

"Steady on. I know the smell. It's a moose."

"A moose? What's that? We've never had one visit Shimmering Lake."

"They're harmless. They graze on lichen and moss. You'll see plenty more before you go home."

Adrenalin dissipated through Prism's veins. She shook and stretched her neck and tail, her enthusiasm vanishing like aquadragon bubbles on the surface of a lake. Disappointed that the creature wasn't the one behind the troubles that they sought, she continued in search of water, guided by the fresh sweet scent. A tiny trickle burbled from a stone mound, forming a small pool near the edge of the clearing. Instead of draining away in a creek, the spring soaked into the soil, thick with bladderworts. Prism savoured the rich treat until Kodi caught up and drank his fill.

The croak of frogs resumed as she led the way back into the trees, so different to her home, the shadows forming weird shapes. A woodpecker tapped far below as the climb steepened, the first she'd heard. Was life in these woods a good or a bad sign? Did these animals belong here, or had they escaped the horrors to the west? At least she hadn't imagined the monstrous creature. Keen to experience everything she could, Prism threw herself into the climb, barely increasing her breathing as the slope increased.

"Wait for me…at the top." Kodi's puffing fell behind.

Prism emerged from the forest and powered up the rocky track, the first time the trail led onto the ridge rather than following the lowest point through a pass. Trees gave way to wispy shrubs, even those dwindling until the mountain's bones stood bare. A few patches of snow lingered in the shade, pure and white, unmarred.

A rattle alerted her. Then silence. It came again, harsh in the still air. She searched for the source of the sound. A mottled grey and brown shape, barely camouflaged, coiled against the rocks.

She stepped towards it. "I'm Prism. Why are you angry?"

The snake increased its warning, raising its head with open mouth, tail vibrating like dried seeds in a pod.

"There's no need to be afraid. We're only passing through." Prism halted, lowering her nose, hoping to gain information from the snake. "Have you seen a giant golden eagle?"

The snake struck the air with glistening fangs.

Prism snatched her head back. "Don't be like that.'

The snake tightened its coils, shrinking into a clump of solid muscle.

"Have you heard of someone having a magic feather? It would be as long as my horn, and solid gold."

Still refusing to answer, the snake retreated into a crevice in the rock, its rattle hushed.

Once again frustrated but unperturbed, Prism resumed her climb. Perhaps the rattlesnake couldn't understand her. Could whatever was wrong in Westlands be affecting her ability to converse with animals? The moose hadn't spoken with her either.

She bounded higher. A breeze developed, building to a wind that whistled in her ears, whipping her hind legs with her tail, egging her higher. Her hairs rose against the chill. Watching her footing, Prism scrambled up the last of the rocks and peered over the summit. The track wound down the opposite side of the peak, wider and less steep, looping around boulders to the tree-line far below in a clear and easy path. She raised her head to admire the view, staring out across a vista of valleys to an indistinct skyline.

Dizziness overcame her. Her limbs froze. Her stomach roiled. Trembling, she went to step back but couldn't move. She gulped down her fear and shook her head to steady her vision. All around, pine-clad mountains rolled to the horizon. No snow remained on the open slopes. Clouds scudded past the peaks, creating the illusion that the ground moved. A falcon soared, circling on thermals she couldn't see.

Flying.

Prism attempted to open her wings. They wouldn't budge. She pinched her eyes shut and tried again. This time they unfolded, her feathers ruffling as an updraught tugged their outstretched span. She opened her eyes and almost toppled over. She clapped her wings shut and attempted to turn.

Her body refused to obey like it always did whenever she climbed heights. She squeezed her eyes tight and slid down the scree in reverse, stones spitting against her legs like biting fire-ants, retreating until the wind no longer tickled her ears. She opened her eyes and, with a long sigh, relaxed.

She hastened back to Kodi, breathless and sheened in sweat. "We can't go that way, it's too dangerous. We'll have to go back and take the lower path."

Kodi twisted around on the narrow track, grateful that he hadn't regained his full bulk since crossing the mountains in search of help. Prism was in too much of a hurry, although it had been useful she'd gone ahead and discovered the dead end. The less climbing he did the better. His legs quivered from exhaustion, every step a conscious effort, his paws feeling as if they wore boots of clay.

He had lost all the goddess's golden feathers, the precious objects left in his care when she had returned to the spirit world. The final loss left him hollow, without purpose. Even though he didn't know who or what he had guarded the feathers for, his failure ate at his insides as surely as a gutful of worms. He had become the Guardian of Nothing.

Had Blaze stolen the last one in order to fly better than Claw? But as a dragon, Blaze had no need of feathers. It was all too confusing and the great dragon was Prism's friend. Kodi kept his suspicion to himself. He'd proven to be incapable and undeserving.

Useless.

The voice in his skull echoed. He hadn't told any of the unicorns about the strange words that filled his mind, sneaking between his ears when he least expected it, confronting his consciousness. He shivered despite his thick fur, the nape of his neck prickling.

Die.

Were the words from the goddess? Or from his soul?

Seeing Prism waiting for him where the track forked, he ignored the nagging voice and hurried to catch up.

Prism emerged from the trees at the base of the western foothills. Kodi lumbered beside her, the downhill run easier for him. She blew at the rank grass that offered little feed value. At this time of year, there should be sweet new growth and buds on shrubs. Not that she needed to graze as she could draw energy from the land, but a sweet snack was always welcome. She wandered about, looking for anything better. In a sheltered clearing behind a jumble of rocks she found an orderly collection of timber and reeds. "What are these? They look like shelters of some kind."

Kodi stretched up on his hind legs and sniffed the air. "This must be Leeface, the human settlement. I'll go back to the woods while you ask the clan if they've seen or heard anything odd. Both of us might frighten them."

Prism trotted between the buildings, mud flicking from her hooves as she searched for any sign of life. The ash in the fire pits clumped in soggy lumps. Drying racks stood empty, the taint of fish old, and the woven limbs of saplings used for the frame brittle and sagging. A long narrow boat lay on the bank, a hole pierced through its woven side, the reeds already disintegrating, mulching the barren earth.

Prism poked her head into a dwelling that had no cover over the doorway and peered into the gloom. Other than a cracked pot lying on its side, abandoned near a hearth, the place was deserted. She loped back to where Kodi squatted next to a stream. "I'd say they've moved away. Thank the goddess there are no corpses. What do you think has happened?"

Kodi licked one of his paws. "I agree the place has been abandoned. The water here is foul. Not as bad as up at Bearsden, but not good. Look at the algae everywhere. These creeks should be crystal clear this early in the season with all the snowmelt. And there are dead fish snagged along the banks."

Prism sniffed one carcass, curled her lip, and glanced around. The croak of frogs was the only sign of life. "Don't the salmon die after spawning? Perhaps that's what's causing the stench."

"Not at this time of year. And these aren't salmon. I won't be feasting on this rotten flesh."

Prism wandered along the stream and jumped across a narrow spot, sending up a spray of slime. She checked out the surrounding area and admitted something was definitely wrong. "We'd better go further south and see how far this stretches."

A wail rose above the incessant chorus of frogs. Prism pricked her ears and swivelled them to locate the source of the high-pitched ululation. Following the sound, she stepped back across the creek and headed upstream.

The noise grew louder. Prism found its creator, a solitary man, sitting cross-legged on the bare dirt, naked except for a loin cloth and necklaces of animal parts. Eagle feathers tangled in his matted hair, hanging in wisps down his back, the bedraggled ends grey. His browned skin draped on him like bat wings. At her approach, he raised his head and ceased his lament.

Sunlight flashed off Prism's horn as she greeted him and introduced herself. "Why do you wail that way? Where is your clan?"

The man waved his skinny arms to either side and then grappled for a pipe. He puffed on the acrid smoke, tendrils weaving out of his nostrils to linger in the air. "The end! The end! There is no saving us!"

Prism tossed her head. "There's no need to be like that."

He threw his arms wide. "Mother of all, thank you for granting this old spiritman a vision. I served you as best I could. You've seen to destroy your world. I accept your punishment." He renewed his wailing.

"I'm not the goddess! I'm not responsible for the earthquakes and the plague. Stop that noise. I can't make any sense of what has happened with you carrying on like that. Have you seen a giant eagle or heard of a magic feather?"

The old man sat back on his haunches. He placed down his pipe and stretched out trembling arthritic hands. His eyes lost their glaze as he blinked. "Are you real?"

Prism snorted and paced around the collection of tiny bones scattered around. "Of course I am. My friend, Kodi, said these lands suffered a plague. I've come to help."

"I thought you were a vision, though I've never seen one so clearly before. I thought your kind were myths. The Mother is generous to allow me to meet a unicorn before all is destroyed." He rose with his hands outstretched, his mouth agape.

Rather than approach her, he slumped to the ground, sinking back into a stupor. He rocked backwards and forwards, running his fingers among the bones. "Now I know the end is nigh. Surely you are the harbinger of death!"

Prism gasped, shocked, and scattered the bones with her hoof in anger. Taking a deep breath, she calmed herself and prodded the man's shoulder. "What do you mean? Talk to me. Where is everyone? What's happened?"

Blinking, the villager scratched his chin and sucked on his pipe again. "When the earth shook I told them to go south. There's no safety here. I can read them."

"The tremors? Or your clan?"

"The bones. The bones show the end." He keened into his open hands before scooping up and trickling the remnants through his fingers.

"What are these bones? How can they show you anything? Tell me more about your myths and why you think I am the harbinger of death."

The spiritman leapt to his feet and pointed south. "You must go! Everyone must go!"

"Why? What about the animals? We haven't met any for days. All we hear are the frogs." Prism didn't like the glassy look in the man's eyes. He peered as if he could see through her to something far off in the distance.

He coughed, a deep gurgling sound. Spitting out phlegm, he clutched the bones. "All gone. Only the rotten frogs."

"Frogs are usually a good sign. You must tell me what's happened."

The man ignored Prism's probing. "There's no-one here. Only me and the stars. And even they fall from the sky."

Chapter 3

The further Prism and Kodi travelled, the more the country changed. Following the waterway, they encountered marshy ground that eventually led into a series of pools. The wetlands dominated the landscape leaving little ground with firm footing. Algae and dead fish blanketed the water for as far as Prism could see. She lost count of the number of times she leapt onto what looked like short grass only to sink chest deep in the mire. Whenever she broke the surface, great bubbles of noxious gas burst around her.

If only she could fly to understand how far the devastation stretched. She had been too far away, and shrouded by trees, to see anything from the mountains. But the stink on the ground was better than the sense of failure to use her power.

She floundered on and encountered a strange tangle of fallen trees and woven branches across one of the deeper waterways. She sniffed at the mound from the bank, unsure if it was floating or anchored, the heap almost looking neatly ordered. A slight scent of fur lingered beneath the rot that had become so familiar. "This doesn't look like the river carried all these branches here. What do you think?"

Kodi crouched and scratched his rump against a log. "It's a dam. Beavers fell trees to block the flow for ponds." He pointed with his nose. "Look, there's their lodge."

A lifeless island of sticks and bark rose amid the pervading slime. Prism waded in to the pool and tested the mound with her foreleg. The edges collapsed, twigs breaking off and slowly spinning as they drifted away on the imperceptible current. "I don't think anyone's home."

"No, this one's abandoned. Beavers like to keep their homes neat. I wouldn't stay in the water if I were you."

"I'll be alright. The goddess tasked me with sorting this problem out, remember? She won't lead me into trouble." Prism approached another beaver lodge further downstream that looked in good condition and called out a greeting.

No one answered.

Kodi snuffled at the water's edge. "They may not hear you if they're deep inside. There'll be an underwater tunnel."

Doubting answers could be found here, even if creatures resided within, Prism splashed back through the shallows, grateful to return to dry ground. Midges buzzed around her eyes and ears. She shook her forelock to deter them without effect and stamped a front hoof as more swarmed around the delicate skin behind her elbows.

A sharp sting pierced her flank. She leapt high, all fours in the air, swished her tail, and shied across the bank. A multitude of insects sucked her blood, the flies drinking any drop of moisture, tickling and probing her skin. "Let's keep moving."

Kodi shrugged and followed, his thick coat impervious to the bugs.

With her nose low, Prism studied the terrain, hesitating to widen her nostrils to draw in any suspicious scent in case the insects flew inside. No birds swooped and swerved to snatch the feast of bugs. Although Prism had become accustomed to the deafening croak of frogs, she hadn't seen any. Didn't they eat insects? There had to be a reason for the lack of animals. That could be why the vegetation had swamped the waterways; nothing consumed it.

Suddenly, as if she had called one, a frog hopped in front of her. She reared in surprise. Instead of the colourful laughing amphibians she had teased at Shimmering Lake, this frog squelched in a coating of slime. It rotated goggling eyes, glazed and dark. Blisters and boils pockmarked its grey skin. She lowered her face to say hello, fighting back her revulsion.

The frog spat yellow bile at Prism's face, burning her delicate muzzle. She spun around and lashed out with a hind hoof, sending the frog flying before frantically wiping her nose on her foreleg.

Kodi bounded over on all fours. "Don't! Let me." Using his forearm, he wiped the mess from Prism's head, raced to drier ground, and writhed in a thicket of reeds.

Prism hurried over. "Are you alright?"

Standing and shaking, Kodi reassured her. "I wanted to get rid of that guck before it penetrated my fur."

"Thank goodness. I was worried you were having a fit. I feel terrible I kicked that poor creature." Prism trembled, the sting on her nose lessening as her body healed. She had never harmed another living thing before. At Shimmering Lake everyone lived in harmony, even predators with prey animals. None there had a need to kill to eat.

Kodi nudged her neck with his snout. "You acted in self-defence. Don't blame yourself. It attacked first."

Prism wasn't reassured. "It must have been frightened. We're so much bigger, and probably surprised it. There'd be no other reason to act like that. All I did was confirm I was a monster."

Kodi shook his head. "No. That creature wasn't natural. I'm glad you killed it."

Shuddering, Prism hung her head. "Don't say that. I'm supposed to be here to solve the problem, not add to it."

"It seems to me that the frog is part of the trouble. You did what you had to do. I'm sure it won't be the last creature you have to kill before the land returns to health." Kodi drew away, glancing around at the poisoned waterways. "If it ever does."

Prism drew a deep breath. "I'm not here to kill anything." But Kodi was probably right. Who knows what she might have to do to overcome the troubles? "I hope we don't encounter any more rotfrogs."

As if to spite her, a loud belching resounded behind Prism. She swung around. A mass of slimy bodies congregated at the water's edge. Some had limbs missing, others had odd growths on their backs or had three eyes. One by one, they hopped onto the grass and advanced, long tongues flicking amid yellow-green ooze, emitting a powerful stench whenever they croaked.

"Let's get out of here." Prism sprang into a canter.

Instead of the dense evergreens of Rattlesnake Ranges or the open lakes and marshes of Beaver Lakes, the southern forest consisted of beeches and birches dotted in stands across rolling hills. Grass was sparse beneath the canopy though verdant meadows flourished in-between the copses. Ancient towering maples threw elongated silhouettes as Prism trotted along a narrow creek clogged with weeds. Even here, the call of frogs drowned out everything else. There had been no signs of other animals, not even people at the village of Lakespill where the marshes ended.

Searching for any sign of life, Prism flicked her ears and peered into the grotesque shadows. A faint scent of horse wafted amid the sickly-sweet odour of rotting vegetation. Anticipation accelerated her pulse. Having never met normal horses before, she halted, raised her head, and whinnied. Her whole body vibrated, projecting her call as far as possible.

An answering neigh echoed from the trees. An appaloosa stallion emerged into the late afternoon sun, his white rump in stark contrast to his tawny neck, chest, and legs. Black and brown splotches splattered his hindquarters. A few white hairs highlighted his forehead, eyes, and muzzle.

Abandoning Kodi in her excitement, Prism galloped towards the stallion and slid to a halt. She reared, flashing her horn and hooves, and stretched her wings wide. "I was beginning to think no horses remained in the west. I'm Prism."

The appaloosa stallion pranced with his neck arched and tail held high, proud and majestic despite his ribs protruding through a dull coat. "Thank the goddess! I knew she'd send the unicorns even if no-one here believed me. I'm Boldearth of Maple Woods."

Prism admired Boldearth. Despite his hollow neck, he looked magnificent with his rounded crest and powerful rump. From the sparkle in his eyes, she suspected a good sense of humour lay beneath his suffering. "I'm delighted to make your acquaintance. Are there many horses here? What about other animals? Tell me all that's been happening."

Boldearth's eyes twinkled brighter as he drew himself up to his full size, only a bit shorter than Prism. He led the way to where a small band of horses swished away flies under a broad maple. Stirred from their dozing, they faced the newcomer with pricked ears and raised heads. None of them spoke. Boldearth introduced each of them. "There are only a few of us left. The waters are dangerous and the feed scarce."

Prism stepped closer. Horrific scabs and growths covered the horses' coats, reminding her of how Kodi had looked when he'd arrived at Shimmering Lake. Their breathing rasped with every shallow rise of their chests like the rattling lungs of the spiritman at Leeface. But that wasn't the only sound. "I can hear the frogs even here. Are they normal for this territory?"

Boldearth tossed his head. "No. I've never seen their like before, here or anywhere. I used to range White Water Cliffs before Wolfbane chased me off. That was back when bloodwolves ranged there. We haven't dared return in case the beasts still lurk."

Prism had been raised on tales of bloodwolves. "Did you ever encounter King Fleet of Foot? Or Queen Silken Tresses?"

At the latter name, Boldearth threw up his head. "I met Tress. Only briefly, but I remember her well. Hard to forget a black mare like that. How do you know her?"

"She's my granddam. Fleet is my grandsire. I've never met them. Tell me all you can." Prism thrilled at the chance to hear more of those days from someone else's perspective.

Boldearth tilted his head to one side and looked her over from nose to tail. "But you're a unicorn. And winged, too, like the goddess. I didn't know unicorns also had wings. You're very beautiful. How can your grandparents have been normal horses?"

"It's complicated." Prism appreciated the stallion's admiration. She stood a bit taller and raised her tail a little higher. Her blood ran hot. Relishing the chance to spend more time with the handsome stallion, Prism settled in for a long talk and told the tale of her ancestry, fending off any discussion about her wings.

While Prism chatted with the horses, Kodi wandered through the forest. It was too early for the bumblebee queens to have started breeding, so searching for their nectar pots, his favourite food, was pointless. Instead, he grubbed around for tubers and bugs. Created as the guardian of the goddess's feathers, he was able to talk with all animals. That prevented him from snacking on rodents or squirrels like other bears; he couldn't eat someone after learning their name and chatting with them. Only after the salmon run when their carcasses littered the riverbanks, their souls long gone, did he savour flesh, the nutritious fat on their backs enough to see him through the harshest winter.

He tore a strip of bark from a maple tree and peered at the trunk.

Holes at the height of his hips circled the tree. They weren't from a woodpecker—too small and too low. He poked a long claw in the hole. It was deep. Nobody would need to drill so far to look for insects. Curious, Kodi lumbered from tree to tree. Nearly all of them had similar holes. He peered into their branches to check the health of each tree. They looked well enough.

Hurt.

The voice in Kodi's head had been quiet for days. Now it shrieked in his skull, the stillness of the forest magnifying the effect. Only then did he notice how quiet the day was. No birds squabbled overhead and no tiny mammals scurried through the leaf litter. Only the distant croak of frogs broke the stillness. This forest wasn't as untouched as he'd hoped.

Gone.

What made him hear these things? Was the goddess sending him a message? Kodi shook his head, the flapping of his ears drowning out the wailing words.

Dead.

Kodi cringed. He abandoned his quest for a meal and returned to Prism.

Although swapping stories with the horses was interesting, and Bold-earth was very handsome, Prism needed to continue her search for what lay behind the poisoned land. She had tried to convince the stallion to go with her. Refusing, he had insisted on remaining with the small herd of horses, unwilling to abandon them, the mix of mares, stallions, and youngsters too weak to pick a new leader, even though he denied being their king.

That was a pity, as she would have welcomed his company, but maybe for the best. As he was unable to use mind communication he wasn't a warmblood, those horses with unicorn ancestry, so would also be incapable of drawing strength from the land. She couldn't guarantee there would be anything for him to eat where she had to go, so didn't press him to join her.

None of the horses had heard or seen anything of the giant golden eagle, Claw. Nor had they seen Echo, the unicorn who usually lived in the north and protected Westlands. With his ability to create sustenance for those under his care, he had been known to travel south in times of need such as during drought or after fires. This time he hadn't come to help.

Prism feared that what Diamond suspected was true: Echo had moved away, for whatever reason he hadn't shared with the other unicorns. That saddened Prism, both for the animals that relied on his aid as well as her own desire to meet her grandsire, Gem's father.

As Kodi ambled to where Prism rested, she said her goodbyes to Boldearth and the herd. "We'll visit the people at Sweetwood as you suggest." She intended to circumnavigate Beaver Lakes and head north to Bearsden. Visiting the village to the northwest wouldn't be out of her way. After sharing her plan with Kodi, she set off at a trot. The bear settled into a steady rhythm behind her, his shaggy coat swinging from side to side.

The short trek through the forest proved uneventful, with no more signs of horses or other animals, not even the noisome frogs, except for a few birds who didn't linger to talk. When Prism and Kodi reached the village, she suggested he wait as before, unsure of the reception they would receive. Although the spiritman hadn't been frightened of a unicorn and a giant bear, Prism wasn't sure he had believed they were real.

She walked on alone and whinnied at the edge of the clearing where timber huts clustered around a central hearth of round river stones. A massive stone slab topped another fire-pit near the trees, with hollowed out logs like miniature boats arrayed in line on its surface. Clay jars with woven tops stacked nearby. On the other side of the solid shelters a pile of wood towered over the rooftops, presumably for the fires. Unlike at Leeface, everything looked neat and clean, the buildings in good repair, and the ground swept and level.

Tiny people, only half the size of Laila and the spiritman, ran out giggling and waving their arms. Only when larger men and women came out to see what the commotion was about did Prism deduce that the little ones were youngsters. Standing so that the spring sunshine shimmered over her rainbow-dappled coat and sparkled from her crystal horn, Prism kept her wings tucked tight to her back. She didn't want to answer embarrassing questions this time about her ability to fly. As she waited, a small band of people clustered around her, keeping a few horse-lengths distance.

One wizened old man stepped forward. "What trickery is this?

Who is behind this apparition?"

Prism arched her neck and flicked her golden tail over her rump. "I'm Prism, the Spirit Unicorn, daughter of Mystery and Gemstone of Shimmering Lake."

The leader gaped. "You can talk!"

Walking towards the group, Prism studied the wasted bodies of the crowd. "I can communicate with all animals."

A burble of excitement and mutterings of disbelief rippled through the gathering. "A unicorn!" "Is it real?" "Am I sick?" "Our wishes have been granted!"

The old man bowed his head, long braids swinging in grey strands. "I welcome you, Lady Prism, though I still wonder if I am imagining you. What brings you to our village?"

Prism walked closer. "I'm after information. As I am sure you know, there is a plague across the land. I've come to help."

The leader shook his head. "You need to talk with Yaholo Bones, our spiritman, if he's still alive. He stayed at Leeface to study the bones."

"I met him. He has no answers."

A scream rang out. A woman nearest the trees dashed towards them, babbling. People ran to grab spears.

Prism looked in the direction of the commotion. Kodi stood on his hind legs. She reared to distract the clan. "Do not attack! The bear is with me. He won't harm you."

She cantered over and shielded him with her body. "You should have waited for me to prepare them."

The great bear shrugged. "I'm not frightened of their sticks. I wanted to hear what they had to say."

Prism turned back to the crowd and introduced Kodi. "Without this brave bear I wouldn't be here. He travelled far to seek help from the unicorns. Put away your weapons."

With reluctance, the men did as bid, lowering their spears but not releasing them. Small children huddled behind their parents, peeping out with ogling eyes.

The man who had spoken before held up his hands for silence. "We are privileged to be visited by you. I've always believed unicorns to be myths. We'll take your word that we're safe, but would prefer the giant bear didn't enter our village."

Kodi dropped to all fours and strode in front of Prism. "Are you frightened I might steal your berries?"

Prism suppressed her humour at the expressions of surprise, shock, and horror on the people's faces. She doubted any had heard of a talking bear, especially one as enormous as Kodi, even if their legends had prepared them for a unicorn.

An elderly woman, shoulders bent with age and hard work, joined the man who had first greeted her. "We forget ourselves. Forgive us, Lady Prism. I am Istas Sugar and this is Ahote Spear. We are the elders of this clan, the few of us who are left. Please, powerful ones, blessed of the Mother, let us offer you food. We have maple sugar fresh from the harvest. You have chosen a good time to visit."

Not knowing of the foodstuff, Prism waited until a wooden platter was brought forward. Sniffing the sweet block, she was tempted to try some, resisting only because she feared that whatever poisoned the land might have affected the food.

Kodi had no such qualms. His eyes rolled with delight as he tasted the offering. "This must be what they eat in the spirit world! Tell me where you find it. It even makes bumblebee nectar insipid in comparison. And there's so much!"

Istas explained how they tapped the trees and boiled the sap first to a syrup and then a solid block. "It keeps better in this form. Without it the winters would be hard."

Acknowledging Kodi's enthusiasm, Prism tasted the substance. The crumbly block dissolved on her tongue, filling her mouth with an explosion of sweetness. "This is delicious. Is this how you've survived when other creatures have perished?" If the foodstuff were that magical, perhaps it would make an elixir. She could carry it to those in need.

Ahote's shoulders slumped and he lowered his spear. "As sustaining as the maple is, we've lost many people. And many more are sick. Most of us used to live in the north, at Riversmeet and Salmonrun to the west of the lakes, and Leeface and Lakespill to the east. Disease has killed all the game and polluted the waters, forcing us from our homes. Now all of us who remain have established a new settlement here. With the ocean to the south, we can escape no further."

Prism sighed. Her quest wouldn't be fulfilled that easily. "Is there anything you can tell me about the disease? Have you experienced it before? Does any of your lore mention anything similar?"

"No, Westlands has never experienced devastation like we have heard has happened in Midlands and Eastlands. That is why Yaholo consulted the bones. But apart from sending us here, he found no answers."

Prism studied the clan anew, sensing many were near death, their emaciated bodies covered in sores, not obvious at first due to the skins they used as coverings. She couldn't leave them to die without doing something. "I'll contact my sire and ask him to send Laila, a healer woman, to help you. Kodi and I must continue to search for whatever ails the land."

Chapter 4

Summer in Bloomsvale brought an abundance that the villagers in Midlands hadn't experienced for a long time. Oats ripened across the fields and alfalfa swayed on the river flats. Hogs had bred and provided plenty of meat and skins, especially with younger people riding the bachelor stallions to hunt. Gone were the fears from the bloodwolf war and the ravages of the population. Although the loss of family and friends still hurt, hope had returned to the clan.

Except in Delsin's heart. Squatting next to his mother in the dim interior of the hut he felt helpless. The emerald dragon scale gifted to him by Blaze after the stealthcat war hung hard against his chest, but the ability to talk with animals it granted him couldn't help overcome this problem.

Noni Tonic, the clan's healer, rested a bony hand on his shoulder. "There's nothing more I can do."

Delsin clutched the cold husk of his mother's hand, dry as the bark that peeled from the birch trees. Shallow breaths rasped her throat, the only evidence that she lived. "I wish Laila was here."

The old healer harrumphed. "What could she do that I can't? She chose to abandon you and wander the world. Forget her."

That was unfair. The decision to leave Bloomsvale had been forced on Laila. Their bullying father had pushed her too far and the Midlands healers had refused to take her as an apprentice due to her refusal to bear children. Instead, she had gone with Fleet to find Gemstone, and, once at Shimmering Lake, had learnt more from the unicorn than she ever could have at home. With the healer dragon, Meda, she had worked tirelessly to save the Eastlands clans from stealthcat injuries. He was sure she could help, if only she were here.

Not only that, he missed his sister. She had led him through the woods as a boy, pointing out the birds and animals that lived among them; had chased him through the meadows and woven chains of flowers; and had wrapped her arms around him when Jolon, their father, spoke with his fists. Delsin had always known they were different to other children. Laila had little interest in people, preferring animals. And with his blue eyes, pigeon chest, and crippled legs, he wasn't strong. Fortunately, he had no interest in hunting or making weapons, preferring to study the clouds or the stars, imagining the world spinning beneath his lean frame.

Not like their older brother, Bly Tusker. Bly was always the first to enter a fight or race off on a hunt. Big, and tough, like their father. Jolon had high hopes of his eldest son becoming chief one day.

Delsin hadn't noticed Noni drift away. He dabbed at his mother's lips with a damp cloth, the overpowering aroma of the buckbean reminding him of his long trek to the far side of the river to find the plant. It was a pity the tonic had little effect. Venturing alone across River Lifeflow to collect it had been the hardest thing he had ever done, only made possible by riding the warmblood stallion, Rocky. The horse gave him an independence that his deformed legs denied him otherwise.

The room darkened as a bulk blocked the door. "Can't you do anything useful instead of sitting there like a moping girl?"

Delsin didn't bother to respond to Bly. Experience had long ago proven it was futile to argue.

The hulk of a man stomped across the room to where Jolon hunkered in the corner. "Here, fresh liver. I'll bring you a haunch once it's roasted."

Jolon took the wooden platter without comment, his shrivelled and scarred body a mere stick in comparison to his former trunk of an oak. Some days he whittled at arrow shafts or knapped flints, never with good results. He rarely went outside other than to binge on ale with his cronies. Even then he said little. His sole purpose these days was to watch over Macha Gatherer, Delsin's mother, waiting for her to recover. Delsin doubted Laila had done anyone a favour by saving their father after Blaze had scorched him. No wonder Bly never smiled, with a crippled brother, a sister long gone, and now two dependent parents.

On Delsin's return from the war in Eastlands he had built a small shelter on the edge of a distant copse and spent most of his days alone. Mojag Carol, the clan's spiritman, still refused to accept him as an apprentice, claiming Delsin wasn't strong enough to cope with the fasting necessary and afraid that the hallucinogenic plants used when communing with the ancestors would overpower him. At least Mojag shared some knowledge with him in return for Delsin recounting in detail the bloodwolf and stealthcat wars. The spiritman was also the clan's storyteller and composed ballads of important events to sing at annual gatherings.

Delsin wasn't unhappy with his life of solitude. With the ability he'd learnt from his mother to find rare medicinal herbs and edible plants, some of the women brought him meat in return for his help. It also gave him time to study his passion, the night sky. An unusual number of stars had fallen in the west lately, since about the time the tremors rippled the earth. Were the events somehow connected?

He didn't know, and now he was needed here in the village. No longer could he spend all night awake and sleep in the day. The stuffy confines of his old home brought back sinister memories, and the strewn skins and broken pots evidenced his mother's demise. She had borne many children, one almost every year. Few lived beyond a moon or two. Only Bly, Laila, and he had survived to share the brunt of Jolon's wrath. Not that the old man retained any ire these days. Delsin stroked a wisp of hair from his mother's face. At times, it beaded with sweat. Now it was like a hearth stone with the fire long burned away. Needing fresh air, Delsin stretched his back and headed out beyond the village.

The main horse herd would be away on their summer grazing, not needing to stay close for feeding. The mares didn't come for grooming with their foals so young, the fillies and colts taking all their attention. Delsin loved to watch the youngsters play, chasing each other and rearing in mock battle. Later in the season, a few Bloomsvale children would bond with those colts who offered to be ridden once they were four years old. That ceremony was a highlight of Delsin's year, translating between the clan and the herd as each horse selected their future companion. From then on, only that child would handle their colt, grooming them and feeding them, and practising the signals of communication. By the time the horses became old enough to ride, the pairs would understand each other's desires and moods as intimately as a husband and wife.

Now Delsin longed for Rocky, the skewbald he had ridden ever since the bloodwolf war. The horse had become more than a means of transport. Being able to communicate through the power of Blaze's dragon scale, they had become close friends. Rocky never ventured far from Delsin, too old to bother fighting other stallions for mares or showing off in front of the two-year-old fillies waiting to be sent to new territories.

Strolling across lush pasture, rocking in his bow-legged way, Delsin cheered up from the fresh aroma of alfalfa. His spirits lifted further as a white-tailed kite hovered in search of rodents, and hummingbirds blurred among the goldenrod or snapped insects on the wing. Delsin stopped on a slight rise and whistled a shrill call.

Within moments, thundering hooves tremored the ground. Rocky raced up, snorting and rearing as he reached Delsin, his coat gleaming with health. "I was beginning to worry about you. I haven't seen you for days."

"Sorry, my mother is ill. I didn't want to leave her." Delsin ran his hands over the stallion's glossy neck, thickset shoulders, and rump rounded with muscle to check for any sore spots or knots that might need massaging.

Rocky nudged his hip. "Do you have time for a ride? I didn't want to leave with the rest of the stallions without seeing you, but the grass is getting sour and I must leave the alfalfa alone for hay."

"Of course. I'm sorry. I should have come to you sooner." He lightly grasped the base of Rocky's mane and sprang onto the stallion's back, wrapping his legs comfortably around the horse's barrel as if he had been born to be astride.

The wind in his face as Rocky stretched at a gallop across the grassland filled Delsin with joy. The freedom of riding never failed to invigorate him, no matter how demanding the clan became or Bly's bullying infringed on his life. Rocky transported Delsin to another world, one of exhilaration, speed, and strength. Being able to talk with the stallion added to his thrill.

Even so, something niggled at the back of his mind. Something didn't feel right with the world, but no visible evidence offered a clue as to what. Everything flourished, and for once the food stores were full. Women sang as they ground grain and children squealed as they played. Men told tales of hardships with the distance of time enriching their stories and muting the pain. But something was wrong. A feeling of doom hovered over Delsin's shoulder, never quite within sight, like an owl following him at night on silent wings.

Hoping to shrug off his sombre mood, Delsin urged Rocky faster. The stallion needed little encouragement, leaping creeks and pounding across the packed earth. His steady breaths snorted in accompaniment to the rhythm of his stride and sweat slicked his glossy coat. Delsin caught sight of a person ahead in the distance, walking alone through the tall grass. He leant back to slow Rocky who dropped back to a lope and then a trot. Then gave a huge shy.

A wolf bounded from their right, heading towards the person.

Delsin grabbed Rocky's mane and clung tighter with his legs. Why would a wolf be hunting alone? His veins burned hot with adrenalin, even though Rocky could easily outrun the predator. Delsin needed to rescue the walker before the wolf reached him. He squeezed the stallion into a flat-out gallop.

The wolf veered to cut them off.

Rocky spurted towards the man. No, not man, woman. Now Delsin understood. "Laila!"

Thrilled to see his sister, Delsin reassured Rocky, explaining that the wolf was Paws, Laila's friend. They had met her when they had all been in the east. Rocky halted next to Laila, with Paws bounding around like a cub with a rabbit skin.

Delsin slid off and flung his arms around Laila. "You've answered my dreams. How did you know I needed you?"

Paws licked Rocky's nose and smothered Delsin in wriggling fur.

Laila hugged her brother and laughed. "I didn't. I'm not stopping. Let's get to the village and I'll tell you everything."

Delsin remounted and offered his arm to hoist Laila onto Rocky behind him. She always travelled light with only her medicine bag slung over her shoulder, able to gather whatever else she needed along the way. Rocky shied again as a tiny dragon alighted on his crest. Having a high percentage of warmblood, the stallion was one of the few horses who could see dragons. Usually only unicorns and other magic creatures, or those gifted with a dragon scale, had that privilege.

Delsin settled Rocky with a stroke and held out his hand for the dragon to sniff. "Meda! It's great to see you too. Is Blaze nearby?"

Laila handed Meda onto her shoulder. "He stayed at Shimmering Lake. He's happy with all the other dragons. The aquadragons are even trying to encourage him to swim."

Picturing the great fire dragon immersed in the lake shoved aside all Delsin's worries. "I bet he resists that! He hates water."

"I know, but he also wants to fit in with the other dragons. Being so much bigger, he does everything he can to please them and be accepted." Laila snuggled against Delsin's back as Rocky broke into a ground-covering trot.

The return trip to Bloomsvale passed quickly with them sharing news of their friends and delighting in the bounty of the season. When they reached the outskirts of the village, Delsin and Laila thanked Rocky for the ride, and gave him a rub down and a bowl of oats before he wandered off to graze.

Delsin placed a restraining hand on Laila's shoulder outside their hut. "Mama is very unwell and can't leave her bed."

Concern flooded Laila's face. "It's good that I'm here then. I'd hoped she'd recovered with the improvement in the land."

Entering the dim room together, Delsin sensed Laila's shock even though he had warned her. Paws crept in behind them and slunk to a crouch, growling.

"Get that beast out of here!" Jolon's complaint lacked the power of his former self, sounding more like a whine. He squeezed back into the corner against a stout support pole and lashed out with his legs.

Laila called Paws and soothed her by stroking the wolf's ruff. "It's okay, I won't let him hurt you."

Paws looked up at her with amber eyes. "And I won't let him hurt you."

A twitching hand on the skins that formed Macha's bed distracted them. Delsin knelt by her side. "Good news, Mama. Laila is here." Grateful that Noni wasn't with their mother, Delsin looked to his sister with raised eyebrows.

Laila crouched next to him. "I'll get you better, Mama."

Delsin left to get water. Once outside, he breathed deeply, his mood lightening as dappled sunlight warmed his skin and birdsong filled his ears. Now Laila was here, he could concentrate on determining what unsettled him. If only Mojag would let him participate in seeking the spirits.

"What are you looking so happy about?" Bly stomped past before Delsin had a chance to react. Fearing for his sister, Delsin followed his brother inside the hut.

Bly stomped over to Laila. "About time you came home. Get this place tidied up. Father and I will eat here tonight rather than join the communal meal." After dropping flint and sticks to construct into arrows at Jolon's side, he spun on his heel and left.

Laila ignored her elder brother, grabbed Delsin's elbow, and led him outside. "Meda says mother isn't sick, she's given up."

Delsin didn't want his hopes dashed before he had barely raised them. "At least ease her pain."

"She's not in pain. Not physical, anyway. It's her mind. Her body still breathes, but there's no soul inside to save. We're too late." Laila didn't seem upset, rather, accepting of her mother's release from a lifetime of suffering.

"We can't leave her like this. You must be able to do something. And what about father? He's a broken shell." Delsin didn't need to remind her that Blaze had scorched Jolon for beating her up and stabbing Paws.

Dropping contact with him, Laila strode ahead to the shade of a stand of oaks where they had hidden from Bly as children. From there, they had witnessed an old hog die beneath the spreading branches; the one that Bly had shot after it had fallen, claiming it as his kill. He still wore the giant tusks that had granted him his name when he had come of age.

Delsin tried not to think of the whispers among the clan that the chief was getting too old to lead. Bly's gang were gaining support for his rise to power. Maybe Laila, with Meda, could help Gomda Hunter regain his strength even if she couldn't save their mother.

Before he could share his worries, Laila sank to the ground, hugging her calves and resting her chin on her knees. He joined her, leaning his back against the sturdy trunk, positions they'd always adopted and gained comfort from. Laila wasted no time in explaining she was on her way to Sweetwood and that Mystery believed the falling stars were a bad omen. She shared the message from the goddess about a unicorn being the harbinger of death and Prism's departure to seek a solution.

As Delsin listened to her relate the horrors troubling the west, an idea started to form. By the time she reached Prism's request that Laila help the villagers, Delsin had reached a conclusion. "It's not a healer they need most. They need to find out what's causing the problem to enable a solution to be developed."

Laila nibbled at the petals of a buttercup. "You're probably right. Meda and I can heal the people's sores, but they'll get sick again if we don't find the reason. I have no plan of how to even start."

Delsin squared his shoulders and made a decision. "I do. I'll help Prism."

Laila's chin dropped to her chest. "I had a feeling that's what you'd say. All the way here, I've felt a misplaced sense of purpose. Seeing Mama, I feel terrible that I've been away so long. But I can't do anything for her. We should both go west."

Wrapping one arm around her shoulders, Delsin's resolve strengthened. "Rocky will take me, but he's getting too old to carry us both that far."

Her back tensed. "I can't stay here. Especially not without you. You know I can't. And Prism specifically requested that I come. Meda and I can do a lot to make the clan's life easier, even if we can't discover what's causing the plague."

Delsin hugged Laila closer. "I'll be quicker on Rocky than you going on foot. And as a warmblood, he can call her when we get near to find the way."

Laila rummaged in her medicine pouch and extracted a figurine of a horse hanging from a bark plait. "Yuma carved this of Fleet ages ago. Gem has enhanced it so that it will guide me to any of his bloodline, so it works for Prism too. But Prism has left the clan to search for Claw. I'm not even sure where the new village is; only that it is in the far south."

Delsin scrambled to his feet and paced around the tree. "We must discover the cause of the problem, not just cure the symptoms. Did the earth quake at Shimmering Lake?"

"No, but we saw the smoke when the obsidian mountains erupted. On my journey here I've wondered if the ash might be poisonous."

Delsin considered the possibility. "I can contact the ancestors to see what they know. We need to help Prism first, then all the people and animals. After we've discovered the problem, I'll ask Prism to contact Meda. In the meantime, you could make friends with one of the bachelor stallions so you have a mount."

"It would be odd to ride a normal horse after being so used to Mystery. What you suggest makes sense, but I don't like it." Laila's shoulders slumped and she pursed her lips.

Delsin's hopes rose, relief mixing with excitement tinged with a hint of nervousness at the chance to discover his destiny. "Does that mean you agree to stay? I'm sure Noni will be delighted to hand over responsibility for Mama to you."

Meda snuffled her fluted snout into Laila's braid. "If the nasty man or anyone else threatens you, I'll summon Blaze."

Laila stroked the tiny dragon. "Thank you. I suspect the mere threat will be enough to make Bly and Jolon leave me alone."

Chapter 5

The western side of Beaver Lakes proved as desolate as the people had predicted. Nothing was immune from the plague. Even the trees that bordered the marshlands stood silent of bird life. Pine needles pattered to earth and birch leaves hung limp and brown. The village of Salmonrun stank of rotting carcasses of fish, lizards, and small mammals.

Prism trotted among the structures, poking her head into open doorways. "What an awful place. No wonder the clan left."

Kodi squatted on a log near the communal hut, scratching his rump. "It would have been rich with life at one time. The devastation stretches further than I feared."

Prism snorted at the stagnant water in a small pond and pawed the ground. "There are no answers here. Let's keep moving."

"It seems the further north we go, the worse the conditions become. Perhaps we should have started at Bearsden after all." Kodi rolled onto all fours and set off along a well-worn trail that followed the dry ground beside the tree-line, snaking around stumps and rocks, keeping to the highest points.

Cantering to join him, Prism drew strength from the sun. She had long ago abandoned absorbing the energy through her hooves, the tainted ground failing to invigorate her as usual. Her preference had always been to use wind as her source of power, but here no breeze ruffled the few patches of water not clogged with weeds.

Settling into their steady rhythm as they traipsed north, Prism and Kodi fell into companionable silence, all their theories about who or what might be behind the plague long since exhausted. On the rare occasions they encountered life, no-one had seen a giant golden eagle or heard anything about the goddess's stolen feather. Most animals scurried away in fear at their approach. Those that remained begged for help. Anger built in Prism's heart as she witnessed rotfrogs encroaching on the land. Any attempt to communicate with them failed.

She had never imagined that life outside of Shimmering Lake was so different to how she had grown up. Her time had been spent playing and learning. The stories her parents shared of the bloodwolf and stealthcat wars hadn't been real for her, only narratives of her ancestors' glory. Now she realised the pain and trauma they had experienced, and the troubles that non-magical creatures suffered in their normal existence. Life would be hard enough without the plague. She must find its cause and stop it. But how? Her wings lay dormant on her back, niggling her that they held the answer. Why else had she been chosen by the goddess to come west?

But she couldn't fly! She was the Spirit Unicorn, not the Air Unicorn.

She continued north, keeping her pace slow for Kodi's sake, though her legs yearned to race and discover an answer. The infested waterways they travelled alongside gradually dried up. Instead of mats of emerald vegetation lay bare cracked earth. The former rich loam riverbank dwindled to a stony beach.

Prism drew ahead across open ground, keen to make distance before the sun set and Kodi wanted to rest. Boulders hunkered to her left beneath sparse trees like sleeping bears, grey and blotched as if diseased, reminding her of how sick the guardian had been when he had sought help.

One of the boulders moved.

Prism reared with surprise and whinnied. "Who's there?"

No-one answered. Nothing stirred. She blew through flared nostrils, every muscle tense, her body rigid.

Kodi caught up and stared into the gloom. "What's the matter?"

"I'm sure one of those rocks near the bushes moved." Prism stepped closer, her nose lowered and ears pricked.

"Be careful." Kodi stretched up on his hind legs and sniffed the air. "I can't smell anything untoward, other than the usual rot."

Treading her way through a tangle of briars, Prism went to investigate. "I'm certain I didn't imagine it."

"The shadows can play tricks this late in the day." Kodi lumbered back onto the track and sat down.

The long hairs on Prism's muzzle bristled. Something had definitely moved. Whatever it was must have gone. She turned to follow Kodi but caught a flicker of crimson out of her left eye. What had been a grey boulder unravelled in slow muscular ripples and stretched into a sinuous length of reptile, tasting the air with its forked tongue.

Prism leapt backwards and sought the safety of clear ground. "Kodi! Keep away."

The snake, many times Prism's length, uncoiled and slithered towards her. Mesmerised by its fluid muscles, she stared into its black eyes. "I'm Prism. I apologise if we are intruding on your territory."

The snake continued its lithesome approach, raising its head as it neared. It gave no reply.

Prism remembered the rattlesnake on top of the ranges. Maybe she was unable to communicate with snakes outside of Shimmering Lake. She tossed her head to make her horn sparkle. Perhaps the creature would recognise her even if it couldn't understand her. "We don't mean you any harm. We're looking for Claw, the golden eagle."

"He no longer fliesss."

The deep voice startled Prism. She tossed her tail over her hind-quarters and held her ground as the snake advanced. "You know him then?"

The desiccated twigs of a tree rustled.

The snake whipped his head to one side. "Who isss there?"

Kodi loomed next to a mighty spruce.

Prism braced. "He's a friend. Kodi, the guardian of the goddess's feathers. We're searching for the last one that has been stolen." She daren't mention the real reason for her being there in case the snake was somehow involved with the pestilence.

"Ssstolen? Feathersss?" The snake wrapped himself into a coil with his head facing Prism.

Never in any of her parents' stories had they mentioned a giant snake, but surely, this had to be another of Shadow's creations. Was the duocorn behind the troubles after all? Why would he want to destroy Westlands with a plague? Maybe the snake could help her after all. "The land is sick. What do you make of it?"

"Sssick. I eat the corpsssessss. Clean the watersss." His unblinking eyes swivelled with each statement.

"So you don't know what's caused the problem?" Was the snake telling the truth? His expressionless face gave nothing away.

"Nasssty tassste. All there isss. Pity bear belongsss to goddesss. He looksss deliciousss." At this the snake returned his gaze to Kodi, his crimson tongue flickering towards the bear who remained motionless, listening.

Prism stepped between them. "Why don't you introduce yourself and tell me what you know about Claw? You say he can't fly. What happened?"

"I am Lashhh. Falling starsss wounded Claw. Fliesss too high." After unravelling his length in a sinuous stream of grey muscle, Lash rewound himself in a tighter coil, his skin dim without any hint of glimmer as if his body sucked the light into its mass, causing the dusk to darken.

Not trusting the snake, Prism wanted to move on. "Can you tell us where we'll find him? If he's injured, we might be able to help him."

"He'sss at Bearsssden. With sssparkling green eyesss."

"Why is he there? What's happened to his eyes? Kodi didn't see him when he was there before." Was the snake playing tricks with her?

"With emerald hoovesss. Emerald horn like yoursss."

Realisation hit Prism like a lightning bolt. "You're describing Echo? Claw is with my grandsire?"

The change in Prism startled Kodi. Where she had previously bounced with enthusiasm for what she claimed was her great adventure, now she glided with elegance and energy, a performance he couldn't match. With her tail held high and her wings folded above her spine, her neck arched and her steps high, her rainbow-dappled body rippled colour like dragons skimming Shimmering Lake under the noon sun.

He didn't remind her that he had seen no evidence of Echo at Bearsden, let alone the giant eagle. None of the bears he spoke to had either. Admittedly that had been winter and they had been dormant in their dens. But none of the unicorns had been able to contact Echo with mind messages. If Echo or Claw had been at Bearsden when Lash was there, Kodi doubted they still were.

Lash. The giant snake gave Kodi the creeps. As soon as he had seen the serpent talking with Prism, the voice in his head had screamed.

Hide!

He wasn't a coward. In his long life as guardian he had encountered many animals intent on claiming his cave. Other bears, mountain lions, colonies of bats and bees, even people on rare occasions. He had seen them all off with little more than a growl or a suggestive swipe of his paws. Never had he experienced the chill that churned his innards like that unnatural snake.

And unnatural it certainly was—one of Shadow's creations from Obsidian Caves no doubt. He dreaded to think what other monsters loomed from that pit to continue to defile Equinora. Mystery's assurance that Shadow was a reformed character did little to soothe Kodi.

Dark.

Yes, the duocorn was aptly named. Shadow had spent too many generations in the black rock to give up his grab for power so easily now he was free. Living at Eagle's Peak, content with a black eyed mare? Kodi couldn't believe it. Perhaps they'd had a colt and he was the unicorn the goddess claimed must be the harbinger of death. But a new unicorn could only be created if one died. Was that what had happened to Echo? Had Shadow killed him so one of his own offspring could become the Earth Unicorn? But Kodi couldn't share that possibility with Prism. She didn't believe a unicorn could be responsible for this devastation, no matter their ancestry. And now she was certain they'd find Echo.

Scenarios roiled in Kodi's head like leaves trapped in a whirlpool. If Echo had died, the unicorns would have known. They shared the pain when a hotblood departed Equinora to meet the goddess in the spirit world. Unless Echo had been too far away. But Lash declared he'd seen him, so Echo would have been able to hear the unicorns' call at that time. It was all too confusing.

Lumbering after Prism, Kodi puffed as the country started to climb away from the lakes. "Steady up!"

She trotted back to him. "Do you want to rest? I can scout ahead if you like."

Kodi sighed and scratched at his itchy hide. "No, just slow down a bit. I'm still recovering from being sick."

Prism snuffled his shoulder and lipped at his neck. "I thought Gem and the waters at Shimmering Lake had healed you. Do you think you've become re-infected from being here? Perhaps you should return."

Kodi did not intend to abandon Prism. If he was no longer the guardian of the feathers, at least he could look after her. "The sickness never fully went away. But I can cope. I won't rest until the feather is found."

Prism shifted her weight from foot to foot. "We don't know that the feather's disappearance is anything to do with the plague. Why don't you find bears to discover more about Claw's whereabouts while I go ahead and discover how far the devastation stretches?"

Kodi set off up the trail. "We must stay together. I'm not leaving you. If I have to travel faster I will."

"I'm sorry. That's not what I meant. See if you can find something to eat. I'll look for clean water."

Prism's look of remorse did as little to satisfy Kodi as the sparse pickings. He had promised Mystery and Gem to look after their daughter. He wouldn't let them down. Certainty that the stolen feather and the plague were linked strengthened his determination.

His stomach rumbled. A skinny muskrat scampered across the path, its large hind feet thudding in haste, taking refuge under a bramble.

Kill.

Kodi shook his head in confusion. That couldn't have been his thought. He would never kill an animal. The poor creature was a long way from its usual habitat of ponds and marshes, probably driven into the forest by those awful rotfrogs and stagnant water. Before he had a chance to talk with the muskrat and find out any news, it vanished.

Upset by the notions that passed through his mind, Kodi abandoned his hunt for edible greens. What he needed more was to help Prism find the source of the plague and develop a cure. Then his body might recover from the poison that seeped through his veins.

Then he might be free of the voice.

Chapter 6

Delsin cantered westwards along the southern bank of Silverstream on Rocky. The gentle forested slopes of Dark Woods had given way to barren monoliths of near-vertical granite dotted across the flood plains, throwing elongated shadows in the afternoon light.

Rocky slowed to a walk and pricked his ears. "We're nearly at White Water Cliffs."

As much as Delsin delighted in venturing through new territory, he was pleased the first leg of their journey was nearing an end. A chill breeze whistled by, a sign of autumn approaching, and his back ached from days of riding. "Can you hear the falls?"

The skewbald stallion cocked his head. "No. It's Fleet I hear. We must be close for me to pick up his mind messages. I couldn't even hear Mystery when he was out of sight."

Encouraged by Rocky's excitement, Delsin urged him back into a canter, glad the horse's distant unicorn ancestry gave him the ability to communicate by thought with others of his kind. "Had you better tell him we're coming? We don't want him thinking you're a rival."

Rocky blew through his lips in the equivalent of a horse's laugh. "I've already done that. They're coming to meet us."

The thrumming of hooves on packed earth grew louder. Two shining black horses came into view, the stallion with not a single white hair. Fleet had grown even stronger than when Delsin had first met him in the bloodwolf war. The mare with the brilliant white streaks in her mane and tail must be Tress, Mystery's dam. It was hard to imagine, even as magnificent as they were, that this pair of black horses could beget a silver unicorn with a copper horn.

Rocky threw his tail high and pranced as the horses met, almost unseating Delsin with his exuberance.

Delighted, though not surprised, Delsin recognised the rider on the stallion. "Yuma Squirrel. It's great to see you."

"I thought Fleet must be mistaken." Yuma leapt from Fleet, strode across to where Delsin dismounted, and embraced him. "What brings you here?"

"Not a social call, I'm afraid." Delsin patted Rocky before heading to the river for a drink.

The horses would want to talk too. They swapped breath through flared nostrils, squealing in greeting and striking the air with their forelegs, before splashing into the shallows a short distance away.

Yuma waited for Delsin to refresh himself. "It's not far to the village. Tell me what's going on as we walk."

Happy to stretch his legs, Delsin ambled in his rolling gait, easy in Yuma's company. It didn't take long for him to share his news about Prism's quest and what she had discovered, seeking help for the villagers via Mystery. "Laila came by on her way to Westlands."

Yuma stopped and studied him. "Is she coming here? Or has she taken a different route?"

"Neither. She's stayed to care for our mother. We agreed I'd see what help I could provide first." Delsin expanded on his news, including how Jolon had never recovered from Blaze's burns, either mentally or physically, and that Bly had taken over as head of the family.

"Is Laila safe?" Yuma rested a hand on Delsin's shoulder, staring hard into his eyes. "I know she left Bloomsvale to get away from your father. If your brother is as bad, then what will happen to her?"

Delsin chuckled. "Don't worry, she has Paws with her. And Laila told them she can summon Blaze at any time. They won't touch her."

Yuma resumed walking. "Can she?"

"No. But remember Meda? She's still with Laila. The dragons can communicate over long distances. And Blaze is very powerful. He'd hear Meda if she was on the moon, he's that infatuated with her."

As they discussed the best strategy for finding whatever ailed the west, Delsin became aware of the horses catching them up. The dragon scale he wore enhanced more than his ability to talk with animals. He could differentiate the smell of Rocky without even looking. He'd hate to return to the dull senses that he'd had as a boy. It still amazed him that Yuma had turned down Mystery's offer to enhance the scale that Tatuk, a dragon friend of Gem's, had gifted him. The diamond let Yuma see and talk with dragons, but he refused the added power of talking with other animals. He claimed that, as a hunter, he didn't want to understand his quarry's cries. Even so, he could always remove the amulet when necessary like Laila did, with the one Meda had given her, when Paws was on the chase for food.

Yuma fiddled with the dragon scale on its leather thong around his neck as if he'd heard Delsin's thoughts. "I'd offer to come with you, but I can't ask Fleet to leave his herd, especially if a threat lurks over the mountains."

Delsin glanced at the black stallion. Fleet was certainly impressive. The horses strode out, sparkling with river-water. "I don't expect you to. Let me find Prism and see how I can help. My meditations tell me she needs a spiritman more than a healer or a hunter. If it looks as if people must become involved, like we did against the bloodwolves and stealthcats, I'll ask her to send a message to Fleet."

Fleet nudged Delsin's arm. "We'd love to hear about our granddaughter. Neither Mystery nor Gem have said much about her. I suspect they fear who may be listening in."

Having never met Prism, Delsin could only pass on what Laila had shared. After describing her beauty and the fact she had golden wings, Delsin summed up what he believed of her character. "I gather she's bold and brave."

Tress arched her neck in pride, able to follow the conversation through Delsin's dragon scale.

Fleet, being seven-eighths hotblood, didn't need dragon power. "She's young to undertake this mission on her own."

Delsin repeated the argument Laila had shared with him about Mystery's, and Fleet's, own ages when they had ventured into danger. "Don't worry, she has Kodi with her."

If he weren't on a mission to help with the troubles in the west, Delsin would have never been as happy in his life. He rode Rocky south through the foothills between Rattlesnake Ranges and Dark

Woods, beautiful country full of wildlife and birdsong, trickling brooks and fat trout, and an abundance of berries and nuts. The late summer southern sun warmed his bare arms and legs as a light breeze tousled his waist-length hair. He didn't tie it into a braid like the hunters, preferring to let the black strands add to his senses, the ends teasing the roots with any movement. Since he'd started wearing Blaze's scale after the stealthcat war, his bond with the unseen world had been enhanced, not only smell and sound, but his intuition and connection to those who only existed in spirit form. Sometimes in his meditations the Mother spoke directly to him as if she sat next to him by the fire. Yet still none of the spiritmen would apprentice him.

Animals skittered along leafy trails and birds flitted above, training their young in the ways of the wild. Delsin assuaged their fears of his presence as he passed, sharing news from further afield. None had heard of the plague on the other side of the mountains or of a giant eagle with golden feathers. When alone, Delsin and Rocky chatted about their mission and the glorious surrounds, or travelled in silence, each lost in their own thoughts.

They arrived at a fork in the path. Delsin dismounted to give Rocky a break. "I'll see which way we have to go."

After retrieving the jade carving of Fleet from his pack, Delsin suspended it in front of him from his left hand. With his right, he twisted the cord as Laila had shown him, letting it go when the plaited bark tightened as far as it could. The figurine spun in ever enlarging ellipses as it unwound, its arc more pronounced to the west, finally swinging directly between the two tracks.

Rocky dribbled water over Delsin's forearm as he sniffed the talisman. "That doesn't help much."

"I expect it means we can take either path. We'll take the westward track and I'll check again in a while. At least we know we're still going the right way." Delsin tucked the jade horse away and sprang onto Rocky's back.

As they resumed their journey, cantering wherever the ground was suitable, Delsin thought of Laila back at Bloomsvale. She must have enjoyed her life since leaving home, wandering Equinora in the company of the animals she loved, far away from bossy men and spiteful women. She had never fitted in like other girls. The wolf, Paws, and the healer dragon, Meda, were her family now. It was sad that she had to resume her life under Jolon and Bly's watch, but Delsin was certain Prism needed him, not his sister. Did their mother even know Laila was there? Hopefully Macha would die peacefully soon, be able to talk with him again, and free Laila to return to Shimmering Lake or join him in the west.

He thought of Yuma too, another misfit, who resented being chief of Waterfalls, claiming he was too much of a wanderer for the responsibility. He had never fitted in with the traditional role set out for him according to their culture. A talented carver, a great bard, and a strong hunter, he was welcome wherever he went. Especially by the women! They flirted with him unashamedly whenever he arrived at their village to trade flint and jade, singing his stories about horses or deer, or playing his flute in mimic of the animals and birds.

The only woman not enchanted by him was Laila. Was she lonely, despite her animal friends? She and Delsin had been close as children, almost like twins. Although he also enjoyed his solitude, spending a few days with her while he had prepared for the journey had been wonderful.

At least Yuma had his sister, Winona, and his best friend and her partner, Chaytan, to share his dreams and help him rebuild the village since its total destruction in the bloodwolf war. Delsin had talked at length with all three of them the one night he had stayed at Waterfalls. The new couple were happy and respected by the growing clan. Some people had come from as far away as Eastlands to start a new life.

Beneath him, Rocky stretched his head low and coughed with a shudder. Delsin stroked the horse's clammy neck. "Are you alright?"

Rocky drew to a halt and puffed. "It's hard to breathe. I feel awful."

Delsin slid off and rubbed Rocky's forehead. "How long have you been unwell?"

Rocky blew a stream of mucous from his nostrils and coughed again, his ribs protruding with the effort. "It's been getting worse since we last stopped for you to check the way. I was okay before that."

"Did you eat something that could have become stuck in your throat?" Delsin massaged the horse's neck to see if he could find a lump.

Shaking himself, Rocky denied feeling any blockage. "Let me

graze for a bit. I'm sure I'll be alright. We're high up and the air is thin."

Delsin frowned. "You never had difficulty when we crossed Dragonspine Mountains and they're much higher."

"I was younger then." Rocky wandered off.

The stallion soon returned to Delsin's side. The brief rest had failed to ease his breathing. "We can't delay any longer. Mount up and let's get going."

Worried by the pale look in Rocky's eye, Delsin hefted his pack onto his shoulders. "I'll walk. The slower pace will be easier for you. There's no point rushing and making you worse."

Delsin stopped as often as he could, using the excuse to check their direction. Each time, Rocky looked worse, his coat standing in dull patches and sweat slicking his skin. He continued to cough, started to stumble, and hung his head so low that his nose almost brushed the ground. His ears lolled, no longer pricking at every creature they encountered.

They reached a grassy clearing by a narrow creek. Delsin called a halt even though the sun still topped the trees, warm on the hair laying on his back in contrast to the chill that crept down his spine. "This'll make an ideal camp for the night. I'll make a tea for you to help clear your airways. I'm sure you'll be better tomorrow."

Chapter 7

Echo's gaze followed the silver streaks of a meteorite shower as they arced across the night sky. Beside him, perched on a boulder because no branch would hold his weight, a giant eagle dozed. Echo waited to see whereabouts the falling stars descended to the horizon. "Are you watching?"

Claw opened one eye and ruffled his feathers. "Eeerk! I saw. Go to sleep."

"There'll probably be more. We need to see where they land." Echo shuffled his hooves, anxious for morning.

"I'll find them, eeerk!" Tucking his beak beneath one golden wing, Claw refused to pay attention.

Echo paced around the rock, keeping his eyes pointed above the treeline. No more showers splattered the atmosphere with diamond and amber points. The numbers had dwindled over the last moon, reducing his capacity to help those in need.

The death. The rot. The stench. Never before had he witnessed a plague like the one that befouled his territory. Or anywhere else, for that matter. As the original Earth Unicorn, and with Moonglow dead, he had lived in Equinora longer than any other creature. Nothing had prepared him for the devastation of the land. Had Aureana abandoned them? Did she no longer care for her creations?

In the years of wandering before he had settled at Bearsden, Echo had witnessed many natural disasters—floods and droughts, volcanoes and earthquakes, fires and diseases. Even though lives were lost and country destroyed, hope always remained. Water brought fertile silt to the soil. Eruptions spewed rich ash to feed the land. Flames cleansed and opened up the ground to light. He failed to see the benefit of the current algae-suffocated waterways or the amphibians with their vile sores. Water and land animals alike gasped to death, either suffocated by the oxygen-starved water or drowned by fluid in their lungs.

The arrival of the giant eagle had been both a gift and an added disruption to Echo's solitary life. Claw had plummeted from the sky while Echo had been patrolling his southern boundary against intruders. He didn't like coldblood horses venturing into his territory, nor the people that chopped down trees and killed the animals. In his role of protector, it went against his nature to see anything harmed.

So when Claw had asked for help to mend his broken wing, Echo hadn't hesitated to help. Having the power of creating life-healing sustenance, he had transformed rocks to make medicinal meals for the eagle. But over the years, his stock of suitable stones had depleted. How ironic then that the fragments of meteorites that had brought the eagle down proved to be rich in minerals, richer than anything Echo had used before.

Claw had healed well, once again able to soar among the clouds, spiralling in golden flashes against the sun. In return for Echo's aid, he requested the eagle help him find more gifts from above, those rocks he felt sure Aureana had sent. Although Claw was one of Shadow's creatures, he had done all that Echo had asked. The eagle had been able to insert the three golden feathers into his wings and tail at Obsidian Caves, shining bright in contrast to his brown chest and head feathers, so Aureana must have approved of their use. Maybe she hadn't abandoned Equinora after all.

With dawn bringing a pink tinge to the eastern horizon, Echo nudged Claw with his muzzle. "Wake up. It's light enough to see."

"Eeerk! Go away. The sun needs to be higher." Claw rotated on the rock and turned his back.

Echo trotted around the base of the boulder and prodded the eagle with the tip of his emerald horn. "You don't need bright light. Come on, there are sick animals that need us."

Claw's golden wings rustled as he stretched and preened. "I need to clean my feathers."

"You're procrastinating. Let's go. The quicker we find what fell last night, the sooner you can hunt and I can cure the sick." Echo cantered off along a wide trail that led towards where the meteorite shower had fallen.

Claw clenched his wings tight to his sides and swooped into a dive. Echo calculated where the eagle would land and galloped to meet him. With Claw's keen eyesight and additional powers granted by Shadow, he easily detected the bounty. Even so, it had taken days to locate these stones, much further away than Echo had anticipated, but at least it was a large fall and the fragments hadn't scattered too far. Would there be enough to help the ever-increasing numbers of sick? With the plague creeping further south with every moon, Echo required more and more of the precious fuel.

Searching for the final pieces, he skidded to a halt on the hillside and stared at the devastation in the valley below. That wasn't caused by the plague; Aureana had sent him an abundance of rock. Broken limbs hung from pine trees and stumps burned where the blast had hit. Splinters of shattered trunks had sprayed in all directions. This fall must have been larger than the one that had knocked Claw from the air. Echo still marvelled that the eagle had survived, not only the collision, but the subsequent fall to earth.

The meteorite that had caused this destruction proved far too big for Claw to lift. "Eeerk! I'm not carrying that."

"There'll be smaller fragments around. Keep looking." Echo trotted with his nose to the ground, sniffing for the distinctive trace he had come to know well.

Claw screeched.

Echo raised his head.

The eagle scooped up stones in his giant talons and rose above the mountain. He hovered. "Eeerk! Enough!"

"Follow me." Echo pinpointed their location in order to return later before heading further northeast. Winding along the narrow trails through the mixed forest, he kept an eye on Claw, not wanting the eagle to take the shorter more direct route back to their base. Echo hadn't been able to help the creatures this deep in his territory before. He located a clearing where a fresh stream burbled down the mountain and called for Claw to land. Many hoof and paw prints large and small traversed the path. The recent activity was a good sign. He should be able to save many of these residents.

Claw deposited the stones in a jumble without landing, only flying low enough to prevent further damage. He hovered above

Echo, shielding the sun and squawking complaints about the lack of wind, his chipped talons, and the ignominy of collecting rocks.

Echo ignored the eagle's rantings and drew power from the land before blasting his horn against the fragments. They shattered into a steaming pile of rich grains. "Don't block the sunlight. I need the energy. Go back and get another load. I must feed the meat-eaters too."

But Echo couldn't overcome the total effects of the plague on his own. He was tired, a feeling he'd never experienced before. He was getting old. Aureana had never promised that unicorns were immortal. He had tried calling the others for help. None answered, not even Diamond. Didn't they care anymore? Moonglow's suicide must have upset Diamond more than he'd realised. The two mares had always been close. Had she done the same as her friend and joined Aureana in the spirit world? No, he'd have felt her go. She must be far away. With her ability to translocate, she could even be across the ocean. But that didn't explain why none of the others responded.

Before long, Claw returned. This time, instead of hovering low, he dropped his burden from the height of the treetops and climbed back into the sky. "Eeerk! Enough! I've paid my dues!"

"Nooo!" Echo stood amid the scattered stones, afraid of what the eagle's departure meant. It would take Echo a long time to find the fallen stars without Claw. How many more animals in his territory would die? He couldn't help them all, not alone.

Chapter 8

Prism only became aware she neared another unicorn's territory when Kodi pointed out a ridge of spruce, the dense trees forming a dark border in stark contrast to the mixed forest to the south. Rows of mountains rippled like a green sea, their crests tipped with clouds like foam. Sunbeams slanted into the valleys, denying the death that lay beneath. No other evidence indicated Bearsden's boundary, not like at Shimmering Lake where the waters warmed and the plants reflected spring, summer, and autumn simultaneously.

Kodi rose on his hind legs and peered about. "The rot is even worse than when I was here before. I'll see if I can find any of the bears I spoke to."

Prism worried for the guardian's health. "We don't know how this plague is transmitted. You should keep away from infected animals even if you do still show signs of being ill."

Kodi scratched his hide and held up his paw, the fur matted with yellow pus. "None of the healthy animals I've met have caught it from me, and as I haven't become worse, I must have some level of immunity granted by the dragons' healing. But don't worry, I'll take care not to come into contact with anyone. We have to do something to find out what's going on."

Pine cones thunked to the ground around Prism in a gust of wind. A shower of needles smothered her dappled coat, transforming her rainbow colours to a cloak of brown. She shook free of the vegetation, stamped a hoof, and snapped at her flank as a mosquito sank its proboscis deep. "The only things alive around here are these noxious biting insects."

"I'm pretty sure there's a cave over the next hill. Let's shelter there for the evening until the bugs have gone." Kodi dropped to all fours and bounded away with renewed enthusiasm.

Prism didn't blame Kodi for wanting to find his own kind, but she doubted the bears would have any more news than they had earlier in the year. Another insect stung her rump. She broke into a gallop and overtook Kodi. As he'd surmised, she found a cave half way up the hillside, its mouth no higher than her ears and only wide enough for a horse, or a large bear, to squeeze through. No scent of animal emitted from the entrance. She waited for Kodi to arrive and investigate, not wanting to get trapped in a space where she might not be able to turn around.

He caught up. After a quick amble into the cave, he soon came out. "No-one's home. They'll be searching for food in preparation for winter."

Not wanting to state the alternatives, that the bear had died or moved away, Prism kept quiet. She followed him back inside, pleasantly surprised how the cave opened into a much larger airy chamber. After a quick glance around, she settled herself facing outwards. Sheltering in the cool darkness at least gave some respite from the midges. She spotted a movement through the trees below. "What was that?"

Kodi joined her at the mouth of the cave and peered to where she pointed with her horn. "I don't see anything."

Prism studied the terrain. "There. I saw it again."

Kodi ventured a short way down the slope and searched the gloom. "You're right, something large. From the way the branches are moving, it might be a moose."

Prism didn't think so. She caught a flash of emerald. Every hair tingled with excitement. *Echo, is that you?*

No answer. The movement stopped.

She waited. Nothing. She must have imagined it. Echo would have answered if it had been him. Or maybe it was a moose. Disappointed, she retreated to the back of the cave to look for bats or lizards to question. They'd thrive on the bounty of insects in this country, but only hollow echoes answered her greetings.

"Prism!" Kodi called her to come outside. "Look!"

Prism rushed to Kodi's side, scanned the forest, and caught another flash of emerald. The clattering of hooves trotting across the stony creek drove her to crash down the slope, paying no attention to her safety. She slid and skidded in a direct line to the bottom, ignoring the meandering trail they had climbed, not bothering to wait for Kodi. She sent out mind messages as she went. Although she received no response, she sped faster.

A flash of an emerald tail blended into the trees ahead.

"Wait!"

A loam coloured unicorn with dazzling green eyes spun around, his matching horn pointing to the sky. His bright emerald mane and tail contrasted against the dark backdrop of the dying forest, his emerald hooves sparkling as he pranced. "Steady down. Why didn't you announce yourself?"

"I did." Hadn't Echo heard her? "I've been calling you for many moons, even a few moments ago when I saw you."

"Your powers are not as strong as your looks then. I assume you're Prism, daughter of Gemstone and Mystery. What are you doing here?" Echo pranced up, touched his emerald horn against her crystal one, and blew gently into her nostrils.

"I've been searching for you. Kodi, the goddess's guardian, came for help when he discovered the plague in your territory. We thought you'd moved away." Prism drew in the intoxicating scent of her grandsire, delighted to have found him at last. So the giant snake, Lash, had been right.

Echo stepped back and tossed his head. "I called all of you for help. Why didn't anyone answer? I've been fighting the rot on my own, exhausting myself in an attempt to save the animals. I can do nothing for the plants."

What was wrong? They'd each been trying to contact the other with no success. "The air smells musty and thick here. Maybe that's the problem."

"Perhaps." Echo appraised her. "You're even more beautiful than I'd been told. And your wings! Is that how you came here?"

Embarrassed to admit that she had no control of her power, Prism lowered her head. "No, I can't fly yet."

"You will. It takes time for you younger generation unicorns to learn your powers." Echo jumped as Kodi joined them. "So you are the guardian. Why are you so far from Snowhaven?"

After greeting Echo, Kodi slumped onto his hindquarters. "The last of the goddess's feathers has been stolen. I heard that Claw, the great golden eagle created by Shadow, might know of its whereabouts."

"Claw? He never mentioned it. He came to me for help. Fell from the sky, actually. He flew so high, a meteorite crashed into him and broke a wing. Lucky for him the same rock provided me with the ability to heal him."

Prism didn't know what to say. She hadn't known Echo had the power of healing as well as creating sustenance. Before she could arrange her thoughts, he danced around her.

Echo reared in excitement. "Now I see Aureana's plan. She has sent you so I can help with your wings too. We'll need to find more sky stones. Then you can assist me instead of Claw. I've used all the rocks he located."

Torn between the prospect of flying and discovering the source of the plague, Prism left Echo to search for meteorites alone. Would his sustenance help her overcome her fear? She hadn't shared with him the true problem behind her lack of flight.

As Echo had said it might take a while to track down the stones without the great eagle's extra senses, and as Prism didn't know what she was looking for yet, she wouldn't be able to help. Instead, she had suggested that she and Kodi use the time to search the country further north for any sign of the feather or the cause of the problems.

They travelled for days, the cold increasing as they climbed into the ranges. Prism lost all feeling in her hooves, her breath frosted on her muzzle, and her eyelashes stuck together with frozen tears drawn by the wind that blew straight off the icecaps. She'd never visited the polar regions, nor had any intention of doing so. Even so, her heart lifted. The trees here were not as barren. Small animals scampered with cheeks stuffed with nuts, or buried treasures in hidey-holes. None would stop to chat, too busy preparing to hibernate.

Further and higher Prism led the search, through forests and over rocky outcrops. Up and down, she scrambled and slid along the winding tracks slick with mud or loose with scree. The treacherous going forced them to turn back on many occasions. It didn't matter. She could see the forests thronged with vigour, filled with wildlife. Eventually, they encountered larger mammals, including moose. Despite the cold, the land thrived.

Prism emerged onto a stony ledge and surveyed the gentle slope below covered in heathers. Seed heads nodded among the pasture to where the river tumbled and surged in its haste to reach the sea. But this season the salmon wouldn't make it in the opposite direction to their spawning grounds, the suffocating algae downstream drowning all chance of them creating the next generation. She must find the problem. Echo had been unable to help solve the mystery of who or what created the rotfrogs and poisoned the land.

She must find the harbinger of death! The wind tugged her mane and tail in streamers as she stretched out her wings. A gust caught their tips and lifted her, pebbles rattling as her hooves lightened and left the ground. Her stomach roiled. Her eyes blurred.

She clamped her wings tight to her sides and wheeled around. Her power was there. She knew it. But how could she admit to being frightened? Unicorns weren't supposed to be scared of anything. Nothing else daunted her. Her parents would be more than disappointed. She had seen that look in their eyes when they had encouraged her attempts to fly, promising that the power would come when her horn emerged, and then later when she first came into season. But even they had given up finding landmarks in her life to measure her lack of progress. Now they only stated that the goddess would help her when the time was right.

Prism had ventured on this journey in the hope of discovering courage. What was the point of her life if she couldn't use her power? Maybe she ought to kill herself to enable the goddess to create another unicorn in her place. But she had no desire to die, even if she could get close enough to the edge of a cliff to jump like Moonglow had done.

Sunk in despair, Prism joined Kodi who waited on the track, regaining his breath after the steep climb. He stretched up and pointed to a dark shadow amid the rocks. "I recognise where we are. I've visited here before. It's a large cave."

Keen to forget her latest failure, Prism sprang up the narrow trail. As she climbed towards the opening, the overpowering scent of bear wafted down. Someone was definitely at home.

Kodi suggested Prism wait. "This she-bear has cubs. I'll let her know we're here rather than enter unannounced."

Prism fidgeted while Kodi bellowed his presence. The sound of moving bodies carried to them without an answer. She stepped closer. "Please, Lady Bear, can you help us? I'm Prism, the Spirit Unicorn, and I seek advice."

When Prism had almost given up hope of a response, a dark form materialised in the mouth of the cave. "I see you, unicorn. This isn't your territory. I know the Earth Unicorn. What do you want?"

She swiped behind her. A shriek accompanied a ball of fur rolling away. "Don't let that outsized bear step any closer."

Prism held her ground. "Have you seen a giant eagle or heard about a golden feather as long as my horn? Do you know who or what might be poisoning the waters and killing the creatures further south?"

Two pairs of eyes above brown snouts and topped with round furred ears peeked over a rock near the cave entrance. A deep growl rumbled from the mother bear. The noses retreated. "No. But another giant bear came and asked the same thing last winter. He—"

"That was me." Kodi advanced on all fours. "I'm the guardian of the goddess's feathers."

"Get back!" The sow bared her teeth and slashed the air with her claws. "You can't be him. That bear was near death. He wouldn't have lived this long."

Prism didn't want to anger the bear. "This really is Kodi. My dam healed him. We want to save all the animals, which is why we're here. Can't you tell us anything?"

The bear relaxed but kept a wary eye on Kodi. "I've heard of the plague further south. But as you can see, things here are normal. A few more animals have come to winter here, perhaps. Other than that, I haven't seen anything, certainly not a giant eagle or a golden feather."

After thanking the bear for her help, Prism and Kodi retreated down the mountain, disappointed in the lack of news. Prism looked around as if answers would be hanging in the trees.

Kodi stripped berries from a huckleberry bush and stuffed them in his mouth, the juice dripping out as he puffed. "What now?"

Prism hesitated. If she could fly, then finding the problem might be a lot easier, and Kodi could rest rather than traipse after her. Or she could call Echo to see whether he had found any rocks yet— but Echo wouldn't hear her. She had tried several times to swap thoughts with him without success before she and Kodi had left.

The plague might be affecting the air as well as the water.

Was that why Kodi was having difficulty breathing? That could be why the people were having problems with their lungs too. But they were far to the south. If foul air preceded the plague, more than Westlands could be in danger.

She must call her parents. At least she could tell them that Echo was here. There shouldn't be any problem communicating in the fresh mountain air.

Mystery, Gem, great news! Can you hear me?

Prism! Yes, of course I can. The familiar voice of her sire carried clearly to her mind. *Have you found the goddess's feather?*

No, no yet. But Echo is at Bearsden. We suspect the air is befouled and preventing him from hearing us.

Her dam joined the conversation, her enthusiasm evident in her greeting. *Is Echo alright?*

Yes. And Claw has been here but now he's gone. Echo needs help to find special stones to heal the land. Can you locate Diamond and ask her to come? She can translocate him to make his task faster.

Mystery confirmed they would. *But it might take some time. She could be a long way away.*

Gem butted in. *Are you and Kodi okay?*

Fine. We're in the north of Bearsden where things are well. They worsen towards the south. Don't worry if you don't hear from me again for a while. I must go back down to where I can't send or receive messages and help Echo.

Chapter 9

To Delsin, the abandoned village of Lakespill rammed home the devastation in the west more than the lack of animals or the clogged waterways. Where there would have been the soft singing of men and women at work, or the shrieks and giggles of children at play, he heard only the croak of frogs. Nothing of value remained in the empty huts, only broken pots or clothes beyond repair. Even the cold hearths had an abandoned feel, lifeless ash undisturbed by inquisitive creatures. The people had packed all their useful possessions, without tidying up like they would have done when leaving a temporary camp. He hoped that was a sign they intended to return.

Rocky browsed at the bases of the wooden shelters, the few patches where grass still grew. All the other vegetation had wilted or died, the rotting odour hanging on the still air. The stallion tried to swallow but coughed instead, making the ugly wattles that dangled from his head and neck swing. The pus-filled growths had appeared over every part of his body, even down his spine. Delsin could no longer ride.

Frustrated at his inability to help, Delsin twisted the jade carving of Fleet on its thong. His only hope was to find Prism soon. The amulet spun and, for the first time since his journey began, pointed northwest. "I hope this means we're catching up. The direction has never been as clear before."

Having wandered over, Rocky nudged Delsin's shoulder. "That's good. Did you find any clean water?"

Delsin shook his head. "There must be rainwater trapped somewhere. I'll climb that ancient hemlock and see if there are any puddles clear of algae."

From his vantage point, Delsin gaped. In the direction they had to go lay vast expanses of green—not grass, but weed-choked lakes. Reed boats lined the shoreline, half submerged, their hulls rotten. The few unclogged streams reflected glints of sunlight, the only hint of the waters moving beneath a mat of infestation. Mouldy rushes bent over the banks of the meandering creeks that criss-crossed the landscape.

With a heavy heart, Delsin slid to the ground and led Rocky to a cluster of rocks that formed a natural basin, the recent rain as yet untainted. As the horse drank, Delsin filled his bladderskin and imparted the bad news. "We can't go the way the amulet shows. We'll need to detour around the lakes to the south."

Rocky coughed again. "Let's get going then. There's no point standing here."

Delsin hesitated. "I think you should go back. I have no idea how much further we have to go. What if we don't find Prism soon?"

"Back to what? We don't know what's causing the problem. It could be as bad in Midlands by now." Rocky set off at a steady walk, his flanks sweaty and muscles trembling.

"Laila has Meda with her. She could heal you." Delsin couldn't bear Rocky fighting on through the wasteland when he could return home.

Breaking into a stumbling trot, Rocky ignored Delsin's pleas. "I'm a warmblood. I'll be fine."

As they trudged the perimeter of the lakes, Delsin became more and more concerned for Rocky. "You can't go on like this. You can barely walk." His own body shrieked from the days of trekking, his knees swollen and his back aching.

The stallion remained silent.

Delsin headed towards a pile of rocks with the intention of forcing Rocky to rest. They both needed a break. The platform of ridged stones was unlike any he had seen before, concentric circles of ridges between mounds weathered like lizard skin.

The rocks moved.

Losing his sense of balance, Delsin grabbed Rocky's mane. It made no difference. His head swam as the boulders rippled and rolled. Was this another earthquake? If so, it was like none he'd experienced before. Rocky jammed to a halt, throwing up his head in alarm. Before Delsin had time to regain his stability, the boulder at the end of the pile lifted into the air. Two obsidian orbs flashed as a crimson tongue longer than Rocky's tail flicked out like a whip.

Rocky spun and bolted, leaving handfuls of hair in Delsin's hand. Frozen to the spot, Delsin stared as the rocks uncoiled and wove a hypnotic dance a few arms' lengths away. Taking one step back, he kept his eyes locked on the giant snake.

"I will eatsss the horssse."

Shaking his head to try to get rid of the vision, Delsin could only think that he had either eaten poisonous mushrooms by mistake, succumbed to the plague, or his exhaustion was making him see things. He hadn't had adequate food or water for too long.

From behind him, Rocky whinnied and called him back.

The snake changed direction, his muscles rippling as he slithered in pursuit of Rocky. "He isss sssick. A niccce meal."

Delsin fled to a nearby aspen and scrambled up the trunk, his feet slipping as the bark peeled away beneath his moccasins, preventing him from climbing high enough to escape the snake's reach. Grasping Blaze's scale, he hoped he'd be able to make the creature understand him. "Please don't hurt Rocky! We're looking for Prism, the winged unicorn. Have you seen her?"

As soon as he had spoken, Delsin regretted the decision.

The snake changed direction and coiled up at the base of the tree. "Prisssm? Yesss. And the bear. He wasss sssick too."

Delsin didn't know whether to be delighted that the snake could talk with him or petrified at what it might do. He decided a formal approach might be best and introduced himself. "May I have the honour of your name?"

Settling his head among his coils, the snake continued to stare with unblinking eyes, their black depths as unfathomable as a starless night. "I am Lasssh. I eat the poisssoned onesss. Like the horssse."

After greeting Lash with all the politeness he could summon, Delsin begged him to leave Rocky alone. "He'll get better. We're here to help Prism save Westlands from whatever ails the land. Do you know anything about the plague?"

Lash unwrapped his coils and stretched out, his scales rustling like the fallen leaves that coated the slimy mud. "Ssshadow abandoned me. The barrier at Obsssidian Cavesss came down. Who knowsss who essscaped?"

Delsin's neck tingled at the words. Shadow, the duocorn, had created Blaze and Claw, and Delsin had heard the stories of Snag, the giant cave spider. It had never occurred to him that there might be more creatures, and that they were no longer contained. "Could they be behind these troubles?"

While Delsin questioned Lash, Rocky paced to and fro. Delsin worried that the horse would weaken himself with fretting. With no idea how he could save himself if the giant snake decided to attack, he cupped his hands and called over to Rocky. "You need to go."

The stallion refused to budge.

"He'll be dead sssoon. A good feassst." Lash continued to exclaim how Rocky's flesh would fill his skin and make him grow.

"No! He's one the goddess's favoured animals. He has unicorn blood." Delsin instantly wished he could bite back the words as the snake raised its head higher—being a warmblood might make Rocky's flesh more attractive to Lash. "You can't eat him. He's under the goddess's protection."

The branch holding Delsin creaked and cracked, threatening to snap. He couldn't think what to do with Lash ranting on about consuming rotten flesh and how it made him strong. In a flash of inspiration, Delsin removed Blaze's scale from around his neck. At least that way he wouldn't be able to hear the snake's sickening words. But the only difference it made was that the snake retreated. Delsin could still understand his words.

The tree swayed as the setting sun brought the evening breeze. Delsin hung the scale back around his neck. He needed to distract the snake from Rocky. "So, you have your own powers. Do you know where Prism is now? Can you swap messages with her like the dragons? Is she near?"

Lash coiled up a short distance from the tree. "You have one of Blazzze's ssscalesss. A gifted one, not ssstolen, I can tell. I'll not harm friendsss of the dragon. Where isss he?"

This was more than Delsin could have hoped. With relief that the dragon scale gave him protection, he risked loosening his grip on the swaying branch and dropped to the ground. With another insight, he grappled for the jade carving of Fleet and explained that Blaze now lived at Shimmering Lake with many dragons. He didn't add that the others were tiny and gentle. Clutching the braid that held the carving, he held it out at arm's length and spun it. "This can show me which direction Prism is, but not how far. Can you tell me? I need to get help for Rocky."

Lash whipped his head forward and grabbed the jade. The thong snapped as the snake backed away, wrenching Delsin's shoulder. He staggered as he was almost flung to the ground. As he recovered, Lash glided away and slithered into the forest, his chiselled head held high, mouth gaping, gulping down the jade figurine. He disappeared as if he'd never been there.

Delsin lugged an armful of flat stones down the hillside to the hollow he had prepared in the mud. Already the fire in the base had burned to glimmering coals, perfect for heating the stones. He had hunted far to find suitable rocks, equal in size and as dry as possible. Those near the swamp, being wet, could explode and injure him. Having placed the stones to heat, he gathered armfuls of soaked branches and constructed a frame over the hole. He had already stacked wet bark and pine fronds ready to make a roof.

Rocky dozed nearby, one hip dropped as he rested a hind leg. His coat had started to fall out in patches, revealing sores that wept with pus. Growths hung like leeches from his tender skin. He blinked and raised his head as Delsin approached. "There's no point asking again, I'm not going."

Stroking the stallion's neck, Delsin sighed. "I know you won't go home. But why not go to Shimmering Lake? The dragons can heal you. Gem can probably create another way for me to find Prism. Once you're well again, you can come and find me."

The skewbald hung his head. "I don't think I'd make it, even if I could find the way. I've never been there. And don't forget there's a protective barrier."

"But you're a warmblood. Gem would let you in." No amount of arguing persuaded Rocky to leave. Delsin despaired. Returning to his construction, he finished the sweat-lodge and disrobed before sliding into the makeshift space. He hadn't had time to build a proper hut with all that he needed. The temporary shelter would have to do.

Delsin splashed water on the hot stones and breathed in the steam.

He had been unable to find enough fresh water for his liking, not wanting to risk using the precious drinking supply he had hoarded. He choked on the pungent odour of burning algae and pushed away thoughts of what might be entering his lungs, anxious not to fall sick.

Holding an old coney skin over his nose and mouth that he usually used for washing, he expanded his lungs and held his breath. Slowly releasing the air, he cleared his head and repeated the exercise until his heart slowed. His skin prickled as beads of perspiration erupted and dried. Having never been invited to join Mojag Carol or the other spiritmen in their ceremonies, he wasn't sure if he should do anything else. He concentrated on his belly.

Breathe in…hold…breathe out.

Breathe in…hold…breathe out.

Emptying his mind of all other thoughts, he moved his focus to relaxing his toes, his feet, and his ankles. Working up his body, he unwound the muscles in his legs, his back, and his shoulders. He released the strain in his neck, his arms, and his hands.

Breathe in…hold…breathe out.

Breathe in…hold…breathe out.

He let go of tension in his jaw, his nostrils, and his forehead.

Time lost all meaning. As the fire dimmed to ash and the air cooled, Delsin roused. He wriggled out of the confining space and splashed a few precious drops of clean water on his face before crumbling off the dried mud from his skin. Shivering, he dressed.

The ancestors hadn't come, but it didn't matter. He knew what he must do.

Chapter 10

Prism strode into the clearing where she had agreed to meet Echo. A large patch of bare earth had been scraped clear of what little grass remained, and a pile of silver-grey stones glistened in the centre. Their uneven edges had been smoothed as if they had melted, the largest no bigger than her hoof, the smallest as tiny as a mouse's eye. She sniffed at the collection. To her, they didn't smell any different to any other stone. Pacing around the heap, Prism tried to gauge when Echo had last been here. "There aren't any fresh hoof prints, so it must have been before that rain a few days ago."

Kodi leant against a tree, scratching his back on the rough bark. A cloud of pine needles fell as he rocked the trunk. "We've no choice but to wait. He said he might have to go far to find each one."

Prism hated any more delay. She was still no closer to finding out the cause of the plague. All she knew was that it became worse south of here.

A flash of emerald emerged through the trees. "I thought I heard you. Good timing. I'm going to create the sustenance. You can have some before I distribute it to the sick animals."

Echo looked as if he had lost weight since their last meeting, his coat more like mud than rich loam and his hooves dull like autumn grass instead of gleaming emeralds. Prism hadn't noticed before how much shorter his horn was than hers. She had always known that, as the goddess decreed, each generation of unicorns was more powerful than the previous. What she hadn't appreciated was that their horns, the symbol of their power, reflected that strength. Her parents' horns were spiralled whereas the first generations' were smooth, another differentiation. Hers was faceted like dragon scales, the clear crystal reflecting the slightest hint of light in a splash of colour.

After she and Echo snuffled noses in welcome, she pranced and half-reared. "Let me help you feed the animals before I have any. I can eat some of the next batch."

Echo peered at the pile and disagreed. "I fear these are the last ones. I haven't seen another fall and I've searched the entire territory."

The bad news added to Prism's worry. "What will happen then? How will anyone survive? I couldn't find anything strange in the north. Perhaps we should pair up and look further afield."

Ignoring the questions and her suggestion, Echo asked her to stand back. "Sometimes the stones shatter when I change them."

Bracing his legs apart, he breathed in deeply and lowered his head over the meteorites. Red, green, and blue sparks buzzed from his horn like fireflies. He breathed out and touched the tip of his horn to the first stone. A streak of white light shot skywards.

Prism leapt back.

The stone sagged into a flattened cake, steaming with the pungency of burnt hair. One by one, Echo touched the stones and transformed them. "Wait for them to cool before you eat. I'm hoping the residue of my power will trigger yours. The sustenance will certainly make you stronger anyway. Have the largest. It's too difficult to carry far." Echo stepped back, sweat sheening on his coat and dripping from his neck, his horn noticeably shorter and his flanks hollow. His skin sagged over his shoulders and rump.

Prism was shocked at his transformation. "I didn't know creating food took so much out of you."

"It didn't use to. I've always used the earth's power to sustain me before, but with Equinora so sick, I daren't risk drawing energy through my hooves." Echo stumbled, mumbling over his shoulder as he staggered away. "I'll draw on the sun and wind. It won't take me long to recover."

As Echo sipped at the creek, Kodi sauntered closer to Prism. "Nothing comes without a price." He sniffed the air. "I'm glad I don't need to eat that."

Echo returned and stared at the bear. "You should have some too. I can see you're still not fully recovered from the plague. Don't rely on your own powers."

Kodi politely declined and returned to his tree. This time he squatted at the base, not bothering to scratch.

Prism suspected he didn't want to show how uncomfortable his skin remained, though she suspected the wounds from his boils still troubled him. It concerned her that the dragon healing hadn't completely overcome the poison, especially as the guardian was one of the goddess's special creatures. Trying not to worry, she turned her attention to the bubbling and hissing mess of rock. "Do you think it's ready yet?"

"Give it a bit longer. It should stop changing soon." Echo went on to ask what she had found in the north.

"Everything looked normal to me, and Kodi said nothing was wrong. We met a she-bear with cubs. They were healthy with no signs of growths, and no had problem breathing." Prism backed off as the smell of the sustenance Echo had created became stronger, rich in minerals and salt.

Echo shuffled his feet before asking more. "Were you able to call anyone in the clean air?"

"Yes." Prism had forgotten to mention the conversation with her parents. "Mystery and Gem will contact Diamond and ask her to come. They'll let me know when they locate her."

Echo hung his head. "It will be great to see her again, though I don't know what she can do with the supply of stones finished. Look, these are ready. Have that big one."

Prism stretched her neck forward and gingerly lipped the largest cake. She flinched as the sustenance stung her gums, acidic and salty at the same time. Clenching her jaw she gripped the spongey mass and dragged it away from the pile onto the dried grass beyond the burnt area. Having witnessed Echo at work, she now understood why he had cleared the earth.

The transformed meteorite was lighter than she had expected, with an airy soft feel, squishy and damp. She licked the blistered surface; definitely salty. "Are you sure this will help me fly?"

Echo watched with his ears pricked. "Not certain, no. But it can't do any harm to try."

Still she hesitated. The lumpy mass stank of rot. "Perhaps I should leave this large bit for the sick animals and only try a small piece?"

"No. I gave special attention to that piece to help you. That's part of the power—thinking about what I want to achieve. When I created that piece, I pictured you in the air, flying like Claw, your golden wings sparkling." Echo encouraged her to eat while the portion retained his essence.

Closing her eyes, though how that would help she didn't know, Prism snatched at the gooey mess and swallowed it down in three gulps. It didn't taste as bad as it smelled. The sting in her mouth soon numbed. "How long will it take to work?"

Echo nuzzled her neck. "I don't know. I'll leave you to try your powers while I deliver the rest to the nearby inhabitants."

With her tongue furred and stuck to her cheeks, Prism went in search of fresh water.

Kodi watched Prism trot up the hill, her head and tail held high. He envied her enthusiasm and optimism, though he suspected she harboured doubts of her ability to fly. Several times on the journey he had seen her spread her wings. As soon as the wind lifted her hooves clear of the ground, she clamped the feathers to her back as tight as her closed eyes. He hadn't let on he'd seen her attempts. He trusted the goddess. Prism's power would emerge when she needed it.

He struggled to his feet and went in search of any berries that might have survived the foraging of others or the plague. He found little. It didn't really matter, he didn't have much appetite. It was more something to do while he waited. Echo had cantered off, carrying pieces of sustenance in his mouth to feed the needy. Kodi guessed it would be a while before Echo returned as few animals lived in the vicinity. The unicorn had recovered as quickly as he had promised after using his power, though he didn't look as magnificent as Kodi had expected.

Not like Jasper, Prism's great-grandsire, who had been Kodi's friend for as long as he could remember. Now Jasper was dead. And now, with four used, the final feather was missing. He still didn't know its purpose, let alone why Jasper had entrusted the precious objects to him after the goddess has discarded them. With the last one missing, he'd probably never know. A sense of uselessness pained his heart like hunger gnawed at his stomach.

The few berries Kodi found were dry and tasteless. He abandoned his hunt and found a sunny sheltered spot in which to doze. He curled his great bulk around his paws and rested his nose on his belly, the fur warm and familiar, grateful that the smell of rot had dissipated from his sores. Or maybe he had become accustomed to his stench. What must it be like to hibernate like other bears? As guardian, he had never had the luxury of sleeping through many moons.

Cold.

Had someone answered him? Or was it his imagination?

Starve.

Kodi hadn't heard the voice for a while, not all the time he and Prism had been further north. Could it be the effects of the poisoned air muddling his mind? Breathing was certainly harder in Echo's territory.

Groaning, unable to rest with the intrusion in his head, Kodi clambered to his feet and lumbered up the slope after Prism. He wouldn't follow her all the way as she needed privacy to discover her power, but hopefully gaining a bit of height into the clean air would help him rest and silence the voice. Finding a boulder warmed by the sun, he nestled at its base and tried to stop thinking about Westland's plight. He could do nothing to help. He wasn't even the guardian anymore.

Die.

The voice persisted. Abandoning any hope of dozing, Kodi stretched out and watched the sky, waiting to see Prism's rainbow form flying overhead on golden wings.

Prism perched on the edge of the precipice. A strong breeze tugged at her feathers, adding to the tingling through her body that lingered from Echo's sustenance. The muscles and sinews under her outstretched wings burned with energy. Equinora's power surged through her blood from the sun and the wind. She focused on the creek that wound like a lazy snake through the valley way below, reminding her of Lash and the need for her to be able to fly, to locate the harbinger of death and end the plague.

She could do this. She had Echo's strength to help her. As she flapped her wings in slow rhythm, her hooves lifted off the ground. Her tail streamed out, leaving the backs of her legs cool. Her heart thudded. A gust snatched at her body, knocking her sideways. The ground tilted and the world spun. Nausea rose in her throat.

Prism clapped her wings shut and stepped back. Her skin quivered, every hair erect. She blinked and twitched her upper lip. Of course she couldn't fly sideways in these gusts. She needed to have the wind behind her. Or straight on.

She trotted back down the trail and headed to the other side of the hill. When she reached a gentle slope on the lee side of the mountain, she stared at the layers of conifers that spiked the hillsides, speckled with the oranges and yellows of deciduous trees. She pictured what they'd look like from high in the air, like Blaze had described to her, the landscape melding into a multi-hued patchwork rolling to the sea. Renewed optimism buoyed her spirits. She couldn't wait to tell her parents that she'd gained her ability to fly. Finding her grandsire had obviously been what she was meant to do all along.

But what if her power drained while she was still in the air? She'd crash and plummet like a pigeon struck by a falcon. Watching Echo use up his reserves had frightened her. She'd never witnessed her parents suffer when they had used their powers. She dithered, and then decided she needed to seek advice before risking her life. She retreated among the boulders that capped the peak this high above the tree-line. Her parents could ask Blaze questions for her.

Mystery, Gem, are you there?

No answer. Perhaps they were busy communicating with Diamond, or were swimming deep and couldn't hear her. She'd wait a while.

She tried again. And again. Still no answer.

Now that the autumn days had shortened, dusk came early. As the sun sank below the horizon, Prism gave up calling her parents. She would attempt a short flight, not one that took her over the trees. A few horse lengths would be enough to prove she could.

Using a different strategy to her previous attempts, Prism located a long run of open space. She broke into a canter and stretched her wings, beating them like a goose lifting from a lake. The ground blurred beneath her. Wind whistled in her ears. Dizziness swamped her. Her heart pounded and her legs flailed, desperately seeking solid earth.

She stopped flapping, hit hard rock, and stumbled to her knees. It was no good. Technically she could fly—she had always known that—

her problem was fear. That's why Echo's sustenance wasn't working. He'd said he needed to think of what he wanted to achieve when he used his power. He had imagined her flying, not overcoming vertigo. But she had never admitted her weakness to anyone. After she had flown once, she would be fine; she only needed to gain confidence.

Night darkened with no hint of a moon. Cloud soon smothered the few stars that blinked into view. The darkness became total. This was her chance. Unable to see the land or any horizon, Prism galloped as fast as she could and used her other senses to guide her. The hillside had no obstacles that might obstruct her take-off. Timing her wingbeats to her breathing, she lifted off.

A flash startled her. Sparkles of orange, green, and white arced across the sky, one streak so dazzling that the image remained on her retina long after it fizzled out. She had never witnessed meteorites in so many colours. The light was so bright she caught a vision of trees lying on their sides and water running up hill. The ground smacked into her side and one wing bent beneath her body. Pain seared her spine and blood trickled from a graze on her hind leg. Gasping for air, she struggled to her feet. Failure dragged heavy on her soul.

Chapter 11

Myriad colours from dewdrops twinkling on the autumn leaves reminded Prism of the dragons at Shimmering Lake. A pang of homesickness twisted her innards as she trotted down the hillside. Already her scrapes and cuts from the fall had healed. Only the damage to her pride and her fear of flying remained. And the worry for Westlands. She was no nearer to finding the cause of the plague than she was to overcoming her vertigo.

Determined not to let her angst show, she cantered across the clearing where she had left Kodi and Echo. They stood nattering under a giant pine on the far side. The bear stopped what he was saying as he spotted her and lifted a paw in greeting.

Echo walked over to meet her near the dwindling pile of transformed rocks. "We were starting to worry about you. How far have you been? What did it feel like? We'd hoped to spot you overhead."

Prism snuffled his muzzle and pointed north with her horn. "Did you see the huge meteorite shower? There'll be lots more stones, I'm sure."

Kodi ambled over. "Could you work out where they landed? We didn't see anything from here."

"Yes, I think they came down near the she-bear's cave."

"This is terrific news." Holding his head high, Echo asked her to lead him there. "Have the last of this sustenance before we go. I saved it for you."

Eating more of the salty compound didn't appeal to Prism. It wasn't Echo's power she needed. "There are others that will benefit from it more than me. Leave it for the squirrels and chipmunks.

PAULA BOER

They're sure to gather it for their stashes."

Reluctantly, Echo agreed that might be for the best. "How far do we have to go?"

Before Prism could answer, Kodi interjected. "You two go ahead and I'll catch you up. I'll locate a few more bears in case any have heard about Claw or the missing feather."

Guessing that Kodi didn't want to slow them down, this time Prism accepted his suggestion. Looking at her grandsire, she decided to keep the pace slow anyway. He appeared dull in both eye and coat. His emerald mane and tail hung in thin wisps and his horn appeared shorter every time she looked. Maybe he was just old.

Heading back the way she had come, Prism trotted alongside Echo. Now that she had the opportunity to ask about his life and that of the other first-generation unicorns, she didn't know how to start. He'd never been part of her dam's life. "What made you choose Bearsden for a territory?"

Echo needed little prompting and chatted away, describing how he'd wandered Equinora for many seasons after the unicorns went their separate ways. "When I reached here, the dragons revelled in the water. It was as good a place as any to make a base."

The mention of dragons surprised Prism. "So you had dragons in the early days? What happened to them? Don't they live as long as us?"

Puffing from the steep climb, Echo stretched his head and neck low. "Many generations lived here, raising their broods in the warmer waters of the beaver pools. Winters were hard on them as they don't like the cold. Some would hibernate, though many would go down to Tern Island during the snows. But they always came back each spring."

Prism hadn't seen a single dragon since leaving Shimmering Lake. No wonder Echo looked so sad. He must miss their cheerful playing. "So where are they now?"

Echo scrambled over the loose footing on the ridge of the hill and drew a deep breath. "Gone. All gone."

Imagining dragons succumbing to the poison filled Prism with horror. She hadn't believed that the goddess's magical creatures could become ill until she'd met Kodi. "That's terrible. Couldn't the healing ones help the others?"

Echo halted and looked around as if he might suddenly see a

flock of dragons. "I don't know. I haven't seen a single one since the start of the plague."

"So they could be somewhere safe, not dead?" Prism's hopes rose. Perhaps the dragons had sought refuge at Tern Island until the plague was eradicated. It still sounded strange. At Shimmering Lake, the dragons always found those creatures that needed help and called one of the unicorns to help them. Either she, Gem, or Mystery would send the healer dragons love to replenish their energy and enhance their powers. Surely Echo's dragons would have done the same? It was peculiar that they had vanished when they were needed most.

Understanding that Echo had no answers, she changed the subject, describing the colours of the meteorite shower and how bright they had been. "There must be a lot of stones. Hopefully we'll be able to prevent the plague from coming this far north. There's no sign of it up here."

Prism gathered the fragments of rock that had survived entry into Equinora's atmosphere, their tiny size impossible to compare to the show they had made arcing across the night sky. Having found a great store of them scattered far over the hills and valleys, she wondered if they had shattered into many pieces. She was sure she hadn't seen that many fall. For days now, she had cantered back and forth to Echo, building up his stores for him to help all the creatures. At first he had gone out in search of animals to feed. Now the birds carried word that Echo was here. All manner of animals large and small sought him out. For all their lives, he had been the protector of Westlands, though many this far north had never met him. Like so many tales since the goddess had created Equinora, each species had its own legends of the unicorns.

Carrying her latest find of stones, Prism hoped they'd finish the task soon. Even the smooth edges abraded her tongue and, with her mouth full, she didn't like not being able to chatter to everyone she met. She encountered bugs and lizards of types she'd never seen at Shimmering Lake and wanted to know them all. She wanted to investigate the different plants that grew on the forested slopes and in the dark gullies of rock. She dreamed of finding her courage on another moonless

PAULA BOER

night and accompanying bats and owls in silent flight.

Almost back at Echo's clearing, Prism picked up an unfamiliar scent. No, she had smelled it before, once. A moose wound his way along a well-worn trail through the pine forest. How could she have not seen the one before? It was enormous, bigger even than the handsome appaloosa stallion she had met in the south. The bull balked as she pranced up to him before holding his ground, feet splayed. His pendulous upper lip twitched and a flap of skin wobbled under his throat. Broad antlers cupped the sky like giant human hands. Fat reserves padded his shaggy coat that gleamed like burnished acorns. He tipped his nose skywards and bellowed.

Prism dropped the mouthful of meteorites and flashed her horn. Having not had a chance to talk with the last moose, she was determined to speak with this one. "There's no need to be frightened. I'm a friend."

Obviously taken aback that she could converse with him, the moose blinked long lashes over his chestnut eyes. "I'd heard tell of a unicorn in these parts, but never held much store in the tales. But the stories talk of a brown stallion with a green mane."

"That's Echo, the Earth Unicorn. I'm Prism, the Spirit Unicorn."

"Am I dying? Are you the goddess? She has golden wings, or so I believe." The moose stared around as if checking he really was still in Equinora.

Delighted that the bull engaged in conversation, Prism explained why she was here. "Come and share some of the sustenance Echo is creating. There's a plague coming and it'll help you resist it."

"A plague? I saw sick animals in the south, with horrible growths and pus-filled boils. That's why I headed up here." The moose stretched his head forward and sniffed her neck. "I didn't feel safe staying in my favourite wetlands, and they're overrun with a noxious algae. Is that part of the problem too?"

"Yes, and horrible frogs that burn. I came through there." Prism didn't want to remember the yellow bile that stung her face, and hoped the horses with Boldearth had found better territory away from the spreading disease.

The moose backed up a step. "You're not carrying it, are you? The plague?"

Prism snorted. "Do I look as if I have the plague? Anyway, I'm a unicorn. I can't get sick."

90

"I guess not. You're certainly beautiful, like many rainbows squeezed together."

After the moose agreed to accompany her, Prism picked up her hoard of stones and led him to where Echo worked his magic. A pile already steamed at his feet emitting the salty tang she had become familiar with. He had found a meadow bisected by a narrow creek and cleared an area that wouldn't set fire from his sparks. Nearby, at the edge of the forest, crossbills searched among the white pines for seeds, and warblers flitted for insects. Prism caught glimpses of squirrels scampering up the rough bark. The sense of well-being all around satisfied her. For too long she had travelled through plague-ridden country, devoid of life.

The moose waggled his lip as he sniffed the spongy mess. "Are you sure this will keep me well?"

Echo welcomed the moose and explained how he'd been feeding all the creatures to the south. "For some it was too late. Better you have it now before you get sick."

While the moose was eating, a bear lumbered down the hill, two cubs gambolling behind her with their lips stained purple with blackberry juice. They chased and tumbled down the slope, buffeting each other with their paws, oblivious to everything except their game.

The moose raised his head and scented the air. "That's enough for me." Without another word, he drifted into the trees with barely a sound, melting away with a grace that belied his size.

Prism enjoyed watching the cubs' antics. Certain this was the she-bear that she and Kodi had met in the cave, Prism tugged up a mouthful of ramps and savoured the onions as she waited for the sow to arrive.

The she-bear ambled into the clearing and cried to her cubs. The pair ceased their chasing and tucked in to follow, huddled behind her bulk. "What's happening in my glade? There're more animals passing the entrance to my cave than usual."

Echo explained about his power to transform rocks into a sustenance that would protect her, and encouraged her to eat. Without any hesitation, the bear gorged on whatever Echo offered her. The cubs tried a few mouthfuls too before returning to their play.

Prism wished Kodi could see them; he was particularly fond of young animals. As if she had summoned him, the guardian galumphed into the clearing. With a cry of warning, the she-bear drove her cubs away and headed back up the hillside.

Over the ensuing days, many more creatures came to meet the unicorns and share the providence. Most were busy stashing away food either in secret stores or in their bodies ready for hibernation. Prism could no longer find any more fallen stones and had witnessed no more meteorite showers, even though the night skies remained clear. The moon had risen, delaying any further attempts at flight.

At dawn, Echo had said he was going to seek any creatures that hadn't come to him. Taking what he could carry, he had left to distribute his bounty. A new wave of concern washed over Prism as Kodi shared more news of his enquiries. No-one had seen or heard anything about Claw or the goddess's feather.

While discussing with Kodi what they should do next, the bull moose ventured into the clearing. He stumbled as he crossed the creek, his head low and tongue lolling.

Prism trotted over to meet him. "What's happened? You look unwell. You should have been protected by Echo's sustenance."

The moose raised a head covered in scabs. "The plague has reached here." Pendulous growths hung from his neck and chin. Blood dripped from his nose. His once-glossy hide had large patches of hair missing and boils oozed over his rump. Even his hooves were cracked and chipped.

Prism was shocked to see the haggard bull. "Here, have the last of what Echo left."

The moose shook his head. "No. Save it for those still well. It's too late for me. I must have caught it down south before I met you. Being old, older than I look, I'm more susceptible. I only came to warn you."

Wanting to help the moose, Prism tried to think of the herbs that Gem would use. Although her dam had taught her the healing properties of every plant, she had paid scant attention. Gem, Laila, and the dragons healed any animals seeking help at Shimmering Lake. Prism had never expected to need the knowledge. Now she struggled to remember. Milfoil should staunch any bleeding. She tore up mouthfuls of the feathery plant and dropped them for him to eat. She also searched for agrimony and hypericum, hoping that one of them would at least ease his symptoms. While she gathered enough to deliver to the moose, thoughts buzzed in her brain like angry wasps.

The bull accepted her medications before taking a deep drink. "I'll go now. It's been a delight to meet you. I doubt I'll see you again until we meet in the spirit world. Your coming was the harbinger of my death." Then he was gone.

Harbinger of death! What did he mean? Was she the problem? Was she the unicorn causing the plague? Having taken root, the notion grew until it filled her head, threatening to burst her skull. Is this why she couldn't fly? Was she evil, a throwback to the duocorn? He was Fleet's grandsire after all, which made him her great-great-grandsire. Or did she have bad genes passed down by the crippled Jasper, Fleet's sire?

Kodi laid a paw on her back. "Stop it. I can see what you're thinking. It's not you. It was a bad choice of words. How can you even entertain the idea that you're the cause? The plague was here long before we arrived. Remember, that's why I came to find you in the first place."

Only slightly reassured, Prism paced back and forth, pawing at the ground and twitching her tail. "But what does it mean? Why is the moose sick after we gave him some of Echo's sustenance? Didn't we give him enough? He's very big."

Another worry teased at the edge of her mind. "You don't think—" She couldn't bring herself to say it. Memories sprang from when Gem had related tales of the first-generation unicorns and their powers, even though she had only known her own dam, Diamond. Something nagged at Prism. What was it? "Is it true that Echo can create medication as well as sustenance? Too much of a medicine can be poison."

Kodi slumped to the ground and scratched his thighs. "Yes. But surely you're not suggesting he's to blame? He's trying as hard as we are to make things right."

"Of course, but what if he doesn't realise what he's doing?" The possibility wouldn't leave Prism alone, tweaking other memories.

Kodi swiped a fly away from his face and considered her suggestion. "Did you say he focused his power as he transformed the stones? Isn't that how he added potency to the ones he made to help you?"

And that hadn't worked. Prism thought of all she'd learnt about Echo's powers. She'd never paid much attention, only desiring to meet the older unicorns. Tempest could do something with the weather. That had never mattered at Shimmering Lake where spring, summer, and autumn combined all year round. Her parents had far more power, with Gem creating life merely by swimming in the lake and Mystery able to detect every element he touched, even deep in the earth beneath his hooves. She wished they were here now. But she hadn't been able to contact them since...since eating Echo's nourishment. Could that be why, that it was the food, not the poisoned air?

Before she could ponder the situation further, the she-bear shuffled in to the clearing. The cubs dawdled behind, no longer playful. Keeping a safe distance from Kodi, the sow approached Prism. "Is there more food? I haven't the energy to seek any out on the mountainside."

Prism blocked the bear's path to the remaining pile of spongey mess that Echo had transformed. "There is, but I don't think you should eat it."

The bear growled low in her throat. "Who are you saving it for? I passed many corpses on the way here and I can't eat those. They're diseased."

Kodi rose to his feet, stretching much taller than the she-bear. He had begun to think that Prism was right; something was wrong with the food. He couldn't let the bear take the risk. "Take your cubs back to your den and settle for winter."

The she-bear snarled and checked that her cubs were safe behind her. "What would you know? Have you ever raised two hungry cubs? I need more food to give them milk. We need to build up our reserves. Who knows how harsh this winter will be?"

Prism glanced between the cubs and the sow. "Please, return to your cave. This little bit of food won't make any difference."

Witnessing Prism's distress disturbed Kodi as much as the sick sow and cubs. Until now, Prism had always trusted they'd find a solution. Even when she had been upset by the effects of the plague, or angry when her attempts to fly repeatedly failed, she had never been as distraught as this. She could hardly stand in one spot in her anxiety. Doubting the mother bear would listen to Prism, only one way remained to drive her away. He drew himself up to his full height, slashed the air with his massive claws, and roared. Lunging around Prism, he headed straight for the cubs.

The she-bear screamed a warning before raking him with her claws. Blood erupted from his nose, but at least she spun and chased her offspring up the hillside. Birds ceased their trilling. A silence settled on the glade. Not even a breeze rustled the leaves. Kodi watched the bears go, saddened by his action, but it had been necessary.

Prism gathered up the last of the milfoil and carried it over to him. "I think you need some of this too."

Embarrassed at his aggression, Kodi mumbled his thanks. He had only ever been roused like that before in defending the goddess's feathers. He had never expected to attack another bear, let alone a mother with cubs. "I couldn't think of another way to stop her eating."

Prism nuzzled his shoulder. "You did what was necessary. I couldn't have convinced her. Are you alright?"

His nose stung, but other than that, he had suffered no harm. "Do you really think that Echo's sustenance is the cause of the plague?"

Prism released a long sigh and paced around what was left of the transformed rocks. "It seems too much of a coincidence if it's not."

Kodi sought a patch of shade where he could think the matter through. "But Echo hasn't been as far south as the horse herd we met. They'd have said if he'd been there. They hadn't eaten any of his mush."

Prism wouldn't settle. "What if the rotfrogs ate the food then poisoned the waters? The water flows towards the sea and might have tainted everything that drank from it, animals and plants."

The concept had merit. Kodi scratched his face and flinched as he inadvertently knocked his torn nose. "That would explain the algae perhaps. There's none in the creeks here. I wonder if it'll grow now that the animals are becoming diseased."

Neither of them could come up with a definitive answer. The one topic they avoided was how they would tackle Echo if what they suspected proved to be true. Kodi sought a different solution. "We mustn't forget the stolen feather. What if Claw is using it, either knowingly or not, in some way? We don't know where he is. He might be nearby."

Prism stopped with one hoof in the air, brightness back in her eye. "You're right. That's far more likely." Then her neck drooped. "But that doesn't explain why the goddess told me a unicorn must be the harbinger of death."

"Don't dwell on that. We don't know what that means." Kodi hesitated to suggest that Prism hadn't interpreted her vision of the goddess correctly. After all, she was the Spirit Unicorn.

Instead, he pondered the meaning of the feathers. He had been their guardian all his life. He couldn't ever remember being a cub. He had always lived in the cave where Jasper had carved a niche to protect the treasure. There must have been five for a reason. Were they supposed to be used together? Whenever Prism returned from one of her failed attempts to fly, he suspected the feathers' real purpose had been to belong to her.

All five of them. Now only one remained, and he didn't know where. Even if he did find it, would one alone be enough to help her fly?

Prism guessed Kodi wasn't sharing all his thoughts. "If Claw was to blame, the plague must travel through the air. That would explain everyone's breathing difficulties, and why Echo hadn't been able to contact us."

Kodi cocked his head on one side and paused before answering. "I suppose it's possible. Or Echo's magic rocks could be blocking your mind communications. You only failed to call Gem and Mystery after we found Echo. You didn't have that problem in the south, even where the plague was worse."

Prism thought back. "I've had the same thought, but I hadn't tried to contact anyone for ages before that. I don't know when I stopped being able to." The possibility that a unicorn was truly the cause of all the problems still didn't sit well with Prism. It just didn't make sense. "But why would Echo poison his territory? He said he'd tried to contact us for help." The only explanation Prism could see was that Echo didn't know what he was doing.

Kodi offered an alternative. "He's the oldest of the remaining first-generation. Perhaps he's trying to get to the spirit world. He might think that by doing this, the goddess will come and get him."

Prism couldn't give any credence to such a notion. "I can't believe a unicorn can do deliberate harm. It goes against our very nature."

"What about the duocorn? Look what devastation he's wrought."

Pacing back and forth, Prism muttered to herself then halted in front of Kodi. "Shadow isn't a unicorn. A hotblood, yes, but not a unicorn. His dual horns are evidence of his corruption."

The old guardian shrank against the trunk of the tree. "I still think Echo believes his time is up. I know the feeling well, know what it's like to no longer be of use. I'd happily go to the spirit world if the goddess would have me, but I've failed in my duty. I expect that's why I became sick."

Prism struck the ground with her hoof. "Don't say that. Echo's time isn't up any more than yours. He isn't of no use. Neither are you."

Staring at the distant peaks consumed by heavy snow clouds, Prism stamped again. "We must search harder for Claw. I'm sure he's involved somehow. Why else did he aid Echo collect the first rocks?"

Chapter 12

A cold wind chilled the sweat on Delsin's neck as he tugged on a bark rope. Bracing his feet against the rough timber, he heaved two logs together and lashed the end as tight as he could. The crooked trunks didn't lie as snug as he'd like but they'd have to suffice. That was the last one.

Building a raft had proved harder than Delsin's insight in the sweat-lodge had led him to believe. It had taken him days to find enough bark to twist and plait for ropes. Although he had been fortunate to find a derelict beaver dam as a supply of timber, as he would never have been able to chop down sufficient trees with only his flints, he had still required many hours to lug the logs to level ground. No doubt, his brother would have had a raft constructed in no time, but Delsin didn't share Bly's physique.

Rocky looked worse every time Delsin checked. The horse's eyes had lost their sparkle and blood dribbled from his nose. Delsin was careful not to touch the drool that hung in strands from the horse's lips. "Are you ready? Don't rush."

Rocky snorted a spray of guck in all directions and staggered to the water's edge. "Won't we end up at the sea? That's the wrong way."

Delsin reassured the stallion with a pat and hefted a long pole. "I'll push us like I used to do as a kid, albeit on a smaller creek. Let's go."

As Delsin held the raft steady, Rocky stepped on board. The contraption wobbled as he placed his weight on one hoof. "Are you sure this is safe?"

Shrugging, Delsin held up his hands. "It's this raft or nothing.

You should have left when you still could."

"I know, I know, so you keep telling me. But if you think I'd leave you alone then you don't understand friendship." Rocky jumped the short distance onto the logs and splayed his legs as his hooves slipped. The raft pitched, putrid algae lapping over the edges as it settled beneath the horse's weight. Rotfrogs hopped on board, stinking pus erupting from boils on their deformed limbs. Some had no eyes, others had many. With every croak, they spat bile in a wide spray.

Delsin leapt next to Rocky and shoved the sick amphibians back into the slime with the end of his pole. Balancing his weight to steady the raft, he exhaled a long breath. After a glance at Rocky on the slippery logs, he thrust against the muddy bottom of the befouled pond. A dead fish rose to the surface, its eyes smoky and scales slipping off in a puddle of mucus. As the guts of the fish burst open, the stench threatened to relieve Delsin of his paltry breakfast. He pushed off, heading for clearer water.

At least the algae that coated every surface near the banks dissipated in deeper water. In its place, tendrils of red weed crept below the surface, snagging Delsin's pole or dragging the front of the raft down with its weight. He had to keep sidling to the front to clear the obstruction before creeping back to propel the punt. Meanwhile, Rocky teetered on the unstable platform, trying not to let his hooves slip between the cracks that opened and closed as the logs shifted.

Nimbus clouds loomed over the distant hills, their purple bellies threatening snow, muffling the world so only the tiny splosh of the pole breaking the surface reached Delsin's ears. The absence of the croaking rotfrogs added to the ominous silence. Delsin glanced to either side of the waterway to pick out landmarks to navigate by. With the jade carving stolen, all he could do was head north and hope they'd find signs of Prism and Kodi. "Winter is coming. We'll need to go ashore a few times a day in order to get food. I hope we find Prism soon."

Rocky eased his limbs gingerly to avoid capsizing the raft. "I'll keep sending out mind messages. When we get close enough, she'll guide us."

Delsin hid his concerns, knowing Rocky would do his best. "The trouble is, we have no idea how far these waters stretch."

The skewbald blew a stream of muck from his nostrils. "We can only do what we can do. Focus on today, not tomorrow."

Knowing the stallion was right, Delsin settled into a steady rhythm with his pushing. In order to reach the lakebed with the short pole, as well as to make access to solid ground easier, he had to remain reasonably near the winding bank. Travelling in the clearer water towards the centre would shorten the distance, but was too risky in case they capsized or the lakes had currents that would drag them the wrong way. The rivers looped through the land like the coils of a serpent. Delsin shivered as he recalled his close encounter with Lash, the giant snake. Could the beast follow them through the waterways?

With the darkening clouds and shorter days, the light soon diminished. On clear nights, Delsin used the stars as his guide. Now, unable to see the outcrop of rocks he had picked to guide him, he had to stop. But slime coated the shallow bank, hiding he knew not what. If Rocky became bogged in the mud, Delsin would never get him out. "Watch out for a place to land."

Rocky blinked and shook his mane, causing water to wash up over the logs. "We don't have to stop yet. I can guide you. My eyesight's better than yours."

"Are you sure? I've been keeping that crag to our left. Can you watch it as well as spot any obstacles in our path?" Delsin worried that the horse needed to rest more than stare into the gloom. If they hit a submerged tree, they could easily tip up and both drown, and who knew what rotten creatures might lurk in the depths.

Rocky stretched his neck to peer ahead. "You're right. It's getting too dark to be safe. I could do with a drink anyway."

Locating a dry place to beach took longer than expected. Once Rocky had scrambled to safety, Delsin used the last of his strength to drag the heavy logs up far enough so the raft wouldn't float away, his arms screaming in their sockets from poling all day.

All days blurred into one, an endless nightmare of punting, shoving, and slogging through mud. Rocky's condition deteriorated further. Delsin's concern grew that they wouldn't reach help before Rocky became unable to climb on and off the raft. Already he had ceased grazing on the few course grasses when they stopped. Delsin spent most of his waking hours on land harvesting whatever the stallion would eat. By the time Delsin had cooked his own meagre meal, he fell asleep without even undertaking his usual ritual of thanking the Mother for another day survived.

Time after time, the maze of waterways led them into dead ends or unnavigable stretches, forcing them to backtrack. Once, a thick fog had descended making it impossible to move for half a day. Their only option had been to steer to the nearest dry land and sit it out. With clouds obscuring the sky, neither sun nor moon had offered any reassurance that they still headed north. Only the bitter wind that blew in their faces confirmed their direction, and Delsin had started to doubt that too. What if the winds blew differently in winter this side of Rattlesnake Ranges? Nothing was the same as at home.

Not that he missed Midlands. He didn't have the energy to miss anything. Life had become one continuous struggle to pole the raft, hunt for food and water, and light a fire to huddle round at night. There had been no sign of life to fear, not even the howl of wolves that he would have expected. Delsin used any spare moment to sleep. Even when standing on the rear of the raft he would drift into a doze, his arms pushing without conscious effort. The threatening snow had materialised, coating the countryside in a white dust, further reducing visibility and upsetting his orientation.

Plant the pole, push against the muddy riverbed, retrieve the pole, hands cold and wet on wood, fingers numb. Plant the pole, push against the bed, retrieve the pole. Plant, push, retrieve. Plant, push, retrieve.

A jolt thrust Delsin fully aware. The raft banged against something hard. Rocky scrambled and fell with a thump. The uneven weight tipped the logs up to one side. The raft listed further. Rocky slid towards the water. Delsin leapt to the opposite side to balance the precarious craft. "Don't struggle. You'll make it worse."

Stretching forward, Delsin shoved against the obstacle with the pole. The raft wouldn't budge. He stepped closer to gain more leverage and slipped, landing on top of the skewbald. Not bothering to rise, he thrust his legs against what he could now see was a fallen tree jammed against a rock. The current flicked the raft around and wedged it against the submerged limbs. Delsin fought the might of the water as well as the logs' weight, his thigh muscles popping as he attempted to dislodge the blockage.

The raft spun free, whiplashing his neck, and floated along on the current. Delsin didn't dare stand up so he spread his arms and legs wide to maintain the little balance the raft had. Rocky whickered in distress, still lying prone on the edge of the platform, his hooves dangling in the icy water up to his fetlocks. The raft plunged and twirled as the rapids caught hold and dragged it in their fury.

Nothing Delsin did made any difference. He wrapped his arms around Rocky's neck, more for comfort than stability. He wouldn't be able to stop the horse from slipping off. If Rocky went, he would go too.

The world turned end over end and went black.

Delsin regained consciousness, his legs soaked and freezing. Rocky lay next to him on a stony ridge, the shallow rise and fall of the stallion's protruding ribs the only sign he lived. Delsin vomited, wiped his mouth on one arm, and checked the surroundings. They were stranded on a tiny island. No, more a wash of pebbles built up in the wake of a massive boulder. Water gushed around either side, the spray soaking through Delsin's clothes, adding to his cold. The only redeeming feature was the raft wasn't damaged.

But it propped on end on the bank, across the raging stream, out of reach. There was only one thing Delsin could do. He stripped down to his boots, gritted his teeth, and splashed into the frigid depths.

Rocky raised his muzzle and nickered. "Don't. You'll die."

Delsin sucked in a deep breath as the water rose up his thighs. "We'll die if I don't." He waded to where the raft teetered on end and grabbed hold of one of the ropes.

At least the cold had driven the last of the rotfrogs away. Whether they were hibernating or had moved further south, Delsin had no idea, and at the moment didn't care. One thing at a time. His legs and feet were already numb, making progress difficult. Shivers racked his shoulders. As he hauled the raft onto the water, a protruding stump caught him in the forehead, almost knocking him unconscious again. He shook the stars from his eyes, wriggled the top of his body across the raft, and used his hips to push against the flow of water. For once, luck was on his side and the logs floated ahead like a child's toy.

Getting Rocky back on was a different matter. The horse had no strength left to stand, let along jump onto a moving platform. After much trial and error, Delsin manoeuvred the raft below where Rocky lay and wedged the ends of the logs under the horse's spine. "Grab this rope in your teeth if you can. We can't let the raft drift away."

Delsin lashed another rope around all four of Rocky's legs, just below the knees and hocks. Retreating to the stallion's other side, he waded waist-deep into the water and pulled. Rocky's legs rose in the air. He hovered like a horse stuck mid-roll then, with what little energy he had left, twisted and squirmed until he collapsed onto the raft.

Delsin caught his breath, heaved out of the water, and flopped beside Rocky, no longer able to feel his arms, his fingers blue. His teeth chattered, threatening to bite his tongue. "I'll pull us to the bank and get a fire going. And I need to cut another pole."

Having lit a fire, eaten, and replaced the lost pole, Delsin struggled to determine where they were. "We must have been carried down an offshoot. I don't recognise any landmarks."

Rocky shivered under the pine fronds that Delsin had used in an attempt to keep the horse warm. "It's time you left me. I'm only a burden. If you think there's no risk of catching my illness, kill me and eat my flesh. I'll do you more good as food."

"Don't talk rot. How could you even think such a thing? What was it you said about friendship? I'm not leaving you. The cold's affected your brain." Delsin rearranged his drying clothes as a distraction. Deep down, he knew Rocky was right, he couldn't drag the horse on and off the raft every time they needed to stop.

The idea of dragging sparked a memory from the stealthcat war in Eastlands. Laila had constructed a contraption for the horses to tow, to help the people move their possessions. Perhaps he could do something the other way round. He'd never be able to drag anything as heavy as the raft. Pondering designs, Delsin wrapped his outer jerkin around him and wandered into the forest. Many saplings had fallen over from the wind or under the weight of very deep snow away from the water's edge.

Filled with the energy of inspiration, Delsin hastened back to his pack that had fortunately remained strapped to the raft. He extracted his flint axe and dressed fully. "I'll get you something to eat soon. First I have a sled to build."

He floundered back through the snowdrifts into the trees and cut down what he needed. Then he returned to his camp, stoked up the fire, and laboured to build a lightweight platform big enough to fit under Rocky's dwindling bulk. He'd have to drag Rocky above the ground to prevent injuring him. First, he bent and hardened the two outer poles by heating them in the hot coals and plunging them into cold water. Once the frame was stable, he wove the remaining limbs like a giant basket on runners. As his dinner cooked on the steaming coals, Delsin reused the ropes from the original heavy raft to form a harness for his shoulders, padding it with soft furs from his pack. By the time he'd finished building the odd contraption, his limbs hung like wilted greens. After a short break, he heaved himself to his feet, stretched his aching muscles, and returned to the forest. Gathering enough fodder to keep them going for a few days stole the remainder of his strength. He stoked the fire, checked on Rocky, and settled down.

Tomorrow he would need all the strength he could muster.

Chapter 13

Snow drifts higher than Prism's ears rolled ahead through the bottom of the valley as she continued her search for Claw and answers to the plague. Whichever river flowed beneath her hooves lay hidden deep under thick ice. Unable to feel the earth, Prism drew on the energy of the wind. Even though Mystery had warned her of his experience of snow from when he had crossed Dragonspine Mountains, she hadn't expected to suffer the same way. Without the connection with the ground thrumming life up her limbs and feeding her energy with every step, her balance became disoriented and her sense of space unsettled. More and more she had to rely on her sight and hearing to prevent stumbling, holding out her wings for support when her hooves broke through the frozen crust.

After one such event that left her gasping, she halted, rearranged her feathers to settle along her ribs, and gazed over the waves of white and grey that looked like a great sea frozen in a storm.

Kodi floundered to where she stood, puffing as his eyes followed her pointing horn. "What do you see?"

Prism studied the dark grey shapes that had confused her for a while. At times they seemed to move, then one of the scudding clouds would hasten across the sky, blending the forms into the drifts. Maybe they were an illusion. "I don't know. Can you smell anything?"

Scenting the air, Kodi turned his head to catch sounds too. "I think it's a wolf pack."

"Wolves. Is that a good or a bad sign up here?" Prism had only met one, Laila's friend Paws. Prism loved playing chase with the wolf who could dodge and parry faster than her. Prism could outrun Paws over a long distance but not in a short sprint. "Let's go and meet them."

Indicating a copse of pines that jutted from the deep drifts, Kodi suggested she go alone. "I'll wait here. I might spook them. They're more likely to talk with you."

Suspecting Kodi needed a breather after the long hard climb through the deep snow, Prism set off to investigate, her enthusiasm overcoming her need for caution on the unsure footing. Flashes of sunlight reflected off her hooves as she plunged belly-deep through the powder, sending crystals in a spray with every bound. She descended, squinting against the glare from the snow, unsure at times that the grey shapes were still there. Then they'd take form again, different to the previous view, mutating like Echo's stones.

The closer she came to the valley floor, the more certain she became that what she had taken for two or three shadows was in fact a pack of wolves as Kodi had surmised, clustered around a brown lump. As she neared, she recognised a fallen moose. A pang of despair swept through her veins. A dead moose. Two immature male wolves ceased their tug of war on a piece of its hide as she approached. Slowing down so she didn't scare the pack, she strutted within hailing distance and called out her name. "I desire to speak with you."

The wolves arrayed themselves around their kill, growls rumbling low in their throats. A large male stepped forward, his thick ruff, muzzle, and tail tipped with white hairs. He sat on his haunches between Prism and the pack as if he had not a care in the world, least of all the worry of a rainbow-dappled unicorn entering his domain. "I haven't met you before. Why are you here?"

Prism halted and lowered her nose to demonstrate she was no threat. "I'm searching for one of the goddess's golden feathers, and a giant eagle named Claw. Have you seen or heard of them?"

The wolf licked his lips and twitched his ears. Behind him the yearlings mumbled and squirmed before getting a snap from one of the bitches. He ignored the disturbance. "No, we've heard nothing like that. Is Echo with you?"

"You know him!" Prism was always amazed that so many of the creatures knew of her grandsire.

"Of course. He looks after us all. He'll be busy this winter with the season so hard, though that's good for us wolves. We're well fed."

Prism glanced at the remains of the cow moose, blood-stained snow churned around her torn carcass, her head cranked back exposing a torn throat. Her disembowelled belly gave off whiffs of dung amid fresh meat. "I hope she didn't have a calf."

The dominant male threw a quick glance at his family. "What about my cubs? But don't worry, she was old. That's the way life is. We saved her a winter of suffering. She wouldn't have survived until spring."

Prism acknowledged the natural order of life. If the moose had died of cold and been buried by snow, her body would have been wasted. Even so, the loss of such a once-fine beast still hurt. She was glad Kodi didn't eat animals like other bears did. She wouldn't be able to cope with hearing their cries as they died, or seeing him crunch on their tiny bones. At Shimmering Lake, Gem's favourite dragon, Tatuk, created food for newly-arrived carnivores.

Why had Echo's dragons left him? Surely, those who created food or performed healing were required more than ever. Echo could send them love to aid them as Gem did with her dragons, yet he had seemed unperturbed about their disappearance. One possible answer reflected Prism's major fear—that Echo was behind the troubles, he was the harbinger of death.

Prism and Kodi had waited for Echo's return before venturing north in pursuit of Claw, but she hadn't been able to raise her doubts with him about whether he was creating the poison behind the plague, unable to confront her grandsire with such an accusation. He hadn't been surprised that she had wanted to keep searching for Claw, and had only asked her to remember the locations of any more meteorite falls they witnessed before he left again.

The wolf waited for Prism's response, head cocked to one side and tongue lolling.

She thrust her doubts aside and explained about the plague to the south and her worries it was spreading northwards.

The leader rose and padded to each of his pack, introducing them as he went. "As you can see we're all well, thriving, in fact. You need to ask the birds about the eagle and the feather. But most of them have flown south."

Another fear stabbed Prism. What if the birds had migrated into the worst of the plague, never to return? She couldn't imagine a forest in spring and summer without birdsong. The empty skies and quiet of winter were bad enough. Even the few birds that remained huddled deep in the forest were silent from the cold, or their songs were muffled by the snow. Only the wind spoke among the branches and soared over the ridges.

After discussing more about the land and inhabitants around them, Prism decided the wolf was right. There was nothing for her up here other than bad weather. She needed to get back to Kodi.

She found the guardian nestled at the base of a cliff in a clump of prickly shrubs near the copse of pines. Red saliva dribbled from his mouth, scaring Prism that his condition had worsened, until she saw him feasting on the desiccated remains of autumn's last berries. Few drifts had built in the lee of the wind and, from the broken stems she could see, the bear had been able to reach higher than any other inhabitants.

She shared what she had learnt from the wolves. "I think we need to move on."

Slobbering, Kodi licked his paws and nodded. "Pity, as this is the best meal I've had in a long time, but I agree. The weather will only worsen. We need to find somewhere to wait out the winter."

Prism didn't intend abandoning their search. "We can't do that. We just need to look elsewhere, maybe further west."

Kodi clambered to his feet and accompanied her back the way they had come. "There's no point searching while the snow is so deep. It makes the going hard and we're unlikely to find anything. I think we should go back to the she-bear's territory. If we can't find another cave nearby, hers is big enough for us all."

Prism doubted the lady bear would welcome Kodi in her domain, and doing nothing for moons wouldn't fulfil her mission. "Let's head that way and decide what to do when we get there."

Going back took less time than their climb through unknown territory, partly because they didn't need to side-track in search of answers or easy trails, and partly due to the wind that blew from behind. If Prism's head hadn't been buzzing with worry, she might have enjoyed the strength of the blow pushing her along, carrying her as much as the energy it filled her with, teasing her to open her wings. She kept them clenched to her sides.

Kodi had picked up speed from his feast, or maybe from the

possibility of denning in a sheltered cave. The sky smoothed into a solid grey hide, shielding the peaks of the mountains. More snow was coming. A dark speck caught her eye. Was that an eagle? She skidded to a halt in a cloud of white and pointed out the circling shape to Kodi. "What do you think?"

He squinted, his nose twitching as if to smell the bird. "It's certainly an eagle, but I can't sense any power, or see any gold."

Disappointment washed over Prism like the water that trickled beneath the frozen waterfalls. None of the forest birds had known anything of Claw. Her only hope was to talk to another eagle. But the birds of prey soared out of reach, never responding to her calls. Her only chance to speak with them was to join them in the sky. To fly.

Pushing on in frustration, Prism formulated a plan. She'd pretend to settle for the winter in a den with Kodi and, when he was deep in hibernation, steal away. She'd find somewhere she could stretch her wings through the long dark nights, somewhere the soft snow would protect her if she failed, somewhere no eyes could observe her attempts.

By the time they reached the familiar landscape around the she-bear's cave, Prism's determination had built into a force of its own. They had been unsuccessful in finding another cave nearby. Now they crept into the entrance, not wanting to disturb the bear if she was already asleep. Prism blinked while her eyes adjusted to the dim interior. Turning a corner into the deeper recesses, she expected darkness to close in. Instead, a white orb glowed across the full width of the cave. Confused by the image, Prism halted.

The orb moved. Six legs rattled against the stone floor. Another two held a net of fine silk, large enough to encompass Prism's head. She backed up, bumping into Kodi in her haste. The giant spider glared at her with eight crimson eyes, its mouthparts opening and closing with a clatter.

"Die."

Kodi reeled as the order shrieked through his head. As he caught his balance, he realised the spider had spoken aloud, not in his mind. But it was the same. The same voice. Joy at the terrible words not being his own mingled with the horror of what stood before him.

Ignoring their presence, the spider turned her back and advanced deeper into the cavern.

Kodi had no doubt that the spider was intent on capturing one of the cubs. "Stop!"

"No!" Prism's shout echoed his despair.

The spider rotated back to face them. "Hungry."

Prism advanced, her horn lowered. "Please. Talk to us first." She introduced herself and Kodi, and explained their mission. "Who are you?"

Kodi related how he had ventured from Snowhaven, far away in Dragonspine Mountains. If they kept the spider's attention, the noise might wake the she-bear and she'd take her cubs to safety. There might be a back entrance to the cave, or at least an opening which the spider couldn't fit through. Bigger than him, bigger even than Prism, the spider's body looked like a giant boulder with a tiny stone for a head. Already a suspicion came to his mind, confirmed when the spider said her name.

"Snag."

He had heard the tales of the monstrous arachnid. "Why aren't you at Obsidian Caves, or with Shadow?"

"Gone."

Prism took a tentative step forward. "Has the barrier come down since he left? Is that how Lash came here too?"

"Cold."

Kodi didn't know whether Snag was referring to the home she'd left behind or here. "This cave's warmer than outside, but there are others. This one's already taken. You must find a new home."

"Eat."

Exasperated by the one word sentences, Kodi remembered how he'd heard Snag over the last few moons. He tried using his mind to communicate with her. Perhaps she could tell him more that way. *Why are you in Westlands? How long have you been travelling?*

No. Go. Light.

That made sense. With her lack of pigment, Kodi suspected Snag could only travel at night. It would have taken her a very long time to reach here. He didn't think she could have arrived early enough to have anything to do with the plague. But what else had escaped Shadow's territory? They had already suspected the barrier had come down from meeting Lash.

Prism nudged his forearm. "What should we do?"

Knowing that Prism couldn't hear his thoughts, he quickly explained about being able to communicate with Snag like unicorns did between themselves and with dragons. "Surely that must mean she's one of the goddess's special creatures, like me."

As soon as Prism recognised the spider from her parents' stories, she had stared not at the throbbing white body but at the gossamer fibres between Snag's front legs. They looked so delicate, so pretty to have been made by such a grotesque creature. Then as the spider shuffled back into the bear's den, Prism saw how the stretching strands glinted with power. "Please don't hurt a cub. I'll find you something better to eat."

She had no idea what. Had Gem and Mystery located Diamond yet? But even if she could call them, they wouldn't get here in time to save the cubs, even if Diamond was able to transport them. Prism had to work this out. She was the one who had come west to save the lands. Grateful that Snag had turned back toward her, Prism waited for Kodi to translate her queries and the spider's responses into mind messages, easier than vocal communication.

His upper lip curled as he passed on Snag's replies. "She likes sweet things, like I do. But there aren't any berries left near here. And there certainly won't be any bumblebee nectar."

Stretching her brain like the spider's threads, Prism struggled to find a solution. She remembered the sugar that the humans had made from maple sap in the south. There were no trees like that up here. Perhaps pine would be similar. "Kodi, keep her talking. I've an idea."

Relying on Kodi to distract the spider long enough to prevent her capturing the cubs, Prism dashed outside and ran to the nearest tree. A blob of resin stuck to the trunk where a branch had snapped off, its tart scent pleasant. She licked it, but the smooth surface had little taste. She struck the blob with her horn to knock it free. The tiny globule fell to the ground, almost lost in the pine needles. It didn't look big enough to satisfy a giant spider. A deeper hole was required, like a woodpecker would do, like the people used to tap the maples, but Prism wouldn't be able to chip enough bark and wood away with her horn and biting the tree might damage the sap wood.

She placed the tip of her horn against the wound to extract more. Now what? She couldn't blast power like Jasper had done to carve rock. Drawing on Equinora's power, she summoned heat from the wind, narrowed the energy through her horn, and concentrated hard. A small wisp of smoke spiralled upwards. She jerked back from the smell, not wanting to hurt the tree. But the tree could heal a small wound; a small injury wouldn't kill it. If she didn't get the sap, then Snag would devour the young bears.

Prism placed her horn back against the trunk and drilled a hole with the crystal tip. A sticky substance seeped down the rough bark. She tasted it. It wasn't sweet, but gummed up her lips. If Snag didn't like the tree essence, at least it would stick her web into a useless mass. Not having any other ideas, Prism continued drilling. The weeping slowed almost to a stop, with only a few beads solidifying large enough to remove and adhere to her horn.

Frustrated, Prism rushed to the next tree and tried again. Another droplet of amber liquid oozed from the trunk before crusting over. She tried again at the next tree. And the next. At each one, she only managed to extract a tiny amount. It would have to do. At least the stickiness made it easy to collect. Returning to each tree she'd harvested, she was relieved to see the seeping had recommenced after she had moved on, but then stopped when the nodule had hardened. Good. She would return and gather the lumps if she needed more.

Prism returned to the cave. Tension drained from her muscles as she found Snag still in the front chamber with Kodi. He had eased past her to block the passage to the interior. From the tapping of the spider's legs, Prism suspected the creature was getting impatient, so rubbed the sap from her horn with her front leg to deposit the nodules on the smooth ground. The tiny pile didn't look enough. She stepped back in case the spider reacted badly to the offering. "Try this."

Snag clattered against the cavern walls as she turned, the web net still held out in her front legs. She tucked it away beneath her body, leant down, and grasped the pine sap in her mandibles.

Prism held her breath, not knowing if the tree's essence would gum up the spider's mouthparts or even poison her.

The globules disappeared into the spider's maw. She lowered her head and sucked up the remainder. "Good. More."

Surprised, yet delighted that the spider relished the food, Prism bided for time. She couldn't gather a lot of sap without damaging every tree in the area. She had already selected those that she considered big enough not to harm. "Maybe tomorrow. Can't you draw on Equinora's energy like Kodi? He doesn't need to eat much, and he tells me you are one of the goddess's blessed family."

Snag reared on her back four legs and clacked her mandibles. "How?"

So the sap hadn't stuck them together. Prism peered behind the spider to Kodi. "Can you explain?"

Kodi nodded.

Prism jolted as a voice called into her mind. At first she wondered if she could hear Snag after all. But that was ridiculous; she had never been able to communicate like that with Kodi. And she recognised this voice, one she thought she might never hear again.

Diamond!

Replying to Diamond's call, Prism raced down the hillside from the bear's cave, her mind in turmoil like the snow flying beneath her hooves in all directions. Diamond had arrived, which meant Prism's parents had been able to reach her. Continuing to send mind messages as she had descended into thicker air, Prism didn't worry that her granddam didn't respond. Maybe her power to communicate by mind was coming back slowly and she could only hear, not send. Regardless, she could tell where Diamond was by her stream of messages, and reaching her far outweighed any other consideration at the moment.

A flash of silver broke the whiteness of the drifts that cloaked the far hillside as Prism reached the valley. She increased her pace and neighed so loud it caused thuds of snow to drop from laden branches. Diamond's pristine white form became visible as she turned towards the sound, her black hooves slashing the air like obsidian knives as she reared in welcome.

The two mares raced together, skidded to a halt, and snuffled their noses close in greeting. Prism backed up a step, in awe of the Light Unicorn, barely remembering her from when Prism had been a foal. Her granddam had been present at her birth but had left soon after, leaving her education to her parents.

Diamond's silver mane and tail shimmered like a frozen waterfall dusted with fresh snow. "Let's take shelter and you can tell me all that's happened."

Prism glanced over her shoulder back up the hill to the cave, torn between wanting to ensure Kodi and the other bears were alright and beginning her tale. Only by sharing her suspicions about Echo could she lighten that burden. "It's been awful. The plague has killed so many, and all the waterways are polluted."

Walking next to Diamond as they headed for the comfort of the forest, Prism recounted all she and Kodi had experienced since leaving Shimmering Lake. Diamond listened with patience, only interrupting to seek clarification on some minor point, such as the number of rotfrogs and the types of algae. Prism answered as best she could, glad of the excuse to delay the worst news she had to impart, yet at the same time wishing to rush and get it over with. After describing how Claw had located the meteorites, and how Echo had transformed the stones into salty cakes of sustenance, she told Diamond how her ability to communicate had been lost after eating the mush. She told of the moose and the bear becoming sick, and how the land to the north, where Echo had yet to visit, remained unscathed.

She paused, chewing a mouthful of nothing before yawning in trepidation. "So...as you can see...the trouble might be...without him realising of course...that Echo is poisoning—"

Diamond's head snaked out and bit her hard on the neck, drawing blood. "How dare you accuse my partner, your grandsire?"

Prism squealed and backed up in alarm, catching her hocks against a branch and falling to her hindquarters. She staggered back to her feet and trotted behind a tree, shaking as much as the limbs over her head as Diamond pursued her. Bites stung her rump.

Prism sought safety behind a wide trunk. "Wait! I'm not blaming him. I just don't know what else can be causing it."

Diamond ceased her attack, but her ears remained flat back on her neck and her teeth bared. "And did you find Aureana's last feather? Have you spoken to Claw? The eagle could have poisoned the stones."

Quivering with fear, Prism acknowledged there might be another answer. She had yet to tell of discovering Snag in the cave. That reminded her that she needed to get back in case Kodi was having trouble convincing the giant spider to leave the cubs alone. "I, I, no, but—"

Diamond swished her tail and advanced. "No. You're quick to cry for help but you didn't think things through. Why Mystery sent you rather than coming himself I can't imagine. You're far too young."

She relaxed and beckoned Prism to come out. "It's not your fault. Come and finish what you were saying. Tell me everything the wolves up north said."

One small step at a time, Prism crept back to where they had flattened the snow before, keeping further away from Diamond in case of another attack. Going on to share the discovery of Snag, and remembering she hadn't told her granddam about Lash either, Prism rushed the story out.

Diamond's eyes for which she was named gleamed with anger, though no longer directed at Prism. "You see. It must be the duocorn again. It's always the duocorn."

Keeping her head low in submission, Prism explained how Mystery didn't think he was the threat this time. "He says Shadow is—"

"Don't say that name to me. He lost the right to that name when he murdered Dewdrop."

Prism didn't want to have that argument now. "But what of the last part of my vision? The goddess told me a unicorn must be the harbinger of death. Shad…the duocorn isn't a unicorn. It obviously isn't Gem, Mystery, you, or me. That only leaves Tempest or Echo."

This time the fury in Diamond's eyes pierced Prism like a bolt of lightning. She reeled back, fearing another painful strike.

Diamond shimmered. Sparks flew from her horn. And then she was gone.

Chapter 14

Echo couldn't remember a time when exhaustion had drained him before. His bones weighed heavily inside his withering muscles, his skin sagged, and his hooves dragged at every step. Aureana's power had seeped away from Equinora, leaving him bereft. He couldn't even communicate with the other unicorns to see how they fared. Were they all dead? Surely he would have felt them passing, like those terrible moments when Dewdrop had been slain by Shadow, when Jasper had plummeted to his death, and later, the tragedy of Moonglow's suicide, all of them joining Aureana in the spirit world

The time had come for him to follow them. His willpower, like his desire to continue protecting his land, had dried up like a creek at the end of a long hot summer. Only the plight of those who depended on him kept him going. One step at a time. One rock at a time. One pile of sustenance at a time.

As he couldn't use his power until he had recovered his strength, Echo sought out the one place that always cheered his spirits. He entered the gorge and broke into a trot, his spirits lifting already. The trail twisted and turned along the course of the brook that burbled over stones polished smooth. His muscles relaxed as he saw no corpses as in the other waterways, no vile amphibians belching noxious bile, no clogging algae or weed.

His favourite glade nestled in a narrow gully sheltered from the wind. Although the high walls meant the sun rarely shone to the base, the protection prevented the majority of the snowfalls blowing in. Those few flakes that fell soon melted from the radiated heat of the rock walls. Hot water steamed from a pool at the far end, bubbling warmth from deep below, feeding the lush vegetation that cloaked the valley in a flush of flowers for most of the year. At least the geyser still blew, even higher than in the past, providing an oasis of warmth around its perimeter. He had hesitated to come here before this, partly because he had been too busy, partly because he feared his haven may have been destroyed by the recent earthquakes.

But something was missing.

The dragons. Of course. This had also been their favourite place. So they hadn't taken shelter here. The last glimmer of hope that they had sought refuge in this sacred place evaporated. They were truly gone. Echo's pleasure at returning to his sanctuary diminished even further—no animals lived here anymore. At the start of the plague, he had constructed a protective shield around the glade and pool to keep out all creatures, other than the dragons, in case any visitors carried the poison. Now he missed the cheerful songs of birds and the delight of the tiny mammals that used to relish a warm swim. The larger herbivores had rarely come, not wanting to be trapped in a narrow valley with no escape. Occasionally a bear had arrived but, like him, they preferred to be solitary and respected his domain.

Wondering whether he should drop the barrier so those animals seeking respite could enter, Echo reared in surprise as a flash of sunlight reflected from a sheet of white on the other side of the pool, against the cliff where the gully ended. Had a snowdrift fallen from overhead? Another flash outlined a white mare with a silver horn.

Diamond!

She didn't answer.

"Diamond!"

"Echo! I trusted you'd come eventually. I've been calling and calling you." Diamond pranced to join him, her knees high and her black hooves flashing like wet obsidian. Her eyes sparkled and her mane and tail mirrored a spring waterfall in the sun.

Echo's demeanour lifted like the steam rising from the pool. The first-generation unicorns didn't usually spend long in each other's company, not being able to shield their thoughts in close proximity, stealing the privacy they all craved. Now Echo had no such concern. "It's wonderful to see you. You look as beautiful as ever." Memories of their last time here rushed through his loins, the time they had mated, a joining that had resulted in the birth of Gemstone.

"I'm sorry to say I can't say the same for you. You look terrible. And your land—everything's sick. Whatever has happened?"

Diamond lowered her head and nuzzled Echo's muzzle, snuffling down his neck and shoulders before stepping around him, sniffing at his protruding ribs, and lipping at his jutting hips before standing back to look him all over.

Relieved to have the company of his long-time friend and former lover, Echo sighed and shared all he knew of the plague, saving Claw from a meteorite accident, and discovering that the sky stones made an excellent source for his sustenance. "I don't know where Claw is now. Returned to Obsidian Caves I presume."

Diamond shook her head in a cascade of silver hair and snorted. "Why the duocorn let the eagle have Aureana's feathers she alone knows. I'm sure they weren't meant for Claw, one of the duocorn's gross creations."

Echo was reminded of their granddaughter. "I suspect Aureana intended Prism to have them. You know she can't fly?"

Diamond reared and pawed the air, rolling her eyes and lashing out with a hind leg. The look of ire on her face would have melted a glacier.

Her reaction shocked Echo. "What's the matter?"

Diamond stamped in a circle around him. "Don't talk to me about our granddaughter. I have no idea why Mystery sent her here to help you. She has no plan. No training. No power."

Echo turned on the spot to keep his head pointing towards Diamond. "We were all young once. She means well. I suppose I should have tried to help her more, but I was so busy. She'll find her power when Aureana deems the time is right."

Diamond came to a standstill, her coat rippling as if flies tormented her, and glared at him. "It's not her power that's the problem. She thinks you're creating the troubles. In your own land. As if any unicorn, especially you, would harm another living thing."

Echo blinked, dumbfounded at the suggestion. He couldn't absorb this news. Out of habit he tried to respond to Diamond with his mind.

Silence.

Was he so sick he was imagining her? His own desire for company may have created a hallucination.

Diamond, or her apparition, twitched her upper lip and flicked her ears. "We can't tackle this alone. I'll fetch Tempest. He must come and help."

Now Echo accepted he was imagining things. He closed his eyes. Tempest would never leave Seashore. He shuddered with relief—it was only a bad vision brought on by his exhaustion—he'd never seen Diamond angry. She'd never say he looked terrible. And Prism, not only another unicorn, but his granddaughter, would never accuse him of being behind the troubles.

He opened his eyes. No-one was there, only the drifting mist from the pond, sparkling in the noon sun.

Chapter 15

Hot shafts of pain lanced Delsin's shoulders as he threw his weight into the harness and heaved. Towing Rocky on the sled had become easier since the waterways had frozen, even navigating the lumpy ice, but the wrenching of earlier drags over snow had torn muscles he hadn't known he had. Sticking to the edge of the banks to maximise the level ground, knowing he could never halt the sled with Rocky's weight downhill let alone have the strength to heft the stallion up any form of rise, had meant their journey had meandered far longer than if he'd been able to ride.

At least the sun shone today, its position reassuring Delsin that they still tracked north. His legs shook with weariness, his knees threatening to buckle. He couldn't let that happen. If he stopped he wouldn't get started again. The intense cold that permeated his furs whenever he took a break soon sank to his feet once he traipsed on again. He had long ago ceased knowing where his fingers ended and his mittens began, his flesh numb at all his extremities. He didn't dare touch his nose in case the frostbite he feared had already damaged the delicate skin. Rocky was in a similar state, lying dormant behind him, unable to move to keep warm, swaddled under boughs of pine for shelter that added to the weight Delsin must tow.

Thirst threatened to crack Delsin's tongue. His chapped lips, muffled behind a mask of woven grasses, prevented him from opening his mouth more than a fraction. His eyes peered through frosted lashes, stuck together as he daren't open them wide to the glare. As comforting as the sunshine was, the light reflected from the snow, blinding him to a world of white.

It was no good. He had to stop. After using the last of his strength to aide Rocky to roll off the sled onto firm ground, Delsin flopped to the horse's side. "How're you feeling?"

"Thirsty."

If Delsin didn't rise and set about his chores at once, he wouldn't have the heart to stand. Groaning, he pulled himself to his feet using a brittle shrub for support. The branch snapped in his hand, sending him reeling back to the ice. Regaining his balance with much waving of his arms, he bent his body and rested his hands on his knees, gasping, still holding the stick. "There's the first bit of kindling. I'll get a fire going."

Delsin's body went into automation as he collected firewood, lit a fire, and set a small clay pot containing a handful of icicles on the flames. At least the ice provided sufficient water for them to each have a sip. Before the big freeze he had used snow, not daring to risk the poisoned water, each handful only melting to a dribble and taking a long time to provide enough to drink. Eating unmelted snow would only cool his body and chap his lips, though he had seen Rocky lipping at the drifts around him.

After they had both drunk enough to rehydrate, Delsin searched the immediate surrounds for anything edible. Close to the waterways very little remained in the way of berries or nuts, the bare shrubs mere sticks from where the wind had blown away the snow. He trudged deeper into the forest, gathering armfuls of lichen for Rocky.

A shadow crept over him. Turning in alarm, Delsin's fear immediately changed to delight as Rocky plodded behind him. "You must be feeling better."

The skewbald puffed, steam emitting from his nostrils in plumes. "The good...water and...clean...food—"

"Don't talk." Delsin dumped his horde in front of Rocky and hugged the horse's neck. "Enjoy that while I find more. Don't come further yet."

Thrilled that Rocky had managed to gain his feet on his own, Delsin's spirits lifted higher than they had been for a long time, mainly for the horse's wellbeing but also his own. He wouldn't have been able to tow such a weight for many more days. He tried not to let what might lay ahead drag his mood down again, pushing away worries of how they'd ever find Prism in this vast land of white that stretched forever. Now Rocky was regaining his strength, they could follow a more direct route north across the frozen lakes. Then that idea melted away like snow in his pot. If a blizzard hit when they were exposed, they would perish.

A movement to his left froze Delsin more than the cold that wrapped around him. A pair of long white ears, tipped with grey, cast a shadow against a small drift. Keeping his hands behind him, Delsin manoeuvred a stone into his sling, a weapon he had become accustomed to carrying on his belt, before swinging round as he fired. The hare fell where it squatted. At least there would be a hearty meal tonight, his first meat in a very long time.

Delsin trudged alongside Rocky, his head bowed into the wind, sleet stinging his eyelids when he sneaked a peek at the way ahead. The storm tried its best to batter his spirits to no avail. Since Rocky had started to recover, Delsin's belief that he was meant to be here had grown ever stronger. Last night he had built another temporary sweat-lodge using materials from the sled that he no longer needed. He had let his soul float among the stars where the ancestors had given him comfort, assuring him he headed in the right direction and encouraging him to keep going.

Rocky halted and bent his head round to speak in Delsin's ear, the shrieking wind preventing normal conversation. "There's shelter to our right. We should head that way."

Agreeing with a nod of his head, Delsin clutched Rocky's mane as the stallion guided them to whatever he had seen. Within a few strides, the gale lessened enough to allow Delsin to walk upright. Dark mounds loomed out of the swirling snow that took shape as giant boulders scattered like children's conkers over a flat landscape. The snow around them had been whipped away to form drifts on their northern flanks, leaving bare ground on their lee sides. Relieved to be able to breathe easily, Delsin rested for a moment before following Rocky further into the moraine. A shallow basin led to a steeper but smooth slope, only a thin crust of frozen snow sheeting whatever vegetation lay dormant beneath, tips of reeds and sedges pointing through like spear-tips.

Rocky pawed at the ground and nibbled with delicate lips. "This doesn't taste tainted."

Relieved, as they had left the forest with its nutritious lichen behind a day ago, Delsin extracted his digging stick from his pack and scraped for tubers. The frozen earth made the work hard and soon he had warmed enough to want to strip off his outer skins. As that would be madness, he paced himself to work slow enough not to draw a sweat. The moisture would crack his skin and soak his clothes, chilling him all the colder when he stopped.

As they foraged, the blizzard abated, the sleet turning to large fluffy flakes that stuck together and quickly coated everything in a thick blanket. Delsin brushed off the clinging wetness from his arms. "We need to find shelter. It must be close to nightfall."

Rocky had led them along the valley in his search for food. "There's a crevice between two rocks a short way away. We might be able to fit inside."

It didn't take them long to discover that the narrow gap opened into a wider area clear of snow. A few shrubs, long dead from failing in their struggle to reach the light, offered fuel for a small fire. Delsin soon had a tendril of smoke spiralling from the dried moss he had saved. There wasn't enough wood to warm him, but at least he could heat water to cook the roots.

While his dinner stewed, Delsin rummaged in his bag for the teasel he used to brush Rocky. He ran his hands along the stallion's sides, pleased to feel the flesh returning. Hair had grown back over the bald patches and only a few pendulous growths remained around his throat. "How are you coping?"

Nudging for Delsin to keep massaging his muscles, Rocky confirmed he felt much better. "I was sure I heard equine thoughts while I was grazing. I responded, but no-one answered. Maybe it was only the wind."

Excited by the prospect that they might be getting close to Prism, Delsin applied a new vigour to his brushing. By the time he had finished, he was more than ready to eat and sleep. He snuggled into his furs and huddled between Rocky's warmth and the wall. The rock radiated heat. From where? If the earth tremored in the night, he'd be buried under the stone. But he hadn't felt a rumble for a long time. Making associations between the rocks, he realised that on clear nights he hadn't seen any more falling stars. Were the events related? While pondering the mystery and wondering if he should leave the comfort of the gully, drowsy from consuming the thick broth, he fell into a deep slumber.

After waking more refreshed than he had felt for many moons, Delsin tidied away their camp and stashed the few remaining twigs on top of his pack.

Rocky poked him with his nose. "I can carry those. I'm much stronger. Sling them over my withers so they hang evenly down my shoulders."

Not wanting to burden him, and doubting the horse's strength had returned as much as he pretended, Delsin reluctantly agreed to share the load; he also needed to regain his strength. As they set off back to the frozen waterway, he took the opportunity to add whatever timber he found, taking care to keep the branches well away from Rocky's healing sores. After they left the land to trek once more on the sheet ice, they could collect nothing more. At least they moved faster.

The morning had dawned still and bright, the sky a solid blue and everything pristine under a layer of fresh snow. Light twinkled from the surface of the frozen lake, dusted with crystals, as if all the stars had settled to earth overnight. With a spring in his step, Delsin headed towards a contorted branch poking out from a drift.

As they drew closer, Rocky slowed and snorted. "Something's dead."

Keeping a wary eye for any sign of lurking wolves or other predators attracted by the smell, Delsin carried on to the firewood. The broad branches would make a welcome blaze, especially now that Rocky could help carry the heavier pieces. The tips of the sticks promised a large pile under the snow, the form of a large log outlined in the drift. He hoped the fallen tree wasn't stuck in the ice, assuming it had drifted here in warmer weather or had been part of an old beaver dam.

Only as he reached out to tug on the first branch did Delsin acknowledge his mistake. This was no fallen tree. How could it be, out here on the frozen lake? He should have known better. The branch was actually an enormous antler of a type he had never seen before, broader than his hands spanned together, longer than his legs. Brushing aside the recent snow, Delsin revealed the emaciated body of a giant deer. It must have been old or sick. He slumped to his knees to investigate more, his mood sinking as his belief dissipated that they had left the plague behind. The beast had died recently, hence the smell, but the hide wasn't worth saving. Besides, Delsin daren't risk touching it, having seen the telltale yellow pus erupting from boils on the bull's neck.

Delsin withdrew on his knees. "We should move on."

Without a word, Rocky veered around the carcass and stepped out. Delsin jogged to keep up. Neither of them wanted to remain near the diseased corpse. Pondering what the dead beast meant for them, Delsin failed to notice Rocky's head raised, his nostrils distended, until the stallion whinnied.

"Can you hear someone?" Delsin's excitement bubbled out of him like a hot spring.

"No, but look. Hoof prints."

"Do you think it's Prism?"

Rocky trotted along the spoor, his tail swishing and nose low to the ground, tracking like a wolf. "I've called, but there's no answer. Whoever it is can't be far. These prints are fresh on last night's snow."

Even a normal horse in Westlands, going at a fair pace from the spacing of the stride, was good news. Delsin hurried to catch up, puffing with exertion.

Rocky halted, his skin quivering with excitement. "Mount up. We need to move fast."

"Are you sure you're ready? I don't want to cause you to get sick again." Delsin longed to be on horseback, though not at the expense of his friend's health.

"Yes, yes, hurry."

As soon as Delsin had settled on Rocky's back behind the bundle of firewood, the stallion took off at a ground covering trot, floating in the air with his hooves barely touching the ice, his toes flicking out as he stretched forward.

The winter sun reached its zenith as Rocky's energy faded. Dropping to a walk, he continued to follow the random tracks that had no obvious destination. Delsin was concerned that Rocky was exhausting himself for no effort. This couldn't be Prism. "Let's take a break. We both need to eat. We must get back to land while we still have plenty of light."

Rocky didn't want to leave the trail. "We must have almost caught up. We—"

A dark shape loomed ahead. A mouldy green tail drooped from a hollow brown rump. The horse didn't seem to have noticed them approaching.

Rocky whinnied.

Delsin gasped as the horse turned. The animal's patchy coat hung on a skeletal frame and his eyes looked not at them, but at some distant image that only he could see. His broad forehead, that could have been noble at one time, sported a stubby horn covered in what looked like the algae that cloaked the waterways in autumn. Delsin wasn't sure if it had always been stunted or whether it had snapped off, the end a rough knob. This must be a deformed warmblood. He leant low on Rocky's neck. "Is this who you heard earlier, do you think?"

Rocky was silent for a moment. "No, he doesn't seem to be able to hear me, and I can hear nothing of his thoughts."

Delsin was horrified at the sight of the horse. He had never seen an animal look so sick and still be on its feet. He slid from Rocky's back and walked with his hands outstretched, introducing himself as he neared. "Wait a moment. Let us help you."

The horse glanced over his shoulder, continuing on his way as if they were no more than apparitions.

Delsin called out louder in case the animal's hearing had been affected by his illness. He checked that Blaze's emerald scale lay snug against his skin, the dragon's power enabling him to talk with all animals. "We're looking for Prism, the Air Unicorn, rainbow-coloured with golden wings. She's come to help save Westlands."

The revelation had no effect on the horse. He continued to weave across the ice, nose low to the ground.

Rocky attempted to make contact too. "Have you seen her? Do you know anything about the plague? We want to help. Please stop and talk with us."

The bedraggled horse wandered on as if searching for something lost. When he did speak, his cracked voice sounded like he was choking on ice, grating on each word. "Find the fallen stars. That's all anyone can do. Find the fallen stars."

Delsin remounted in order to follow. "Have you seen a unicorn? Or Kodi, a giant bear? He's the guardian of the goddess's feathers.

One's gone missing. Or have you seen a huge eagle with golden wings and tail? We need to find them."

The horse didn't seem interested in talking and kept his rump to them as he tracked a path only he could see. "Not them. Find the stars. Find the stars. I must find more stars."

Realising the horse was mad and that they were unlikely to get any useful information from him, Delsin and Rocky turned north, saddened at the horse's plight, yet helpless to offer aid. But the presence of one horse might mean others lived nearby. As they left the ice to find solid ground for the night, Rocky sent out mental calls to any warmbloods, or with luck, Prism.

Chapter 16

A cold chill swept over Prism that had nothing to do with the weather. She couldn't believe Diamond had attacked her and then vanished. Not knowing whether her granddam had gone in search of Echo or abandoned Westlands to its fate, Prism recalled their conversation, searching for an answer. She needed to talk these issues through with someone, like her parents did with each other when they had a problem to solve. She only tangled her brain in knots trying to work out what was behind the plague. She wanted another equine to share her ideas with, not a bear. What a pity that Boldearth, the handsome stallion in the south, hadn't accompanied her.

Had she been wrong to suspect her grandsire of being behind the troubles? But the evidence was so strong, with her losing the ability to communicate by thought after she'd eaten the transformed meteorites, and the moose and bear both succumbing to terrible sores after doing the same. She shuddered at the thought of becoming plagued herself, imagining her coat marred by scabs and her hair falling out. She had seen how Kodi constantly scratched at his thick hide and how weak he became from any exertion even after the healing he had received at Shimmering Lake. Grateful that she could draw on Equinora's power, especially here above the thickened air that assailed the lower land, she drew a deep breath and felt her power rise.

Her power. What good was her power? She was too scared to use it. If she could fly she might be able to find Claw, or at least see where the troubles were worst, even travel to Obsidian Caves. Thinking about Diamond's assertion that Shadow was behind the troubles, Prism shivered to consider there might be more giant creatures like Lash and Snag. But Mystery had been able to convert Blaze to the side of good. Could she do the same? Perhaps she should have sent Lash and Snag love so that they wouldn't feed on animals—alive or dead. But she'd been too busy trying to track down Echo and Claw, and discovering what had happened to the stolen feather. And what if she'd failed?

Despite knowing she should go back up to the cave and help Kodi with Snag, Prism wandered in the opposite direction, following the valley until she stood exposed to the bitter winds that drove stinging sleet into her face. She deserved the pain. She should stop drawing on Equinora and let the winter take her.

Instead, the sun broke through the clouds and the wind ceased. Power poured into her without conscious effort. She broke into a trot to dispel her excess energy. Determined not to go back to the protection of the cave, she set out with no other direction in mind, ploughing through deep drifts, sticking to the hardest tracks, and skidding on the frozen river. She scrambled up rocky banks that broke away beneath her hooves. She slid down bare slopes of scree on her haunches. Sweat crusted her delicate coat to become a layer of ice that melted almost as soon as it formed. Cold water trickled down her neck, her flanks, and around her tail.

In the midst of her misery, Prism heard her name being called, a faint whisper that wouldn't go away. The insistent plea reverberated like her hoof-steps, her imagination adding words to the rhythm: Prism, failure, Prism, useless, Prism, stupid.

Ice cracked beneath her, throwing her into cold water. Splashing with knees high, she struggled to save herself, slipping on the snow towards the banks as it gave way under her panic. She sought escape along the frozen rim, broken off ice slabs cutting into her chest and legs as she heaved. Her hooves gripped solid ground. With a mighty lunge, she scrambled to safety. Trembling, she exhaled with relief. She didn't want to die after all.

Pri...sm! Pri...sm! Pri...sm!

She hadn't imagined it. Someone was calling her. Someone she didn't know. *Who are you?*

The answering silence was more unnerving than the incessant chant.

Then it was broken. A warmblood stallion searched for her.

This couldn't be Boldearth as he hadn't had the power to communicate by mind. Excited at the prospect of meeting another horse, Prism explained where she was and gave directions to find her. She shook herself free of a spray of sparkling frost and fluffed out her feathers before folding her wings tidily to her back, then set out at a canter to meet the stranger, her golden tail flicking and streaming behind her as she leapt and bounded.

A skewbald stallion emerged over the ridge, his white patches distorting his shape against the snow, the brown and black splotches of his coat bouncing like stones in a rock fall as he descended towards her. Another creature followed at a more sedate pace, a man from the look of it, carrying something on his back. Prism ignored the latter and galloped to meet the horse.

She skidded to a halt a few lengths away and studied the newcomer. He was much taller than Boldearth and very strong, despite evidence of the plague lingering in growths around his neck and throat, and patches of new hair stubbled over his rump. She definitely hadn't met this stallion before, hadn't even known that horses could be so varied in their markings. "I'm Prism. You were looking for me?"

The stallion introduced himself and bowed low on one leg. "It's a pleasure to meet you. We've come a long way to find you."

Glancing behind Rocky, Prism watched the man struggle up. She introduced herself to him before addressing the stallion again. "You're a welcome sight. Did Boldearth send you?"

Rocky nuzzled the man who had said he was called Delsin and suggested they seek somewhere to rest while they shared their tale.

The man agreed and pointed to a line of trees at the edge of the valley where the slopes steepened and were clear of snow. "How about we make camp there? I'm ready for a meal and would welcome a fire."

The man looked starved. Obviously humans couldn't draw on Equinora's energy, but this stallion must have been doing so to be in such good condition if he had suffered the plague. She knew little of warmbloods, or any horses really, only what her sire had told her about whom he had met in the east. And the skewbald had to be a warmblood to be able to use mind communication.

She knew even less about people and dropped her pace to walk next to Delsin. "Talk to me as we go. How is the clan in the south? Did Laila, the healer woman I sent for, reach you?"

The man shook his head. "We're not from the south. We're from Midlands. But yes, Laila came, but I asked her to remain at Bloomsvale to care for my mother in my place. Laila is my sister."

Prism tossed her head. Her surprise couldn't have been greater. Not having any siblings of her own, it had never occurred to her that she would ever meet any of Laila's family, and especially not here, so far from Shimmering Lake or Laila's original home. "Why are you here?"

When Delsin explained, Prism was torn between disappointment that the healer woman hadn't gone to help those people in need and wariness about whether her brother could aid with Prism's quest. "How can you help?"

The man paused in his stride and turned to her. "I don't know yet. But I've met Claw, in the stealthcat war—"

Prism jumped sideways in shock. "You must know my sire! And Blaze!" At the memory of the giant dragon, Prism's pleasure at having company disintegrated like smoke in a gale, her heart heavy from missing her friend.

Rocky broke into her sorrow. "We know them, and fought alongside them. That's partly why we're here."

They reached the shelter of the trees. Delsin made camp with practiced ease while Rocky shared the rest of their story. The more Prism heard, the more she felt utterly hopeless. She refrained from mentioning her fears when she recounted her own travels to try and locate the source of the plague and find the missing feather.

They talked until well after dark, the crackling fire sending sparks against the black sky, obliterating their sight of anything beyond the trees. By the time they had shared all their news, only a single log remained to keep the man warm who had settled into his furs. The stallion rested a hind leg and dozed. The night silenced, not even the whoosh of owl wings breaking the still air.

It pained Prism to admit that the plague and whatever, or whoever, was behind it was beyond her ability to discover and overcome. From what the man had said, he had no idea how to help either. He hadn't even been able to hang on to the jade carving of Fleet when Lash had snatched the totem. Admittedly he had been brave to face the snake who was many times his size, and one of Shadow's creations too, but if Lash was the enemy, what good could a man do?

This was unicorn business, but Diamond had been no assistance either. Was Echo inadvertently the problem? Or, the dread that lingered over Prism like the suffocating air of the wetlands, was she the harbinger of death? But how could that be? The goddess's statement made no sense.

Prism had no choice. She couldn't do this alone. She had failed. She must call Mystery and Gem again.

Chapter 17

With Prism away, Kodi took on the responsibility of feeding Snag. He used one set of claws to scrape the sticky sap from the rough bark of the pines and stuck the globules onto the fur of his other forelimb. Already he looked like he was covered in blisters, the weight of each tiny blob adding up to a surprising amount. When he daren't leave the mother bear and her cubs unattended any longer, he hurried back to the cave.

Snag waited for him where he had left her, all eight legs tucked beneath her massive body in the centre of the cavern. "Much?"

"This should keep you going for a while." Kodi extended his arm and braced against flinching as the spider sucked the goodness from his fur. He didn't know how much more the trees would offer at this time of year. Already the original holes had dried up and he had to travel further afield each time to gather the nutrition Snag needed. Fortunately, his claws were long and sharp enough to tap the trees without Prism's help, but it was slow and tedious work.

Withdrawing to rest against the cave wall, before Snag might get carried away and extract his own juices, Kodi struggled to come up with an alternative solution. "Can't you draw energy from Equinora? I always feel better out in the sun."

"Dark."

Kodi scratched at his ribs while he considered Snag's predicament. He had learnt she couldn't cope with light which was why she moved around at night. "What about the wind? That's a powerful source of energy too."

No answer.

He had to do something. He left Snag to digest her meal, confident the bears were safe after the spider had feasted so well. Clambering up the rocky hillside above the cave, he searched for a new home for her; somewhere he could keep an eye on her but safely away from the cubs. A narrow entrance between sheer granite walls offered a possible option. He squeezed through the gap and peered up at the dim light that seeped into the chimney overhead. Would it be dark enough? A chill breeze blew through the opening and whistled as it escaped out of sight. Following the thread of air, Kodi shook off rock dust as the space widened.

He stopped. A solid wall confronted him. Peering at the stone, he detected a darker space up to his right and searched with his paw. Stretching up on his hind legs, he located a ledge by feel. By hefting himself with both front limbs, and scrabbling with the claws of his hind paws digging into the rock-face, he peeked over the edge. As his eyes fully adjusted to the dimness, he made out a hollowed space, large enough for Snag to nestle inside. This would do.

By the time he returned to the bear's home, dusk had settled on the land. He explained to Snag about the possible new location and encouraged her to follow him, luring her out of the cave with a few more globules of sap he had gathered on the way back. "It's a much better place than here, closer to the trees that produce this food."

Snag's feet tapped against the rock as she followed him, scampering up with far more ease than he navigated the climb. When he showed her the crevice, he had a moment of fear that her bulbous body wouldn't fit through. He needn't have worried. She elongated her abdomen to accommodate the narrowness and slipped in without touching the sides.

Immediately, she set about attaching silk to either side of the gap, presumably in the anticipation of capturing anything that flew through, such as the bats he had heard squeaking in similar places in the past, though it was doubtful that any creatures lived here now.

As she finished the framework, Kodi admired the skill with which she wove the gossamer into a wall, the strands billowing as they stretched with the wind. Unlike the white net she had constructed to snare the cubs, this delicate web glowed amber. After she tightened the corners and completed the intricate design, Kodi sensed the power captured from the breeze. "Can you draw from the energy?"

She didn't respond. Had she understood? After a frustrating number of attempts to explain again how to draw power from Equinora's elements, Kodi waited.

Snag twanged at the long threads that suspended her work. With one long leg she gently touched the centre of the web and plucked a loose filament, reattaching it further out. She did the same with another, then another, until only a few strands remained crossing the very centre. A low whistle emitted from the hole, changing pitch as she altered the structure fibre by fibre.

Kodi listened with pleasure, the sound as musical as a forest of songbirds, eerie in the near darkness. Tiny nodules glowed on the threads like miniature suns. "That's beautiful. Can you feel any power?"

Her countenance didn't change. Kodi waited in vain for Snag to speak. Instead, she extracted a single filament from the spinneret on the end of her abdomen and scuttled into the hole that Kodi had discovered earlier, dragging out the fibre behind her. When she had squashed into the recess, she totally disappeared except for one foot clutching the end of the thread as if waiting to snag a victim, like a man trying to catch a fish with a worm.

With nothing more he could do, Kodi retreated from Snag's new lair and returned to check on the she-bear and her cubs. As he descended the slope, taking care not to lose his footing on the precarious rocks, he stopped and listened.

Power. Feed. Good.

Satisfied that his efforts had proved worthwhile, Kodi's thoughts returned to the loss of the feather. He still had no idea how to locate the last of his treasures that he should be guarding, the treasures entrusted to him by the goddess before she had departed from Equinora for ever, the treasures that Jasper had endured enormous pain in order to carve a niche in solid rock for their protection. Then inspiration hit him. If he could hear and speak with Snag via his mind, he might be able to converse with Claw. How close would the giant eagle have to be in order to be in range?

Prism escorted Rocky and Delsin to the cave, relieved to find that Kodi had safeguarded the bears and must have found Snag a new home as neither of them was here. A twinge of worry wormed through her veins like the borers that chewed tunnels under the bark of ash trees, then, like the grub emerging into its adult form of a moth, the feeling flew away. Kodi could communicate with the giant spider with the powers granted by the goddess. He would be safe.

Unless the spider had trapped him and dragged him away. No. Kodi had explained the spider couldn't go out in daylight. Despite the heavy cloud cover, the day was still bright. He must be safe. She'd know if he wasn't. Wouldn't she?

How could unicorns communicate with other hotbloods and dragons, yet not with the goddess's other special creatures like the guardian? Was it because Snag was one of Shadow's creations, enlarged in the caves where he had festered in anger for eons?

Did this mean Kodi was one of Shadow's creations? Maybe he wasn't one of the goddess's creatures after all. Maybe he was part of the evil. Maybe he had abandoned her. Was he to be trusted? But he had fallen ill with the plague. If he were part of the evil that caused the disease, he wouldn't have been susceptible. Or was he the one spreading the plague? She trembled in horror with what that would mean for those back at Shimmering Lake. But neither Mystery nor Gem had mentioned any outbreak of disease at home.

Delsin broke into her troubled musings. "Shall I set up camp in here?"

Before she could answer, several things happened at once: Kodi lumbered up the slope; Rocky screamed a warning as he reared and leapt in front of her; and Delsin scrambled onto a boulder, abandoning his pack at the base.

"It's alright! It's Kodi!" Prism hastened to introduce them all. Rocky and Delsin relaxed but retained their distance, listening with interest as Kodi described how Snag had settled into a crevice not far away. The fear and doubts that had been growing like a vine around Prism's throat shrivelled away as if hacked off at the base.

Kodi reached up a massive paw to help Delsin back down the rock-face. "How is Laila? I didn't travel with her for long, but I enjoyed her company."

Delsin accepted the bear's assistance with no more fear and slid the last little way to stand opposite the bear, his head only reaching halfway up Kodi's chest. "She always spoke of you with affection and told me you were with Prism. I'm sorry for my reaction. I wasn't sure if you were another bear who lived in this cave."

Looking towards the entrance, Kodi waved towards the right hand wall. "There's a she-bear with cubs inside. I think there's a crawl space behind the entrance that might be better for you than at the back, in case she wakes from hibernation when I'm not around to introduce you."

It had never occurred to Prism that a bear might prove dangerous to a man. At Shimmering Lake all animals lived in harmony, and Laila's best friend was a wolf. There was still much for her to discover about the wider world. But how could she learn from all the different creatures when none were around? Corpses didn't talk.

The memory of all that she and Kodi had encountered since leaving home plunged her back into despair. She was supposed to be here to fix the problems, solve the riddle of the plague and put things right, find the stolen feather and return it to Kodi. Why then was everything still so wrong? What was she supposed to do?

Leaving Delsin to talk with Kodi as he set about doing whatever it was people did, Prism set off towards the valley. Mystery and Gem were on their way, on foot as Diamond had disappeared and wasn't responding to any of them. Prism couldn't think of anything useful she could achieve while she awaited their arrival, and had no idea how long they'd take. At least they didn't need to go all the way around the lakes, and could travel day and night drawing on Equinora's power to sustain them. Part of her wanted them to arrive soon and part of her dreaded them seeing what a failure she was. She hadn't even overcome her problem with flying.

She tore into a gallop and surged across the frozen ground, her wings clamped tight to her back, her head and neck stretched low. Pounding the ice, she empathised with the groans and creaks coming from beneath her hooves that reflected her sorrows. Faster she fled, her tail streaming behind her, tears stinging her eyes from the cold. Faster, faster, she thrust her frustration into every stride, her feet striking harder, harder, as her anger at herself grew.

Steam erupted from her nostrils with every stride, sweat crusted on her neck and flanks. Blind to the world, Prism drove herself beyond feeling, the only sounds the drumming of her hooves, her thumping heart, and the wind in her ears. Her muscles shrieked as the ice prevented her from drawing power from the land. Her breath came in gasps, each inhalation drawn by the rhythm of her stride. Her lungs burned. Her throat stung. A trickle of blood from her exertions dripped from her nostrils, leaving a trail of crimson splashes. She didn't care. She welcomed the pain.

The world gave way beneath her. Prism scrambled to regain her footing and neighed as something sharp sliced her leg. Her ears rang from cracking ice. She gasped as freezing water engulfed her. Her legs thrashed in panic as she floundered to regain a firm footing. Each time she tried to get her front hooves onto the surface of the ice that surrounded her, the frozen surface of the lake gave way, plunging her into the frigid waters. Time and again she lunged. Time and again she went under. With each attempt she weakened, her brain numb, unable to save herself.

She sank. Belatedly, she spread her wings. Too late. Her water-logged feathers clumped with ice. The weight dragged her tired body deeper into the lake, engulfing even her head. Prism stopped struggling. She wasn't any use to Equinora. Let her join her ancestors in the spirit world. Let the goddess take her. Or she could sink without trace to become sludge at the bottom of the lake. She wasn't worth the goddess's effort to take her to be with Moonglow, and Jasper, and Dewdrop. Darkness swamped her.

A muffled whinny pierced her misery. Was that a call from the unicorns who had died? Was she on her way to the spirit world? Another neigh reverberated through the water. An avalanche rumbled in the distance. Or was it another earthquake, or only the blood in her head? She had no way to tell.

Where was she? She concentrated. She was in a lake. Drowning.

Reawakened into a flurry of paddling, Prism resurfaced. She blinked away icy crystals and spotted the skewbald stallion at what must be the edge of the lake, bashing the ice with his front hooves. He'd fall in like her! She must stop him. "Don't come near! You'll drown!"

Rocky ignored her plea, sending jagged shards flying as he broke a path through the ice from the bank. "Head this way! You can make it!"

Had the goddess sent the warmblood to save her? She couldn't let him risk his life for her. Prism dragged air into her lungs. With a fresh burst of energy, she struck out with her forelegs, snapping the ice, this time not trying to mount the surface but to create a path so she could swim to shore. With each slab she broke off, Rocky broke two. Already he was in to his chest, rearing and bashing his weight down on the next piece of ice.

The stallion couldn't retain that effort for long. She had to reach him before he killed himself. "Stop! That's enough!"

He ignored her shout, or perhaps her voice hadn't the strength to reach him.

She renewed her efforts to escape the clinging ice. The sun broke between the clouds. As the warmth hit her face, Prism received a burst of energy. She sucked the power offered by the goddess and surged onwards. Potency raced through her veins, melting the ice on her wings and giving strength to her muscles.

Rocky must have seen her renewed vigour. He turned and stumbled out on the bank, shaking in a spray of ice crystals before stamping his feet and shivering.

Prism heaved herself up beside him, blowing warmth from her nose over the length of his body. "You shouldn't have come in. You aren't strong. You're still ill."

The stallion nuzzled her neck as his body warmed. "I'm sorry I couldn't reach you earlier. You're much faster than me."

"I didn't want company, not then, but I'm glad you're here now." What Prism had at first meant as only solace was actually true, thankful that Rocky had prevented her from allowing the water to overcome her. That didn't lessen her misery, but somehow the warmblood's presence heartened her.

Rocky pawed at the thin ice that crackled at the edge of the lake. "Spring is on the way. Westlands may recover now."

Prism didn't think a season of snow would eradicate whatever had caused the rotfrogs and cloaking algae. "Do you think so? Will there be any animals left to have young?"

"There are a few survivors, though not in good condition. We met a stallion on our way here. He was quite mad. He kept going on about looking for rocks. We couldn't make any sense out of him. Did you experience the same with other sick animals?" Rocky started to walk back the way they had raced, his legs wobbling and his weariness evident in his low head carriage, his tail clamped between his buttocks.

Trying to absorb his words, Prism fought the darkness that threatened to overcome her again. A mad stallion? "What did he look like?"

Paula Boer

As Rocky shared more about the encounter, she recognised who he and Delsin had met. "That was Echo, the Earth Unicorn. He must be really sick." Her grandsire wouldn't do that to himself. So he wasn't the problem after all. Diamond was right. Echo had told the truth about saving Midlands with his stones. "We must find and help him."

Chapter 18

Splashing through the slush, Prism cursed the wet conditions brought on by the spring thaw. One moment she cantered on what looked like firm snow, the next she floundered up to her chest when the crust gave way. Along the waterways, the ice slid and creaked as it broke apart, preventing her from using the rivers and lakes as byways. The land looked so different from when she had passed through before. Where she expected hills, the land was flat. Where she anticipated level ground, she had to scramble through rocks. The further south she headed, the more lakes she encountered, treacherous with sunken trees that snagged her legs if she navigated the shallows. Weaving her way around the obstacles confused her even further. She had no idea how to find Echo.

And that was only part of her problem. When she had finally succumbed to the inevitable and called Mystery and Gem, she had only intended to ask them for advice. Instead, they had insisted on coming. Many times she had considered calling them again to tell them not to come, that Echo wasn't, as she had feared, behind the troubles. But if she couldn't find him, she'd still need their help, and they'd be in Westlands soon.

When Rocky had described his encounter with Echo, Prism had decided to set out to find her grandsire and instructed Rocky to return to Kodi and Delsin to inform them what she was doing. Saving her life had weakened him and she didn't want company to hinder her efforts or see her failures. Now she wasn't so sure she had done the best thing. She didn't like being alone. She loathed Westlands. And she hated her inability to do anything right.

A few green shoots struggled through the melting snow. Without the need to eat, Prism denied herself the tender treats. She was in no mood to graze anyway. Slogging on through the bogs, she dreaded encountering any rotfrogs that might emerge after a winter of hibernation. Hopefully, they had all perished in the cold and the land would recover with the coming warmth.

A shaft of sunlight broke through the clouds. Prism blinked at the bright reflection from the water, puzzling over the light. She had roamed for half the day at least, intent on heading south, but the sun was over her left shoulder. She was heading the wrong way. The meandering waterways had confused her sense of direction, swinging her back towards the cave.

Cross that she hadn't paid more attention to where she was going, lost in her misery as she had been, Prism abandoned her search for Echo for today. So close to her companions, she'd stay with them for the night and head out again tomorrow. Then she'd keep going until she found her grandsire, no matter what else she encountered.

She shuddered as the sun slunk behind a cloud, cooling her coat. Then a flash of colour caught her eye. She raised her head to peer at what might have caused such a dazzle. The shadow hadn't been a cloud. A broad span of wings flashed with rainbow colours as the shape passed overhead, sunbeams once again slanting across the mountains. Prism had no doubt who blocked the sun with that sweeping glide, his long neck snaking to search the ground, and his tail lashing behind him as he turned to dive towards her.

Prism reared with excitement that her friend had come. *Blaze!*

The mighty dragon swept in ever-decreasing circles as he lowered into the valley, his scales sparkling and twinkling like coloured stones tossed in a stream. He landed, skidding in the slush, arching his neck as he braked, his wings held out to slow him down and legs thrust forward.

Prism whinnied a greeting. "I'm so glad you're here. How did you find me?"

Blaze folded his wings to his back and stepping high with taloned feet. Once alongside Prism, he wound his neck around hers in a hug. "Mystery and Gem needed a guide so I flew flew flew and saw you your beautiful coat like mine far far below! Meda my Meda gone gone with Laila to follow her destiny me to follow mine with you my friend my Prism!"

At news of Mystery's and Gem's pending arrival, a fresh pang of regret pierced Prism that she had failed in her mission. At the same time, she wanted to see her parents and was delighted Blaze had come too. "How far away are they? There's no point them coming here. We should meet at the cave where Kodi is waiting."

With the other unicorns so close, Prism hesitated to call them. No brief mind message would be adequate to explain the situation, and now that Echo was not the cause of the problem, she didn't know who might be listening in. She was no closer to solving the mystery of the troubles than when she had left home all those moons ago. With dragging hooves, she set off at a trot to return to the she-bear's lair, her heart only lightened by the sight of Blaze skimming overhead to guide Mystery and Gem to meet her.

Prism waited a short distance in front of the cave, down the hill on a level glade free of snow where she could watch the tree line to the east. Her parents' progress was marked by the soaring dragon circling above them, diving and spinning in a flash of many colours as he cavorted in the air. Prism's heart soared with him, wishing she could fly alongside him, seeing the world from above laid out in miniature as he had described to her so often in his attempts to encourage her to join him. Mixed feelings squirmed in her guts like the wakening worms in the earth beneath her feet: delight at having the company of her friend and parents; despair that she had not found her power; and worry that even with Mystery's and Gem's help they may not be able to save Echo.

As Blaze swooped along the ground and rose to meet her, Prism spotted her parents emerge from the pines, Gem's emerald coat and ruby mane and tail a bold contrast against Mystery's silver body and copper hair. Light reflected off their opal and copper horns as they cantered with ease up the slope, both looking as if they had been out for a pleasant lope rather than racing for days over the mountains.

Rocky stepped up beside her and whickered. Kodi and Delsin remained at the mouth of the cave, standing quietly.

Prism couldn't resist bolting down to meet her parents, joy overriding her fears. "I didn't expect you so soon! And spring is here too."

After they greeted her with snuffling noses, they cantered up to the cave. There, Mystery and Gem thanked Kodi for taking care of Prism, and introduced themselves to Rocky and Delsin. Gem sniffed at the stallion's neck before glancing around at Prism. "Rocky is sick, and Kodi still carries a taint of the plague."

Prism suggested they share information from their adventures on their way to find Echo. "We can't linger. He's in a really bad way. I'm sorry I suspected he was the problem. I didn't expect you to come. But now we must hurry."

Mystery turned from where he had been talking with Delsin, no doubt asking after Laila and how he came to be here in her stead. "There'll be time to find him. Blaze can look while Gem tends to those here. There's no point scouring the country aimlessly."

Prism paced as she fretted, nervous energy fizzing in her veins. She halted next to Gem, fidgeting. "What can you do for Kodi that you couldn't do at home? Even swimming in Shimmering Lake didn't cure him completely. Echo needs you more."

Ignoring her daughter's concern, Gem nuzzled Kodi's shoulder. "Head down to the river. I'll swim in the waters and give them power. You are much better than you were. Hopefully now you'll heal completely." She pivoted to face the skewbald horse. "And you, Rocky, come too. If nothing else, a swim will restore your strength."

Without waiting for agreement, Gem cantered down to where the melt revealed a wide pool. Large segments of ice still floated near the banks, making entry difficult. "Blaze, can you help?"

The dragon had flown down with Prism and now stood with his neck outstretched over the frozen waters. As the unicorns sent Blaze love, his scales changed from multi-hued to crimson, his lungs swelled as he held out his wings, and then he huffed fire over the pool. Even before the ice had finished melting, Gem plunged in, gasping as she did so, and swam out to deeper waters. Paddling around in circles, she suddenly disappeared as she dived without a ripple, leaving no trace of where she had been.

Rocky whinnied in horror.

Prism was quick to reassure him. "She always does that. Don't worry. Go in."

The stallion tentatively slipped into the waters, followed by Kodi.

Prism crossed to Delsin. "My dam's power transforms the water into sustenance for all who drink it, and it becomes a healing balm on the skin. You should swim too, even if you're not sick."

Delsin crossed his arms and shook his head. "Even though Laila has told me about Shimmering Lake, I'm not sure I want to risk going into these waters. I don't have hair or fur to keep me warm. Gem didn't invite me too. I'll ask when she emerges."

Prism agreed to the wisdom in waiting to see what Gem thought. She watched as Rocky waded out of his depth and started swimming. Kodi was more reluctant, lying in the shallows and wallowing instead.

In a surge of white-water, Gem erupted through the surface, her horn shattering the last of the ice and her coat glistening. She spoke to Rocky as she swam past him, climbed out onto the bank near to Prism, Mystery, Blaze, and Delsin, and shook in a shower of freezing droplets. "The goddess only knows what has happened here. The water is foul. No fish, no plants, no sign of any living thing. Even the water itself lacks vigour. I told Rocky not to stay in too long."

Obeying her instructions, the stallion and the bear clambered out and shook as Gem had done.

Prism searched for signs that they were healed. "How do you feel?"

Kodi rubbed at his rump before looking at his paw. "The sores are drying up, but I don't feel invigorated like when I swam in Shimmering Lake."

Rocky added his own verdict. "My throat no longer hurts, but I'm tired from swimming in icy water."

Gem nodded as if she had expected this. "You'll need to swim every day. I'll go in as often as I can, but I don't know how we can bring life back to the area."

"But we can't stay here. We must find Echo, and Claw. And get to the source of the problem." Prism couldn't believe Gem was talking about hanging around for a daily swim when so much needed attention.

Mystery calmed her down by blowing a stream of warm air into her face. "I've told you, Blaze will search from the air. When he finds Echo, I'll go with you. Gem can stay here with the others. There's no point us all rushing off until we know what needs to be done."

Kodi was relieved he didn't have to go traipsing south to find Echo. The brief swim had left him slightly refreshed and he was sure his sores would heal, but it had been a long year from when he had discovered the last of the goddess's feathers stolen. Following the rumours nattered by the birds and murmured by the bears, he had travelled far west to this land, only to become sick and struggle to survive seeking help back in Midlands. Then he had accompanied Prism back here only to find matters worse with no obvious solution. Three unicorns were here now, four if you counted Echo, wherever he was. And Diamond had come and gone. Finding the source of the plague was up to the unicorns now.

He needed to follow his own quest to retrieve the last feather. First, he must build his strength. The best way for him to do that was to eat. Seeing Rocky looking lost in the presence of the unicorns, and with Delsin busy telling more of his tale to Mystery and Gem, Kodi invited the warmblood stallion to join him. "I know a place where the snow will have disappeared and there should be fresh grass. The shrubs may even be budding."

Rocky needed no further convincing. "Grateful as I was of the lichen Delsin gathered, I'd relish some sweet clover."

Unable to promise anything quite so luxurious, nevertheless Kodi led the horse to the spot he had found when looking for a new home for Snag. The giant spider had settled into her crevice, rarely venturing out except to consume the sap that had started to flow from the trees now that the days were above freezing. Last time he had visited her, Kodi had been surprised to find Snag had changed colour, darkening to the amber of her threads instead of being as white as new snow, and now able to venture out at dawn and dusk as well as through the night.

He and Rocky said little as they navigated the stony path to the eastern side of the mountain. When they arrived at the place Kodi had been searching for, he stared around in confusion. There was no grass. Bare earth that looked as if it had never grown anything lay exposed wherever the snow had melted. Scratching at the last pockets of ice, Kodi revealed new shoots barely long enough to nibble. "That's odd. It looks as if someone has been here before us, but who could graze so close to the ground?"

Using a front hoof, Rocky dug away a drift and lipped at the old grasses beneath. "There's no nutrition in these. Let's look further afield."

Carrying on their search, Kodi rounded a wall of rock. A buzzing sounded a short distance away. "If that's from pollinators, there must be flowers."

Following the noise, Kodi and Rocky increased their speed as the volume grew. The buzz became deafening as if the whole mountain was formed of insects. Rocky hesitated and let Kodi draw ahead. "Can you check it out? I don't want to be stung and you have thick fur."

Kodi dropped to all fours and lumbered towards the sound, ready to turn and flee if the swarm decided to attack. As he came out between a jumble of rocks, the day darkened. A thick mist hung in the air, swirling and pulsing like a living thing.

Indeed, it was a living thing, or rather, many living things. For as far as Kodi could see, the cloud of insects hummed and rasped, flying steadily away from him. They looked like no insect he'd ever seen before, not wasps or winged ants, not bumblebees or grasshoppers, and left the ground barren wherever they passed. They swarmed the barren slopes in a metallic glimmer of blurring wings.

Then they changed direction, back towards him, and attacked.

Kodi swatted at the bugs as they entered his ears and drank the liquid around his eyes. Racing in frenzy, he bounded around the hill, looking for the edge of the swarm. Unable to outrun the pests, he headed up into the rocks from where he hoped to see the extent of the horde. Unable to penetrate his coat, the majority of bugs lost interest and sought fresh growth. The living mist swept down the valley, washing around the hillside like waves on the shore, flooding up into crevices wherever greenery grew. The storm of mouths stripped everything bare—ground, shrubs, and trees.

Kodi hurried back to Rocky via a higher route above the remaining insects and explained what he had witnessed. "This new plague will undo all of Gem's work. It's worse than the rotfrogs. Gallop back and tell Mystery, Gem, and Prism."

Rocky wasted no time in fleeing back to the cave.

Kodi slumped onto his haunches and considered his options. He was no help in fighting this type of enemy. He had his own role to pursue. Now was as good a time as any to see if his ability to share mind communications with Snag extended to Shadow's other creatures. *Claw! Hear me! Oh mighty eagle who flies to the sun! Claw! He with the golden wings and tail, and eyes that see so far! Claw! Come to me! In the goddess's name, I seek you!*

Delsin dumped another armload of wood near the mouth of the cave. He was likely to be staying for a while. Mystery and Prism would try and bring Echo here once Blaze had located him. Until Rocky had come galloping into camp, the spring weather had raised Delsin's spirits, even though trudging through the mud and snowmelt sapped his strength. Birds had started to return from their winter homes, filling the dawn with song as the days lengthened and warmed.

Rocky's news about the gorgebugs had come as a shock and counteracted everyone's high hopes that things were improving. And then Gem discovered rotfrogs emerging from the bogs, having lain dormant through the winter submersed deep in the slime, oblivious to the cold. Every time Westlands began to recover, a new peril threatened.

Delsin had set about establishing a more permanent camp. He had stripped the bark off springy elder saplings and fashioned baskets. He had created stone tools that had been too much to carry before but made life easier. He had built a lean-to shelter outside the cave, preferring to spend his days out in the light where he could watch the land transform. The low tunnel that led to his sleeping hollow, safe from the she-bear, made that haven stuffy and dark. After Kodi had explained to the mother bear that Delsin was under the protection of the unicorns she had ignored him, spending longer outside each day as she awakened from her winter slumber. Even so, he didn't want to risk upsetting her. It helped that, with the aid of Blaze's emerald scale hanging around his neck, he could at least talk with her.

Now the cubs tumbled and tussled with each other in the sunshine, ignorant of Equinora's troubles. The sow wandered in search of food, trusting the unicorns to care for her young in her absence. Delsin loved watching the balls of fur investigate their world, one male one female, discovering that ants can bite delicate noses or discovering the sweetness of tender new buds. For now, the plague of insects had left the area around the cave alone, perhaps because of the power of the unicorns or, more likely, because Blaze had blasted one swarm with his fiery breath.

Delsin was stunned to see the magnificence of the enormous dragon who had grown much larger than when Delsin had met him in the east. Delsin was also in awe of the unicorn mares. He had come to know Mystery well during the Eastlands war, and had heard of Gem's beauty, but nothing had prepared him for her and Prism's shimmering auras of glorious colours. It was no surprise that Rocky was enamoured with Prism. Delsin had seen little of the stallion since they had arrived here, the warmblood shadowing Prism's every move, trying to cheer her up with titbits or grooming, enticing her to gallop for the sheer joy of movement.

As much as Delsin would have loved to ride, to revel in the speed and feel the wind in his face, he didn't want to intrude. Instead, he took pleasure in seeing Rocky so well and happy after moons of being sick. The horse had grown strong with Gem's healing. Besides, Delsin had his own tasks to fulfil. Determined to build a proper sweat-lodge, he had scoured the hillsides for suitable logs and branches. Now he twisted the last of the bark in his hands into a strong rope to finish off the roof.

With the last of the pine boughs lashed securely, Delsin lit the small fire he had laid ready in the centre of the low hut. He folded himself into a comfortable position with his ankles crossed in front of him and his hands resting on his knees, naked save for a loincloth of his softest deerskin. As dusk descended and the fire shrank to embers, he drank the tea he had brewed from a concoction of dream herbs—anise, eyebright, and mint leaves, with honeysuckle flowers and lotus root. Hopefully he had the quantities right, having only helped Mojag Carol, Bloomsvale's spiritman, gather what was necessary, never partaking of the tea himself. Next, he added pinches of dried sage to the coals that warmed the river rocks he had selected earlier in the day from a clean stream, each of them rounded and of similar size. As pungent smoke filled the enclosed space, he flicked drops of water from Gem's swimming place onto the hot stones, allowing the hissing steam to permeate his sinuses, drawing the aroma deep into his lungs.

Breathing slowly and deeply, Delsin emptied his mind. He focused on the beat of his heart, the blood flowing through his veins, and the air expanding his chest. He lost all concept of where his body ended and his surrounds touched him, blending with the earth beneath his seat bones, becoming one with the spinning planet on which he rested. He let his mind drift with the stars, crossing the heavens in the wake of the sun, towing the moon in its nightly dance.

PAULA BOER

A towering pinnacle pierced his vision, black rock rising above the clouds, erupting in flame with smoke spiralling into the firmament to escape in the dark. The vortex built into a column of stone, growing the mountain higher, rocks piling skywards like an avalanche in reverse. The peak spun, surrounded by flying creatures of gold, wings shimmering and beating a divine music. A cascade of jewels rained from the mountain top, transforming into a snake that wound to the top, erupting from the summit as a dragon that laid an egg, which morphed into a spider spinning golden threads, casting those lines to the pastures below and hauling horses and bears up, up, up into the flames.

Chapter 19

Needing time alone, Prism cantered up above the cave that had become their base. The climb steepened forcing her to drop to a trot, then to a walk, and finally to bounding from rock ledge to boulder, scrambling on the slippery surfaces wet with mist. Low cloud shrouded the mountaintops, formed droplets on her coat, and ran in rivulets down her flanks. Power coursed up through her legs with every stride, driving her harder and higher. Her crystal hooves made no sound as she ascended, the effort needed to navigate the treacherous terrain not even raising her heartbeat or quickening her breathing.

Rocky had wanted to accompany her, as usual, but she had snubbed him with a curt word. She had too many things to think about. Delsin had shared his vision with them, a vision that made her shiver with dread. One image he had described kept slithering into her mind: a great jewelled snake wrapped around the mountain.

It had to be Lash. But the giant serpent she had encountered had been grey. Grey, like Blaze had been when Mystery had first met the dragon. She shouldn't have disregarded Lash so easily. She'd been sent to Westlands to discover the source of the plague and solve the problems. Instead, she had cavorted around as if on a treasure hunt. Why hadn't she worked out that the great grey snake was behind the terror? She had taken his explanation of being there to tidy up the corpses at his word, a good thing for him to do. But he must poison them in order to feed. How could she have been so stupid?

Her insides twisted in horror that she had suspected Echo, her own grandsire, as being behind the problem. No wonder Diamond was furious with her. Prism had to find Echo and make him well, make things right. And now she had to find Lash too and put an end to the troubles. But how? The only way to locate either of them was from the air. Neither Mystery nor Gem had raised the issue of her lack of flight, content to send Blaze to do what should obviously be her job. Each day saw him return with no news. He couldn't even ask any of the surviving creatures about Echo's whereabouts as they fled as soon as they saw his shadow.

Reaching the summit, Prism stretched out her wings, feeling the tug of air that licked the crest of the mountain range. The slight breeze wasn't enough to lift her. She'd need to run like she had before, when she'd crashed on her side and given up. That would be impossible up here on the peak. With Westlands cloaked in fog below her, her mood soured even more. She shouldn't have come up here. Even without being able to see the scope of the wasteland, so vast, the destruction in her mind daunted her even more than flying.

A strong gust shoved her off her feet. She caught her balance with her wings. At least they were good for something. A clap like thunder cracked beside her. She startled and pivoted on the rock.

Blaze shuffled sideways towards her on the precipice. "My friend my beauty my Prism why don't you fly fly fly with me and we'll own the skies and glide soar swoop together!"

"Oh Blaze, we've been through this before. As soon as I try, I freeze. My stomach sickens and my head spins." Prism hung her head in shame.

Pointing his snout skywards, Blaze wouldn't be deterred. "Fly fly fly with me in my talons and I'll carry you high high high so you can see the joy the power the glory!"

The notion of being carried had never occurred to Prism, yet that was how Shadow had escaped his prison of Obsidian Caves. Claw had swept the duocorn over the barrier in return for three golden feathers. At least it would give her a chance to participate in the search for Echo and Lash. But her eyesight wasn't sharp like that of an eagle, or a dragon. She'd need to fly low, skipping the treetops and landing in clearings to talk with the animals. Blaze wouldn't have the strength to carry her like that. "It's a nice idea, thank you, but I don't think that will work."

Without answering, the massive dragon leapt into the air.

Sorrow from hurting her friend's feelings added to Prism's self-loathing. But her fear was something she had to overcome on her own. Another gust of wind rocked her.

Blaze swooped low. Instead of landing, he ducked over her with his legs spread and talons open, snatching at her like a bird of prey grabbing its victim, his sharp claws tucked in behind the back of her wings. He lifted her effortlessly.

Prism choked back a scream. Up, up, they went into the clouds. She didn't need to close her eyes; the thick mist blocked her sight, disorienting her to where they flew. Faster and faster Blaze drove away from the mountain until Prism hung far away from all security, shrouded in white, buffeted by a wind the like of which she'd never experienced on the ground. Her dangling legs swept away from her as if she stood in a raging river, her tail streamed as if tugging her back to land.

The cloud pulled apart to reveal the landscape below, tree-clad slopes like lush pasture, the forest mere stubble, with broad waterways trickling like mere brooks through the valleys. Safe in Blaze's grip, Prism studied the land, amazed at the beauty of the world in miniature.

Blaze dropped her.

She tumbled head over heels, rolled from side to side, and plummeted. Air sucked out of her lungs. She gasped in a vacuum.

Fly! Fly! Fly! Blaze's demand whizzed through her mind as she fell through the elements.

All became blue, then green, then blue again, then white as she rolled through the sky, one wing out and back to her side then the same with the other one. Her feathers flapped against her side, beating her to take notice.

She fell. And fell.

Priiism! Nooo! This time the scream came from Gem far below her, shortly joined by cries of despair from Mystery.

In a flash as she spun towards earth, Prism saw her parents staring up at her, rearing and pawing the air. It made no difference, she couldn't save herself. Didn't want to save herself. This was better, to end it all, to let the goddess take her to the spirit world and have someone else save Westlands. She was useless, powerless.

Another voice intruded. *My queen, my beloved, don't leave me so soon after I found you! Fly! Fly!*

Rocky's words shocked her. Queen? Beloved? Did the handsome

stallion care for her that much? The treetops beckoned, their spiked tops pointing accusing fingers at her failure. The ground rushed towards her, stones growing into boulders. She gasped at the closeness of death. Would it hurt? Would it be quick? Would she join the goddess even though she'd failed her purpose?

Prism held out both wings, stretching them wide and letting the wind tease out her feathers. The world stopped spinning, her legs dangling beneath her. She curled up her knees and hocks as if springing across a stream, thrusting her hooves against an imaginary platform. She flapped her wings as she had watched Blaze do on countless occasions and fought against the pending impact.

Nothing happened. She plummeted to the ground, certain she would strike right in front of her parents and Rocky. She couldn't let them see that. She had to fly. She flapped. She kicked. She screamed to the goddess. Nothing worked. She continued to plummet.

Coldness swept over her body, matching the ice running through her limbs. Then she jerked to a halt mid-air. Sharp talons once again grabbed her spine and lifted her. She exhaled with relief. *Thank you, Blaze!*

Try try try to fly fly fly you must you must go with me and we'll go high high high!

They climbed and climbed. Prism's heartbeat steadied. With a clear head, she studied the ground and searched for Echo and Lash.

Blaze dropped her again.

That was no accident. Fury ran hot through Prism's veins. Why did Blaze save her just to let her fall? Prism bared her teeth, her anger rising, determined to drag the fickle dragon by the tail and bring him down. She stretched her head forward and snapped at his tender belly. Nimble in the air, Blaze out-manoeuvred her with ease, rising above her. She turned in an ungainly spin before righting herself. He wouldn't get away with this! She chased after him and rose to attack.

He dodged and dove. She followed him down and angled to cut him off. He rose again and twisted over her back, cackling at his escape. She pursued, determined to get in a kick at his shimmering scales.

He swooped in front of her nose. *You're flying you're flying! Fly with me and we'll go higher higher and beat that bird that feather thief Claw who thinks he's so much better than me! Fly fly fly my Prism my friend!*

Flying? She was! Her anger dissipated like the clouds that Blaze had carried her through. She scanned the ground below her. No hint of dizziness afflicted her. No longer did her stomach roil. No more did she quake with fear. She'd found her power. Every hair tingled with exhilaration, the caress of the wind soft, her skin absorbing energy quicker than she used it. Nuances of air currents filled her ears like the song of a nightingale, the pressure changing as she rose or descended. The very air smelled of freedom, carrying hints of the rich forests of Rattlesnake Ranges, distant sandy deserts, and the far off ocean.

Prism burst with strength and glee, the quickness of her breath evidence only of her thrill, not of effort. When she had peeked at the world when hanging under Blaze's talons, the landscape had appeared flat and unreal. Now, as she shifted her angle to turn or bank, the full dimensions of trees and hills, rivers and valleys came into sharp focus. Her parents and Rocky appeared like horse-shaped ants, scurrying in a miniature world. Memories of her vision of the goddess flooded back—was this how the goddess felt, looking down on her creation? Prism had never dreamed flying would be like this, the sense of superiority to all those destined to remain forever on the ground. No wonder birds sang and Blaze revelled in the glory of flight!

Prism soared alongside the dragon, sharing his joy, learning how to delicately flip the tips of her wings to adjust her height, to bank to either side, to speed up or slow down. Now, now she could accomplish her task and find out who, or what, was behind Westlands' problems.

After touching down her hind feet with delicate grace, Prism cantered a short way, folded her wings, and dropped to a walk. Her first landing had been disastrous; full of the joys of flight, she had crashed in an ungainly heap and skidded on her nose. Although her bruises had quickly healed with Gem's help, it had taken days for her feathers to straighten.

Every day she practiced flying with Blaze, his suggestions overflowing her head as he shared a lifetime's wisdom of aerodynamics. In good weather she could hold her own, keeping up with him at high speeds and able to skip over the treetops or soar into the clouds, but the twisting and rolling he accomplished so adeptly was far from her strength or skill. When the wind gusted or when visibility was poor, she struggled to keep on target or orient herself.

Having watched her land, Rocky trotted along the river to meet her. "Did you find anything today?"

The stallion always met her on her return from the day's searching. So far, Gem had insisted she return every evening to share any news, though Prism suspected her dam was more concerned about her crashing or getting lost. "No, nothing again, just more devastation."

The joys of finding her power—even if it had been through Blaze tricking her into flying—washed away like melting ice as Prism described the deserted forests, not only empty of creatures but now bare of vegetation. The only things alive were the slime that choked all the waterways as the weather warmed and the incessant rotfrogs with their venomous spitting. That was another good reason to return to the cave each night. Gem's presence kept away the foul amphibians from the water and the destructive gorgebugs from the new grass.

Keeping abreast of her as they strolled back to camp, Rocky leant over and nibbled at her withers. "Why don't we go down to the glade before we go back? It's not as if you have fresh news to share."

Simply grazing amid the haven Gem had created appealed to Prism. Following Rocky's lead, she changed direction and broke into a lope, keen to forget all that she had witnessed that day.

When they reached the clearing, Rocky rolled in a sandpit that Mystery had dug and then stood and shook from nose to tail. Prism daren't copy him for risk of damaging her wings. Instead, she sipped from the fresh brook and nibbled at the grass, the sweetness on her tongue an elixir against the tang of corruption elsewhere.

Rocky commenced grooming her as had become their habit, using his teeth to scratch her neck all along her mane, grasping mouthfuls of skin and tugging at her tired muscles. He worked down her shoulder and around her chest, gaining vigour with every stroke of his tongue.

Prism sensed a change in the routine, one that normally calmed her. This time the blood rushed through her body, tingling every hair along her spine. Rocky was a magnificent stallion and had called her his queen. His beloved. There was no doubt he was as aroused as her. Reciprocating the grooming, she turned the attention into playful nips, flicking her tail across her back and spinning around to avoid his touch. He chased her, his muscles rippling, driving her before him, and then became gentle and affectionate once more, drawing out the anticipation with the experience of age.

Prism couldn't wait any longer. Standing with her rump to his chest she thrust backwards, no further message necessary. Rocky consummated their relationship with enthusiasm, coating her with his hot sweat.

Having searched far to the south without seeing any trace of Echo, Prism decided to head west to determine where the influence of the plague ended. Not that it was easy to tell from the air. Only where gorgebugs had stripped the vegetation clean or algae fouled the waterways could she sense if animals had become diseased or perished. Wherever she could, she landed and sought out any inhabitants, querying those few she found about whether they had seen Echo, Lash, or Claw. She couldn't forget the need to find the great eagle for Kodi's sake, and she housed a suspicion that more than one of Shadow's creatures lay behind the evil that swept the land.

Once Blaze had become confident of her flying abilities, he had suggested they split up and search for Echo and Lash in different directions. Hopefully Blaze would be able to communicate with the massive snake over distance in the same way Kodi could with Snag. Poor Kodi. She worried for the guardian. Despite his sores healing, he had been very quiet since Mystery's and Gem's arrival, and spent most of the time wandering alone.

Delsin also spent a lot of time alone, but she didn't know if that was normal for people. Since having his vision, he had spent a lot of time closeted away in his lodge seeking answers to what he had seen. She shoved the memories of what he had described aside. For now she must focus on finding her grandsire.

The forest beneath her became so dense that nowhere offered a place to land for as far as she could see, but drawing power from the sun and wind she had no need to rest. The pines and spruce that clad the gentle slopes hummed with birdlife, a good sign that all was well this far west. She turned north and headed back to the area where she and Kodi had encountered the wolf pack. Back then the territory had been deep in snow and none of the animals sick.

Now was a different matter. Prism couldn't believe what she was looking at. Corpses littered either side of the winding river and slime coated its banks. A bedraggled wolf limped from one body to the next, sniffing each before rejecting the opportunity to feed.

Prism dived through the air and made a perfect landing alongside the wolf, his tattered fur barely covering his skeletal frame. The nails of his paws had shredded and bled, the result no doubt of digging for roots gauging from the one that hung stuck to a broken canine.

The wolf looked up at her with glazed eyes. "It's you. You fly now."

Shocked, Prism took a step back. "Are you part of the pack I met here in winter?"

"All gone. Only me left. I told them. Don't eat the dead." The male wolf slunk along the river, sniffing at rotting fish that had washed up the bank.

"Tell me what happened. I'm trying to find the cause. How long has it been like this?" Prism slowed her pace to stay level with the scavenging wolf who winced whenever he chewed on a stick or bulb.

"Why should I speak with you? A unicorn did this. He brought the death. Forcing everyone to eat his cure."

This last word was spat out with such venom that Prism flinched. "You mean Echo? He was here? So far north?"

"He murdered my family. Leave me alone. I'm hungry." Refusing to say another word, the wolf drifted away, his lank tail stuck with burs all that he would show to Prism.

With her mind whirling, Prism lunged into the air, not bothering with the long run that made take-off easy. Pummelling her wings, she laboured as high as she could go and still detect movement on the ground. She swooped down near the trees and flew back and forth, hunting for a glint of emerald that would reveal Echo's location. Then she remembered Rocky describing what a pitiful state her grandsire was in and looked instead for any equine shape.

Deep in the forest, with nowhere to land, Prism found him. Her grandsire doddered with his nose to the ground, weaving between the trees, giving her glimpses of a wasted body with unkempt hair. His horn had almost gone, but it had to be Echo. It could be no-one else.

Noting the nearby landmarks, Prism rose and headed for home. She wouldn't confront him on her own this time. She would return with Mystery and Gem via the ground, and fast.

Chapter 20

Rain slashed into Echo's face as he dragged his crumbling hooves through the mud. Clouds loomed low over the treetops turning the interior of the forest into a cave, one that had centuries of bat droppings on the floor, choking the air with mustiness and rotting fungus. Barren branches whipped at his shoulders and rump as he shoved past their mouldering bark, their needles and leaves long devoured by swarms of insects. Never before had he witnessed such a dismal spring: every new bud chewed before it unfurled; the snowmelt clogged with stinking algae; no sounds of birds calling for mates. The few animals he encountered barely had strength to drag themselves along, let alone mate and raise young.

With his body torn and bedraggled, Echo pondered why Aureana had allowed Equinora to become so tainted. The unicorns had resumed their protective role. Why had she abandoned them? Or had the deaths of Dewdrop, Jasper, and Moonglow disheartened her? Maybe she frolicked with them in another world, like she once had here, before she'd created the duocorn.

While Echo plodded on through the storm, his memories sparked like the lightning sheeting overhead, illuminating his desolation in flashes of stark white, accentuating the blackness. It was time he also joined Aureana. Let Equinora decline into ruin. He would escape to the spirit world. He had seen many seasons, experienced the joys of exploration, and dwelt in peace at Bearsden. Now his friends were gone, the animals of his territory doomed. Even his granddaughter had turned against him.

But he couldn't abandon his charges. He must go on while he still had strength to search for the stones. He probably couldn't die anyway. If he lay down and did nothing, Equinora's power would course through his veins and invigorate him. He couldn't allow himself time for even that luxury now. The voles and squirrels were gone, the moose and wolves dying. The trees creaked without the chatter of leaves or birds.

A small meteorite shower had fallen last night, back towards his haven. The valley to the east of the gorge was the most likely spot. The larger pieces would bounce and tumble down the bare slopes, the smaller ones captured by the rocks. As he pictured where the sky stones might have fallen, the welcome of his steaming pool lifted his stride. Heading south, he kept his head low and nostrils distended, attuned to the whiff of Aureana's gifts. For what else could they be? He'd never known stones fall from the sky before. Maybe she hadn't abandoned them after all.

His swollen tongue stuck to the roof of his mouth. The stench of corpses drew him to a stream. He shared the desperation that drove predators and prey alike to water, the need to plunge their muzzles into the coolness overcoming their usual stealth. Since eating of the sustenance he created, he had experienced the same urge. That was to be expected. Healing bodies needed cleansing.

Splashing to find a deeper pool where the water would be less tainted, Echo sniffed at the surface. Algae swilled into his nostrils. He sneezed. He couldn't drink here. Fat insects buzzed over his skin, stinging as they drew blood. Not bothering to swish them away, he continued south, aware the world was out of balance, not knowing what else he could do other than nourish those he encountered. When he and Diamond had fed and relocated creatures after the devastating bloodwolf war, the lands had soon recovered. He doubted life would return to normal as easily this time.

As Echo had predicted, the gullies near his home displayed the burnt scars of destruction from meteorites crashing to earth. He gathered the miniscule fragments and built a cache. Once he had found all he could, he set about transforming the pile into sustenance. The work was hard, harder than he had ever experienced. Where had his power gone?

Unable to transform all the stones, and dripping in sweat that mingled with the continuing rain, Echo puffed from exertion and pain. His legs trembled and he gasped for air. The clouds bore down on him, forcing him to his knees. He collapsed, rolled on his side, and sprawled on the soaked ground. Gravel washed into his lips and silted his eyes as rivulets eroded the bare earth around his shrivelled body.

Cold. So cold.

The ground shook. Another earthquake? Or had Aureana come for him? Echo absorbed the vibrations, welcoming the jarring of his bones. Thudding accompanied the trembling earth, pounding a rhythm in his head. Recognition struck. Cantering. Someone was cantering towards him. And not the splayed hooves of moose, but horses. No, not horses. He could smell her now. Aureana! No, more than one set of hooves. Unicorns. Dewdrop? Jasper? Moonglow?

Excitement propelled Echo to his feet. He shook off his misery in an aura of mud.

A trio of unicorns burst from the trees, whinnying when they saw him. Nothing had prepared him for a vision like this. A silver stallion with a copper horn. An emerald mare, her hooves and horn pure opal, her mane and tail crimson. And a golden-winged rainbow, half galloping, half floating on the swirling mist that twisted around her legs.

"Prism?" The other two must be Mystery and Gemstone. His daughter. His beautiful daughter. But she had never been known to leave Shimmering Lake. How would her charges survive without her? What was she doing in Bearsden? Or had they all died and gone to the spirit world? But he recognised the valley where he had stopped to drink, the clogged stream reflecting his disappointment.

The three other unicorns skidded to a halt and formed up abreast in front of him.

"Gemstone? Thank goodness you're here. Help me take this sustenance to feed the remaining animals. Heal the sick while I transform the sky stones." Renewed enthusiasm welled in his heart like water burbling from a spring.

"No. This must stop." It was Mystery who answered, stamping the ground with a shiny hoof, copper light sparkling through the puddles. "Look at yourself. You can barely stand. This is no way to solve the problem. You must stop creating this so-called sustenance. You must cease feeding the creatures who still live."

What had been delight changed to anger in Echo's soul. He quaked with indignation. "How dare you interfere in how I care for my territory? What gives you the right to order me around? You're barely old enough to be weaned."

Prism trotted forward with her wings outspread and halted between them. "Stop this. It's all too confusing. We need to talk. I've listened to the animals and seen them suffer. We must find out who, or what, is causing the plague, why the waterways are infested, and why the air teems with bugs."

Echo gathered what little energy he had and strutted around her to face Mystery. "I see you've not taught my granddaughter any respect for her elders. I know how to fix the problem. If you're not here to help, leave."

Gemstone nuzzled her mate and must have passed him a message.

Damn whatever it was that prevented him from hearing their conversation. That's why he had been taken by surprise by their arrival.

His daughter gazed at him with loving eyes. "Of course we want to help. Why else would we be here? Lash, a giant snake, feeds on the corpses. We presume he's one of the duocorn's creatures. He must be poisoning the waterways. Perhaps he's even creating the rotfrogs and gorgebugs. But we don't believe your sustenance is working. It's killing those who—"

"Nonsense. You don't know what you're talking about any more than my granddaughter. Now, I say again, if you're not going to help me, go home." He turned his back on the three of them. Collecting a mouthful of his sustenance, he cocked an ear to listen for someone to take it to.

A movement caught his eye. Another unlikely trio emerged from the forest behind Mystery—a man on a skewbald horse and a giant bear. He recognised them all, but the bear had been with Prism. The man had said he was searching for her. Echo had forgotten all about them. He summoned the last of his strength and surged towards them, intent on reaching the track, passing them, and being on his way.

The mighty bear held out one shaggy foreleg and blocked his path. "Wait. You're sick. Let us help you."

Fury boiled within Echo. If he could, he would rear and strike at the beast with his hooves, bite his tender nose and kick his furry legs from under him. But he had no energy left. Instead, he drew himself up with all the dignity he could muster. "Get. Out. Of. My. Way."

Gemstone wove around him to also block the track. "Echo, please. I can smell the putrefaction that plagues you. Let me heal you. Let me give you strength."

Shutting his ears to the pleas of those around him, Echo spun in an attempt to find another way past. The four equines and the bear surrounded him. He didn't have the strength to fight his way through.

Gemstone touched her horn to his neck, flinched, and sent power blasting through his body. "Once you're better, we'll talk the situation through. We'll come up with a solution."

Energy streamed into his numb limbs, building his muscles and quickening his pulse. Instead of the effort draining her, Gemstone glowed with power, sparks zinging from her horn. Yet the look in her eye suggested pity and blame. What did she know?

Echo's ire grew in direct proportion to the strength that returned to his weakened limbs. How dare these youngsters presume to take charge? He rose on his hind legs, piercing the air with his scream, and snaked his teeth at Gemstone, sending her reeling, her horn still sizzling. He lashed out with his forelegs, striking Mystery, before dropping to the ground. He spun and thudded his heels into Prism. "Go! All of you! Go like Diamond left me! Get out of my territory!"

Stunned more from shock than the pain in her side, Prism staggered back. Concern for Kodi as he tried to grapple Echo around the neck changed to fear as Rocky plunged in to the fight. "Don't! This isn't the way!"

A piercing neigh from behind Mystery and Gem distracted them all. Through the haze of drizzle, two sparkling figures emerged, glinting despite the lack of sunlight. Diamond, her horn pointing straight ahead and thrust towards the fighters, broke into a gallop. A sapphire unicorn, presumably Tempest, charged after her, his snow-white mane and tail streaming behind him.

Echo ducked away from the younger generation unicorns, slipping in the mud as he hurried to greet the newcomers. Prism gaped as her parents joined her, all three of them shaking from Echo's attack.

Diamond braked and strode around Echo and Tempest, eyes blazing. "What in Equinora is going on? It's a good thing Gem didn't block her message to Mystery, else I'd never have found you. We've been waiting at Echo's haven."

Gem stepped forward with her head held high. "I broadcast that message aloud in the hope that Echo could hear me. As you can see, he is poisoned and unable to communicate other than by speech. He is extremely sick and must not be permitted to continue his work."

Prism straightened with every muscle tense, every sinew stretched, and her heart thumping fit to burst from her chest. She watched for Tempest's reaction, ready for further conflict.

He avoided her gaze and scanned the surrounding country, nostrils flared and standing rigid. Tension hung in the air like the aftermath of an electric storm. Rocky fidgeted behind Prism, and Kodi retreated on all fours to Delsin's side. A shadow circled overhead, the only sign that Blaze had not deserted them. She gazed up at her friend, comforted by his rainbow dazzle, glistening wet like a creek-bed of precious gems.

Tempest snorted and pranced to the centre of their gathering. "What nonsense is this? Believing Echo responsible for this devastation? Not even the duocorn would do this to the land. Where has this ridiculous notion come from? Why isn't anyone looking for the source of the problem?"

His accusations hit Prism hard. No doubt, the tirade was directed at her. After she had shared with Mystery and Gem the wolf's claims that Echo was poisoning the animals, they had reluctantly agreed with her reasoning. But still a suspicion lurked that Lash was somehow involved. She described her discoveries to Diamond and Tempest. "And look how ill Echo is. Surely that's a sign what he's doing is wrong—"

Diamond lunged forward and bit Prism on the neck. She squealed. Before she could retaliate, Rocky leapt to her defence, rearing above Diamond to drive her away with his chest.

At the same time, Tempest and Mystery engaged in battle, their necks entwined and teeth snapping as they stood on their hind legs, their forelegs locked together. Echo slammed into Gem, who only moments before had given him strength from her healing power. Growls and shouts erupted from Kodi and Delsin where they hovered out of reach of kicking hooves.

Amid the bedlam, a loud trumpeting that Prism had never heard before echoed from the hills. The sound hurt her hears, confounded her senses, and upset her balance. Heat welled around her and the other struggling unicorns. Flames leapt from the treetops to every bare bush, igniting them in a flash. A circle of fire grew ever higher, burning everything even in the rain, driving the fighters apart in order to save themselves from the encroaching flames.

Prism gaped.

Blaze swooped and dived, all his scales bright crimson. His chest expanded as he prepared to spew fire. The mighty dragon shrilled again, his great wings fanning the flames as he breathed fire over the already scorched land. Rocks cracked and split with the sudden change in temperature. The earth sizzled and steamed.

Prism searched for an escape. "Blaze! Stop! Pleeease!"

Somehow, her cries penetrated the dragon's panic. He rose higher in the air, beseeching her to join him. As he became a mere speck against the grey sky, Prism's feathers curled and crisped in the heat. She couldn't escape by air, not without having to run through the flames to take-off, and she couldn't tell how much damage her wings had suffered.

Quivering with fear, she looked to the other unicorns for help. Gem and Mystery raced side by side, looking for a gap through the flames. Stripped branches exploded, their popping sap spreading the fire. Echo stood with his nose on the ground, Diamond by his side, comforting each other as if the end of the world had arrived. Tempest reared and pointed his horn to the sky. Streaks of power shot from the smooth tip, striking the clouds high above.

Thunder rumbled and the wind roared as mighty stormheads built. Midday turned as dark as a winter's evening. Torrential rain poured down, dousing the fires that raged through the dead forests. Tempest sent bolt after bolt of power skywards, broiling the clouds thicker and darker into swirling masses. Lightning seared Prism's eyes. With an ear-splitting crack, the ominous thunderheads released a deluge beyond belief.

Drenched in moments, Prism could only blink and watch as rivulets grew to streams, her limbs paralysed in shock. Water poured from the hillsides in silt-laden rivers. Flood waters transformed meadows into lakes. Mesmerised, she shivered without drawing on energy to keep warm.

A tug on her mane broke the spell. Delsin grabbed her in a struggle to stay upright. He cupped his other hand to his mouth and shouted in her ear. "We'll be swept away! Head for the cave!"

He leapt onto Rocky's back and waited for her to move before urging the skewbald to higher ground. Jolted into action by another clap of thunder, she followed, sending out a message to Gem and Mystery. Trusting them to make their own way, she slogged against the force of water that already rose above her knees, splashing her belly with freezing pellets. Sleet pounded into her face, obliterating her sight. She squeezed her eyes tight and relied on her sense of smell and the touch of the earth to guide her.

Chapter 21

Seeking the welcome shelter of the cave, Prism shook off as much rain as she could before squeezing through the narrow opening without doing further damage to her wings. The she-bear had long since stopped being threatened by sharing her home with unicorns, relishing the sweet waters that Gem created and thankful that Prism had saved her from eating whatever had poisoned the animals before winter. Blaze, however, still caused the bear to sweep her cubs behind her, a feat not easily achieved with their burst of growth.

Mystery and Gem arrived soon after Prism, the cavern a tight fit with all of them sheltering inside. Rocky crowded in behind Prism and nudged Delsin on the leg who then slipped to the ground and set about building a fire. The rain had drenched even his store of dry tinder, penetrating the crevices of the cave and pooling in the deep recesses. Blaze crept forwards and lit the stack of wood with a gentle huff.

The she-bear stumbled backwards. "Does he have to do that in here?"

"I'm sorry. I didn't think to warn you." Delsin held out a reassuring hand to the cubs while suggesting the dragon retreat to a more comfortable distance.

A twinge of remorse pricked Prism at the look of contrition on her friend's face. "Thank you, Blaze. We'll all be glad of the warmth to dry out. But why did you burn the forests?" She couldn't come to terms with what he had done.

The dragon curled his tail around his nose and huddled to the stone floor. "Prism my Prism was in danger which scared angered threatened me so I fought power with power with flame to stop the bad one from hurting my friend Prism my friend Delsin their friend Rocky the guardian fear danger—"

"Yes, I see. It's okay. You did what you thought was right." Understanding the truth in what he said, Prism sighed and accepted that Blaze had only been trying to help. It was probably a good thing that so much poisoned territory had been destroyed, first by the fire and then by the flood.

Mystery squeezed past Gem and dropped a stone at Prism's feet as if to change the subject. "I brought this with me. It's one of Echo's untransformed sky stones. I've never encountered anything like it before. It's almost solid nickel, not a metal I know much about, but the corpses I checked reeked of it."

"What does this mean? Are the stones poisonous?" Prism was keen to learn more.

He cocked his head to one side. "It's possible. When Echo transforms them, they probably release nickel into the air, and then the waterways, as well as a substantial amount remaining in the food."

Prism perked up at this suggestion of the source of the problem. "So he wouldn't know he was doing it? He might not be deliberately creating poison?"

Gem had been listening intently and came to the defence of her sire. "Of course not. Why would he? I knew there had to be a rational explanation."

After her first surge of enthusiasm, Prism thought through the implications. "So how do we get him to stop? And how do we cure the land? The plague has spread far. And what about the rotfrogs and gorgebugs?"

Kodi rose from where he had nestled on the other side of the fire to dry his fur. "The insects would have grown in number due to the huge amount of food available with the herbivores dying. Plagues like this are not unheard of. And perhaps the rotfrogs have always been there in small numbers, but were able to thrive in the altered conditions."

Delsin had stripped off his garments to hang on nearby ledges to dry and sat huddled in his bed furs. "We may never know. What's more important is how to restore life to Westlands."

Gem conceded that she had no knowledge of how to cure diseases such as these. She could only treat the symptoms.

Blaze straightened his wings, making the she-bear race to the rear of the cave, and stretched his head high to the roof. "Meda my Meda she'll know she's a healing dragon where is she my Meda?"

Prism perked up. "If Meda doesn't know, then the clan healers might. Delsin, is Meda still with Laila? Do you know where they are?"

The man rose and wrapped his arms around Rocky's neck. "Of course, they should still be at Bloomsvale. But Rocky can't travel in this weather, and it'll take us a long time to go over the mountains."

Undeterred, Prism pressed on. "Rocky can't, but Blaze can. What if he took you to fetch them? Or at least ask their advice?"

Blaze snorted, threatening to set them all alight. "Not leaving Prism my Prism with threats everywhere bad unicorns floods danger poison bugs—"

"Stop it, Blaze. You caused the fires which is why we have the floods. I know you didn't mean any harm, but here's your chance to really help. Do you think you could carry Delsin?"

Squirming like a wolf pup with a stolen bone, Blaze snaked his neck along the ground to Prism. "Hang on hang on hang on through wind and rain and over mountains if he can I can I'll carry my friend Delsin he with my scale to his home."

Relief drove the last of the cold and wet away, enabling Prism to relax for the first time in ages. "That's good then. We have a plan. While Blaze and Delsin go to Laila and Meda, the rest of us will contact Diamond and Tempest to let them know what Mystery has concluded about the stones."

Quiet until now, Rocky nuzzled Prism's neck. "What about the horses down south? And the clans? The floods will wipe them out. They won't know that wall of water is coming."

"You're right." Prism's mind raced. Only one solution offered the speed required. "I must warn them. While Mystery and Gem contact Diamond and Tempest, I'll fly south."

"No!" Gem's reaction was instant. "You know you can't fly in bad weather. And look at your wings. I've never mended burnt feathers. They may not heal properly."

Prism stood firm. "I have to go. This is for me to do, no matter what it costs me."

The flight south proved to be the hardest thing Prism had ever tackled in her life. Time and again the wind buffeted her to the ground, sucking away her strength as much as providing her energy, her sodden wings heavy and taking all her energy to beat. No updrafts helped lift her high and the flooded ground left nowhere for her to rest. Blaze had tried to help her by explaining how to use the power of the thunder and lightning to draw energy into her flagging muscles, but either she wasn't doing it right or even that source of power was insufficient for the arduous journey.

Thankfully, Gem's healing had restored her feathers, new leaders growing to replace those burnt, though they hadn't regained their full length, increasing the effort of every wingbeat and reducing her ability to glide. With the country changed dramatically by swollen rivers and dying forests, recognising Sweetwood proved challenging. By the time she reached the village, it was all she could do to speak.

Instead of the excited babbling of the clan when she had visited with Kodi, the people stood with mouths agape, malnourishment evident in their loose skin hanging from stick-like limbs.

Istas Sugar emerged into the central clearing as Prism prepared to land, and signalled the few children to stay back by the huts. "Welcome, Lady Prism! We had started to think we had dreamed you. You fly!"

Prism folded her wings and used what little strength she had to prance in order to hide her exhaustion, not wanting the people to witness her weakness. She returned Istas's greetings and accepted a welcome mouthful of maple sugar. "You must evacuate the village. There is a great flood coming that will wash you to the sea."

A wail from one of the women cradling a baby with two ragged children hugging her legs preceded an eruption of questions.

Ahote waved for quiet. "Where are we to go? This village is our last stronghold. All the others are overrun with stinking frogs."

Any trek would be hard on the starving clan, but Prism had to remain positive. "Rattlesnake Ranges are high enough to be safe, and there is no sign of the amphibians in the mountains. From there you can go to Waterfalls. I'm sure the clan that lives with my grandsire, King Fleet of Foot at White Water Cliffs, will give you shelter."

Delsin had told her that Yuma still lived there, a man she had heard many tales about. He would know what to do for these people.

A middle-aged man stepped out from the crowd. "Our children and our elderly won't be able to climb the ranges. We should head for Dark Woods."

"What about the wolves?" Another man joined the debate, his voice rising in fear.

Many of the people started to argue at once. "We can't stay here, floods or no." "The sap won't rise with the buds stripped from the maples." "We're better off going further west." "There's no point going anywhere, we'll all be dead soon with the plague."

Prism could take no more. "Stop! I've seen the land from the air. Crossing the mountains to Midlands is your only chance. You must go straight away."

The leaders needed no more convincing. The only reason they hadn't left already was the lack of agreement among the council of where to go. Between them, Istas and Ahote directed people to gather their few possessions, and strap the old and sick onto drags. Children carried bundles of meagre possessions and their parents collected weapons and cooking utensils. At least they had plenty of warm clothes, and spring offered a reprieve from the bitter conditions.

Flying ahead to ensure she didn't lead them into danger, Prism guided the clan to safety. As soon as she had them out of the flood's path, she gave them directions to Watersmeet and left the band of hungry travellers to continue their journey.

Now she had to find Boldearth and his herd, and warn them too. Contact with the ground had renewed some of her strength, but time was running out before the floods would consume everything in their path.

Having sent a quick reassuring message to Gem that the people were safe, Prism continued to search for the horses. At last, the worst of the treacherous weather created by Tempest was over, with patches of blue sky struggling through the cloud cover. Prism welcomed the warmth and the energy to further renew her depleted reserves. Flying further east, she found plenty of places to rest.

The rain had also sweetened the few meadows that had not been devoured by gorgebugs, giving her hope that Boldearth's herd would have been able to find enough feed to survive. Wondering how Blaze and Delsin were going with their mission, she missed the dragon's company in the air, his incessant chatter removing the isolation of the empty sky. But she wasn't surprised that she hadn't heard from him. Blaze couldn't swap messages with unicorns over a long distance.

She landed for a rest and to check for horse droppings or any other sign the herd had been here recently. That reminded her of Rocky. Her heart faltered. Having only had her parents as equine company all her life, Prism regretted every moment away from the stallion. He had a charm of coltish enthusiasm tempered with worldly experience, and had taught her more about the lives of normal horses and people than Mystery and Gem ever had. But she mustn't let herself become attached. She had generations of life ahead of her, and he would die in a few more years. Even a warmblood as strong as him couldn't live as long as a unicorn. But she missed him. She wanted to make the most of the time they had together.

Hoping that Rocky, Blaze, and Delsin were all safe back at the cave with Gem, Mystery, and Kodi, Prism nibbled at fresh shoots and scented for clean water. She wandered across a glade and encountered a small cliff where the land had slipped away, presumably in the floods, exposing the raw rock face. She paused, one hoof raised.

Something shifted within the rocks. Was an animal trapped?

Raising her head, she couldn't detect a whiff of anyone. Curious, she sauntered over. Had she had imagined the shift? There had been no rattle of falling stones. There it was again. Were shadows causing an illusion? It had been so long since she had enjoyed sunshine; her eyes might be playing tricks on her.

No, the cliff had definitely altered. Moving more cautiously, Prism advanced, calling out her name.

"Gooo awaysss."

Prism recognised that hiss. Lash! So this is where he had ended up. Stepping with more confidence, Prism called out a greeting to the snake and reiterated who she was. Now that she knew what to look for, she identified the great coils of Lash's muscles tucked among the rocks. "Are you alright?"

A giant head with forked tongue unwrapped from a slab of

granite. Milky-blue eyes blinked and a long hiss accompanied the hypnotic waving of his raised body. "Don't come clossser."

Prism halted, her neck arched. He had grown so much! With a body now thicker than hers, Lash must have doubled in size since she had last met him. "I need to talk with you."

"No. Go awaysss." Instead of his former silvery-grey, Lash was a dull brown, lumpy like piles of acorns, his underbelly as dark as dried blood.

Prism ignored his continued gyrations and crept closer. She had to find out more. "Are you sick?"

Lash's body rippled around a protruding crag, revealing his full length as he straightened across the glade, slithering in a curve to circle around Prism.

She turned with him to keep facing his swaying head. "Everything's dying, and there's a mighty flood on the way. You must get to higher ground. Have you seen any horses? Alive, that is. I'm searching for Boldearth's herd."

Remembering how Mystery had sent Blaze love to befriend him during the stealthcat war, Prism swallowed her repugnance of Shadow's snake and opened her heart. Lash's opaque eyes started to clear, the milky-blue dissipating like scum blown from a fetid pool. Jet black orbs stared back at her, bottomless wells of darkness. His crimson tongue tasted the air, up and down, flickering in and out. The tip of his tail thrashed against the sodden earth.

Prism lowered her head, unsure whether she had transformed him in any way. "Please, speak to me. Do you know where the rotfrogs and gorgebugs come from? Can you explain what's happening and why?"

The giant snake's only reply was a louder hiss. He returned to the cliff and scraped his body along the rough wall, dislodging earth and stones to tumble over his writhing form.

Prism trotted alongside, continuing to send him love in an attempt to engage him in conversation. At least it appeared he was taking her advice to climb to safety. He reached the end of the stone wall, turned in one fluid movement, and rubbed his head up and down the rock. Wet skin peeled away from his face. Prism halted in horror. What had she done? Or had the rains rotted Lash? Had he fallen foul of the poison like so many others?

Lash's skin peeled back from his wedged head. He squirmed

and ground his body against the hard surface, wriggling like an enormous worm caught in the sun. Not believing what she witnessed, Prism gaped. The dark brown outer layer of Lash's body remained stuck to the cliff as he slithered forward.

Almost hypnotised by the shedding snake, Prism could only stare. That's why he hadn't wanted to talk. She'd forgotten how reptiles discarded their old coverings as they grew, and with the number of dead animals caused by the plague, and his overgrown size, Lash must have gone through this process frequently. The used husk curled down his body as he shucked his old skin. She would get no answers from him in this state. Prism retreated to graze while Lash finished his transformation.

A hiss that sounded more like a sigh brought her back to the cliff. Stunned, she was lost for words. There before her was exactly what Delsin had described from his vision: a jewelled snake, every scale a glistening ruby, emerald, or sapphire among diamond, topaz, and amethyst. His new skin matched that of Blaze, and, she had to acknowledge, her own dapples. Her love had worked, or did her colouring, the same as Blaze's and Lash's, indicate that she was some form of throwback to Shadow? Her fears renewed that somehow she was the harbinger of death.

Before she could ask Lash any more questions, he flexed his full length and departed with a speed Prism couldn't believe. "Don't leave! I need to talk to you!"

Her cries went unanswered.

Prism trotted over to the shell of Lash's former self. She flinched back in horror. Already bloated rotfrogs covered in pustules devoured his shed skin. Was this how they became so foul? She took to the air in a hurry and set off after the snake. She needed answers, not least of all about Shadow's influence in the plague. Lash was bound to know.

Too late. The snake was gone.

Flying over the treetops reinvigorated Prism, the joy of being airborne overriding her revulsion at the repulsive creatures she fled and her possible role in the problems facing Westlands. Lash could wait for another time. With his new jewelled colouring, she would easily be able to find him again. Even if he paled, all she had to do was transmit her love to brighten his scales. That would be easier now she had witnessed him in all his glory.

For now, she must locate Boldearth and warn the stallion of the impending flood. Tempest's storms would have melted the last of the snow, possibly even on the highest peaks where the ice lasted well into summer in normal years, adding to the volume of destructive water.

Without the constant rain, Prism relished her journey. The freedom that came from being airborne, and the relief of not having to consult with anyone, removed the pressure that had driven her. Until now, she had always had Kodi, or her parents, quizzing her motives and beliefs. Even Blaze had chastised her before she had learnt to fly, and she still held a tiny grudge at the way he had dropped her twice, even if it had worked.

Only Rocky, her handsome consort, never questioned her actions. She wished he had wings too. Then the places they could go and things they could see! But he was a horse. There was no point wishing for what could never be, and she had more immediate problems. She still couldn't make up her mind whether Echo deliberately poisoned the stones he collected, and whether Lash had anything to do with the plague. How could the snake be evil if he had morphed into a jewelled creature like Blaze? The dragon had never been evil, only doing what he needed for survival at Shadow's demand. And she had never deliberately harmed anything or anyone. Nothing made sense.

Was another hotblood behind the troubles? Shadow could have sired a strong warmblood, or empowered and corrupted other creatures. She shuddered at the possibility so much that she almost crashed into a towering fir. Swerving at the last minute, she decided to land in the next clearing and think through the issues while standing on firm ground.

The forest provided several opportunities for her to land, its natural sparseness offering small clearings with little to obstruct her run-up for take-off. After choosing one that looked free of rocks, she landed gently, proud of the grace and control that had come from long practice. She steadied to a walk.

About to drop her head to graze, she shied at the smell of horses. A pair trotted over. "Boldearth! I've been looking for you. Where's your herd?"

The appaloosa stallion nosed her extended muzzle and swapped a nicker of greeting. "We split up long ago. There's not enough food in any one area for more than one or two horses."

Boldearth looked healthy, if rather thin. He was much smaller than Rocky, and nowhere near as handsome. The mare at his side was heavy in foal and didn't look in as good condition. Prism worried how far the other horses may have spread. "You need to move further east. There's a great flood coming. It isn't safe here."

Boldearth turned to his companion. "We can't travel fast with Patches so close to foaling. We can't fly like you. And magnificent you are too! We hurried here as fast as we could when we saw you. What other news do you bring?"

Prism didn't want to waste time describing all that had happened since she had first come to Maple Woods. "You must get to higher ground. Make your way back to White Water Cliffs. You should be safe over there, and Fleet will surely allow you and your mare to share his territory if you say I sent you."

Boldearth scratched at his ear with a hind hoof as if he didn't have a care in the world. "We'll head towards Dark Woods. That should be safe enough and avoid the steeper hills."

"But what about the wolves? The clan fear that many still lurk there."

The stallion twitched his upper lip with disregard. "We've outrun bloodwolves. I doubt normal ones will give us trouble. And neither of us wishes to live in a herd again. But thank you for the warning. Don't worry about us."

Having hoped to save all the horses, not just two, Prism wasn't sure what to do next. She couldn't scour the country for every member of the dispersed herd, especially not knowing how many others still lived. "Will you at least warn any other horses you see? I'd hate for any to be caught and drowned."

Both Boldearth and Patches informed her that all of their former friends were long gone, or dead. "Are the clan safe? They're slower than us."

Prism shared how she had led the people to the trail through Rattlesnake Ranges.

"What about the old spiritman at Leeface you told us about? Did he die?"

Shocked that she had forgotten the old man, Prism promised to seek him out.

Flying over what had once been the village of Leeface in the foothills to the east of the lakes, Prism circled to find familiar landmarks. Everything looked so different from the air. Deciding the only way she would find the right place was to retrace the path from the mountains, she surged on an updraft and soared on layers of warmer air. The ground dwindled beneath her, enabling her to see the pass where she and Kodi had crossed the ranges. Gliding lower, she followed the trails until she came to the spot that had to have been the village. The strange rock formations she remembered remained solidly anchored in the bowl-shaped valley.

But no sign of the village remained. Instead, a beach of silt coated everything in sludge. A rim of tangled branches and uprooted trees denoted the high water mark. The flood had been through already. And it had come so high! Nothing would have withstood that rage of water. Not a single hut remained. Not even a circle of stones marked ancient fireplaces. Not wanting to land in case the mire sucked her into its gripping depths, Prism alighted beyond reach of the destruction. The only good that had come of the torrent was the lack of foul beasts polluting the waters. Not a croak reached her ears.

A screech like that of an owl echoed through the pinnacles. Wanting to know what had occurred when the flood came through, Prism sought the source of the sound. The song became louder, ululating to a pitch beyond that of any bird she had ever met. Reaching the ancient fir from where the sound emanated, she halted at the base and called out her name.

The sound immediately ceased, followed by a scrabbling on bark as if a racoon scurried from branch to branch.

Prism waited for the arrival of whatever had been making the noise, ready to launch into the air if the eerie noise came from one of Shadow's creations. She needn't have worried. Instead of some monster, a frail old man slithered out of the tree. She whinnied when she recognised the spiritman. "You're alive! I can't believe it. How did you survive?"

"Is it really you again? My unicorn! Let me touch you. How did you cross the floods?" With hands outstretched, Yaholo Bones tottered towards Prism, groping the air.

Sensing his problem, Prism stepped forward and dropped her horn to his hands. "I flew. What blinded you? How have you survived?"

"The bones! The bones! They were right!" The spiritman ran his hands over her body, delicately stroking her wings and ending at her tail. "The stars have stopped falling! The rotfrogs are gone! The bread of ghosts has been found!" He waved his skinny arms over his head and cavorted around her, flapping as he imitated her flying. "The winged one has come! All will be well! All will be well!"

Surprised yet delighted at the health of the old man, Prism tried to tease answers from him about what the bones had foretold and how he had been blinded. All he would repeat were sentiments about the stars sending the bread of ghosts until her arrival. Even if he hadn't been before, he was obviously quite mad now.

Chapter 22

Delsin stripped the ribs from bulrush leaves and plaited them to weave into wide bands, the repetitive work soothing, allowing him to think of what lay ahead. Excitement mingled with fear at flying, and enthusiasm for seeing Laila mixed with what he might find at Bloomsvale. Expectation that Laila and Meda would know a cure for nickel poisoning overlaid everything, tinged with worry that they wouldn't.

But one step at a time. First, he had to rig something to secure him to Blaze. With an armful of strong straps, he called Blaze and met the dragon on a flat meadow. "Tell me where you want these. I don't want to strangle you."

Blaze raised his head and stretched out his wings. "Chest belly shoulders not neck don't wrap wings or legs or throat!"

Fashioning a harness, ensuring the reeds lay flat against Blaze's scales so as not to cut into him, proved a challenging process. If Delsin didn't position the ropes individually around each scale, the diamonds cut into the braids. When he tightened the knots, Blaze fidgeted, adding to the difficulty. "I'll need an extra length to reach around your stomach. You're even bigger than you look. Have a break while I plait more."

Delsin returned with another armful of straps, enough to stretch around Blaze's girth below his wings, across his chest above his wings, and loop around the top of his tail for extra security. When Delsin had finished, he stood back to check the overall effect. "Apart from you looking like a ptarmigan ready for the pot, it should hold." The harness didn't fit as snugly as those that Laila had constructed for horses to tow travois, but a giant dragon was a very different shape.

Blaze hopped like a wounded duck, testing his mobility. "Try try try to fly fly fly with me! Let's go and I'll show you the glory the wonder the beauty from the sky!"

Delsin grabbed the shoulder strap and tried to scrabble onto Blaze's back. He couldn't get high enough to swing his leg over. He slid back to the ground. "You'll have to crouch down. I can't jump around your belly like I can with Rocky."

Even when Blaze flattened himself, his head and neck a mirror of his draping tail along the ground, Delsin struggled to mount, the weight of his pack unbalancing him. In the end, he used Blaze's scales as steps while hanging on the rope with both hands and walked up the dragon's side as if he climbed a rock face. This time he managed to swing his leg over the base of Blaze's neck, about where he imagined the dragon's withers would be. "How does that feel?"

"Too far far forward I won't be able to go up up up!"

Using his hands to lever himself over the ridges of Blaze's spine, Delsin worked his way towards Blaze's tail. With each serrated plate that Delsin bumped over, his legs spread wider to accommodate the dragon's width. "I can't go back much further. Will this do?"

"Too far far back I can't lift my wings can't flap can't fly!"

Delsin crept forward again, one ridge at a time, like playing leapfrog as he and Laila had done as small children. "How about here?"

Blaze opened his wings and ran forward. He stretched his neck out like an arrow and prepared to launch.

Sharp scales bit into Delsin's backside. "Don't fly yet! I won't be able to stay on like this."

Blaze jerked to a halt, thrusting Delsin's crotch onto the bony ridge of his spine. Delsin sucked in air, his eyes smarting. When he had recovered, he swung his right leg in front of him and slid to the ground, still hanging onto the shoulder strap, wrenching his arm. "I'll fetch something to sit on."

He'd need to discover a better way of getting on and off if he were to fly regularly, though the second time was easier now he knew where to position himself. With a padded coney skin under his seat bones, Delsin wriggled from side to side. "That's more comfortable, but I still don't feel stable."

"Hurry hurry hurry we fly we go to Bloomsvale to my Meda my

friend I can't wait any longer!"

Delsin hooked the toes of his boots under the straps around Blaze's neck and settled between his shoulder blades. The dragon's wings lifted either side of him like the giant petals of a jewelled crocus. In a powerful surge that left Delsin's stomach behind, Blaze took to the air, gaining height to leave Rocky dwindling below them. Delsin only had a brief moment to feel sad at leaving his other friend behind before the cold numbed his concentration. The wind sucked away his breath and roared in his ears. "Do we have to go so high?"

Blaze turned his head to regard Delsin with crimson eyes that crinkled in glee. "Higher higher higher easier to glide quicker to arrive sooner to see my Meda my friend!"

Delsin clutched the extra rope he had looped around Blaze's shoulders, thankful he had added the reinforcing. Closing his eyes removed his ability to balance. Leaving them open increased his insecurity. In an attempt to relax, he shifted the pack on his shoulders that dragged him to one side. The weight swung back, grating against his spine. Why had he insisted on bringing food and water? At this speed they would be at Bloomsvale before nightfall. He chuckled, half with nerves, half with genuine humour as he remembered almost packing his fire-lighting flints and kindling, much to Blaze's chagrin.

Once accustomed to the wind whistling past his ears, and with his face rigid with cold like a death mask, Delsin snuck a glance at the ground. They had reached a point, higher than the peaks to the east, where Blaze only needed a flick of his wingtips to keep moving, yawing slightly to left or right as the unseen air currents shifted. With the land no more than a dream panorama sliding below, Delsin's curiosity overrode his fear. "The earth is curved! What's that dark mass to the south?"

Blaze banked, almost unseating Delsin in his haste. "The sea the ocean the waves of water the homes of aqua where dragons emerged to land!"

The ocean! Delsin had never visited the coast. No wonder the remnants of the Westlands clans could go no further south. At no time had Delsin dreamed the sea was so vast, to stretch forever. And that was only the surface. What swam beneath, in depths unimaginable? The sky, too, shrank Delsin's perception of his significance, like a tiny spiderling carried over the world by a silken thread in search of a home, or a dandelion seed blown wherever the weather dictated. Moving within a third dimension left life on the ground as mundane and restrictive. No wonder Blaze wanted Prism to fly with him in his element.

With the landscape spread before him like a giant's map come to life, Delsin recognised landmarks where he had travelled. Already they crested Rattlesnake Ranges. Far to the northeast the glimmering verdancy must be Gem and Mystery's territory, Shimmering Lake at its heart twinkling like a raindrop caught in the sun. Joy welled in Delsin's heart, the best he had felt since leaving Bloomsvale with Rocky all those moons ago. It was as if someone else had experienced the pain of that journey, the long slog through the snows, and Rocky being on the verge of death. The algae and rotfrogs, the rotting corpses, and vegetation stripped by gorgebugs, weren't evident from this height.

The reality of his journey brought back his sombre mood. He hoped Laila and Meda would know an antidote for nickel poisoning. If that was what the problem truly was. A lump of sky stone and a small piece of Echo's sustenance that Mystery had snatched were packed snugly in a clay jar in his pack, their presence burning a hole in his back.

The land changed from mountains to foothills to rolling plains. Blaze glided lower. River Lifeflow threaded through the land like the veins on the back of his mother's hands. To the south, Dark Woods brooded in sombre silence, impossible to tell if any creature lived within. As they followed the path of Silverstream, Delsin recalled his visit to Reedmarsh and his hunt for the herbs necessary to concoct the tonic for Macha Gatherer. Was she still alive? Soon he'd know.

Suggesting to Blaze that he land away from the village in order not to scare the clan, Delsin anticipated their arrival with mixed feelings. The bliss of flying and being free of land-based cares contrasted starkly to his aching body and concerns for his family, Equinora, and all its inhabitants.

Giving him no more time to worry, Blaze landed with a grace that belied his size and the speed of their flight. "Meda my Meda is here my first beloved my friend my saviour!"

The tiny dragon alighted on Blaze's neck like a brilliant butterfly, their many-coloured jewelled scales sparkling from an abundance of love.

Delsin extracted himself from the tangle of straps and dismounted.

Laila grabbed him in a fierce hug. She hugged Blaze too before laughing and crying at their arrival. "I never dreamt anyone could ride a dragon! What's happened? Why is Blaze with you? Where's Rocky? Did you find Prism?"

"Whoa! Let me get my breath." Delsin returned Laila's hug and thanked Blaze for the safe trip. "Flying was amazing. So different to being on horseback, though that's fantastic in a different way."

Laila's smile did little to hide the haggard lines of her face. "Meda told me you were coming, which is how we're here to meet you. But neither of us could make sense of anything else Blaze told her."

While the two dragons swapped news, incongruous as they were with one larger than a family hut and the other as small as a squirrel, Delsin and Laila retreated to their familiar tree where they had spent so long as youths. Glad that he had brought something to eat and drink after all, Delsin opened his pack and shared his meal. "I'd better tell you all I can before we get mobbed by everyone from the village."

Laila nibbled at a handful of pine nuts and shook her head. "Don't worry, I told them Blaze would burn anyone that came close. We've as long as we want."

The question that lingered like a shadow over Delsin's heart escaped his lips. "And Mama?"

Laila's smile slipped from her face. "No change. Bly insists I feed her. I keep her clean and massage what little remains of her body. But she's not there. Her soul has fled. It would have been kinder to let the winter take her."

Delsin nodded. It would be impossible for Laila to go against Bly's demands. "Can the other healers do nothing? You know—" He resisted putting into words that a potion or other means should ease Macha Gatherer to her next life.

Laila shook her head and grasped Delsin's hand. "Father watches like a hawk. He'd know. If something happened when he wasn't there, even naturally, he'd blame me. I think he'd kill me, no matter the consequences."

Desiring to change the subject, Delsin regaled Laila with all that had happened since he had last seen her and why he was there.

"Mystery is sure that the creatures are being poisoned by nickel, either from what they consume or what they breathe. The waters must carry the plague and the rotfrogs survive because everything else is weak. We believe that's why the gorgebugs multiply so rapidly too. The plants don't have their usual natural defences to protect against the insect numbers."

Meda flew over and settled on Laila's shoulder. The healer dragon hung her head and nuzzled Laila under the ear. "I don't know cures for poison. I only know how to fix broken bodies."

Laila stroked Meda's snout with a finger. "Don't worry, I've asked the clans' healers about Kodi's symptoms and what he witnessed."

She rested her other hand on Delsin's knee. "One of the elders visiting from Oakvale says there's a fungus that treats lung and skin diseases. Apparently, agarikon is only found in old growth forests."

Delsin sat upright, thrilled to hear of a possible solution. "What does it look like? How do we use it?"

The frown on Laila's face belied the good news. "That's the problem. No-one has seen any for many years. They didn't even have any dried remnants to show me. The ravages of the bloodwolf war destroyed many of the ancient trees."

Delsin's heart dropped as if he'd plunged over a waterfall. "We'd need a lot to cure everyone in Westlands. We must find some and test it out. If it works, perhaps we can grow more. The plague must be stopped before it can cross the mountains and reach here."

Chapter 23

Without Prism, Blaze, or Delsin around, Kodi had plenty of time to rest and heal. Gem gave him all the help she could between her ventures to improve the waters and pasture. Mystery spent most of his time seeking out Echo without luck. Neither Diamond nor Tempest had responded to their many calls.

The peaceful days accentuated Kodi's sense of loss of the missing feather. It was time he resumed his search. Claw had failed to answer any of Kodi's calls. Whether he didn't hear, or was ignoring Kodi, he didn't know. He promised himself that he would leave as soon as the others returned. The unicorns must save Westlands. If nothing else, he could use the she-bear's discomfort at his presence as a reason for moving on. She spent the lengthening days out foraging with the cubs, wary about being near him, only returning to the cave at night. Not even the spring storms drove her home to shelter.

The only thing that kept Kodi from heading off was his worry over Snag. Even though she now drew energy from Equinora, harnessing the breeze in her web, each morning and evening he fed her resin to ensure she didn't trap and kill the few animals who had survived the plague. She had become so used to his visits that she waited outside the crevice, her amber body darkening with every meal, enabling her to be out in daylight. If he left, he dreaded what she might do and where she might go.

He ambled up the hillside to her nook, laden with glowing nodules of pine sap that had become easier to gather with the flush of spring, relishing the sun on his coat. Having rubbed away his heavy winter fur, and with his skin refreshed by Gem, it really was time to move on. But how could he insist that Snag collect her own nourishment without killing?

A shaft of light reflected from something in the rock, dazzling him. He blinked away his surprise and gasped before greeting Snag. "You're golden. Truly golden." Was this a sign? Was the goddess telling him to trust the spider?

A screech overhead pierced his wonder. He twisted around and stared into the glare, swivelling to catch the movement. An eagle screeched again, accompanied by the mewl of whatever was pinned in the giant talons, its wings and tail flashing in mirror of Snag's new colouring. Claw!

Shocked at the arrival of the one he sought, Kodi froze, paws dangling at his sides.

The she-bear bounded past, roaring and bellowing.

Her agonising cries drove Kodi to look closer at the eagle's burden. One of the cubs squirmed beneath the giant bird, bleating and whimpering. "Claw! No!"

At the call of his name, Claw peered down but continued to climb, circling with the heavy weight clutched in his talons.

Kodi stretched up high as if he could grab the cub and drag them both to the ground. Impossible, of course. The eagle was already above the tops of the highest trees. There was no point shouting. The wind would whip away his words. *Stop! Return that cub! I am the guardian! I must talk to you about the feather!*

Whichever of his words made an impact, the giant eagle turned and glided back to Snag's rocks. The she-bear shoved her other cub behind her and bared stained teeth.

Landing with a flap of golden wings, bright against his tawny chest, Claw retained a clutch on his catch. "Eeerk! What do you know? About the feather?"

Kodi asked first about Claw's health, relieved that the eagle was prepared to talk. "You look healed from your accident with the falling star. You must be very strong to fly so high. Echo told me how you helped him gather the stones."

Claw preened a pinion, keeping one eye on Kodi. "Eeerk! Should go higher! To the sun! With the final feather! But it won't stick, eeerk!"

"You still have it?" Delight fought with anger that the eagle had stolen the feather. Kodi still knew nothing of its true purpose.

Although Shadow had assisted Claw to insert the other three feathers in his wings and tail, Kodi wasn't at all sure the eagle was meant to be the recipient. "What have you tried?"

The bear cub struggled beneath Claw, mewing to draw her mother's attention. The sow fretted behind Kodi, growls rumbling from deep in her chest, drool dangling from her open mouth.

Claw adjusted his perch. "Eeerk! Many wounds from trying. Feather won't go in. Must need unicorn magic."

Kodi brightened as a way through this dilemma occurred to him. "Gemstone is nearby. Give me the bear cub and I'll fetch her. She'll be able to heal your sores and might help you with the feather."

Claw hopped backwards. "Eeerk! Stay away! Stay away!" He dragged the bleeding cub across the rough ground, increasing her cries of distress into ear-piercing yowls. "Keep the cub. Until she comes, eeerk!"

Kodi dithered. If he didn't get Gem now, the cub was doomed. If he fetched Gem, she might be able to help Claw. But he didn't trust the eagle. Who knew what greater harm would result.

A rush of golden legs shot past Kodi. Snag scuttled over to Claw and waved her mandibles at his head. The eagle released the bear cub and rose on outstretched wings, flashing gold, cawing with indignation.

Before Kodi had time to be thrilled, Snag wrapped the youngster in silk, rolling the cub over and over beneath her legs.

"Snag! You mustn't." Kodi could sense the she-bear about to rush the spider. He blocked her passage and grasped her to his chest. "Let me deal with it."

Snag stopped her spinning. "Not. Eat. Hold."

With relief, Kodi released the cub's mother who stood on her hind legs at a safe distance, calling to the captured youngster, the other one hiding behind her bulk.

Snag gathered the cocooned bear under the shelter of her body. "Go. Get. Gem."

Glancing around as if the unicorn would miraculously appear, Kodi still wasn't sure he could trust Claw, or Snag. Or, for that matter, the she-bear.

"Snag. Hold. Go."

Kodi had no choice. He lumbered as fast as he could in search of Gem. Suspecting he'd find her at the lake, he raced down the slope, almost tumbling head over heels in his haste. He called to her as he ran and prayed to the goddess he'd see an emerald equine in the waves.

The lush beach that had sprung up from Gem's ministrations came in sight, the glint of an opal horn emerging from the depths. "Gem! Come quick. Claw and Snag have one of the cubs."

Gem galloped out of the water in a fury of spray. "Where? Tell me!"

Kodi quickly shared the location and let Gem surge ahead, unable to keep up with her greater stride. When he arrived back at Snag's rock, the bear cub remained alive, still enveloped in silk. The she-bear pined from a distance, pacing back and forth on all fours, the male cub bounding alongside to stay close.

Gem had her horn pressed against the eagle's underbelly, sparks flying as she healed the wounds caused by the many times he had tried to insert the last of the goddess's feathers. The feather itself peeked out from the down on his chest, unaltered. Gem either couldn't or wouldn't aid Claw like Shadow had. Kodi wasn't sure whether to be pleased or disappointed. He flopped onto his hindquarters, puffing from the run.

Gem finished healing Claw and trotted over to Snag and the cub. Claw stretched out his wings, flew by her, and pecked at her neck with his hooked beak. He snatched the cub from Snag's protection, still wrapped in silk, and launched into the air.

Flying on Blaze as if he'd been born to ride a dragon, Delsin searched the area around the cave for Rocky. There was no sign of any of the inhabitants. Thinking the stallion might be out grazing, Delsin scanned the hillsides for the skewbald or any of his other friends.

He spotted them clustered around the rocks where Kodi had found Snag a home. From the way they huddled in a tense group, something troubled them. He hoped the giant spider hadn't resumed catching animals in her web.

Blaze banked and surged, his neck stretched out and wings beating hard, and veered away from where the bears and equines stood.

Delsin grabbed at Blaze's harness, his heart pounding. "What's happening?"

"My enemy the eagle the thief the servant of Shadow is here here here!" Blaze powered across the sky, oblivious to Delsin's cries to remember he rode aboard.

Delsin had no trouble identifying their target. Claw! The massive eagle's wings and tail glinted in the sun, dazzling Delsin. He shielded his eyes with one hand, keeping a tight grip of the harness with the other, and peered at what the eagle carried. A golden cocoon hung suspended in his talons. Was this Snag's egg sack? That would explain the commotion, though Delsin had no idea how she would have found a mate, or what it would mean for her to have young. He shivered. He had no fear of spiders as a rule, but he didn't relish encountering a horde of giant ones with magic powers.

Blaze closed the distance on his foe. Delsin wrapped both hands in the cord around the dragon's chest and wedged his feet hard against the jewelled sides, fearing that an impact would unseat him and send him to his death. "Blaze! Take care. We don't know what's happened."

The dragon didn't slow or alter course. "Claw the thief the stealer of the feathers that should have been mine mine mine again stolen from Snag. She told me yes in my head the spider speaks so does Claw he taunts so I chase chase chase!"

Delsin had no hope of altering Blaze's intent to hunt down the eagle. He tensed his body while relaxing his mind. If this was how his life was meant to end, then so be it. The only pity was that no storyteller witnessed the fight to relate the spectacle in a song. What a sight the golden eagle and jewelled dragon must be, chasing high over the hillside. With Claw's burden, the eagle had no hope of outflying Blaze. With the air whizzing all sound away, Delsin prepared for the attack. His stomach lurched as Blaze swooped over the top of Claw instead, spinning as he did so to fly back into the eagle's face.

An instant before contact, the scales between Delsin's legs grew hot. A glance down confirmed his suspicion. Blaze's scales glowed crimson as he called on his power. With a blast that seared the hairs from Delsin's arms, Blaze shot a spout of fire at Claw. The eagle tumbled, his chest feathers singed, and released the cocoon. The bundle plummeted to the trees far below, spinning end over end.

Blaze's sudden change of direction prevented Delsin seeing

more. Eagle and dragon battled in the air, talon and claw, fire and beak. Lower and lower they spiralled as all the years of pent up rivalry erupted. "Blaze! Let me off!"

His desperation must have penetrated the dragon's fury. With a swoop, Blaze dived to the ground, scraping the grass with his toes. Delsin released his grip and leapt for safety, hitting the earth with a thump as Blaze soared back up. Delsin rolled to minimise the impact, an action he regretted when his pack dug into his spine, knocking his breath out with a huff.

Gasping from a mixture of fear and effort, he clambered to his feet and hurried as fast as his crooked legs would allow to where Gem and Rocky lingered with the bears around a tree. The cocoon had caught in a branch half way up. By the time Delsin reached the base, Kodi had started to climb, his heavy body rocking the thick trunk as each paw clawed the bark and heaved him higher.

With only one cub fretting behind the she-bear, and her low moaning as she watched the cocoon in the swaying branches, Delsin soon figured out what the golden sack held. He stared in horror as Kodi crawled along the branch that held the precious parcel, the creak and groan of the tree loud in the expectant hush of the waiting crowd. Kodi paused, shifted his belly, and braced a hind paw against the trunk. He slid one foreleg through the pine needles and hooked the cocoon with his claws. Slowly, slowly, he drew the wrapped cub towards him.

With a loud crack, the branch on which Kodi lay canted down, catching on the one below. Kodi abandoned all caution, scooped the cub to his chest, and scuttled down the tree as if he were a squirrel, not an oversized bear.

Feeble cries emitted from beneath the wrapping. The she-bear raced to nuzzle her youngster and scrabbled at the clingy threads. Instead of tearing, they tightened around the cub.

Delsin recalled the story of Yuma rescuing Fleet from Snag's web. "Stop! You'll make it harder." He shrugged out of his pack and rummaged for his obsidian knife, the one he kept for special needs when flint was insufficient. Too precious to use all the time, he kept it encased in a stiff leather pouch to protect the sharp edge. He eased it from its case so as not to cut his hands, knelt beside the cub, and tentatively sliced at the cocoon. The threads parted like a soft fruit, not at all sticky as he had expected.

The cub wriggled free and scampered to her mother, ignoring her barging brother. Gem tested the little bear with her horn for injury and neighed in surprise. "She's perfectly alright. There are only a few scrapes from Claw. The silk protected her when she fell."

Kodi sniffed at the rescued youngster. The look of gratitude from the sow more than made up for the effort of climbing the tree, a pastime he had long since abandoned. After reassuring the she-bear, he left her in peace, joining Delsin and Gem where they waited. "She says Blaze and I can den in her cave any time we like."

"I should think so!" Delsin reached up and scratched Kodi's favourite spot between his shoulders. "That was very brave. Foolhardy, but brave all the same."

Pleased with the affection, Kodi looked to Gem. "You're sure the little one is okay? That was a long drop."

Gem tossed her head and snorted. "She's fine. It seems you may be a guardian of more than the feathers."

"The feather!" In the panic over the cub, Kodi had forgotten Claw's story and the last feather tucked among the down on his chest. He searched the sky for the eagle, hoping that Blaze's fire hadn't damaged the last of the goddess's treasures.

The pair of Shadow's giant creations ducked and dived around each other overhead, the jewels of the dragon's scales flashing against the silhouette of the eagle. Kodi gaped. Claw's whole body had turned gold, every feather on his head, his chest, and his back the same as his beautiful tail and wings.

Delsin watched beside him. "What are they doing? It's an odd way to fight."

Kodi listened to the mind conversation between Blaze and Claw, stunned, surprised, and confused. "They're not fighting. They're celebrating. Blaze's fire burnt the final feather into Claw. They've put their differences aside, revelling in the joy of flight."

Even as Kodi comprehended the true nature of the aerobatics, the pair of previous adversaries shot skywards, racing to see who could fly the fastest and highest. He sensed no animosity in their actions or thoughts. They had become friends.

And now not a single feather remained for him to find and guard. His purpose for living was over. No more searching to be done. No point returning to Snowhaven where a shelf carved by Jasper to hold five golden feathers waited for him, empty.

Chapter 24

From the slump of Kodi's shoulders, Delsin suspected the bear wasn't as pleased about the alliance of Blaze and Claw as he made out. That made sense. Kodi had been chasing Claw for the return of the feather for a long time; suffering the plague, travelling far from home, and witnessing the devastation of Westlands. Although Kodi had never said as much, Delsin also suspected the guardian believed the feathers belonged to Prism. But hers were soft and supple, not hard and rigid as he had heard the goddess's were, made of solid gold. There again, they must have become normal bird feathers when their power was triggered, else Claw wouldn't be able to manoeuvre as he did.

Relieved that the cub was safe, and Blaze and Claw no longer fought, Delsin pushed the relevance of the feathers aside. He needed to focus on the fungus, the agarikon that Laila had described. She had said little to go on other than it grew near old stands of firs and larches, and could be eaten raw or ground to a powder. Mixing it with goose oil created a salve that could heal sores, but he hadn't seen a goose in a very long time.

First, though, he had to find the fungus. After asking Gem whether she had heard of the treatment the clan healers used, with no success, his only option was to seek aid from the ancestors. He gathered enough timber to heat his sweat-lodge, pondering how Snag, and now Claw, had become golden. That could only mean they were the goddess's creatures now, not Shadow's, the same as when Blaze had come good after being fed love by Mystery.

And what about Prism? She was both jewel-dappled and gold, symbols of the goddess. So Echo had to be the harbinger of death, even if he intended good with the sustenance he created from the meteorites. Or had Prism misunderstood her vision? And what about Delsin's vision, the dream of a giant snake climbing a mountain? Perhaps Lash, the enormous grey snake, was behind the plague carried by the rotfrogs. And now all plants suffered from veracious gorgebugs. As spring progressed, new life slowly emerged, only to be devoured or poisoned.

Kodi and the other bears had gone foraging. Blaze and Claw still showed off to each other, their antics flashing across the sky. With Prism searching for Lash, Mystery hunting for Echo, and Gem conversing with Snag, Delsin had the cave and its environs to himself. After a quick welcome, Rocky had sensed Delsin needed to be alone and wandered off to graze. He'd make it up to the stallion soon; in fact, he guessed they'd be doing a lot of travelling to collect the amount of agarikon needed to save so many creatures.

Evening had fallen by the time Delsin had prepared the hot stones to produce steam. He undressed and slipped into his lodge. Having not eaten since the day before with Laila, the herbs he drank took immediate effect. His mind grew to embrace the universe, connecting with the stars, stretching to eternity. His pulse became the rhythm of life, his breaths the flow of seasons. He walked among the forests, greeting trees and hearing their stories of generations past. He rose from his body and welcomed the ancestors gathering around him.

When Delsin emerged from the sweat-lodge, he was surprised to find the sun had risen overhead. Shaking the cloudiness from his brain, he sought Rocky and groomed him before leaping aboard. It felt great to be back on the horse again, his legs wrapped around the warm soft barrel. He'd enjoyed flying on Blaze, but a dragon's scales and spiny back were nowhere near as comfortable.

They located Kodi dozing in the shade of a copse of larch. "Do you want to come with us?"

Kodi stood and stretched. "Of course. Where do you want to start?"

Sharing with Kodi what he had learnt from Laila, they headed for the forests on the lower slopes. Delsin kept a lookout for sick animals. They encountered none. Away from the green sward nourished by Gem, the stripped meadows and barren shrubs offered no sanctuary or food for the ill or healthy. When they reached the ancient trees that Delsin remembered from his trip to find Prism, he scoured the ground for fungus.

With light able to penetrate the canopy due to the gorgebugs' destruction, the usually damp forest floor had dried. The rains from Tempest's storm had only added to the devastation, not provide a moist environment for mushrooms and toadstools to thrive. The few specimens Delsin did find were small and shrivelled, hardly enough to save every animal in Westlands. Some he recognised as poisonous so discarded. Others were of food value but not medicinal. One type he hadn't encountered before had the rough texture and colour Laila had described. He tested a small piece on the tip of his tongue. Experiencing no immediate ill effects, he gathered those to sample again later. He and Kodi picked what they could, finding very few, before returning to the cave despondent from their afternoon's efforts.

At least Mystery had returned. Hoping the silver unicorn had news of Echo's whereabouts, Delsin encouraged Rocky into a canter, the rolling stride and breeze on his skin lifting his spirits. When Rocky halted next to Mystery, Delsin greeted him before noticing that a variety of small animals sheltered among the rocks: two skunks and a racoon, a few mice and squirrels, a tangle of snakes, and a small deer. Birds perched on the branches of a nearby tree, incongruously quiet. All the animals bore the marks of sores and starvation. "Did you find Echo?"

Mystery nosed a confused mouse away from where it wandered towards the snakes. "No. And these were the only animals I could get to return with me for Gem to heal. She's away swimming, but shared with me what's been happening. Did you find the fungus?"

Delsin held out his meagre gathering to show Mystery then slid from Rocky's back. He had suffered no adverse symptoms from the larger piece of fungus he had eaten on the return journey. Kneeling beside a fox that had crept out to sniff Rocky's hooves, he held out a small slice. "Eat this. It'll make you better."

The fox nibbled at the offering, licked her dry lips, and gulped the mushroom down. Encouraged, Delsin fed the other creatures, with Mystery encouraging those reticent to eat what was offered. "We shouldn't let Gem heal them or we won't know if it works. I don't know how long it will take to have an effect, nor if it's enough, but there's no more close by."

Prism glided towards the cave, glad to see everyone was gathered. She couldn't wait to tell them about Lash's transformation. But something looked wrong. Why were they all ranged along the cliff wall?

She landed and quizzed Gem mentally as she trotted up the track.

Her dam sounded miserable. *The animals we tried to cure are dead, or dying. The mushrooms that people use didn't work. I've cured a few, but for the others I was too late.*

Prism strode up to Delsin, her glee from her news dampened by the tears trickling down his face.

He crouched by a small deer, its mouth foamed in red. "It's my fault. I must have collected the wrong ones."

Rocky nuzzled the man's shoulder. "Don't blame yourself. The specimens were old. Maybe they'd lost their potency. It's the plague doing the harm, not the fungus, or else you'd be sick too."

Sadness hung over the group like a rain cloud. Prism snuffled at the tiny corpses dotting the ground. "Blaze should cremate them. We don't know how contagious their bodies might be."

The gloom of the moment overrode Prism's former optimism. She had set such store in Meda and Laila coming up with a cure after Mystery had discovered the problem was nickel poisoning. "The southern clan are on their way to Waterfalls, and Boldearth is taking his mare to Dark Woods."

Rocky shot her a glance. "Only two horses?"

"That's all I found. They said the others are all dead or scattered." Relating her return journey, Prism shared about discovering the man with the bones and how well he had been. "Quite mad though, raving on about ghosts."

Kodi remained slumped against a boulder. "He did well to survive the floods."

Prism recalled more of the crazy conversation. "He said he climbed a tall tree. That's where he found the bread to eat."

Delsin leapt to his feet, his face alight. "Tell me what he said. Exactly!"

As she struggled to recall the spiritman's rantings, Delsin became more animated, waving his arms and rushing over to Kodi to drag the great bear to his feet. "Bread of ghosts! I should have known. Stupid, stupid. That's what agarikon is."

Confused, Prism followed on his heels. "What do you mean?"

Delsin hugged her around the neck. "Laila told me that the fungus grew in old growth forests. I assumed she meant under the trees. She meant on the bark, hanging from the cracks in the ancient trunks and branches."

Kodi pointed west. "I think I know what you mean, large pendulous growths. I saw a few on the giant firs when I was hunting resin for Snag. Is that what we need?"

Delsin's excitement bubbled out of him. "Yes, yes. Why didn't I work it out before? Agarikon will be what the healers call the fungus. Spiritmen call it 'bread of ghosts'. We must find the conks."

Prism hesitated to become too excited by Delsin's enthusiasm. "But the old man was blind. What if this bread you talk of was the cause?"

Waving her worries away, Delsin remained ebullient. "I've never heard of it doing that. This is the answer. I know it. Trust me."

Prism had no reason to doubt his word. The reversal in everyone's mood turned into a flurry of planning. Delsin would weave paniers for Rocky to carry any conks that Delsin and Kodi found. Gem would gather any of the animals that came to the lake to feed. Blaze would search for more of the sick and call Mystery to fetch them. With her ability to scan from the air, Prism would travel further afield and carry back any small creatures she found. At the moment, they couldn't help the larger creatures like the wolves and moose, but Delsin could test the fungus on the smaller animals first.

Prism flew low over the trees, the joy of flight and the warm spring battling with her worry for Westlands and the need for her to complete her mission. At least the goddess's words about a unicorn being the harbinger of death had proved to be about Echo, even if he didn't intend to harm his victims.

A brown shape waddled along the edge of a swollen river far to her left. She banked and circled to confirm the sighting. A beaver splashed into the water as she passed overhead. She sought a level place to land and trotted to the water's edge. "Are you sick? I can help."

A ring of ripples expanded from a whiskered face breaking the surface. "Are you the goddess? Am I dying?"

Keeping her wings slightly raised above the paniers that impeded her from folding her feathers flat, Prism entered the shallows and lowered her nose to the surface. "No, but I can treat you if you come with me. Let me carry you to safety."

With a bit more encouragement, the beaver waddled out to the bank, wheezing as he clambered up the gentle slope. Raw sores oozing pus matted his fur. One front tooth had fallen out. His tail that should have been thick with fat trailed behind him like a piece of dead skin. "My partner is nearby. I can't leave her."

After reassuring the beaver that they would find his mate, Prism gripped his loose coat in her teeth and hefted him into the left-hand basket. Even in his poor condition his weight dragged on the restraining ropes around her neck, half-choking her. She couldn't fly like this. The sooner they found the female beaver to provide balance the better.

As Prism walked downstream, the beaver moaned about how hard conditions had been. First they had sickened from the poisonous water. Then the swarms of insects had decimated the aspen, willow, and birch they fed on. "And I don't have enough energy to drop the large trees that might still hold old leaves. We've been living off bark and roots."

The female beaver wasn't far away and was in poorer condition. Too scared to speak when Prism approached, yet unable to run away, she cowered under a sodden log until her mate popped his head over the edge of the basket and encouraged her out. A weak squeal as Prism lifted her by the neck was the most noise she made.

Still unbalanced due to their difference in size, Prism took great care as she launched from a fast canter. Once airborne, the effort of carrying two squirming bodies was worse than their differences in weight. "Please be still. I won't drop you." She soared higher, hoping the further away the ground became the less the land rushing beneath them would unnerve her passengers.

Relieved to see the cave ahead, Prism descended in a spiral so as to not drop too suddenly, changing direction as a flash of emerald revealed Gem down at the lake. As Prism's hooves hit the ground, she let out a long sigh; the effort needed to fly encumbered with two beavers had taken all her concentration. The notion of returning to fetch more creatures daunted her, both the enormity of the task and the knowledge that she wouldn't be able to carry the larger ones.

After leaving the beavers in the care of her dam, Prism set off to find more of those in need. Her next trip rescued a pair of chipmunks and a coney in one basket, and a mink in the other. She couldn't risk putting them together to make room for a porcupine, and the sick rattlesnake basking on a rock couldn't ride in either basket. As clever as Delsin's solution had seemed at the time, fetching the sick for him to cure wasn't going to work. She hid her despair when she returned as Mystery had also arrived with a variety of animals.

Delsin and Kodi were unloading Rocky's paniers. The conks, fungal growths longer than Delsin's arms, piled near the cave entrance in a pile as high as her chest, layers and layers of rings on each revealing their great age, their surfaces rough from many different seasons. But how much would they need to cure each animal? Prism unloaded her latest batch of patients.

Gem led the beavers up the winding path. They struggled to keep up with her, not accustomed to climbing or being so far from water. Gem spoke to them before cantering the remainder of the way to inspect the newcomers. "I should heal them now, not let them continue to suffer."

Prism shared her dam's concern. "They're very weak. But if you do that, how will we know if the ghost bread works?"

Gem looked back to the huffing beavers. "I know, but I hate to see them like this. Perhaps I could just help them a little?"

"That still wouldn't answer the question. We wouldn't know if your healing started their recovery and then they got well on their own." Prism pricked her ears as Rocky joined them, the stirring inside her at his presence always a surprise. She pushed the feelings away, unable to face the implications with Westlands still in dire need.

The stallion dropped a slice of conk at her feet. "I can take this and carry the beavers back to the lake. There's no need for them to come further."

At first the idea of the struggling animals not having to finish the climb pleased Prism. Then she realised her mistake in leaving them at the lake. "If they swim in the waters, they'll be healed from Gem's powers."

Gem flinched. "They've already drunk and swum."

Prism nuzzled Rocky's shoulder. "Then take them back, but don't give them the fungus. We'll need to test it on these other creatures."

Several days later, no doubt remained that the creatures who ate the agarikon slowly put on weight. Their sores had partially healed and they breathed more easily. However, they complained about their eyesight becoming poor, a disaster for when they must fend for themselves after they fully recovered. Squabbles broke out among the animals as they improved in health. Prism had intervened on several occasions to prevent the predators from eating their prey, and had threatened to ban them from the sanctuary Gem had created if they didn't behave.

In comparison, the beavers had fared very well. Their sores had completely healed from the waters where Gem still swam every day, their eyesight remained sharp, and their bodies were already plump. However, their breathing hadn't improved.

Prism found Delsin where he checked on a young deer. "What are we going to do? We can't heal everyone in the lake."

Delsin sat back on his haunches and doodled in the sand with a stick. "One of the conks we found was so old we couldn't slice it for food. It crumbled into dust when I touched it. I kept the powder to use as a paste for the sores if needed. We could try that for their lungs."

Not sure what difference eating dust rather than slices would make, Prism shuffled from foot to foot. "Won't it still make them blind?"

Delsin shook his head, stood up, and pointed to the creatures all around them. "What choice do we have? Breathing the fungus in rather than eating it might make a difference."

Prism hadn't considered that. "Let's try it with the beavers first. I'll ask them if they want to risk it."

Prism trotted down to the lake with Rocky and Delsin and called the pair over. "We've something for you."

Paddling with their strong hind feet, they swam to the edge and popped their whiskered noses above the surface, not bothering to scramble out in the mud.

Delsin knelt as close as he could without slipping into the water. "We want you to breathe in this dust. It might ease your lungs."

Prism explained about the risk of damaging their eyes.

The female beaver heaved onto the bank and nosed forwards. "I need to breathe more than I need to see. Without you saving us we would have died. I'll try it."

The male agreed too and joined his mate in front of Delsin. Before they could change their minds, he shook a broad leaf at their faces, coating their fur with a fine dust.

Both beavers sneezed and ducked back into the water in a synchronised performance that would have impressed Prism at any other time. "Are they alright? Will they have inhaled the powder?"

She paced the shore, watching for signs of life. There were no bubbles, no ripples. "Where are they? Do you think we've killed them?"

Delsin shielded his eyes against the glare and peered out over the lake. "Give it time. I can't believe such a small amount could harm them."

Continuing to stare across the water, Prism started to panic. "I should fly over and see if I can spot them below the surface."

Before she could act, rings formed further out in the lake. The beavers broke the surface. After gasping lungs full of air, they submerged and disappeared again.

"There they are! What are they doing?" Watching from the bank, Prism fretted. She jumped back in surprise when the male beaver erupted from the water's edge.

He bounded up to Delsin, leaping around like a kit. "I can breathe! I can breathe!"

Delsin ruffled the beaver's coat and laughed at the animal's antics.

Prism heaved a sigh of relief. It worked. Now they had to find a way to get dust to every animal in Westlands, and stop any more from getting sick. And they must stop Echo from continuing to transform the meteorites. Echo! If they could cure him, he'd have to see the error of what he was doing. They had to find him.

After asking the beavers to let her know if they started to feel unwell or their eyesight faltered, Prism led Rocky and Delsin back up the winding track. Mystery waited with Gem, having already unloaded his baskets of sick creatures. The sores on a marmot had left his skin bare making him almost unrecognisable. Then a heaving mass of amphibians croaked.

Prism shied. "What are they doing here?"

Mystery used a gentle hoof to herd a straying rotfrog away from a gopher. "We also have to cure these creatures, or else everyone may get sick again."

Agreeing with the wisdom even while still reeling with revulsion, Prism nodded to Delsin. "Try the dust on them. Be careful not to touch them."

Delsin sprinkled a small amount of powder over the amphibians' bodies from arm's length, not cradling the rotfrogs as he would the other animals he cared for. The vile creatures inhaled the dust and burped, their breath reeking of putrefaction. But none of them spat their foul bile.

The dust absorbed into the rotfrogs' pus-riddled skin, sizzling and hissing like cold water hitting a hot rock. The stench from bursting boils drove Prism back a step. Before her eyes, the poisonous creatures transformed into frogs she recognised. No longer the engorged bog-eyed villains of the swamps, they shrank to become tree, wood, and bull frogs. They hopped in frenzied circles, clinging to each other with sticky toes and stretching out their hind legs to test their refreshed skin. Prism's heart soared with the success. She whickered with excitement.

A draught ruffled her forelock. A shadow hid the sun's warmth.

Blaze landed in a rush, the usual clap of his folding wings drowned by his news. "I've found him the unicorn the cause of strife poison rock changing Echo come come I'll show you where!"

Prism grasped a leaf-pouch of agarikon dust in her teeth and launched alongside Blaze. She climbed high and followed him south. There was no time for cavorting in the air today. She must get the cure to her grandsire.

With a strong wind in their favour, Blaze soon led Prism to a canyon she had never seen before. High walls hid whatever lay between them until she was directly overhead. Steam wafted up from a pool at the far end where a waterfall tinkled over the clifftop. Ferns and mosses cloaked the rocks. The greenery would have merged with the forest had the trees not been stripped by gorgebugs. Now the lush haven glowed like an emerald surrounded by a pool of mud.

Prism peered into the depths of the winding canyon full of shadows as she circled lower and searched for Echo. She had almost given up, thinking he must have left since Blaze had seen him, when Echo raised his head from where he lay. His legs twitched as he struggled to heave his wasted body from the ground without success.

Frustrated that she couldn't land in the narrow space, Prism swept as low as she dared and shook the dust from the pouch. A light breeze snatched the agarikon and spiralled in an updraft, stealing the powder and whisking it away over the dead forest. In an instant, it was gone.

Chapter 25

Steam rose around Echo's ears where he stood mostly submerged in the centre of his pool. The warm water soothed his muscles and the sand beneath his hooves massaged his soles as he shifted his shoulders and hips. His skinny neck could barely hold up his head even with the loss of his horn. He had never noted its weight before. Now the stub dragged his forehead down so his lips rested on the surface of the sweet water that bubbled out from vents in the rocks.

His territory was doomed. He could do no more for Westlands. No more meteorites had fallen scorching to the earth. No more animals would consume the sustenance he provided. Even if more stones fell, he didn't have the strength to transform them. His power was gone.

Vibrations through the water interrupted his gloom. He stared along the canyon for the cause. His granddaughter cantered up to the edge of the pool, her magnificent wings held out in splendour, light flashing from her hooves and horn. Her mane and tail shimmered with health and her eyes sparkled as she gazed at him.

He sighed. Not again. He couldn't take any more confrontation. Unable to summon the energy to argue, Echo waited for her to harangue him about the plague.

Instead, Prism knelt on one knee and touched the tip of her horn to the water. "Grandsire, Echo, I have come to apologise. I know now it's not you who has been causing the damage to your territory."

Taken aback, Echo lifted his head and shuffled his feet. "Of course it isn't. What changed your mind?"

Prism straightened up but kept her head low in submission. "I know you've been doing your best to save Westlands. The plague has been too strong. I should never have doubted you."

Although the news pleased Echo, it made no difference. "It's too late. Equinora is doomed."

"No! That's why I've come. We must call the goddess." Prism pointed her nose back to the entrance to the canyon. "My parents will be here soon. I flew ahead to guide them, but I couldn't land between the cliff walls. Blaze is here too and he can light the fire for us."

The great dragon entering his haven was too much for Echo. Finding a reserve of strength he didn't know he had, he lunged out of the water. "I won't have one of the duocorn's creatures here. He has to be behind the plague somehow, I know it."

Prism retreated, chewing her lips. "That's alright. The man is here too. He can light a fire."

Anger boiled through Echo. "What good will that do? We need all six of us to call Aureana, even if she'd deign to answer, which I doubt. And we don't have the mushrooms, they only grow on Tern Island. I can't travel there, even if Diamond offers to translocate me. Accompanying her draws more power than I have left."

Echo's initial joy at Prism's apology washed away with all he'd lost—the freedom to roam his lands, the pleasure of caring for his charges, and the bond of sharing thoughts with Diamond. All gone. In stark contrast to his mood, Prism burst with life and vigour.

She paced through the knee-high flowers that graced the clearing around the pool. "We don't need all six of us. Mystery, Gem, and I have called the goddess before. And we've found another fungus, one that grows in Westlands. Delsin is bringing some."

A tiny spark of hope kindled in Echo's heart before being snuffed out as he considered Prism's words. "So why are you here? Why didn't you conduct the ceremony somewhere else without me?" He knew the real reason for his hesitation. "If Aureana wanted Equinora saved, she would have sent me more sky stones. They have stopped falling. She's abandoned us."

Prism reared and sprang like a grasshopper in the air, flapping her wings and hovering before landing with her nose touching his. "You mustn't think like that. I came to apologise, and we want you as part of the ceremony because this is your land. And you have more experience than us, and—" Prism shook her mane in agitation as if trying to find more reasons why they had come.

Echo stood dumbfounded at the reaction from his granddaughter. Before he could respond, Mystery, Gemstone, and a man on a horse cantered towards them. Echo braced for further conflict until he recognised that the others also came in submission. The last of his energy drained away. A ceremony wouldn't do any good. Their visit was a waste of time, disturbing his final moments as he waited for Aureana to collect him when he died. If she'd do even that.

After their initial greetings, the other unicorns and the man set about gathering sticks for a fire. Echo watched without interest. It would do no good, even if the man could light it without using dragon flame. Instead, Echo's memories roamed back to the days when his dragons cavorted by the pool, chasing each other and singing their happy songs. Where had they gone? He missed their cheerful company and cheeky games. Even the aquadragons that blew fountains in the pool were missing.

Once the pile of timber reached no higher than the man's knees, Prism strutted back, her tail held high and nostrils flared. "We're ready. Will you come and eat the fungus?"

Echo suspected he'd get no peace if he refused. "You'll need a much bigger fire than that. That's barely enough for the man to cook his dinner."

Prism denied the need. "Remember, we've called the goddess before. This will be fine, and we don't want to risk burning your haven."

Echo doubted the lush ground was under any threat. "If you insist on doing this, we should call Diamond and Tempest. It will be better with all of us. But I can't contact them." He didn't need to add that he had lost the ability to communicate with anyone via his thoughts.

Prism nuzzled his neck. "We've tried to call them too. They won't answer us."

Unsurprised, Echo would have ignored this trio too, if he had been able to hear them. Nothing would be gained by voicing his beliefs about why the first-generation unicorns refused to respond. "I told you there's no point. Return to Shimmering Lake. There's nothing you can do here."

"Please. You must help." Prism stamped her hoof and looked at the others gathered around the pyramid of branches. "Delsin, do you have the fungus?"

Echo didn't like the smell that emanated from the basket that the man cradled in both arms. Standing his ground, Echo snorted. He doubted any other mushroom would aid them call Aureana. She had told them what to use before she left Equinora, and it could only be found on Tern Island. That's why Moonglow had made her home there. How could something else work?

Prism gently propelled Delsin forward with her nose and then circled behind Echo. He tried to step away from her, not wanting to participate in whatever they had planned. Prism prevented him from returning to the pool. The man sidled closer, shaking the basket and filling the air with dust.

It didn't contain mushrooms. Suspicious of what was happening, Echo dodged away. Prism blocked him. As he struggled to escape, the man continued to cast dust over him. The powder settled on his skin, making it tingle. It blew up his nose and made him sneeze. His eyes watered and his guts churned. What was this?

Disoriented, Echo spun on his hindquarters to avoid the continuing assault of choking dust. Prism maintained her guard, forcing him to remain near the man. The ground churned beneath his hooves, power coursing up his legs that he hadn't felt for a very long time. His lungs expanded and inhaled more of the powder, great gasps of air thrumming oxygen through his veins. His skin tightened as energy poured into his body, clearing his vision and humming in his brain.

...ing...look...muscles...mane is grow...working...horn...back

Words in his head that weren't his. He couldn't block them, couldn't stop the voices.

Prism, what have you done? Gemstone, can you hear me?

It's worked! Prism bucked and kicked out with joy. "Delsin! Enough. Don't use any more."

The rain of dust ceased. Echo's body burst with strength as power surged into him from the sun, the wind, and the land beneath his feet. "What magic is this? I'm cured! We can heal the rest of Westlands!"

Prism cantered in circles of joy, neighing with delight.

Echo couldn't resist—he lunged into a gallop and raced down the valley, kicking up his heels and throwing clods of earth as he thundered with renewed life. The others chased after him, thrilling in the power and joy of hope.

He reached the mouth of the canyon and drew to a halt. His newfound pleasure evaporated as he viewed the devastation of the land. Not a single green leaf or blade of grass remained. No birds sang. No animals scurried with pouches of food.

Prism skidded to a halt beside him using her wings to brake. She had worked wonders for him, but she couldn't heal all of Westlands. His land was still doomed. "It's too late. There's nothing left to save."

Quickly recovering her breath from the mad gallop, Prism disagreed. "We can dust your whole territory from the air. We've found many conks, and we don't need to use as much on the ordinary creatures to heal them. Even the rotfrogs get better. And once the land is back in balance, the insects won't be a problem."

Echo's desire to believe that all would be well was squashed by the reality of what he saw. "You can't cover the whole land. Not in time. The plague will bounce back as quick as you can cure one place and move on to another."

Prism wouldn't be defeated. "Not if we enlist Tempest's aid. You can call him now. He'll listen to you."

"You never did intend to hold a ceremony, did you?" Echo almost refused, angry at Prism's deceit, but he wouldn't let his territory suffer for his own inadequacy.

Chapter 26

Delsin clung to the rough bark of the tree with his knees. With his twisted legs, he'd never been one to climb in the woods with the other lads at the annual competitions at Oakvale, preferring to seek out the spiritmen and listen to them discuss the sun, moon, and stars, even if they did ignore him. Even so, none of the trees at Oakvale loomed like this ancient fir, its tip so high it made him dizzy when he craned his neck to select the next branch to reach.

Already he had climbed higher than any of his previous attempts to gather agarikon. Only Kodi's exceptional eyesight had identified this conk suspended from a limb close to the trunk, its cream-brown lumps almost invisible against the gnarled bark. Kodi was a great climber, but didn't have the delicacy to harvest the bread of ghosts without waste. The first conk he had grabbed in his powerful forelimbs had snapped off and been crushed to pieces. Fortunately, they'd saved enough to make the find worthwhile. Kodi had also tried kneading the lumps into dust, but too much became lost in his fur.

Pressing his moccasin against the tree trunk, Delsin smiled at the memory of climbing aboard Blaze in a similar fashion. Then the lichen beneath his feet reminded him of gathering handfuls for Rocky to eat. Those days of dragging the stallion through the snow seemed eons ago, as if someone else had lived through that hardship, only related to him in a song. Thanks to Gem's continued treatment, Rocky had fully recovered, but she couldn't possibly save all the animals individually. Now, with the agarikon, more plague-affected creatures might have a chance.

The bark beneath Delsin's feet gave way. He slipped, flailed out, and grabbed for a branch. The limb whipped through his hand, ripping his palm as he fell. The next branch slowed his descent but snapped, too spindly to take his weight. He crashed from limb to limb, collecting scratches and bruises as if the tree berated him for accessing its heights.

He landed on his backside, all the air knocked out of his chest. Other than his heaving lungs, he lay motionless, gauging the pain to figure out what damage he had incurred. His smarting buttocks and stinging hands he could cope with. His right arm was a different matter. Already it was turning red and purple, and stuck out at an unnatural angle.

Kodi hunkered beside him, sniffing him all over. "Can you mount Rocky? We can leave the baskets here. You need to get to Gem."

Delsin breathed deeply and slowly to gather his wits before shifting his weight and testing his legs. "No. We can't go without that conk. It's the largest we've found. We'll need it."

Rocky lipped Delsin's hair. "You're hurt. We can come back for the fungus."

Determined not to leave without their find, Delsin shook his head. "Can I use your tail to help me up?"

The stallion obliged, swinging his hindquarters to Delsin. Hanging on to the horse's dock with his left hand, Delsin dragged himself to his feet. Searing pain shot up his other arm from the movement. He groaned in agony and staggered over to the base of the fir where he had propped his pack, swallowing back the urge to vomit.

Kodi followed and blocked his path. "There's no way you can climb that tree today. If you can't do it with both arms, how will you do it with only one?"

"I must. I've something in my pack that will help." Delsin rummaged with his good hand to locate his medicine bag. The knots around the pouch that contained his blend of white willow bark and birch leaf refused to come undone for his trembling fingers. He used his teeth to pull the string apart, stuck his tongue in, and gagged on the bitter compound. After guzzling a long swill from his water flask, his racing heart calmed.

Once the pain had deadened as much as it was likely to, he untied a rope from Rocky's paniers, bound a splint to his broken forearm, and strapped it across his chest. He looped a longer rope around the tree trunk and passed it behind his back. Holding it with his good hand, he leant back against the rope, his feet wedged against the tree, and caterpillared up the trunk, resting at frequent intervals to allow his shaking legs to recover. Sweat streamed down his face, salty on his lips.

The climb took forever. When he finally reached the agarikon, the conk was even larger than it had appeared from the ground, longer than he was tall and almost as far round. He couldn't carry such a load back down the tree. If he dropped it, it would likely disintegrate and be useless. He peered down at Kodi far below and whistled to get his attention. "You'll have to catch it. Use a panier. Line it with leaves. So we don't lose any fragments."

The shouting and pain left him breathless. He took a moment to recover, then, trusting Kodi to sort out what was necessary, set about slicing the conk with his flint. It would be foolish to harvest the whole thing at once. As he neared cutting free the first piece, he waited until a bellow from below told him Kodi stood ready. Delsin slashed at the remaining section holding the chunk on and asked the ancestors to help it fall true. The fungus plunged straight down, right into the waiting basket. Kodi straightened from bent knees, the fungus intact, cushioned from the impact. Rocky neighed from the success. With renewed enthusiasm, Delsin hacked at another piece of agarikon. This conk alone would fill both baskets.

Getting back down the tree should have been easier than going up, but the swelling in Delsin's arm and the lack of need to concentrate quite so hard increased his awareness of his injuries. Every movement jolted his arm, sending shrieks of pain from his wrist to his shoulder.

Finally he reached the ground, his face clammy and sweat trickling between his shoulder blades. He took care not to jar his body as he untied the rope that supported him. Kodi gave him no chance to recover, lifting him onto Rocky where he straddled between the full paniers.

The journey back to the cave seemed twice as far as coming, even though now they travelled as straight as possible and had previously wandered in search of the next conk. The bone in Delsin's forearm ground against itself at each step. Despite his agony, Delsin was more concerned about whether there would be enough agarikon for the whole of Westlands. He suspected they had cleaned this area out. The fungus took many years to grow, some of the specimens probably older than his grandparents.

Despite his worries and throbbing arm, Delsin couldn't help but experience the thrill he always did when he arrived back at the cave. Six unicorns! Diamond and Tempest had come at once when summoned by Echo, transporting them all to assist cure the land. With Prism's rainbow dapples and golden wings, Gem's emerald and ruby with opal horn and hooves, and Tempest's ocean blue, they covered every spectrum of colour. Add to that Diamond and Mystery's silver coats and sparkling horns, plus Echo's earthy hues of brown and green, the sight defied the imagination. If it weren't for his pain, Delsin would have thought he was dreaming.

Maybe Westlands really did have a chance of recovery.

First light seeped over the hilltops. Today would be the first test of Prism's strategy. The excitement had Delsin up well before the chill had lifted from the night. He added dry pine cones to the remnants of his fire and gathered an armful of logs from a stack near the front of the cave. Gem had healed his arm without any problems the previous night. A refreshing swim and a hearty broth had finished his recovery.

Whatever she had done had strengthened his legs too, though they remained crooked. Or did they? His leg muscles pulled and his hips grated in an unfamiliar way. He walked back and forth in front of the cave, every stride longer and less like the rolling gait of a fat goose. All doubt erased from his mind. His legs were straightening. Bullied by Bly and avoided by all people other than Laila and his mother, he had never dreamed that one day he would no longer be a cripple. And certainly, he'd never thought that he'd meet six unicorns and fly on a dragon as part of his healing journey.

As soon as he had a chance, he would spend a night in his sweat lodge and thank the ancestors. Many people believed that the Mother controlled fate, but now Delsin wondered whether Aureana, the winged unicorn goddess, looked after people too. Or were the Mother and the goddess the same? Whatever, he would thank them all. He no longer felt tired. In fact, he had never been as strong in his life.

But for now, he had preparations to make for the healing of Westlands. He finished weaving and filling packages for Prism to carry aloft. With a sense of anticipation thrumming through the gathered unicorns, Delsin hung the pouches of agarikon from Prism's neck where she could reach them. Diamond had already left to position herself as observer where they had picked to try out the aerial healing, a place swarming with rotfrogs.

Tempest strutted up to Prism. "Don't go too high. I'll let you know when to release the powder."

With Delsin's part complete for now, he retreated to sit next to Kodi where the bear relaxed against a rock. He rubbed his right forearm, still amazed that no pain remained, not even any bruising. "Do you think the agarikon will work?"

Kodi emitted a noncommittal rumble. "We must trust the goddess."

They watched as Prism cantered down the slope, easing into flight with no more effort than strolling along a trail. The morning sun caught her wings as she banked, headed for a ridge, and adjusted her direction and height as the wind strengthened. As she reached a point directly above the divide, she must have received a mental command from Tempest as she commenced tearing at the parcels.

It was too far away for Delsin to see the dust released. Waiting for Prism to return, he calculated how far the powder might travel. They still didn't know how much, or how little, would do the job. Had he gathered enough?

A joyful whinny came from Gem. She trotted over to their boulder, neck arched and tail high. "Diamond says Tempest's breeze did exactly what we'd hoped, weaving the powder through the trees and following the valleys, settling on the streams and dusting everything."

Prism landed and joined them, with Mystery, Tempest, and Echo close behind. The latter glowed with health. Gem had concentrated her healing on him since his cure of nickel poisoning by the agarikon dust, though doubted his horn would ever regrow. Neither Diamond nor Tempest had mentioned, at least not aloud, about the battle between the first and younger generations of unicorns. Hopefully all was forgiven with the success of finding a solution to the plague.

So why didn't Prism look happy? Delsin waited for her to

explain, anxious that he might have made the parcels too heavy, or too difficult to open.

"Where's Blaze?" Prism looked around as if the giant dragon with all his sparkling scales could be hiding nearby.

Delsin hadn't seen Blaze for days. That wasn't unusual. Since befriending Claw, he and the eagle often flew off, revelling in their powers and keen to test each other out. Sometimes Prism joined them, though he suspected her sense of duty to the older unicorns rather than her lesser agility stopped her from participating in their acrobatics, remaining behind to plan how to distribute the agarikon to the whole of Westlands. In the days leading up to this trial, while Delsin, Rocky, and Kodi had gathered conks, Prism had flown many reconnaissance missions for Tempest so he could determine, with his intimate knowledge of the weather, how best to cover the vast area.

Kodi roused beside Delsin. "I've called Blaze, and Claw. Blaze says they'll be here soon."

No sooner had he spoken, two pinpricks glinted in the sky, growing larger as they descended. Claw's golden feathers and Blaze's rainbow scales dazzled Delsin. He looked away from the glare to see Diamond appear in a shower of crystals, her horn still shimmering with power from her translocation.

Echo trotted to meet her, then veered to where Blaze and Claw landed. He reared, flattening his ears and baring his teeth.

Prism shot him a look of anguish before welcoming her friends. "I need your help. The area the dust covered is much smaller than we'd hoped. It'll take me more than the summer to cover the whole of Westlands."

Blaze pointed his snout at Delsin. "I can carry he who carries my scale high high high we'll fly fly fly to anywhere and do what Prism my Prism wants!"

"Eeerk! Claw doesn't need man. I carry pouches. I tear with beak."

Echo reared again and snaked his neck towards the pair. "No! I don't trust them. They're the duocorn's creations. They're not having anything to do with healing my territory."

Despite Echo's reticence, Delsin didn't believe the unicorn had anything to fear. "Blaze and Claw are no longer Shadow's servants. You can see how transformed they are, Blaze by Mystery's love and Claw by the goddess's feathers. We need them."

Echo would not back down. "You haven't met the duocorn. You don't know his wily ways. This so-called transformation could all be part of his plan to throw me out. He's already taken over part of Diamond's territory in Eastlands."

Diamond denied she had lost any land. "He lives at Eagle's Peak in Dragonspine Mountains. I know Aureana imprisoned him at Obsidian Caves, but for some reason she has let him remain free since Claw helped him escape. She must trust him now."

Mystery agreed. "He wasn't evil, only lonely. Who can blame him?"

Echo snorted. "You're too young to comment. You weren't there when he murdered Dewdrop. How many creatures do you think he tortured before he succeeded in making these monstrosities? I won't have them involved. And Aureana won't return to lock the duocorn up again. She's abandoned us."

If Echo didn't permit Blaze and Claw to help, then his territory could still be doomed. Delsin couldn't think how to overcome the unicorn's fears. He addressed Tempest. "Didn't you say we need to do this while we have the last of the spring breezes? Once summer comes, the weather will change."

Tempest agreed. "We need their help, Echo. And I don't want to stay here too long. Seashore, my own territory, needs me. I can't linger in yours because you don't like Blaze and Claw. You were happy enough for Claw to fetch meteorites for you. Why reject his help now?"

Echo lashed a hind leg at the eagle. "Exactly for that reason. He gathered poisonous rocks for me to change into food and medication. The duocorn must be behind this somehow."

Prism butted between the arguing unicorns. "Whether Shadow was behind the poisoning is not in question here. We have proved the agarikon works. I accept Blaze's and Claw's aid whether you like it or not."

With Blaze and Claw to distribute the agarikon dust as well, Prism's confidence grew that they would be able to cover all of Westlands. Tempest's knowledge of the terrain increased with each day as he directed the winds to drive the healing powder into every crevice and gully, along valleys and over hilltops, across open grasslands and deep into forests. Between them, they dropped the bread of ghosts onto waterways and high into mountain caves—anywhere that could sustain life.

Each noon, when the sun was too hot for Tempest to tame the breezes, they returned to the she-bear's cave for Delsin to replenish the pouches. Each evening, Gem filled Prism, Blaze, and Claw with additional power to supplement the little they drew from Equinora, leaving the land to recover as quickly as it could. The only time they couldn't work was during rain. Not only did poor weather hinder Tempest's control of the winds, the powder clagged, making it wasteful to drop.

Now, a light drizzle misted the valley below the cave, obscuring the flush of growth that had sprung up after the gorgebugs had moved on. Only one more load of parcels remained to distribute. Cosy out of the weather, everyone took the opportunity to rest. Rocky strode over to Prism and commenced grooming her with his teeth, massaging her neck with vigorous strokes, sending shivers of pleasure down her spine. About to return the favour, Prism hesitated as Diamond interrupted them.

"Westlands has recovered well. All the animals I met that had been treated in the area where we started are going about their lives as usual."

Sensing the older mare had something on her mind, Prism stepped away from Rocky. "That's wonderful news. It's a pity there are so few of them left."

Diamond agreed. "They'll soon breed up with a good season. The trees and shrubs are already covered in buds again. Some of the meadows are in flower. You've done a good job, worthy of being one of Aureana's six protectors of Equinora."

Prism didn't want to mention that one of the first-generation unicorns had caused the trouble in the first place, or that the goddess had told her that a unicorn must be the harbinger of death. "It's Delsin we must thank, and his sister Laila. Without them, we wouldn't have known how to counteract the nickel poisoning."

Diamond didn't appear as happy as she should have from bearing such good tidings. "I know you still believe Echo is responsible for—"

So this was what troubled Diamond. Prism wished she could take back her harsh words that accused her grandsire of deliberately causing the plague. "I know now he didn't mean harm. The rotfrogs arrived before Echo created his first sustenance from the sky stones."

Echo sidled up next to Diamond. "There was definitely something wrong with the meteorites other than their high nickel content. It wasn't only that they fell from the sky. While you've been out during the day, I've discussed this with Mystery. We think they had been tampered with in some way. What we disagree on is who could have done that. I still believe it was the duocorn."

The unexpected accusation took Prism by surprise. "How? That can't be possible."

Mystery had also wandered closer. He nuzzled her as if in apology but had no answer.

Echo stretched his nose to Prism's and blew in her nostrils. *Have you reconsidered that Claw or Blaze could be working for the duocorn?*

Fury boiled through Prism's veins. *Not this again. They've worked tirelessly to heal Westlands. How can you blame them? Because they were created by Shadow? They're my friends. They wouldn't do such a thing to Equinora.*

Not wanting to hear more, Prism stomped out of the cave into the rain, welcoming the cold and misery. How ungrateful could the first-generation unicorns be?

Kodi lumbered out beside her, his massive body fully recovered and his coat thick and shiny. Impervious to the water that beaded and ran down his back, he sheltered her from the wind that lashed at the mountainside. "We've done all we can. It's time for us all to go our own ways."

Prism agreed. "Echo can have Westlands back to himself. How dare he think Blaze or Claw could have been behind the troubles? He seems to have forgotten that Claw was injured by a meteorite in the first place."

The guardian acknowledged her outrage and tried to soothe her with his warmth. "All the conks have been gathered and distributed. There's nothing more for me to do here."

Prism let go of her anger and focused on the great bear who had come to Shimmering Lake all those moons ago to seek help. He had been cured, and found the last of the goddess's feathers, but nothing had turned out as they expected. "Will you go back to Snowhaven?"

Kodi shook his head. "There's nothing for me there. And I have no wish to stay here and tackle the other bears who will be drawn by the powerful musk of the sow."

"She won't come into season while she's feeding her cubs, will she? I thought bears only had young every few years."

Kodi sniffed the air. "Gem's power in the feed and waters must be boosting fertility. There's no doubt the she-bear is ready to mate. But not with me. It's time for me to join the goddess."

"Don't be ridiculous. You're healthy and would father strong cubs."

Slumping to the ground, Kodi groaned. "I am no longer a guardian. I have lived longer than a normal bear. I don't know whether I've fulfilled my purpose or failed. Either way, my life is forfeit."

"Rubbish." Prism circled the bear. Had he exclaimed his desire to die when he sought the unicorns' aid, she could have understood that. But to feel that way now, after struggling against unbelievable odds and being a key participant in ridding Westlands of the plague, was beyond her comprehension. "Even if you have no desire to breed, there will always be a home for you at Shimmering Lake. There are other precious things than the goddess's feathers to look after. What about Snag? Why don't you escort her there? That way she won't ever have to trap another creature to survive."

Gem had crept out of the cave during their conversation. "Blaze and Claw are also welcome to live at Shimmering Lake. It's fitting that my sanctuary becomes the home of creatures with power. But standing out here solves nothing. Come back inside out of the rain."

With her temper dampened, Prism did as suggested and sought shelter, keeping her distance from Echo. After sharing Gem's invitation with Blaze and Claw, Prism joined Rocky near Delsin's hearth. For days she had been worrying about their relationship. As much as she thrilled at his company, she feared losing him to old age. Better to part now while he could still build a herd of his own and raise foals as a horse stallion should. She didn't want a foal, not if it could only be a warmblood, and six unicorns already held the mantle of each element: earth, air, and fire; water, light, and spirit.

Before she could raise the topic, Echo lugged over one of the baskets that they had used to carry the agarikon, the heavy weight stretching the woven reeds to the point of breaking. He dumped it next to the small fire at Delsin's feet. "Now your role is complete, it's time to give you these as thanks for all you've done."

Delsin remained seated, looking stunned. "What are they?"

Prism couldn't resist peering into the panier. "Dragons' scales? Where did these come from?"

Echo lipped at the emerald hanging from Delsin's neck, the one that Blaze had given him so they could communicate. "They're from the dragons who used to live in my haven, shed when they grew. I asked Diamond to bring them here. I want you to have them."

Delsin ran his hands through the scales: rubies and diamonds, emeralds and sapphires. "These are too precious. I can't take these."

Prism squealed in excitement. "Yes. You must. You can share them with your people so they can talk with animals. We can enhance them, the same as Mystery did for Blaze's scale for you."

Resting a mighty paw on her back, Kodi tempered her enthusiasm. "When a unicorn passes on the ability to communicate with other animals, their own ability weakens. If you empower the whole basket of scales, you may lose that power altogether."

Prism wouldn't be deterred. "In that case, I will only do enough so each clan can have one. Don't forget, I'm third-generation, and have far more power than even my parents."

The frown on Delsin's face grew. "It would be wonderful to talk with all animals, and make it much easier for people to care for the herds and ride the bachelor stallions. But I fear that will put some animals at risk if just anyone has use of a scale. Can I ask that you enhance two for each village? That way every healer and spiritman can protect one. Many of them are vegetarians anyway and wouldn't use the scales to aid in hunting."

Prism nudged the basket. "Of course. Select the scales you want. I'll empower them now. The rest can go to Shimmering Lake in case you need more in the future."

Rocky whinnied in delight. "That's perfect. Blaze can fly Delsin to every village. That'll be quicker than riding me. And I can remain with you, knowing Delsin has the dragon to keep him safe."

Startled by Rocky voicing what she feared, Prism braced herself. There would be no other suitable time to say what she must. "You can't stay with me. You must return to Midlands with Delsin."

"But I must be with you. We, you, I mean…Delsin will be fine." Rocky shouldered against her, his intent clear.

"No. I'm not your mare. I'll go my own way. I don't want you."

The lie hurt Prism like no other pain she had ever experienced, the response on Rocky's face lancing her heart.

Tension filled the cave until Gem broke the silence. "Will you come home with us, Prism? Or do you have other plans?"

Until then, Prism hadn't considered her future. She only knew she mustn't share it with Rocky, or risk a greater agony when he died. Returning to Shimmering Lake to live with her loving parents, watching them together and knowing she could have had a bond like that with Rocky, however short-lived, was no longer an option. "There are still questions to be answered. Where did the rotfrogs come from? Why were so many meteorites falling? Curing Westlands with the agarikon only treated the symptoms."

She had to discover what caused the troubles in the first place. "I need to talk with Lash."

Chapter 27

Echo cantered alongside the river, his strides easy, his hooves barely touching the ground. Thick silt from the floods fed the rich grasses. Varicoloured butterflies flittered above dandelions and daisies. The early summer sun warmed him like the return of his territory's health warmed his heart.

In all the waterways, beavers industriously built new dams and lodges. Fish splashed in crystal-clear shallows, their scales glimmering silver as they broke the surface. Coots and moorhens paddled between reeds, already with chicks in procession behind them. Frogs croaked and frothy spawn floated in bubbles, nothing like the slime and putrefaction of the rotfrogs that had infested every creek, pond, and lake.

Echo left the river and crossed the floodplain where deer and moose grazed, tails flicking in contentment, bellies swelling from lush feed and pregnancy. Fat glossy bears turned over rotten logs in search of grubs and termites. Finches and honeyeaters twittered among the pink-white huckleberry blossom along the treeline. Further into the forest, chipmunks dug up forgotten caches of nuts, darting out of Echo's way as he trotted between oaks and spruce, their branches aglow with new growth. Even the breeze sounded cheerful as it whispered through the branches.

Everywhere Echo roamed, plants and animals recovered, the fresh scents of flowers and buds mingled with the sweet tang of female mammals in oestrus. The barren wastes of mud and slime had transformed to green and gold under a cloudless azure sky. Energy pulsed through every cell in Echo's body. So why did uncertainty of the future hover over him like one of Tempest's storm clouds?

He climbed higher into the rolling hillsides and patrolled the western border of his territory. Nothing appeared to be amiss. He looped back and headed south, through the valleys and gorges until he reached the gully with the steaming pool. His haven remained the same, yet memories of the confrontations with Prism, Mystery, and Gemstone lingered in the air like the dust that Delsin had thrown at him. Echo couldn't deny the agarikon had cured him, and the rest of Westlands, but something niggled at the back of his mind.

All thoughts raced from his head as a dazzling rainbow flashed past his ears. Two, three, multiple bat-sized creatures winged overhead, giggling and cavorting in the air. Dragons. His dragons. His spirits lifted with their wings as he pranced the remainder of the way to his pool. "You're safe and have returned. Where have you been? Are you all well?"

One by one, the dragons alighted on every perch, from rock ledges to branches, even along his spine. The leader of the colony rode Echo's crest, his red legs testimony to his ability to create fire. "We sought refuge at Tern Island. We were safe from the foulness there, but with Moonglow gone, no-one sent us love. We're glad to be home."

Echo poured his joy into his friends, their presence all the reassurance he needed that his territory no longer suffered. Maybe his uncertainty had come from the light weight of his horn. Still only a stump, his symbol of power hadn't regrown as he'd hoped. He doubted he would be able to transform rocks into sustenance or medication, not that he intended to use meteorites again. But this was his territory. There would still be creatures in need of his help over the generations to come.

A green-legged dragon, a healer, hovered in front of his face. "We can fix your horn. It'll take time, but there are many of us here."

Embarrassed that the dragons might have heard his thoughts, Echo raised his mental block. Then he realised that here were friends who he could discuss his worries with, friends who wouldn't judge him. "Do you think I was responsible for the devastation?"

The squeals of indignation from the whole colony of dragons did more to reassure Echo than if Aureana had comforted him herself. But he still couldn't shift his concern about Prism's claim that Aureana had said a unicorn must be the harbinger of death.

Could his granddaughter have misunderstood her vision, and Aureana meant the duocorn? Shadow. Echo hadn't used that name since Dewdrop's murder. Should he go to Eagle's Peak and confront him? Not that he had ever been strong enough to fight the duocorn, and certainly couldn't now with his depleted horn.

The lead dragon tweaked Echo's mane. "Something else troubles you. Tell us so we may help."

Echo gazed around the gully, at the jewelled dragons arrayed on every surface, at the vigorous growth of the shrubs, at the mice scurrying among the grass collecting seeds. How could a unicorn, the protectors of Equinora, ever harm the land, unless Shadow manipulated someone to act on his behalf? "Prism calls Blaze and Claw her friends. Even Kodi, though he may not realise it, is one of Shadow's creations, not Aureana's. I know. He was there when Dewdrop died. Shadow had been enlarging him from a cub. That's why Jasper asked him to guard the feathers, partly because of his great size and partly to save him from more of Shadow's enhancements."

The dragons waited for him to say more.

"What if Prism has always been able to fly and, inadvertently or not, caused the plague in Westlands? Why did Kodi, Blaze and Claw, plus Snag and Lash, end up here with her? Why does Prism seek Lash now? Is she the harbinger of death?"

Chapter 28

Prism circled over the old site of Leeface and selected a place to land as close as possible to the tree where she had last seen Yaholo Bones. Lingering here held no appeal, but Delsin had asked her to deliver one of Echo's dragon scales to the spiritman in thanks for his unwitting help in identifying the agarikon. The old man probably wouldn't even still be alive. How could he survive, blind and frail, unable to hunt, let alone with the added threat of wolves returning? If not from starvation or predation, he might have died of despair.

She empathised. Her hooves thudded to the ground and her heart thumped in her chest. Abandoning Rocky had taken all her courage. Now she could barely draw energy from Equinora. The sight of Yaholo leaning against the base of the mighty tree did little to cheer her.

His sinewy form leapt up and ran to her, waving his arms in glee, as she trotted over. "You're back! The bones told me you would come."

Amazed that the spiritman had regained his sight, Prism brightened up. "I've brought something for you. Wear this dragon scale and you'll be able to talk with animals, even with dragons if one should come by."

Yaholo accepted the plaited thong from her mouth and hung the sapphire scale around his neck with trembling hands. "I thank you, it's a pleasure to receive a gift from one as magnificent as you, a visible legend. I will treasure this beautiful gem. But I've always been able to talk with you and I've seen the mighty dragon fly overhead."

It hadn't occurred to Prism that anyone left alive would watch her, Blaze, and Claw on their mission to dust the land. They had flown low to align with Tempest's winds. "I don't mean only us. I mean all animals, especially horses. If you make contact with a herd, they'll help the clans in return for grooming and feed. And Blaze isn't a normal dragon. They're usually small, the size of a squirrel, invisible to all bar the goddess's other creatures or those who touch one of their gifted scales."

"Really?" The spiritman stroked the dragon scale that hung against his bronzed chest, his skin hanging loose over protruding ribs. "That must be why the ancestors don't speak of them. Where do these dragons live?"

Not wanting to stay longer, Prism refrained from explaining the history behind dragons. "Anywhere they want."

But that wasn't true. The only remaining colony she knew of lived at Shimmering Lake. Residing somewhere without the companionship of cheeky dragons like Tatuk, or the gentle Meda, didn't appeal to Prism. There might still be some at Tern Island, but who would be feeding them the love they needed since Moonglow's passing? Where would Prism claim as her territory? Remaining alone, with no other unicorns and no dragons, added to the pain of living without Rocky. But she couldn't bear to see the stallion grow old and frail while she remained vigorous forever. Perhaps she could encourage a small flock of Gems' dragons to join her wherever she eventually settled.

The spiritman must have been asking her something because he looked at her as if waiting for an answer. "Sorry, I was distracted. I have to go. But tell me, how is it that you can see again?"

Yaholo waved his arms over his head. "That's what I was saying! The land is recovering. The fish are clean, and the water fresh. There are goose eggs and lily corms. The vile rotfrogs and algae are gone. I knew you could do it! When I no longer needed to consume the bread of ghosts, my eyesight returned."

"Was your blindness a side effect of the agarikon? Does that mean that all our work to heal the land will render animals blind?" The thought that she might have replaced creatures' suffering with another form of crippling disability racked Prism's heart.

The spiritman rested a hand on her shoulder. "It takes a lot to have that side effect. I was eating nothing else. It kept me alive, but at a price. And as you can see, and I can see…" he chuckled, "…the effect dissipated as soon as I ate other foods."

Relieved that she hadn't further poisoned Westlands and not wanting to take all the credit for the cure, Prism briefly explained how Delsin had collected the conks for her to dust the countryside. "Now I really must go. I hope your people return."

She spun about and galloped along the lake shore, spreading her wings and letting the breeze lift her in a steady climb, the tips of her feathers ruffling as she adjusted their angle. So much had happened since she had overcome her fear and learnt to fly. What did her life hold now? Where would she go after she found Lash?

Days of flying, alone and with no success in locating Lash, exacerbated Prism's misery. Refusing to return to the she-bear's cave where her parents remained to oversee the recovery of Westlands, she spent the dark hours grazing in the renewed meadows, needing the food as much as the activity with her decreased ability to draw power from Equinora. The sun and earth failed to refresh her as usual. She had lost her capacity for love. If she couldn't have Rocky, she couldn't let the memory of the skewbald stallion seep into her core and torture her anew.

Prism? Where are you? Have you found the snake? Gem's cries had become more insistent each day, begging her to give up the hunt and return.

No. I must keep searching. She had tried ignoring her parents' calls at first, until she accepted how that distressed them. There was no point making them share her pain.

Rocky is waiting for you. He won't leave until he's said goodbye. The message came from her sire this time, the tone one of admonition. She was too far away for the warmblood stallion's own communications to reach her.

He mustn't wait for me. I'm not coming back. Tell him to take Delsin home. Having let her parents know she was safe, Prism ignored their further attempts to get her to change her mind, blocking her mind from them. If only she were able to block her own thoughts as easily.

She flew up the face of a cliff, labouring hard to take her mind off those she had left behind. New growth covered the shrubs and trees in a haze of green, obscuring the ground beneath the branches.

No wonder she couldn't find Lash. He would be easily hidden, his splendid scales blending in with the flowers that carpeted the meadows, or camouflaged by the verdant forests.

The barren rock-face emitted heat from its dark surface, making flying an exercise in concentration as well as strength as she climbed higher. Then the thermals shoved her from below, raising her high above the peaks. Prism glided on outstretched wings, her tail streaming like a wisp of golden cloud.

A pair of falcons matched her loop for loop, their well-being evident in their effortless joy of freedom, living for the moment. No matter the deprivation they had suffered during the plague, they had put that behind them. All that mattered to them now was the present. Food was plentiful and nesting sites available. They had nothing to worry about.

Neither did she. She could live her life as she wished. Go anywhere, do anything. She could live like Gem had done before Mystery had arrived, taking lovers to fulfil her needs and sending them on when she tired of their attentions. She could travel, visit Diamond, and explore Tern Island. Anything! She would always have Blaze to race across the skies and share the miracle of flight. Her spirits lifted. Power coursed through her veins, her body absorbing strength from the sun and wind.

Satisfied at the success of beating the plague, healing her grandsire, and now overcoming her depression, she gazed at the world beneath her. Jewels sparkled along a rocky ledge like a row of dragons on a branch. Lash! It must be. Her renewed sense of love for life must have brightened his scales. Swooping low, she confirmed that indeed the giant snake lay sunning on a rocky outcrop. Nowhere nearby offered a place to land.

She dived and hoped he would hear her yell. "Can you meet me on top of the mountain?"

The giant snake immediately rippled up the cliff, climbing where no apparent crevices offered him purchase. His muscles hugged the rocks as he glided in a liquid flow first left then right, gaining height with every curve of his body. A giant jewelled snake slithering up a mountain—exactly as Delsin had described from his vision.

By the time Prism had found a safe landing place and trotted to the edge of the cliff, Lash had wound himself into a coil. He raised his head and observed her with crimson eyes. "You sssearch too long. I wasss near all the time."

Taken aback that the snake knew she had been looking for him, Prism remained out of reach. "What do you mean, near?"

"The guardian told me you sssearch. I find you through ssstone. You didn't sssee me. You were sssad and I wasss pale." Lash changed position, unwrapping and rewrapping his coils in a sinuous curl.

Of course Kodi would have sent a message ahead. "What stone? Can you detect my presence through the rock beneath you?" She understood little of Shadow's creatures and why the guardian could communicate with them as unicorns did with dragons.

Lash's tongue flickered in and out as his head stretched out towards her. "The green ssstone. The one the man usssed to find you. Itsss inssside me."

Prism remembered Delsin telling her that Lash had stolen the jade carving of Fleet. It was why Delsin hadn't found her until Rocky was near enough to make contact. Rocky. She couldn't think about him now. "So why did you wait for me to find you? Didn't Kodi tell you why we're looking for you? Gem has invited you to live at Shimmering Lake, with Blaze and Snag and Claw." Had her search been a waste of time? If the guardian could talk with Lash, why had she come?

Lash tightened his rings. "Not sssafe. I don't want to lossse my jewelsss."

"What do you mean?" She wished the snake wouldn't talk in riddles. This was worse than Moonglow's prophecies that her parents had told her about.

"Ssshadow. He might ssssteal them if he ssseeesss me. That'sss why I hid until you sssearched."

"Shadow? Why would your creator steal your scales?"

"He'sss upssset. I can feel his sssorrow. He wantsss to dessstroy all beauty. He'sss never ssseen me like thisss."

Echo had always believed that Shadow was behind the plague. But the goddess had said that a unicorn must be the harbinger of death. Shadow was a duocorn. Or had he lost a horn? Is that why he was upset? "Did Shadow send the rotfrogs to Westlands?"

Lash rewound himself in a different coil, his scales paling from Prism's uncertainty. "Frogsss came from the sssky. Like the ssstonesss."

How could frogs come from the sky? The snake didn't make

sense. And Shadow couldn't create meteorites, could he? But why not? He was the goddess's shadow. Why was he upset? Maybe Lash was mistaken. Anyway, it was Echo, albeit inadvertently, who had transformed the stones and poisoned Westlands. A cure had been found and the land was recovering.

No longer concerned about any danger from the giant snake, Prism walked up to him and blew gently on his jewelled body. "Don't worry about Shadow stealing your scales. You'll be safe at Shimmering Lake. Blaze and all the other dragons have scales like yours, and they're fine."

She wasn't going to find out who or what was behind the plague from Lash. But as Spirit Unicorn, the duty to resolve the issue was hers. She would go to Tern Island, Moonglow's former home, and contact the goddess.

Chapter 29

The sweet aroma of freshly scythed alfalfa greeted Delsin as he rode Rocky into Fleet's territory of White Water Cliffs. With Rattlesnake Ranges between them and Westlands, the horrors of the past seasons dissipated like morning mist on a hot day. With the recovery of Echo's territory under way, the only dampener to Delsin's pleasure was Rocky. The stallion had remained subdued throughout their journey, even when they had galloped the open spaces that once would have sent their spirits soaring.

Delsin still didn't understand Prism's rejection of Rocky. The horse may only be a warmblood, not a unicorn, but they had been so close, spending time together whenever they could. Rocky had spoken little of their antics, but Delsin had seen them mate frequently, and there had been no arguments he was aware of.

With the familiar songs of thrushes and robins announcing his arrival, Delsin pushed away his worry. The company of other horses might cheer Rocky up. Delsin was certainly ready for some human company despite his usual preference to spend time alone.

Rocky jogged alongside the creek that provided drinking water for Waterfalls. Bumblebees burdened with pollen hovered over the meadows. As Delsin neared the village, children raced up in excitement, all shouting at once and asking whether he'd found the unicorn. Delsin smiled and told them they'd have to wait and hear his tales that night, after he'd met with the chief. He halted in the central clearing and dismounted.

Yuma abandoned a large pole he was carving and strode over to meet him. "We didn't expect you. Fleet never mentioned you were near."

Surprised that Rocky hadn't informed the king of his arrival, Delsin slipped from the stallion's back and accepted the offer of the children to wash the horse down. "I'm sorry, it didn't occur to me to send word on ahead."

Yuma slapped him on the back and grinned. "Don't apologise. You're here, and safe. That's all that matters. Come and quench your thirst then tell us your news."

Delsin accepted a flask of ale and sat with Chaytan, Winona, and Yuma outside the chief's hut. Other people trickled into the communal clearing, keen to listen too. Visitors were always welcome, especially when they came from outside Midlands, even more so as all had heard of Delsin's mission to seek and help the winged unicorn.

An old woman approached and held out both hands, palms up, in greeting. "I'm Istas Sugar, of Sweetwood. Lady Prism saved our lives. Is it safe to return home?"

Having forgotten that Prism had told him the Westlands clans were seeking refuge at Waterfalls, Delsin was surprised to see her. "The lands are recovering well, the remaining animals are healed, and everything is growing back. But it might be a while before there is enough to feed you all without harming the recovery."

Her long braids swung as she nodded. "And what of Yaholo Bones? Do you have news of our spiritman?"

"He's well. He not only survived, he's the reason Westlands is saved." Delsin quickly told her about the bread of ghosts, but he would wait until later to mention the gift of dragon scales from Echo.

Fleet trotted into the village and halted next to them. The magnificent black stallion greeted Yuma before nudging Delsin with his nose. "I've been keeping track of your progress. My granddaughter has excelled herself. And thanks to you, Echo's territory is safe."

Delsin stroked the sleek neck. "Not just me. Everyone played their part."

Fleet acknowledged his modesty with a cock of his head and a twitch of his upper lip.

In as few words as possible, Delsin briefed those gathered around him. "I can fill in the detail tonight, after the meal, so everyone can hear."

Wielding an obsidian blade, Yuma pointed across to the pole he had been working on. "I'm carving the story of the bloodwolf war. I plan to do another pole for the stealthcat war too, though I'll do that one in Eastlands."

Surprised that Yuma would consider travelling when he had so many responsibilities, Delsin swung his arm to indicate the gathered people. "Who will lead the clan? Will you come too, Fleet? Can you leave the herd?"

Yuma sauntered over to his carving and stroked the figure of a horse's head. "Chaytan is chief now, with my blessing. He and Winona are far better to lead than me. I've almost finished this pole of totems. But you're right, Fleet can't accompany me. I'm happy to walk if you're not in a rush. Will you rest here a few days and let me travel with you?"

Happy to relax among company and give Rocky a rest, Delsin agreed, delighted that Yuma could follow his passions for carving and travel. "We can always double up on Rocky if he wants a run. He's fitter than ever since Gem's healing."

Istas addressed Yuma. "Will you come west after you've carved the pole for the Eastlanders and do one for us? By then we should be harvesting the maples again and you can sample the treats I've told you of."

"Of course, I'd be honoured." Yuma reminded Istas that Westlanders were also welcome to make permanent homes at Waterfalls.

She thanked him. "Those with young children will stay. Us older ones prefer to return home."

Fleet nudged Yuma. "When you leave for Bloomsvale, I will provide an experienced stallion to carry you. He's escorting a few fillies to King Streak at Oakvale. With you along, they'll be safer from wolves, and this'll mean you won't have to walk. I suspect he'll be happy to journey on to Eastlands, and then to Westlands to establish a territory. I'll grant him the mares that Streak is sending me."

Travelling with Yuma at his side added to Delsin's pleasure of being back in Midlands. Summer filled the air with the hum of activity. Blaze's scale around Delsin's neck accentuated the sounds he could hear—animals chattering, birds squabbling, ants ordering. Rocky, in contrast, remained silent and withdrawn, barely talking with the stallion who carried Yuma or the mares who trotted out in front. The small herd was an impressive sight, all solid blacks heavy with muscle, with thick manes and tails. No-one could doubt that Fleet was their sire. Bands of white laced the youngest filly's mane. This one must be Tress's daughter. She was destined for King Flash at Oakvale.

The exciting scent of hot horse wafted over Delsin and warmth seeped into his thighs from Rocky's sides as they reached Flowering Valley. The river crossing had been easy with the waters low at this time of year and they had enjoyed a gallop on reaching the river flats lush with flowers. As they neared the outskirts of Bloomsvale, Delsin rode up close to Yuma. "Let's walk the rest of the way. The horses can find the herd and King Streak."

Yuma wasted no time dismounting. "I could do with a walk to stretch my legs. It's been a long time since I rode so far. Fleet and I don't do much together these days as he doesn't like to leave the herd for long."

The two men strode in companionable silence into the village. An unnatural quiet lingered in the air as they walked between the huts to the central compound. No children ran around, screaming in their games of chase or trying to best each other in their chores. Women ground corn with grim faces, only acknowledging their arrival with a brief nod. Delsin presumed all the men were out hunting, until his brother swaggered out of a new hut, far larger than all the others. Its stout timbers must have been lugged from Oakvale as no trees that size grew near here.

Bly halted in front of Delsin, muscled arms crossed and legs apart. "You're not welcome here. Find another clan that'll take you in and believe your lies."

Not understanding Bly's meaning, and concerned about more important matters, Delsin held his ground. "How's Mama?"

"Dead. Now turn around and go before I have my men escort you. And believe me, they won't be gentle."

Yuma slipped his pack from his shoulders and dropped it to the ground. "Hang on. I'm sorry about your mother, but that's no way to greet anyone. Don't you want to know what's happened in Westlands?"

Bly took a step forward so his nose almost touched Yuma's forehead. "Don't interfere. You can tell us once this trouble-maker has gone."

Delsin wasn't sure whether to be sad or relieved that Macha Gatherer had passed to join the ancestors. "Where's Laila?"

His brother turned to face him and waved his hand as if swatting at midges. "None of your business. Now get out of here. This is your last warning."

Delsin copied Yuma and unloaded his pack, standing his ground. "Let me see Laila. I'll talk to the chief about this."

"Ha! You're talking to the chief." Bly shoved Delsin's shoulder, sending him reeling.

Taken aback, Delsin grasped what lay behind the dismal air that hung over the village. "So what's happened to Gomda? And what makes you think I'm a liar?"

Bly snorted a laugh that was echoed by a group of young men who had materialised from the central hut. "Claiming to ride a dragon? Flying around with a winged unicorn? You've been taking too many of your concoctions to commune with the afterlife. No wonder the spiritmen don't accept you. You live in a fantasy world."

So Laila had mentioned his visit. Delsin was curious about that. "Where's our sister?"

"Where she belongs, doing women's work."

Delsin could take no more. He attempted to step around Bly.

His brother kicked out a leg to trip him, like he had done so many times in their youth.

Delsin avoided the foot with ease, his inner strength from his travails matched by his healed legs. "You're not going to bully me anymore. Get out of my way."

Yuma joined Delsin as Bly's thugs lined up behind him.

Two against six were not good odds. There was only one way to overcome this. Delsin asked Yuma to stay back. "Bly, if you want to fight, let it be just you and me. Keep your buddies out of it. If you win, I'll leave."

Laughter erupted from the men ranked behind Bly. Bly, however, spat on his hands and rubbed them together. "Now?"

Delsin handed his pack to Yuma and nodded. "Right here, where the whole village can witness the outcome."

For answer, Bly swung a fist at Delsin's head, not even waiting for the ritual of drawing a circle around the fighters. Bly's men retreated, jeering and egging them on. Yuma hurried to carry both packs out of the way.

Bly had always beaten Delsin in the past, his greater size and strength overcoming Delsin's frail body that was more used to meditating than hunting. Their boyhood squabbles had always ended in Delsin either running away or begging for forgiveness and doing whatever his older sibling wanted.

Now, however, was a different matter. Delsin had spent many moons trekking across mountains and pulling Rocky on a sled with barely enough to eat. He had the healing of Gem thrumming in his body and a dragon scale that aided his senses. And most of all he had the bottled-up hate for a brother that could so casually announce the death of their mother and think to drive Delsin from his home.

Delsin watched Bly's movements with all the knowledge he had gained from moons of studying animals defend their territory or seek a mate. He noticed every twitch of muscle and cast of eye, every breath drawn and finger curled. Bly was a powerful fighter, strong and fit, but he lacked finesse. Delsin hoped his nimbleness and brains would make up for his lack of skill as a fighter.

Bly threw punches without regard to where they landed. Each blow shook Delsin, his head a punch-bag. His fists stung from defending himself. Pain shot from his guts to his shoulder. His left knee cracked. Blood scent stung his nostrils. Sweat slicked his skin, the saltiness sharp on his split lip. Thirst haunted him, his throat hoarse as he tried to reason with Bly while they circled each other.

Concentrating on staying out of reach rather than attacking, Delsin tensed as Bly raised his fist over his head. Expecting a downward strike, Delsin braced his feet, almost toppling when no blow came. Bly snatched something from the air, thrown by one of his men. A spear! But weapons were never allowed in this type of combat.

Taunts surrounded him: "Kill him!" "Show him who's chief!" "Send him to his ancestors!"

Delsin blocked the cries out and prepared for a drive of the spear against his ribs. Instead, Bly stunned him by barging him to the ground, throwing his weight over Delsin's trapped body. The wooden shaft pressed against his throat, choking him. Through the ringing in his ears he heard Yuma shout, trying to gather support from the villagers to stop the brawl or to make Bly fight fair. He briefly saw Yuma pinioned by Bly's bullies, thrashing his legs to get free.

No-one came to Delsin's aid. His sight faltered and the roars of the watchers dwindled, muffled as if by distance. His heart pounded in his ears. Sharp stones pressed into his back. His mind drifted, visions of jewelled dragons and golden spiders mingling with unicorns swimming in twinkling waters.

The earth stirred. Warmth seeped into his skin and through his veins. His head buzzed and the world spun. The sun grew hot on his exposed legs and wind teased his hair. Nothing existed except the need to breathe, the desire to rise and strike out. Delsin saw nothing, smelled nothing, heard nothing. His body pulsed, energy coursing his limbs, power filling his soul. A glaring golden light dazzled every nerve in his body.

He leapt to his feet, arms spinning and legs dancing as if possessed. He snapped the spear shaft across his knee, cast aside the weapon, and lunged for Bly's throat. His brother reeled back, slipping through his grip. Delsin pursued with fists flailing, pounding Bly back, kicking his feet from under him.

Bly toppled.

The thugs holding Yuma released his arms and ran to their chief's side. Yuma joined in the fight, tackling the largest of Bly's bullies. Then all Delsin could see was his brother's face, all he could feel was his rage. Prepared to die, Delsin pummelled his foe, oblivious to his own pain as Bly struck back. Delsin fell backwards and staggered to regain his feet.

No-one remained to oppose him. Screams came from the onlookers as Bly and his gang fled the village. The compound cleared. Only Delsin and Yuma remained standing in the middle, bloody and gasping for air.

A rush of hot wind swept leaves across the clearing, almost knocking Delsin off his feet. He wiped the blood and sweat from his face and glanced over his shoulder. Blaze swooped low, dipped his wings, and chased after the fleeing men, his crimson scales glowing and his lungs expanding. Claw arrowed overhead, talons extended, and dropped towards the ground. No matter how much he loathed his brother, Delsin didn't want to see Bly and his accomplices fried or torn to shreds. But before he could call the dragon, everything went black.

Something wet washed over Delsin's cheek. Blood? No. Squinting through swollen lids, Delsin saw a long pink tongue at the same time as his nose told him the answer—wolf. "Paws!"

"Lay still. I can't stitch your arm with you wriggling around like that, and Meda's trying to heal your internal bleeding." Laila administered to Delsin's wounds, swabbing away the crusted blood and dirt.

"What happened?" Beneath him a bed of hay smelled sweet and fresh, a deerskin soft against his back.

Yuma offered him a drink. "You're quite the hero. The whole village is waiting in the main hut. They won't come out with Blaze guarding outside."

Struggling to remember what had happened, Delsin shook his fuzzy head. "Bly! Is he dead?"

Yuma barked a laugh. "No, but I bet he's running as far as he can. I doubt he and his cronies will be back."

Groaning, Delsin tried to sit up. "He will. You know he will."

With a hand on each of Delsin's shoulders, Yuma encouraged him to lie back down. "Don't worry about him. The elders will sort that out. The good news is that you've come round. You had us worried when you collapsed like a toppled tree."

Paws wriggled under Delsin's hand, asking for a scratch. "Thank you, my friends. I think the ancestors helped me draw on Equinora's power, like the goddess's creatures do. How did Blaze and Claw know to come?"

Laila patted at his brow with a damp cloth. "Blaze said you called him and he felt your pain. You're bonded through his scale."

Delsin didn't want to think about the full implications of that at the moment. "Mama. She's gone."

"Yes." Laila wrung her cloth out in a basin and resumed washing his face. "I would have followed you when she died, but Bly captured Paws. I had to do as he said or he wouldn't feed her. If I disobeyed, he beat Paws."

Hearing his sister swallow the gulps of anguish, Delsin attempted to sit up. "He must pay for this. I thought Paws was thin. And you too, look at you."

Laila paused her nursing and stroked the emerald dragon who huffed over Delsin's belly. "If it wasn't for Meda we'd both be dead. Jolon went berserk when Mama died. I think Bly only stopped him from killing me so he could make me suffer more."

The clan gathered around the communal fire, the elders seated on carved logs and the remainder resting on the ground. The council needed little time to debate the issue.

Gomda Hunter, the chief who had been ousted by Bly, rose to his feet. "In one thing Bly Tusker was right. I'm too old to lead Bloomsvale." He held up his hand for silence as murmurs of dissent rumbled among the crowd. "It is obvious to all that the new chief must be Delsin, or rather, Delsin Dragonrider."

Cheers erupted and people chanted his name, stamping their feet in accord.

Delsin rose, his back still sore and bruises blossoming on his arms. "Thank you for this honour. I'm truly grateful. But I can't lead the clan. My life is dedicated to the spirits. Choose another, I beg you."

The crowd fell silent then all started to talk at once. No-one had ever turned down a position of power before.

The old chief held up a feathered staff, asking for quiet. "Delsin, your modesty does you credit. Enough of this refusal, it's you we want."

Still on his feet, Delsin made a point of looking at every man and woman, pivoting to face each in turn. "I'm not being polite. I've fought bloodwolves here in Midlands and stealthcats in Eastlands. I've aided a unicorn to rid Westlands of the plague and flown on a dragon. Do not tether me. Gomda is a better leader. I have another path to follow."

To ensure the people didn't try to cajole him further, Delsin left the gathering. The hubbub of voices rose as he departed. Yuma and Laila walked either side of him, Paws bounding around all three of them.

Yuma rested a hand on Delsin's shoulder. "What are you going to do?"

Delsin continued to walk towards his and Laila's tree without answering. When he reached the mighty trunk, he huddled down and rested his head on his knees. The others sat too, waiting for him to speak.

Renewed by the tree's energy, Delsin smiled at his sister and friend. "I have a task to fulfil. Do you remember I said that Echo gifted dragon scales for people? As much as I would prefer to stay here in contemplation with the spirits, I need to visit every clan to distribute them and teach them how to use them. I selected enough for one healer and one spiritman in every village."

Rocky walked towards them, a tiny dragon resting on his crest. Laila leapt up to greet them. "I wondered where you were."

Meda flew to Laila's shoulder and snuffled under her hair. "I fetched Rocky. He needs to be here."

Delsin went across to the horse and stroked his neck. "I'm sorry, old fellow. If you don't want to go then I'll go on foot. It's too much to ask you to travel all of Equinora again."

The stallion tossed his head and nipped at Delsin. "Rubbish. I've never felt so full of life. Don't discard me so soon."

Yuma interrupted their banter. "You needn't go, Delsin. I intend to keep travelling. I can take the scales to all the clans."

Laila joined them. "I'll go too. I have no wish to stay here. And Meda can help them get used to dragons and their abilities."

Something in Laila's expression made Delsin hesitate. His sister and friend swapped looks and reached for each other's hands, their fingers entwining. The old animosity between them had evaporated. Maybe caring for him had brought them together. They were certainly well suited. Paws sat at their feet and pounded the ground with her tail, looking from one to another with a great wolfy grin. That made up his mind. "If you're sure you really mean it, that would be wonderful."

Laila couldn't suppress her grin. "I know you're surprised, but Yuma and I have talked it over. Neither of us wants to settle with a clan. Yuma accepts Paws and Meda. All I'm missing is Mystery to ride."

Delsin hugged her and shook Yuma's hand before addressing Rocky. "My friend, would you carry Laila?"

"Are you trying to get rid of me again so soon?" The stallion flicked his tail before shoving Delsin with his nose. "I may have a few good years left in me yet, but I'd prefer to spend them grazing my home meadows." He paused. "Where Prism knows where to find me."

Delsin translated the horse's words for Yuma. "You really should have one of the unicorns enhance Tatuk's scale for you."

Yuma shook Delsin's hand again. "No, I still wish to hunt. As for a mount for Laila, I can't ask the stallion who carried me here to go all the way to Eastlands when he intends to establish a territory west of Rattlesnake Ranges. We're happy to go on foot to each clan and explain how to work with dragons. We're not in a hurry. I'll share the stories of the wars wherever we go. I've already composed a few songs. Laila can teach the healing skills she learned from Gem."

A weight lifted from Delsin's shoulders. "And I can stay here with Rocky. Mojag Carol is bound to be interested in the dragon scales."

Laila gave his shoulder a gentle squeeze. "The clan will more than likely make you their spiritman instead of Mojag. The one who rejected you can become your apprentice."

Chapter 30

Despite her initial intentions, Prism hesitated to go straight to Tern Island. Using the excuse of checking for further evidence of the plague or recent destruction by meteorites, she flew west over Rattlesnake Ranges and far beyond Echo's territory. She flew north and crossed over Obsidian Caves, where the goddess had incarcerated Shadow until Claw lifted him over the prison's barrier. She flew across the vast marshes of Diamond's territory and south over the grassy plains where the stealthcats had lurked until Mystery battled Shadow. She flew back across Dragonspine Mountains and over Midlands where bloodwolves had ranged until Fleet had confronted Shadow. Shadow. Shadow. Shadow. All the past troubles led back to the duocorn.

Delaying no longer, Prism headed along the coast and circled above Tern Island to gain perspective of her potential new home from the air. An open windswept landscape on the southern peak sloped down to thicker forest on the northern side. Craggy rocks bordered the majority of the rugged shoreline, interspersed with a few sandy beaches where seals dozed. A small pool glistened in a rock basin at the western end of the island where sheer cliffs fell away to the crashing surf far below.

She landed nearby on a grassy strip that appeared free of sticks and stones. If she intended to deny herself Rocky's company, the isolation here would suit her. And, thanks to Tempest's close proximity, the climate would remain mild all year round. She'd had enough of snow and freezing rivers. Not that she intended to socialise with the Water Unicorn. Prism suspected that Tempest and Moonglow had been lovers, but his formality and age failed to excite her like the skewbald stallion.

Rocky. How many times during her investigation of Equinora had she almost returned to him, only to quash her desires by reminding herself of the pain that parting would bring? He was already old, and she was young even by horse standards. And she couldn't allow him, or her own pleasure, to distract her. Maybe here, on Tern Island, prophecies would come to her like they had to Moonglow, or at least she might gain an understanding of who or what was behind the rotfrogs and poisonous meteorites. She was the Spirit Unicorn. The time had come to fulfil her destiny.

Keen to investigate the island from the ground, she cantered downhill, empowered by the warm sun and the invigorating breeze from the sea. The ocean stretched in every direction, not a hint of land on any horizon. Gulls cawed overhead and the sharp tang of spearmint rose from under her hooves. After moons of rotting corpses and stinking water, the freshness of Tern Island was a welcome relief.

A flurry of jewelled wings rose above the escarpment. Dragons! Prism neighed in response to their welcome, her mood lightening that a colony remained in Moonglow's territory. No, her territory now. The presence of dragons solidified Prism's intention to make this her permanent home.

The dragons chased each other through the air, zipping through the stunted shrubs along the clifftops and dodging among a copse of trees that crowned the island. She cantered over to join them, sending out love, their scales dazzling in response.

Prism skidded to a halt and held out her wings to reflect the sun, revelling in the power that poured into her. The chattering dragons all talked at once. Other than understanding that they were delighted with her arrival, she couldn't make out what any of them were saying. It didn't matter, she was happy to share their joy.

A single dragon with purple legs broke away from the mob and flitted to her crest. "Prism! It's me!"

"Tatuk!" The appearance of the cheeky dragon who accompanied Gem everywhere plunged her soul into despair. "What's happened?" She couldn't believe that he would be here unless trouble loomed.

Glowing with all the colours of the rainbow, the little dragon didn't look distressed. "I've come to see if any of the dragons want to move home."

"Move? Whatever for? I'm here now. I can give them plenty of love." Prism scanned the branches where the dragons had settled, quiet while she conversed with their visitor. No wonder they had been so excited, it would be rare for them to have dragons from other territories visit. Maybe they didn't need her. They'd certainly survived, thrived even, in the absence of a resident unicorn.

Tatuk reassured her that all was well at Shimmering Lake. "But with Echo's dragons having fled here during the plague, there are many hatchlings. Some might want to start new colonies elsewhere."

Tatuk was right. No wonder the dragons shone with love. The fresh blood had triggered a new generation, so many that the surrounding trees pulsed with gemstones. "Where will they go?"

Tatuk didn't hesitate. "Yuma and Laila are going to visit all the clans to deliver the enhanced scales, scales from the ancestors of these youngsters. It's only right that the healer women and spiritmen have dragons to live with them too. The dragons can help people with healing, and making fire and food when necessary."

The news delighted Prism. "So are you here to escort them to the villages?"

Relieved when Tatuk confirmed he had volunteered to be the young dragons' guide, Prism queried him about everything at Shimmering Lake. She still blocked mind messages from her parents, not wanting the reminder of Rocky waiting for her, but she was desperate to know all that was going on.

Tatuk chattered on until the sun dipped towards the ocean, subduing the light and turning the horizon mauve and pink, then deep orange and red. He told how Shadow's creatures had settled in well, with Snag living in Laila's jade cave and Lash sunning himself on the rocks above her in the day. Blaze and Claw had made Mystery's and Gem's territory their base but, like her, spent most of their days soaring over Equinora.

Prism couldn't delay her pressing question any longer. "Is Rocky there?"

Tatuk rearranged his wings and curled his tail. "No. He carried Delsin home like you instructed him to."

Although that was exactly what Prism had asked, the fact of Rocky's leaving stabbed her heart. She thought back to all they had shared, racing down steep hillsides and neighing with the wind, rolling after a swim in the invigorating waters, and seeking solitude to graze, groom, and mate. She squirmed with the memory. Rocky had called her his queen. She'd never have flown without him crying out his love for her. And she had abandoned him. Had she done wrong?

But she couldn't worry about her personal troubles until she had a sign from the goddess about what her role as Spirit Unicorn required next. She still needed answers. Many moons ago, dying from the plague and searching for the last feather, Kodi had sought help from the unicorns. Westlands may have been saved and the feather found, but was that really the end of problem? "What of Kodi? How is he coping now he has nothing to guard?"

Tatuk's demeanour drooped. "Dying. Since accompanying Snag safely home, he won't do anything. He doesn't eat or drink. Only Gem's power keeps him alive. He rarely talks to anyone, spending his days and nights curled up like a hibernating bear."

Prism's heart lurched. "That's terrible. If it weren't for his bravery, Westlands and possibly all of Equinora would still be suffering. I must go to him." Without Rocky there to distract her, Prism might be able to directly contact the goddess from Shimmering Lake, or perhaps Mystery and Gem would agree to participate in another ceremony.

Returning to Shimmering Lake held both pleasure and pain for Prism. She enjoyed seeing her parents, yet the love they shared only accentuated her lack of a life-long companion. After their initial greetings, she hurried off to find Kodi.

The great bear was, as Tatuk had stated, curled up in his den, his forepaws over his head with his hind legs tucked around his belly so that he looked like a giant hedgehog rolled in a ball. Only the shallow rise and fall of his chest showed he lived.

Prism scraped the floor of the cave with her hoof to let him know she was there. "Kodi, I've come to see you."

Without lifting his head or opening his eyes, Kodi muttered a brief hello. "Leave me in peace. I'm calling the goddess to come for me."

No wonder her parents hadn't stirred the bear from his dormant state. It would be rude to interrupt if he truly sought the goddess. But could he? He'd never mentioned the ability before. It sounded more like an excuse to sleep. In a quandary as to how to shake him out of his somnolence, Prism paced outside the cave.

Snag scuttled out into the sun, her body dazzling in the light. "Prism. Take. Home."

Stopping her pacing, Prism puzzled over what the spider meant. Did Snag want Prism to go home? But take what? She couldn't take Kodi with her. "What do you mean?"

The clatter of Snag's legs as she crabbed to a higher vantage rang loud in the peaceful setting. "Let. Bear. Die."

Would Kodi go to the spirit world if they let him die? Would the goddess collect him? It was obviously what he wanted. Perhaps Gem should stop feeding him power. Prism galloped down to the lake and waited for Gem to emerge from the healing waters. Since nearly drowning when the ice had cloaked her wings, she hesitated to swim alone. And Rocky wasn't here to save her. Pushing her memories of him aside, she concentrated on why she had come.

Gem sprung from the water, Mystery by her side. Prism shared with them what Snag had implied.

Gem's eyes filled with pain. "It goes against my nature to let any creature die, especially one as precious as Kodi."

Prism understood her dam's reticence. "But it's no life he leads now. He's no longer the guardian. We must let him go if that's what he really wants."

Gem acknowledged that Snag had told her the same thing. Reluctantly, she agreed to no longer keep the guardian healthy. "Let the goddess decide. He deserves that much."

Together they led a procession up the hillside, other animals sensing the seriousness of the occasion and following them to say goodbye to a good friend. Foxes, martens, and mink scurried to keep up. Birds, bats, and dragons provided an overhead escort.

On reaching the cave entrance, a chill seeped from the den into Prism's bones, cooling her heart as much as her flesh. She'd known what they would find. As soon as Gem had accepted the inevitable, Prism had experienced a shift in Equinora's energy. She entered the gloom of the cave, heavy with sorrow. Kodi lay dead where she had left him, his body limp as if still asleep, his lips fallen back to reveal ancient ivories stained with berry juice. Snag stood guard next to his reposing body, and Lash coiled against the walls of the cavern, his scales dim.

Prism stared. Why hadn't the goddess taken the guardian?

When Jasper and Moonglow had died, their bodies had vanished immediately. Why was Kodi still here, one of her special creatures? Prism sniffed at his dormant form. He was definitely dead.

Snag ran a silken cord between her front legs. "Wrap."

Did the spider mean to cocoon the bear like she had the cub? That wouldn't bring him back to life, but it might preserve his remains until the goddess fetched him. Prism looked to her parents. "We can't leave him like this."

Mystery didn't approach. "You were closest to him. You decide."

Prism thought back to the early days when Gem had insisted Kodi accompany Prism to Westlands. She had resisted his company and he had been so slow, but he had given her emotional strength, always calm and able to see things in a different way to her. Guilt had racked him over the loss of the goddess's feather, yet he still suffered through his illness to aid those in need in Westlands. And then when Delsin had identified a possible cure, Kodi had searched the forests for the giant conks. He had guided Snag to live a life without the restrictions of her colouring. He had rescued the bear cub from Claw. He had already done more for Equinora than any other creature she had met.

If he now desired to leave for the spirit world, who were they to deny him? Making up her mind, Prism nodded to Snag. The spider extracted more golden silk from her spinnerets and tried to encase the giant bear. Her legs weren't powerful enough to roll him as she had the bear cub.

Lash slithered over and grabbed the end of the fibre with his tongue. In one long slow movement he rolled his body round and round the bear, turning the furred figure within his coils, coating Kodi with the silk as Snag created more and more thread. When they had finished, the guardian lay like a giant golden chrysalis, his body totally enwrapped. But his body couldn't remain in the cave for eternity. What if the goddess didn't come?

Prism ushered everyone out. "Now what?"

A loud squawk sounded overhead. Claw and Blaze plummeted from the crest of the hill, scattering the small creatures arraigned around Prism.

"Eeerk! Take to Eagle's Peak. Near the goddess, eeerk!"

Blaze flapped his way over to her. "Come come come my Prism my beauty we will say goodbye goodbye to our dear friend the guardian where eagles soar and dragons fly and you you you my Prism can be with him!"

While Prism dithered, Claw dragged Kodi's cocoon out into the light and took to the air, the guardian in his claws. Blaze also took off, beseeching her to join them. Delsin's vision flashed into her mind. Could the mountain the jewelled snake had climbed be Eagle's Peak, not the one where she had found Lash? She launched after them. With such a heavy burden, Claw climbed slowly. The hills and mountains gradually shrank beneath her. Once at gliding height, they made quicker progress.

The obsidian mountain jutted from Dragonspine Mountains like a giant stalagmite, except its point had been blasted flat during the stealthcat war. Prism landed with a clatter, leaving her wings outstretched to balance against the wind. The rock glistened as if from recent rain, yet no moisture in the air dampened her parched tongue.

Claw set Kodi down with care in the centre of the platform before hopping back to the edge of the mountain. Blaze circled above, his shadow cooling Prism like the cave's atmosphere when the guardian had died. She filled with love for Kodi, remembering all their travels together, and all that had been achieved thanks to him.

Blaze landed behind her. "Prism my friend my Prism time for you to say goodbye goodbye to our friend Kodi the guardian the bear one of Shadow's family like me like Claw like Snag like Lash! Goodbye goodbye goodbye!"

One of Shadow's family? That would explain why Kodi had been able to communicate by mind with Shadow's other creatures. But Kodi had been the guardian of the goddess's feathers. Is this why she hadn't collected him? Prism stiffened. Regardless of Kodi's creator, he had been a good soul and had never harmed another creature. He deserved a respectful send off. The guardian would live for ever in the stories related by all the unicorns and all the dragons, all the people and all the animals of Equinora. She launched into the air and flew in circles like Blaze had done only moments ago.

"Oh mighty Kodi, who defended whatever needed protecting, your long reach proved the precious lineage of your ancestry

Go with moose whose courage gives energy to the brave, hiding in full view and shapeshifting to bat, regenerating from life to death to life

Go with beaver whose broad tail smacks in warning of danger, whose skill builds lodges and moulds the terrain to provide shelter and food

Go with otter who embraces youngsters with love, and play with friends in celebration of this wonderful world

Go with eagle whose wings carry messages to those gone before, returning with visions to any who are open to receive them

Go with salmon whose bonds of blood and place are strong, swimming the sacred waters against all that prevails

Go with snake who watches in silence for wrongness and untaps intellect, turning experience into wisdom

Go with spider whose creativity and persistence bridges life across realms with her web and aids those lost to find their path to destiny

Go with squirrel who mixes work and play to gather stores for hard times ahead, trusting that the more given the more gained

Go with butterfly who flits by, sharing beauty and gentleness, knowing not all is as it seems and sacrifice is necessary

Go with mouse who whispers of safe trails in the woods and guides you

Go with ant who honours and respects community and welcomes you

Go to the spirit world, where you shall live forever."

A blast of hot air rose around Prism. She flew away from the platform and looped around the peak. Next to Kodi's silken wrap, Blaze glowed crimson. Fire spewed from his snout and he huffed a great spout of flame over the cocoon. Kodi's body flared and vaporised. Golden smoke spiralled upwards, containing dazzling specks of emerald, ruby, and sapphire, twisting and dancing like dragons in play, a mist of gems rising to the sun.

Prism thrust higher into the air, following the trail of jewel-dust.

Higher and higher she flew, leaving Claw and Blaze far beneath. Up where the air thinned and the sun's rays filled her with power. Up through layers of cold and heat and mist and light. Up where her body lost all sense of form, her spirit soaring aloft alongside Kodi's.

Chapter 31

Prism drifted in a daze, surrounded by mist. No longer did she need to flap her wings, her feathers floating weightless above her back. She stretched her neck down to peer towards the ground. Cloud blocked her view. Her hooves dangled, but at the same time, firmness permeated her soles, preventing her suffering from disorientation. The buoyancy of her body was as if she swam in Shimmering Lake, not needing to breathe.

A blur caught her eye to the left. Kodi stood on his hind legs, his coat glossy, and his eyes sparkling, though he shimmered as if he were a mirage, transparent like ripples on a pond. He pointed a forelimb to Prism's right. Without conscious effort or any sense of movement, she changed direction and stared into gossamer threads wafting in all directions. Golden light permeated their veil, outlining a winged unicorn twice the size of Prism.

The goddess approached, closely followed by a white unicorn with golden mane and tail, and sapphire eyes. Moonglow? Next, a dappled grey mare with black eyes and horn trotted up with a crimson stallion. These could only be Mist and Jasper. Dragons flitted around the unicorns, above and below, singing a welcome to Kodi.

Prism shook her head, not knowing if she dreamt or the goddess had sent her a vision. Or had she flown too high and died, the air too thin to sustain her? Whether real or imagined, she had no doubt she was in the spirit world.

The goddess blew into Prism's nostrils in greeting. "Thank you for escorting Kodi. Since I became unable to visit Equinora, I haven't been able to bring home those created with my power. Unicorns and dragons found their own way, but the guardian didn't share their ability."

Too many questions roiled in Prism's mind. "Am I dead?"

"Gracious, no. You're the Spirit Unicorn. You can cross between Equinora and the spirit world any time you wish. Moonglow, too, could have returned if she had desired until you were born. But now you carry the mantle." The goddess nuzzled Prism's neck. "You may stay as long as you wish, or return to Equinora. Your body will rematerialize on your return."

More confused than ever, Prism studied the spirits around her. Contentment oozed from their essence and their auras radiated love. No wonder the dragons sang. "Why can't you return? How do I get back? Is Kodi one of your creations or Shadow's?"

The goddess paled and shrank to Prism's height. "When I created Shadow, I lost half of my soul. I am missing the dimension that enables me to take physical form. That's why I can't return to Equinora and help protect the land. As to Kodi, I gave him life, and Shadow enhanced him, but as Shadow is my other half, anything he does is of my doing."

Shocked, Prism backed away without using any effort or moving her limbs. She had to be dreaming. "But that would mean you created the bloodwolves, and the stealthcats. You sent the rotfrogs and poisoned meteorites. I can't believe you would harm your world in such a way if you are really the goddess."

The goddess hovered closer. "First, now that you have met me face to face, please call me Aureana. Second, I didn't say I could control what Shadow did in Equinora. It is true that it was he who sent forth corrupted beasts, but as he was formed from part of me, I take responsibility."

More confident that she really faced the goddess in the spirit world, and wasn't dreaming, Prism's desire for answers overcame her timidity. "Who was Kodi guarding the feathers for?"

Aureana nibbled Prism's crest, the gesture intimate like a dam with her foal. "I didn't have a particular plan for them."

Uncertain whether to groom the goddess in return, Prism remained tense, questions still roiling through her mind. "So why was Kodi guarding them?"

Aureana must have picked up her reticence. She walked away, suggesting they go for a stroll. "I never intended to abandon Equinora.

When I couldn't save Dewdrop and lost those five feathers, I couldn't bear to stay any longer. That's when I created the dragons and aquadragons so that at least some of my essence, my power, remained behind until I felt strong enough to return. But then I discovered that without my shadow, I couldn't."

Prism hastened to catch up, following the goddess through the mists.

Aureana continued her tale. "The feathers had to be guarded so that Shadow couldn't usurp their power. Jasper rescuing Kodi from his clutches created a perfect opportunity."

Prism tried to follow what the goddess was saying. "But one of the feathers healed Jasper. Why did Claw get the rest?"

Aureana's nicker tinkled like a cascade of jewels in a waterfall. "Why not? As long as Shadow didn't have them, I had no objection to the giant eagle improving his flight. It never occurred to me that he'd help Shadow escape his prison."

Now even more intrigued, Prism was about to ask more when a cry entered her head.

Priiism! Priiism! Where are you my queen, my beloved?

Rocky! How could she hear him here?

Aureana watched her in silence.

The cry came again. Prism had no idea what to do. "Is Rocky here?"

"No, but he's nearing the end of his life. He still pines for you."

A hot flush flooded Prism. "But how can I be with him? The pain of his death will be too much to bear."

Aureana snorted and stamped a hoof. "Go back to Equinora. Fetch your soul-mate here, then you can be with him whenever your duties do not call you."

"My duties? What do you mean?" Hope rose in Prism's heart along with a fear that she had misinterpreted Aureana's meaning. Could she and Rocky be united for ever?

"Remember, I've lost my ability to return to Equinora. You are the Spirit Unicorn; you know when those with power are ready to die. I gifted you wings and granted you the honour of crossing between the two worlds to escort them. As I told you, a unicorn must be the Harbinger of Death in my stead."

Prism jolted to a halt and trembled. "Does that mean I bring death? Did I cause the devastation in Westlands?"

"No! Of course not. Being the Harbinger of Death merely means you are there in time to guide the spirits home."

Ever since Prism had spoken with the goddess in her vision, Prism had believed the Harbinger of Death was someone evil. How wrong she had been. The honour of working for the goddess overwhelmed her.

Aureana nudged Prism's shoulder. "Go now and fetch Rocky."

Prism gasped air into her lungs as she rejoined her body. Sensations of the wind tugging her mane and tail oriented her back in Equinora. She had no concept of how long she had talked with the goddess. Aureana, the name rang rich in Prism's mind like the sweetest alfalfa, but Rocky's cries still echoed in her head.

She glided across the mountain range and headed southwest to Flowering Valley, Rocky's home, the territory of the horse King Streak. It was this stallion whom her grandsire, Fleet, had been sent to warn about the bloodwolf war before even Mystery, her sire, had been born. Although she knew the tales, visiting the places and meeting the characters would feel as unreal as her time in the spirit world. Now that she was back in Equinora, she still wasn't certain whether she truly had met the goddess or had dreamt her.

The land below opened out into rolling meadows. To the south lay dense deciduous forest. Far in the distance, River Lifeflow bisected the terrain. She glided lower and scanned for herds of horses. She needn't have bothered. A thread as strong as Snag's silk pulled on her heart, guiding her down to where a skewbald stallion lay amid an open grassland. Rocky! Her heart thumped and her pulse raced.

Prism landed a short distance away and cantered over. No other horses were in sight, but Delsin sat with Rocky's head in his lap, stroking the stallion's forelock. She walked up and nuzzled the man's shoulder. "You have been a good friend to him, but it is time to let him go."

Tears trickled down Delsin's face. "I knew you'd come. Can you save him?"

"Not in the way you would wish." Prism lipped Rocky's neck and licked his withers. "I've come to take him to the goddess."

Rocky raised his head a fraction then let it slump back on Delsin's legs. "Prism, my beloved. If only we had met when I was younger. What a life we could have had."

Prism nudged Delsin and asked him to move away. When the man did as asked, she turned her attention back to Rocky. "You don't need to be younger. Let me guide you and we can be together forever in the spirit world."

With a long sigh, Rocky died. No light shone from his eyes. His tail and ears hung limp.

Before Prism could think about how to guide his spirit, Snag and Lash arrived. As they had done with Kodi, they wrapped him in golden silk. While they finished the last laps, Blaze and Claw landed. After greeting them, Delsin stood next to Rocky in his golden cocoon and placed a hand on his wrapped head. "Go safely, my friend, and thank you for all you did for Equinora. You will be remembered in songs as a valiant hero."

With Prism and Delsin sending their love for Rocky to Blaze, the dragon's scales transformed to crimson. With a mighty huff, he cremated the cocoon.

Prism galloped into the flames and took flight, Blaze and Claw beside her. Up, up, they followed Rocky's spirit until only Prism remained beside him. When they emerged from the clouds, next to Aureana, Rocky had become a young stallion again, full of vigour and gleaming with health.

Aureana greeted Rocky and praised Prism for a job well done. "But there is something else I wish you to do before you and Rocky go off together."

Prism licked her lips. Was this a dream after all, now turning into a nightmare?

"Don't look so glum. This will benefit you too." Aureana shimmered in a golden haze, as if she trembled with excitement or anticipation.

Prism waited.

A buckskin mare appeared behind Aureana. She was no unicorn, though shared Dewdrop's black eyes. Could she be Dewdrop's filly? "Who is this?"

Aureana didn't need to look. "This is Chase. She's a warmblood."

Confused, Prism's head spun. "But if only unicorns and dragons can find their way unaccompanied to the spirit world, how did she get here?"

"Chase was empowered by Shadow. No other warmbloods can cross into the spirit world alone." The goddess sounded sad, as if she regretted the existence of horses with unicorn blood. "And I can't return to fetch them or rectify Shadow's mistakes."

Moonglow approached and stood shoulder to shoulder with Aureana. "That's why you, Prism, are Equinora's hope. We have great faith in you."

"Me?" Prism looked to Kodi for support, but the great bear had drifted away to talk with Jasper.

Aureana grew in stature and glowed brighter, her golden horn sizzling with sparks. "I need you to bring Shadow to the spirit world. Once we are reunited, all will be well."

"Shadow? Is he dying too? Why would you want the duocorn here? How will that benefit me?" Prism had no desire to meet the evil creature behind the terrors that had lain over Equinora for years, though without Shadow in Equinora, perhaps life could settle back the way it had been before he started the wars.

Aureana moved around Prism like early morning mist wending through a valley. "Don't mistake Shadow's anger and devastation for evil like I did for so long. His early rampages were due to him having no mastery over his power, far more power than any unicorn wields. When Dewdrop died and I imprisoned him, I mistook his grief for rage. Again, when Chase died, he caused earthquakes and plagues in his suffering. Shadow is my other half. If we are reunited, I will be complete again and able to teach him to use his powers for good."

Prism still couldn't accept that Shadow had no malice. But realising that she had no choice, and grateful that the goddess had enabled her to be together with Rocky, Prism lowered her head in acceptance. "How do I bring him here? Do I have to kill him?"

"That won't be necessary, or even possible. Return to Eagle's Peak. Shadow goes there every evening to grieve Chase. Listen closely while I will tell you what to do."

Prism landed on the obsidian platform and turned towards the scent of a stallion. A black horse with crimson mane and tail clambered above the edge of the rock face. Stones clattered back down the track from his haste. He halted and lifted his head, shaking his thick forelock out of his eyes, revealing twin horns curled around his ears.

Shadow flared his nostrils and pranced over. "What are you doing in my territory? No-one is permitted up here."

Prism held her ground. "Aureana sent me. She invites you to join her in the spirit world."

Shadow reared and neighed, pawing the air with hooves as red as flame. He strode across to Prism, his breath hot on her face. "Does she now? She grants me immortality, then offers me death. How do you intend to kill me?"

Pretending to be unruffled, though inwardly quaking, Prism arched her neck. "Not death. Aureana wishes to be reunited with you, so you may thrive in the spirit world. It isn't necessary for me to kill you. I am the Spirit Unicorn. I can escort you."

Shadow paced around the rim of Eagle's Peak. "Have you been to the spirit world? Is Dewdrop there?"

"I spoke with her before I returned and she is well. She also wishes you to join her." Prism refrained from explaining the nature of her existence.

Shadow swallowed. "How can I trust you? You may be here to kill me using Aureana's powers so she can destroy me once and for all."

"Not at all. She says she is incomplete without you. You are her shadow, her other half. Without you she is desolate." Prism turned on the spot to keep facing the duocorn as he paced around the platform, the scent of his power almost overpowering her. Wind tore at her mane and tail and whipped her forelock into her eyes.

Shadow halted and snorted. "So how are you to manage this amazing feat? Am I supposed to jump off this pinnacle again and be smashed to pieces?"

Prism gasped in horror. "All you have to do is allow me to convey you, without fighting. I have already transported Kodi, the bear you enhanced, to be with Aureana. And Chase is there too, waiting for you."

Shadow tossed his head and his eyes lit up. "If you know about Chase, then you must be speaking the truth. So be it. I have no desire to remain in Equinora. I will go, though I don't believe Aureana truly wants me as a companion. Do what you will."

Although Aureana had given Prism specific instructions, anxiety flooded her heart from the close proximity of the duocorn. "Please remain still."

She launched into the air and flew a circle around Eagle's Peak, calling out the words that Aureana had instructed. Around and around she flew, drawing on the energy of the wind and the sun, dizzying from the power.

"Shadow, rise, return to she
Whose soul is split apart
Let fire burn in your hot blood
True power comes from the heart"

Tighter and tighter, she lapped Shadow, the force of his nature darkening her mind.

"Let water erode your pain
And earth comfort grief
Let air blow away your hate
And light redeem belief"

Louder and louder, she screamed out Aureana's words to draw Shadow from this realm into the next.

"Let spirit join creators
Be lifted strong and bold
Ne'er to be apart again
Black and red with gold"

All her senses dwindled to nothing. Even her sense of self disappeared in a black fog, spiralling into a thunderhead like one of Tempest's storms. Lightning flashed in her mind and nausea clogged her throat. Still she flew and cried out the goddess's commands.

In a flash of golden light, a weight lifted from her soul and she burst into the spirit world. White mist hung like smoke on a still day. Aureana emerged through the vapour, her golden body solidifying and glowing like the sun. She glided across to Shadow who had materialised nearby, his obsidian body shining like the wet rock of Eagle's Peak, his mane and tail flowing like hot lava.

Aureana joined Prism, even more beautiful than in her visions, radiating power from every hair and feather. "Thank you. You have achieved what I could not."

Thinking that Aureana meant bringing Shadow to the spirit world, Prism was about to respond that it was the goddess's words that had succeeded, not her, when the mist dissipated. Solid ground lay beneath her hooves. Birdsong trilled in her ears. A verdant land splayed before her, filled with sparkling brooks and lush meadows, coated in trees heavy in fruit, and flowers dancing with butterflies. "Are we back in Equinora?"

Aureana fluffed out her wings and trotted through deep grass. "No. Thanks to you, I am whole. Shadow's coming has enabled me to create a new world. I shall name it Auresha, merging our names as acknowledgement of his return to me, a place where all those with power may live in harmony for eternity. Come and drink from the lake to restore your strength. You'll find it even more powerful than the waters that Gemstone nourishes."

Prism stared at her reflection in the crystal lake, amazed at the warmth flooding her veins, filling her with love. Kodi scratched his back in delight under a massive pine nearby, and Jasper carved a magnificent sculpture of a unicorn mare in rock. Moonglow played with the dragons.

Shadow pranced between Dewdrop and Chase, greeted them cordially, and returned to Aureana's side. "Do you truly wish me to be your partner?"

Aureana blew into his nostrils. "Yes, but you don't need to choose me over Dewdrop and Chase. Be my King as I am Queen, like the horses live in Equinora. All the unicorns and warmbloods in Auresha will be our herd. We will rule together, return to Equinora when we wish, never to be apart again."

Shadow pranced in splendour around his new territory, tail over his back and head held high. On his return to Aureana, he neighed loudly into the wind. "Let them be free. I am content with only you, my equal."

Aureana glowed brighter, her lifemate by her side.

Prism's stomach churned. Where was Rocky? She whinnied long and loud, anxious to reunite with her own soulmate.

In a thunder of hooves, Rocky galloped across the lush meadow, his muscles rippling beneath his glossy hide, power oozing from every pore.

Prism galloped to meet him.